THE SINGULAR EXPLOITS
OF
MR SHERLOCK HOLMES

By the same author

The Singular Adventures of Mr Sherlock Holmes

Sherlock Holmes and the Singular Adventure of the Gloved Pianist

Mr Dickens & Master Betty

Matchbox Puppets *(with Brenda Stockwell)*

Finding Sampson Penley

THE SINGULAR

EXPLOITS

OF

Mr Sherlock Holmes

ALAN STOCKWELL

ISBN 978-0-9565013-5-6

Published 2012 by Vesper Hawk Publishing

www.vesperhawk.com

www.mrsherlockholmes.co.uk

CONTENTS

PREFACE

In recent years interest in Sherlock Holmes has burgeoned due to new cinema films and television series. Unfortunately, these have distorted the beloved originals by either making Holmes and Watson action-heroes, transplanting them to modern times, or both. In print, some authors have let their imaginations run riot and Holmes has been involved with Jack the Ripper, Dracula, the Titanic, and flying saucers to name but a few. He has been placed in modern America, into the future and far into the past; we have been given his schooldays, his biography and various clones. Poor old Holmes has been mangled and distorted to provide fodder for many ludicrous yarns and unbelievable concepts.

However, some authors have sincerely attempted to imitate the authentic Conan Doyle style and many of their tales are credible and entertaining. The conventions are observed and the author who knows his job ensures that nothing anachronistic appears in his work. A sense of period is essential if the reader is to find himself comfortably at home in the late Victorian era.

The true joy of these pastiches is to imagine that Sir Arthur, once more taking up his pen, has given us a further batch of splendid Sherlock Holmes tales.

I published my first collection of new Sherlock Holmes short stories *The Singular Adventures of Mr Sherlock Holmes* in the year 2003.

The idea was to emulate the style of the original stories as closely as possible and the publication received many plaudits from Sherlockian connoisseurs. A new expanded edition with three extra stories was brought out in 2006, and in 2010 the third edition was brought out with the strapline "Seventeen Stories in the Traditional Manner".

Many readers were kind enough to say how much they admired my imitations and the book is still available for enjoyment by new readers. However, there were some *aficionados* who kept asking when I intended bringing out more new stories. Such requests made me wonder how Sir Arthur dare enter into a contract to supply a new story every month to the *Strand Magazine* – no wonder his tales are so variable!

In February 2008 I was asked to write an acting script for a *Sherlock Holmes Mystery Evening* which I was pleased to do as I had a long-held idea which was ideal for the purpose. After the event, I elaborated the original into a 'whodunnit' and in 2010 published a novella under the title *Sherlock Holmes and the Gloved Pianist*. This work also contained the original play script. I freely admit that work strayed from the standard Conan Doyle formula, perhaps even slightly impinging on the Agatha

Christie mode!

However, since 2006 new ideas have surfaced and, not having deadlines to meet, eventually found their way on to paper. So gradually a collection of new stories has accumulated, all related in the time-honoured manner of Dr Watson. The period is the end of the Victorian era and, whilst the work is entirely fictional, as before, certain characters and events of the time have been included for verisimilitude. A few notes at the end will clarify such matters.

Thus I am now able to satisfy some of my readers by bringing out a further collection of "Ten New Stories in the Traditional Manner." I hope you will enjoy *The Singular Exploits of Mr Sherlock Holmes*.

THE CASE OF THE CRYPTIC CAPITALS

We were just about to dine when an unexpected visitor arrived at 221b Baker Street claiming entrance to our rooms. Holmes, who would far rather miss his meal than a prospective client, asked for him to be admitted. The newcomer was a pinched-looking man of around thirty years. I had not realised it was raining outside, but the man's topcoat was saturated with water.

"Do come in, sir. Remove your coat and I will drape it over the back of this chair near the fire. It may have dried a little by the time you leave. I will hang your hat on the post." Holmes spoke these welcoming words as he assisted the man out of his coat before settling him in a chair near the fire.

"Now, Mr Soper, how can I help you?" asked Holmes.

Our visitor stared. "How do you know my name? I have not announced it," he said in surprise.

"It is my business to know things, Mr Soper. Now you did not come in a hurry straight from the City unless your visit was of importance to you."

The man sprang to his feet. "I don't know how you know my name and affairs, sir, but you must have been told about me. Who has been spying on me?" he exclaimed.

Holmes gave a wry laugh. "Pray seat yourself, sir. All I know about you, you have told me yourself."

"But I have said nothing!" the bewildered visitor exclaimed.

"Your name is written in your hat. The rain, though fierce, was a short shower lasting around twenty minutes just after six o'clock. Today the wind is strong coming from the west. Your coat is soaked in front but barely damp at the back. Thus you have been walking in a westerly direction. The City is due east from here. The shower had ceased by twenty-five minutes past six. Your business was of importance as you did not shelter anywhere. I deduced your journey had commenced around six o'clock from the fact that you have walked here rather than taken cab, omnibus or tube. Having a good idea of the most direct route you will have walked, and noting the time you arrived, the calculation is a simple one."

"That is perfectly true, Mr Holmes. But I do not see how you guessed my journey commenced in the city at six." He laughed, "I could have been walking for hours from further afield."

Holmes held up his hands. "I do not guess, Mr Soper. On removing your coat I observed the cuffs of your jacket were frayed. Your collar is grubby and clearly worn for several days. Therefore you do not walk out of pleasure or exercise, but because you do not have money to spare for transport. Your hat, which is a fashionable, but well-worn, low-crown bowler hat such as conventionally worn by young men in business, has your name written inside. If you lived within a large family you might label your hat to differentiate it from your brothers', but in that event you would simply write your Christian name. You have written 'J Soper'. Therefore, you habitually hang your hat with several, perhaps many, others very similar in appearance. A sensible precaution if one's place of employment contains many men with almost identical hats."

"There are two dozen chaps like me in our office," said Soper.

"I deduced you were a shamefully low-paid clerk in the City, Mr Soper. There is a very marked groove worn across the right inner forearm of your jacket where it rubs against the edge of your desk. The left sleeve is practically worn through at the elbow, as you habitually rest your left arm on the desk top. On the inside of the first knuckle of the second finger of your right hand is a pronounced callus where you hold a steel pen. You have even a smudge of ink on the first joint of your little finger. These are all commonplace indications of a clerk. That you are underpaid is certain from the fact that you present this somewhat shabby and, may I say, under-fed figure who is obliged to trudge through the streets of London in the rain. "

"That is amazing, Mr Holmes, you are correct in every particular. I work at the offices of Hardacre and Frostick in Leadenhall Street."

"I am aware it is the common practice for offices to close at six o'clock daily, allowing the staff to debouch into the streets all clamouring for transport together. Having ascertained your occupation together with the other facts, the location of your place of business was indubitably the City. However, one thing I am not able to deduce is the purpose of your visit. Perhaps you will enlighten me?"

"Mr Holmes, I must explain before you become involved that you are quite right. I am a poor man and will not be able to pay your fee unless you succeed in what I require of you."

"Be assured, Mr Soper, that I make no charges whatever for this initial interview. I have many people, from the lowest to the highest in the land who seek my assistance and it is necessary that I hear their story before I decide whether I will take their case. I do not do my work for money alone, sir. I only accept cases which offer some especial interest – an extraordinary situation, perhaps – I seek a challenge to my brain more than anything."

"Then you will certainly be challenged by my situation, Mr Holmes," said the little man shaking his head at the very thought.

"Then let us hear your story," replied Holmes.

"It is a simple one. I bought a ticket for the Louisiana State lottery and it is a winning one. I have won several thousand dollars."

"Congratulations," said I heartily.

"Alas, I am unable to claim the prize as I cannot find my ticket," said Soper unhappily. He said no more so Holmes encouragingly urged him to speak on. "I live in one room only and I have scoured it from top to bottom searching for the ticket. I know I had it and placed it in a safe place, now I cannot remember where that place was."

"Why have you come to consult me?" asked Holmes.

"People say you can do wondrous things. I hoped you would be able to find my lottery ticket."

"I fear you have been reading Dr Watson's accounts that exaggerate my abilities. I am not a miracle worker. If you, who are familiar with your own room, cannot find an object in it, I fail to see why you should think a stranger might succeed."

The poor chap looked as though he might burst into tears at this statement. "You have dashed my only hope," said he gloomily.

"There are only two possibilities, Mr Soper. If the ticket is not in your room you will never find it however long you search. If it is there and you search systematically from one side to the other, floor to ceiling, then you must find it. That is the only advice I can offer you. Except, of course, that buying lottery tickets should only be done by those who can afford to lose money. The chance of winning is very remote."

"But I have won! That's the whole point! I have succeeded where the many fail!"

"I think you will find that the Louisiana State lottery is notoriously corrupt and that many winners do not, in fact, receive their prize."

Soper rose to his feet and sighed, "I am sorry to have troubled you, Mr Holmes. I thought you may have some sympathy for a poor man, but I see you are only interested in serving the great and good."

"You do me an injustice, Soper. I have refused many of the great and good, as you call them. Let me assist you with your coat. I am a student of crime. I only take cases which have some unusual aspect, or where the police refer to me because they are baffled. The crime which is singular or bizarre is the one that interests me. I consider searching for a lost lottery ticket neither a crime nor *outré*."

I offered to show out our visitor and tell Mrs Hudson we were now ready to receive her dinner. Before I closed the door, I put a shilling into Soper's hand.

When I regained our room Holmes was still seated, puffing at his pipe. "A bit sad," I said, "the poor chap was obviously relying on you."

"Then he should not do so. The man's a fool. If he pays money he can ill-afford for a lottery ticket, then can't remember where he keeps it, he doesn't need a detective, he needs a clairvoyant. Is this agency to be reduced to searching for missing raffle tickets?"

"Well, I gave him his fare home," I said.

"So did I," said Holmes. "I slipped a half-sovereign into his pocket." We both laughed.

Our delayed dinner was still enjoyable though the vegetables were now grossly over-cooked through being kept warm. The conversation, however, was limited to Holmes's moaning.

"Where are the criminals worthy of my attention? Where are the crimes that give exercise to my brain? I'm stultifying through lack of work!"

The weather improved no more than Holmes's temper. After a period of lashing rain the temperature dropped markedly and snow fell in profusion. However, Holmes's heartfelt plea was answered when a singularly puzzling conundrum presented itself, followed by a bizarre death. The case commenced with a visit from a very attractive young lady of no more than some twenty years.

"Pray take a seat Miss Jellicoe, here by the fire. It is very cold, is it not?" said I.

"I am Sherlock Holmes, this is my friend and colleague Dr Watson who is always assiduous in the comfort of young ladies. In what way may I be of assistance to you?"

"It is a most peculiar business, Mr Holmes. At first the matter seemed trivial but, as it has developed, it clearly alarms my father and now he will not stir from his room."

"Perhaps you had better relate your story from the very beginning?" suggested Holmes.

"Yes, yes, of course. I must explain that my father and I live a secluded life in the country with a minimum of servants."

"Where is this house?" asked Holmes.

"The nearest town of any size is Thaxted, in Essex."

"Pray continue."

"About two weeks ago, when I went out to release the chickens – we have a few hens that I lock up at night because of foxes, then release them first thing in the morning and scatter corn for them – I found a piece of paper pinned to the door. On it in capital letters were a T and an I."

"Have you the paper?"

"No. I showed it to my father but neither of us could make anything of it so I screwed it up and threw it away. However, a few days later another paper was pinned to the door. That had simply three Is."

"You mean the letter I?"

"Yes."

"In capitals or lower case?"

"Capitals."

"I see. Proceed."

"Then came this one which I have saved because there was surely some purpose in these notes." Miss Jellicoe handed the paper to Holmes. This, in capital letters, bore an R, an L and an S.

"This seems to be a page torn from a small notebook. Were the previous notes on similar paper?"

"Yes, Mr Holmes, exactly the same."

"Hmm, a penny notebook from any stationary shop. Most intriguing. Is this the last one?"

"The last note, yes. But the latest thing is this page from a magazine." She proffered a page that was mainly occupied by an advertisement for a bicycle. Holmes examined both sides.

"This is clearly from a magazine devoted to cycling. I take it that the side with the picture was outermost?"

"Yes. What does it all mean, Mr Holmes?"

"It is impossible to say at present, but these things do not seem alarming in any way, yet you say your father was very affected by them?"

"Yes, he became increasingly anxious."

"Did you not ask him the reason?"

"Of course, but he brushed my concerns aside saying the papers were probably done by children playing a prank."

"Were there no traces of footprints in the snow?"

"My servant Mrs Brinscombe keeps the step and back path clear of snow, but beyond that there were footsteps and they were not those of children."

"How would you describe them?"

"They were definitely the footsteps of a grown man."

"Excellent! One solitary man or several?"

"That I could not determine."

"But you say now your father has taken to his room and does not emerge?"

"Yes, he claims he has caught a chill in this bitterly cold weather."

"All too possible, Miss Jellicoe," I assured her.

"But the change in him came when he saw the magazine page," said our pretty visitor.

"There would appear to be no cause for alarm in these apparently harmless jottings or the page from the magazine – "

"Mr Holmes, I am not a silly girl, I may have only seen twenty summers but I am a level-headed woman. I would not trouble you if I did not think there was something seriously amiss. I say we lead a quiet life but it is a regular one. My father is a man of strict habits. His main occupations are walking and reading. He would only miss his daily walk under the most extreme circumstances. Even in the recent atrocious weather he has maintained his daily commune with nature. That is until the magazine page, after which not only will he no longer venture out, but has had bars placed over all the windows including the upstairs rooms."

"You interrupted me, Miss Jellicoe," protested Holmes. "I was about to say that though the notes would appear to be harmless there is obviously some deep malicious purpose behind them of which your father, having withdrawn himself so extremely, must be fully aware."

"I apologise, Mr Holmes, I feared that you did not appreciate the most peculiar position as one of danger," replied Miss Jellicoe.

"Now you say he has placed bars at all the windows. This surely indicates great fear of some kind of attack from without. You say his other interest is reading? What kind of books?"

"Many kinds, Mr Holmes. There is a particular bookshop in Thaxted that he favours – they order and deliver books at his request on virtually a weekly basis, he devours print so much."

"Are these books novels?"

"He does like what he calls 'a rattling good yarn' – adventure stories about the wild west and so on – Fennimore Cooper is a favourite, as is Rider Haggard with his tales of the African continent. I tease him that he is an overgrown schoolboy. He loves books about foreign countries and peoples. I think in his youth he travelled extensively."

"So now he is confined to his room?"

"He has confined himself. So far as I can see, his health is in no way diminished although he has become querulous and hesitant in manner. Something has possessed him with great fear. He is a man of fifty, not an old dotard; normally vigorous and masterful and full of life. Within days he has become nervous and anxious and seems unable to determine his own actions, always asking my opinion on the most trivial matters, something totally alien to his usual demeanour."

"Have you challenged him over all this, Miss Jellicoe?"

"I have tried but he will no longer talk normally to me. I have to resort to calling through the locked door. He only speaks to order meals, or more coal for the fire, and of course if any books arrive, though because of the cold weather the deliveries have been sparse of late. The most peculiar thing is he keeps demanding to know if there have been any unexpected callers."

"And have you had callers?"

"No. It is total nonsense. We never have any callers. The vicar came once just after we first moved there but, as Father was outrageously rude to him, he has never returned. He calls clergymen 'Godbotherers'."

"You do not have friends in the locality?"

"No. Except the doctor. Dr Gregg is tolerated by my father as they play backgammon together. Being a hale man, Father has no need of a doctor's professional services but Dr Gregg comes once a week for a regular evening of backgammon. I, myself, have several acquaintances in the neighbourhood but no friends. You must realise that our house is very isolated. The nearest houses are but a hamlet and they are some two miles away."

"I see."

"What should I do, Mr Holmes? I am at my wit's end. My father is in some grave danger I am sure of it."

"The circumstances are indeed singular. Your father is clearly taking defensive measures against some unknown threat. Unknown to you, dear lady, and to us, but surely known to your father. If we knew the meaning of these cryptic notes we would have an idea of where we stand."

"I've tried and tried to get him to speak of them but he just dismisses them as childish nonsense."

"A man is not usually afeard of his life by childish nonsense."

"Exactly, my thoughts, Mr Holmes."

"Do you think your father would speak to me if I should visit?"

"Oh, Mr Holmes, it would afford me much gratification if you would come out and see him but I am afraid the visit would be useless for eliciting any information. He seems determined to persist in this hermit-like attitude."

"We can but try. I shall come and see you, and in the meantime I will try and tease out some sense from these enigmatic notes. If I knew something of the meaning it would provide me with a lever, as-it-were, to prise more information from your father. Should any further notes arrive please inform me immediately by telegram."

"I am grateful to you. Mr Holmes."

"I will come tomorrow. Will you accompany me, Watson?"

"Most assuredly, I would be delighted to," I replied.

"Is Thaxted your nearest station, Miss Jellicoe?"

"Yes, we are about three miles along the road to Great Bardfield. There is always a carriage available at the station."

"Excellent! Until tomorrow then."

Our visitor left in a more optimistic frame of mind than she had shown on arrival. Holmes has a knack of instant reassurance even when he is as nonplussed as the rest of us.

"What do you make of it, Watson?" asked Holmes.

"The man is clearly in fear of his life," I replied. "Installing bars at the windows surely indicates the fact."

"So much is obvious. Why does he remain? Why not flee from the impending danger?"

"I should think that his assailant is watching the house for that very opportunity. The possibility of Mr Jellicoe leaving the house is past. To step out would be death."

"Excellent, Watson! I think you read the matter aright. But what is the meaning of these cryptic notes? T and I on one, three Is on another and the three letters R, L and S on the third. Then the picture of the man standing with a bicycle."

"I can make nothing of it, Holmes. But the conundrum should prevent the atrophy of your brain."

The following day we took the train to Thaxted to keep our appointment. As we drove along the country lane, the countryside looked picturesque under the fallen snow. It was charming to see youngsters, and some not-so-young, skating and sliding on a frozen pond as we passed by.

The house, called Prestbury, was an isolated but anonymous affair probably about fifty years old and of no distinguished merit or feature. We asked the driver to wait as Holmes suspected his visit would be a brief one. The door was opened by a pleasant-looking matronly woman whom we took to be the servant Mrs Brimscombe.

"You must be Mr Sherlock Holmes and Dr Watson," she said. "Do come in, Miss Jellicoe is awaiting you." We were shown into a sitting room which, in spite of a blazing log fire, carried an air of gloom about it. Miss Jellicoe rose to greet us.

"Thank you for coming, gentlemen, would you like some tea? It is still very chill out."

"No, thank you, Miss Jellicoe, the carriage driver is outside and we do not wish to detain him longer than necessary."

"Oh, he must step in!" The young lady went to the door and called "Mrs Brimscombe, the driver is outside in the cold, tell him to come into the kitchen until it is time to return." After attending to that business she then said "We will go up to Father's room."

We were taken up to the first floor and along a corridor to a door at the very end where Miss Jellicoe knocked. "Father, there are two gentlemen here to speak with you."

A strangled cry emanated from the room which was enough to chill the marrow in one's bones.

"I told you not to let anybody into the house!" The voice was full of despair.

"But they are here at my special invitation. They are friends of mine."

"Friends! You have no friends!" came the reply from the voice within the room.

"Mr Jellicoe, I am Sherlock Holmes and with me is Dr Watson," said Holmes.

"I don't need any doctors. Dr Gregg is my doctor," was the reply.

"We know that, Mr Jellicoe, but we would like to talk to you. We are friends who wish to help you," said Holmes.

"I don't want you in my house. Adelita was in the wrong to invite you in. She knows I have given strict instructions to admit no one," said Jellicoe beyond the door.

"Will you see Dr Gregg if he comes?" asked Holmes.

"No!" the voice roared, "I do not want Gregg or anybody else! Leave me alone! I shall speak no more."

"Are you afraid of a man on a bicycle?" asked Holmes. There was no reply. In spite of the pleadings of his daughter, to which I also added my voice, there came not a sound.

"I'm sorry my father was so uncommunicative, Mr Holmes, but I did warn you what he was like. It is very worrying," said Miss Jellicoe as we returned to the ground floor.

"May I inspect the rest of the house and the garden while we are here?" asked Holmes.

"Of course."

The house was more or less square. The ground floor had two large rooms at the front, each with a bay window. At the back were kitchen, dining room, scullery etc, the stairs being placed between the two sections of the house. The upstairs comprised four bedrooms, Mr Jellicoe's being on the extreme right as one faced the front of the house. The small garden was all round the house but the front facade, which faced the road, was no more than fifteen feet away from it. The garden areas to the sides and rear were more spacious. Beyond the garden were fields in all directions. I could see a frozen pond and several large trees with icicles like stalactites depending from their branches. It was a forlorn sort of place and the sky above augured further snow as heavy clouds gathered.

"We'd better be getting back, Holmes," I said. "We don't want to be benighted."

"You're right, Watson, we can do no more here."

Before we reached London snow was falling from the sky.

During the following days Holmes poured over the few clues that had been given to him.

"The likelihood is that the three capital Is represent the Roman numeral three as on a clock."

"Indubitably," I agreed, "do you then think it represents the time?"

"Not necessarily. What if it is a reference as to a king? Is it possibly the name of a king in the manner of say, George III? Then what are we to make of T I?"

"Does it refer to a Roman emperor, perhaps? No English king has names beginning with T and I."

"Titus something?" suggested Holmes.

"Tiberius Imperator?" I suggested.

Such were the fruitless discussions we had concerning these mysterious scraps. As Holmes said, should it be a code it provided insufficient material to attempt a decipher. Holmes was, however, convinced that the letters represented initials. But initials of what or whom?

"The logical assumption would be that the initials are those of the putative assailant, but we are told that fear did not arise until after the receipt of the magazine picture. Jellicoe, whilst puzzled, did not seem to take inordinate fear from the initials themselves," said Holmes. "Yet I feel convinced that they refer to a person or persons."

"But then it could be anybody. If the letters were S and H they could mean Sherlock Holmes, or Samuel Hutton," I said. "Sebastian Hardy," I added warming to my theme. "Solomon Howard."

"Very good, Watson, I take your point," said Holmes testily.

"J and W could be John Watson, John Wesley, John Webster, Josiah Wedgwood –"

"Say that again, Watson," interrupted Holmes brusquely.

"What? Josiah Wedgwood?"

"No, no, the one before."

"John Webster."

"Yes. John Webster. He was a writer, was he not?"

"Yes, I think so, wrote plays, about the same time as Shakespeare."

"Make a long arm, Watson, and look him up."

It did not take me long to find the man. "Circa 1578 – circa 1626.

Principal works *The White Devil* and *The Duchess of Malfi*. Mean anything Holmes?" I asked, passing the volume over to him.

"No, but you have planted an idea, Watson. We know Jellicoe was fond of reading, his daughter told us."

"Yes, adventure stories I think she said he preferred."

Holmes eyes sparkled. "Exactly, an ardent reader of adventure stories. And who was the foremost writer of adventure stories until his death recently?"

"Recent death?"

"In Samoa."

"In Samoa? Why, Stevenson! Only last month. Reported in all the papers!"

"Robert Louis Stevenson."

"RLS! You have it, Holmes! Then what about TI? Another author?" I had to confess that the only authors I could think of with surnames beginning with I were Henrik Ibsen and Washington Irving, neither of whom would be T I.

"What about the works of Stevenson? What did he write?" asked Holmes.

"His most famous book is probably *The Strange Case of Dr Jekyll and Mr Hyde*. Then, of course, there is *Treasure Island* –" As soon as I had spoken the words I looked at Holmes, his eyes were sparkling.

"You are priceless, Watson!" he cried. "You may not shine like a beacon but you are a veritable tinder-box that lights the flame for others to blow up into a conflagration." I felt very proud to be of assistance to my friend.

"What about the three IIIs?" I asked excitedly?

"What indeed? Have you a copy of the book?"

"Afraid not, Holmes, and it is some years since I read it."

"Come! To the bookshop!"

Holmes could barely contain himself as we raced to the nearest bookshop. The novel is a popular one and the shop had it in stock. Holmes brushed aside the assistant's offer to wrap it and we both eagerly crouched over it as Holmes turned the pages. Immediately the connection was clear. The contents page had the chapters designated in Roman numerals. Chapter III was called *The Black Spot*. It all flooded back to me – the pirates sent a page torn from the bible with a large black spot in the centre. This was a warning that they were to return to wreak their revenge on a wayward former shipmate.

"The Black Spot! Of course, it all makes sense!" I cried.

"What does it mean, Watson?"

"It means that an ex-shipmate of Jellicoe has tracked him down and seeks revenge."

"A villain's double-cross! How blind I've been! No wonder Jellicoe refused help. He is concealing some awful deed he committed in the past. His past has now caught up with him and he is terrified. He may not fully have understood the import of the notes but the picture must have revealed the identity of the man. It is that revelation that has so terrorised him. Come, Watson, we must get to Thaxted without delay. Now we know what he is about I will speak to him even if we have to demolish his door!"

On the train we once more examined the illustration. There were no words on the picture itself to provide a clue.

"This is the last item pinned to the door. No more have arrived," said Holmes.

"Not so far as we know," I replied.

"I think it represents a signature."

"A signature?"

"Yes. If I sent you a message with a picture of a row of houses, you would know it came from me."

"Would I?"

"Think, Watson, think."

"Houses? Houses . . . I see homes! Holmes!"

"This picture is revealing the sender of the messages. It should tell us his name."

Feeling elated by my earlier success I suggested the chap's name might be Rider. "That's a fairly common name, Holmes. Rider, perhaps with a Y."

"But he is not riding the bicycle, Watson, is he? If you wished to send a picture of a man riding a bicycle I would imagine it would be easier to find, as opposed to one in which he is not doing so."

"That's true. He's just standing with it. Standing? Standish?" I suggested lamely.

"Look carefully, Watson, the man is not just standing, his feet are apart as though walking."

"Walker! That's a common enough name," I said.

"Again I must contradict you, Watson. If the picture were to indicate a walker there would be no need for the bicycle. You would not associate a bicycle with walking. Again there must be many pictures of walking men that would suffice."

"Yes, I suppose you're right," I agreed, somewhat deflated.

"He seems to be actually pushing the bike along," said Holmes.

"So what do you deduce from that? Is he called Pushing? Push? Propelling? Are there such names?"

"He is wheeling the bicycle along the road."

"Wheeler!"

"I think our would-be assassin's name is indeed Wheeler. Jellicoe spotted the reference immediately and went into this terrible decline. Wheeler is obviously a man to be feared."

"Of course, Jellicoe must know the man and why he has sought him out. Brilliant, Holmes, I'm sure you have cracked it." My admiration for my friend knew no bounds, his analytical mind had made connections from the flimsiest of material.

"Let us hope that Jellicoe's window bars and other precautions are strong enough."

"And that Miss Jellicoe is not foolish enough to let anyone in," I added.

It was past midday when we arrived at Prestbury House. There were two horses tied to the gate and our knock at the door resulted in the appearance of a police constable.

"Who are you?" he demanded peremptorily.

"I am Sherlock Holmes and this is my colleague Dr Watson. We have come to speak to Mr Jellicoe."

"Have you indeed? Well you'll find that difficult. He's dead."

I was stunned by the news and I could tell Holmes was discomforted but, as usual, his feelings never showed in his face.

"We must see Miss Jellicoe," said Holmes.

"Must you?" replied the constable. "My orders are to keep everybody out until my superior arrives."

At that moment Mrs Brimscombe appeared behind the constable. "What is it, Josh? Oh, Mr Holmes and Dr Watson, come in, come in."

"Nay, Mrs Brimscombe, I cannot allow anybody in, you know that," said the constable.

"Josh Goodman, I've known you since you were a little lad with your bum hanging out of your trousers, don't try throwing your weight about here. Just because you've had something happen more than scrumping apples on your beat. These gentlemen are from London. Miss Jellicoe has consulted them. Mr Holmes is a great detective. We're lucky he has arrived, he'll get to the truth of all this. Stand aside, come in, come in."

Thus, against the protests of Constable Goodman, we were admitted. "Dr Gregg is upstairs now, I'll take you up and introduce you. A nasty business."

"Miss Jellicoe?" I ventured.

"The poor girl is quite distraught. You would be, wouldn't you, seeing your own father in that state? She's taken to her room a-weeping. Here we are."

I was astonished to see the door wide open and heavily splintered, and perceived an overpowering smell of smoke.

"Dr Gregg, these gentlemen are Sherlock Holmes and Dr Watson, the London detectives."

Gregg was a distinguished-looking man in his mid-fifties with grey hair and, not unnaturally in the circumstances, of a solemn mien. "I understand Miss Jellicoe has consulted you about this affair. I have heard of your reputation. I must say this kind of thing is beyond my customary business and I welcome your advice."

Mrs Brimscombe, looking at the figure on the bed, gave a visible shudder and hurried out.

"What is the cause of death?" asked Holmes.

"A wound directly into the heart caused by some sort of knife. Have a look." Gregg pulled back the sheet covering the body on the bed. Jellicoe had been a well-built powerful man with a broad chest region. There was a gaping hole over his heart. Holmes produced his lens and fell to examination.

"A knife, you say?"

"Something of the sort."

"Surely a knife would have left a smaller, cleaner, more defined hole in the flesh? This is large and ragged and ill-defined."

"True, Mr Holmes, and, more peculiarly, there seems to be traces of sawdust in the wound."

"So I have remarked. What is your explanation for that?"

"I can only think that the weapon was quite a crude blunt affair. The sawdust makes me wonder if it could have been done by a sharpened wooden stake."

"Good God," I cried, "that's how they kill vampires, a wooden stake through the heart."

"If such a procedure kills vampires, it will surely do likewise to a man. Was he in bed, Dr Gregg?"

"No, no, not at all. He was in his nightgown but crumpled up on the floor by the open window."

"The window was open?"

"Yes, the sash thrown fully up. The room was full of smoke, I'm sure you can still smell it."

"Indeed."

"It would seem that Mr Jellicoe found the fire blowing smoke back into the room. He had a fire going non-stop in here because of the cold weather. He must have risen from his bed and opened the window to let the smoke out and get the fire to draw."

"Then he was stabbed by somebody through the open window? Is that what you suggest?"

"Well, he is dead and he could not have inflicted that wound upon himself."

"I see the door has been forced open, surely the assailant entered that way?" said Holmes.

"Not so. The circumstances are that Mrs Brimscombe and Miss Jellicoe arose as usual but becoming immediately aware of the smell of smoke, came together at the door. As you will know from his daughter, Mr Jellicoe had of late been behaving in a secretive manner, never leaving his room and keeping the door firmly locked. They realised the smoke was issuing from within his room and knocked frantically but there was no reply. Eventually, Mrs Brimscombe, being a resourceful woman, went for an axe, used for chopping logs, and attacked the door, forcing an entry. They found the window wide open, the room full of smoke and the body of Mr Jellicoe in his night attire slumped by the open window. Miss Jellicoe apparently fainted away and has taken to her room. Mrs Brimscombe got a message to me and I came instantly, finding things as you, yourself, have seen. With Mrs Brimscombe's assistance I lifted Mr Jellicoe on to the bed. She had also sent for the policeman, Constable Goodman, who arrived shortly after me. We are awaiting officers coming from Saffron Walden. This is the country, Mr Holmes. Things move slowly here; it takes time for messages to be sent and acted upon."

Holmes went to the window, opened it, examined it and looked outside. "Do you know when it last snowed, Dr Gregg?"

"It snowed at dusk yesterday. I do not think we have had any more in the night. I believe it was a clear night with a bright full moon."

"The snow below appears pristine. There seems no way a man could easily climb up to this window. The ability of a man being able to cling to the bars with one hand and stab his victim on the other side with the other, verges on the impossible. His victim would not willingly stand within his reach to be struck with a pointed stake. The blow that struck Jellicoe dead was of great force. It would have been impossible to produce such force in the conditions that appertained."

"You are the detective, Mr Holmes, I am a country doctor. I merely say the poor man died from a stab directly to the heart. How it was done and by whom is not really my concern; that is why we have sent for policemen from Saffron Walden."

"I must examine the grounds. You are welcome to accompany me if you wish, Dr Gregg."

"I have other business to attend to, Mr Holmes, I am only awaiting the officers then I must leave but, in the meantime, I would be interested to see your methods."

Holmes and I descended to be accosted by Constable Goodman. "I can have you two arrested for disobeying an officer of the law," he said.

"I'm sure you can," replied Holmes pleasantly, "but as this ghastly murder is, fortunately, a rare event on your beat, I should think you might appreciate some expert advice on how the crime was committed and who was responsible. My colleague here, Dr Watson, will tell you how I have solved many crimes when all others have failed, how I have assisted the prime minister of our country and several of the crowned heads of Europe. While you await your superiors from Saffron Walden you might like to accompany me outside while I search for clues. I would value your local knowledge which is far in excess of mine."

"Well," said the constable, "perhaps my superiors would like me to keep an eye on you, see what you're up to."

"Come along then," said Holmes heartily, leading the way into the garden. This was most unlike Holmes who usually carried on his investigations with complete disregard for others. Our group must have looked like a bunch of medical students being lectured by an eminent surgeon.

The snow at the front of the house lay glittering in the weak sunlight.

"See there are no marks at all in the snow here at the front. But there – at the side of the house – a ladder!" We went round the side and a ladder was leaning against the chimney stack. Around the foot of the ladder was much trampled snow.

"Aha! Please stand clear, gentlemen." Holmes approached carefully with his lens and examined the footprints generously spread around. "See, they approach from behind those trees, go to the garden shed then return here. They then proceed to the edge of the garden and, see, follow the fence and stop there immediately opposite the window of Mr Jellicoe's room."

"The fellow must have fetched the ladder from the shed, climbed it and then come down again to take up position to stare at the window," I said.

"Just so, Watson. Would you like to climb the ladder to ascertain his purpose?"

I climbed the ladder. Once at the top I could see nothing amiss with the brickwork. The ladder was too short for me to rise any higher so I could not examine the chimney pot itself. The best I could do was stretch my arm to its fullest extent and grope blindly over the rim of the chimney pot. I felt around and my hand clutched something which I grasped and pulled out. It was a sack filled with something soft. I threw it down to Holmes and climbed back down.

"It was stuffed into the top of the chimney," I said.

"Very ingenious. See, constable. How could the murderer get the window opened? He blocked the chimney so the smoke, unable to escape, would blow out into the room. Naturally, the first thought in those circumstances is to open a window, which clearly Mr Jellicoe did. That was all the murderer needed. His victim obligingly opened the window himself. The murderer then shot his victim on a clear moonlight night from a distance of barely twenty feet."

"Shot? I cannot agree there, Mr Holmes," said Dr Gregg. "I was a doctor in the army and saw many gunshot wounds. I have never seen one like my friend has suffered. And where is the bullet? It did not pass through the body."

"Perhaps the post mortem examination will find the bullet," I suggested.

"Bullets leave small, clean holes, not great gaping wounds. Even a shotgun or a blunderbuss would leave a different wound."

"The weapon was neither rifle, shotgun nor blunderbuss," agreed Holmes.

" And what about the sawdust or whatever it is?" challenged Gregg.

"Frankly I do not know," said Holmes. "But I am sure Wheeler did not approach the window any nearer than the edge of the garden."

"Wheeler?" gasped Dr Gregg.

"Do you know the man?"

"No, no, not at all. But I am amazed that you know that name."

"Clearly the name means something to you, Dr Gregg."

"I used to play backgammon fairly regularly with Jellicoe. Once, when he had imbibed freely, he fell to reminiscing about his bachelor days and said he had a pal called Wheeler and they had decided to try their luck in the gold fields of British Colombia. They were young sparks of about twenty and thought it a great adventure."

"Did he say what happened to Wheeler?"

"Oh, no. Jellicoe was a very reticent fellow, normally very guarded. It was only because he had drunk too much and was on a winning streak in our game that he was more expansive."

"Well, Watson, it would seem that our deduction was correct, but, alas, too late."

"Surely the police can catch the fellow?" asked Dr Gregg, turning to Constable Goodman.

"We'll do our best, sir," he replied.

"He has several hours start," said Holmes. "Ah, this must be the police detective." We turned to see a burly man of about fifty with generous side whiskers.

"Which of you is Holmes?" he demanded.

"I am Sherlock Holmes, this is my colleague Dr Watson, this gentleman is Dr Gregg the local doctor and friend of the deceased, Constable Goodman is the local representative of the police."

"The lady of the house says you are a private detective," said the officer.

"We have introduced ourselves, whom have I the pleasure of addressing?" asked Holmes.

"Detective Inspector Glossup. And I do not like amateurs nosing about in my cases, especially before I get here."

"Quite right," said Holmes pleasantly, "fortunately I am a professional and we have disturbed nothing, although Dr Watson climbed that ladder to remove an obstruction in the chimney. The sack at your feet had been stuffed in the pot to block the smoke."

"Stuffed in the chimney pot?" repeated Glossup incredulously.

"It caused smoke to billow out into the bedroom," said Constable Goodman eagerly.

"Why?"

"So that the man in the room would be compelled to open the window," replied Goodman with a kind of glee.

"Huh, an old trick," said Glossup dismissively.

"One does not expect originality in the provinces," replied Holmes. "Well, we must not hold you up or interfere with your investigations. As Dr Gregg has examined the body, you will no doubt wish to consult him. Oh, the murderer is a man of fifty years, strong but with a twisted leg, takes size nine in boots, his original name is Wheeler but no doubt he has an alias these days. "

Holmes made a slight bow and stalked away leaving me to nod and trot after him. We went to see Miss Jellicoe.

"I am very sorry we were not able to prevent this, Miss Jellicoe. You were quite right, your father was in mortal fear of a man called Wheeler. Did he never mention the name to you?"

"Wheeler? No, never."

"I fear he will have got clean away. We have to rely on the police and they are not very speedy in their work. Have you been back into your father's room?"

"No, I am afraid to look upon him. I am trying to be brave."

"You are bearing up wonderfully," I assured her. "If there is anything I can do?"

"Thank you, doctor. I fear his death has not yet fully hit me."

"Would you like me to stay with you? I have my bag should you need a sleeping potion tonight."

"You're very kind, but Dr Gregg is very reliable and a family friend."

"Of course," I assented.

"I am sure we can leave you in Dr Gregg's capable care, and Inspector Glossup is in charge of the official investigation. I fear Wheeler will be well away by now but we can rely on the police to do all that is possible to apprehend him. Perhaps in a few days, when you have recovered, we can speak again," said Holmes. "Then please get in touch with me at Baker Street."

So we bade farewell to the brave young lady but, to my surprise, Holmes returned to the empty garden, the two policemen and Dr Gregg now being within the house. "We still have to find which way Wheeler fled, Watson. Ah, look over there." In the field beyond were clear tracks and though the field was full of tussocks and undulations the track was clear to Holmes even if I did not always make it out. We trudged across one field into another, our trousers getting soaked up to the knees. Then we came to a pond iced over and the tracks led straight to it.

"He's crossed the pond, it's quicker to the road. Hello? No, Watson don't step on to the ice! See!" Holmes pointed. In the exact middle of the pond the ice had collapsed. Wheeler had clearly fallen through the ice. We returned with the news to Glossup who had softened his demeanour somewhat. I suspect Dr Gregg might have said a strong word or two. To give the man his due, he soon organised men to search the pond by breaking up the ice and utilising grappling hooks.

It was not long before the body of a hefty man was dragged out. A man of around fifty years of age with a twisted leg and size nine boots. Strapped across his back was a crossbow.

Back in Baker Street I asked Holmes about some matters that still puzzled me. "I am intrigued as to why you confided in Gregg and the constable and included them in your discoveries. You are usually so secretive."

Holmes laughed. "When you are in a closed community, such as we found out there in Essex, there is a great danger of the locals banding together, clamming up against the interloper from outside. With all due respect to Gregg and the local peeler, neither seemed the quickest horse in the stable and seeing Glossup did not convince me he would be much different. I had, of course, seen the ladder on our arrival and as soon as I looked out of the window and saw the foot tracks it was obvious what had taken place. It's a pity I don't have snow on all my cases. A child could have read the clues. By confiding in them I avoided their hostility."

"I presume the footprints told you the man's shoe size, what about the twisted leg?"

"The footprints showed the left foot was markedly turned in."

"You surely could not tell his age from the footprints?"

"Certainly not, Watson," Holmes laughed. "But Dr Gregg told us Wheeler and Jellicoe were both young sparks of twenty years when they went adventuring so they must have been of similar age. Miss Jellicoe told us her father was fifty years old."

"Did you realise the shot was from a crossbow? I have heard of such a weapon but never actually seen one."

"I suspected a crossbow."

"But where was the arrow, Holmes?"

"Crossbows do not shoot arrows but a much shorter metal object known as a bolt or quarrel."

"But if a small bullet cannot be found surely an enormous thing like this bolt – what is it, six inches? – should be somewhere."

"There was no such thing in the room, Watson."

"Then how do you explain it?"

"I cannot. That is why I did not voice my opinion on the weapon used."

"And that satisfies you?"

"Of course not. But we have not heard everything about this case. We do not know the reason for the enmity between the men. I shall be very surprised if we do not hear from Miss Jellicoe in the next few days."

"You expect that?"

"I do. You see there was an envelope addressed to her on the mantelpiece in her father's room which said 'Only to be opened after my death'."

Once again Holmes was correct and some two days later we had a visit from Miss Jellicoe. At last the cold weather had broken and the snow and ice were gradually melting away when we opened the door to the young lady.

"I have come to thank you, Mr Holmes, and you too Dr Watson, for your efforts on my behalf." Holmes waved his hand airily and dismissively and I inclined my head in acknowledgement. "It is only right that I confide to you a letter that was written by my late father immediately prior to his death. From this letter, which I must confess, was a great shock to me, much is made clear about his death at the hands of the man James Wheeler. I would like you to read it." She held out the envelope that was indubitably the one Holmes had last seen on the mantelpiece in the room that was the scene of the crime. Holmes asked if I may read it out aloud to which the lady consented. This is what I read:

"My Darling Adelita,

If you are reading this missive then it means I am no longer alive. You will have been aware of how afraid I have appeared these last few days and I owe you an explanation that you should, by all that's right and just, have had many years ago. I can only plead that you are still a very young woman and my intention was to reveal all to you when you were a little older, perhaps when a marriage was imminent.

When I was but ten years old I met a boy of the same age called Jim Wheeler. From the start we hit it off and became inseparable. Eventually we pricked ourselves to draw blood and allowed our bloods to mingle thus becoming blood brothers. We chimed together wonderfully and never had a disagreement as we grew up. When we were no more than eighteen years of age we were both champing at the bit to do something with our lives. The pair of us found this country hidebound and constricting so we decided to take ourselves off to the Americas. This was in 1872 and there was lots of talk about gold in British Columbia so we thought we would go out there. We ended up in a wild place called Big Bend river but the quest for gold was hopeless as there were far too many prospectors, many of them old hands from California, the so-called Fortyniners, so we did not bide long but travelled south across America.

We spent fully twelve years traversing that mighty continent, the two of us as close as two men could decently be. The dangers were immense. On more than one occasion each had to thank the other for his very life.

Eventually we found ourselves in Argentina in Southern America and things were booming in the capital Buenos Aires. There were manufactories starting up all over the place and immigrants arriving from many lands. As two smart young men from England who could speak Spanish we were in great demand in business enterprises as well as socially. To be brief, we got in with a crowd of well-to-do young people and it was there where we met Estella, a beautiful girl, an heiress. Her father had owned a bank and had died leaving her a fortune. All the fellows were after her including Jim and me. We did not think we would get even a look in but for some reason she took to us both. Very soon we were both madly in love with her and determined that we would woo and marry her. She admitted she liked us both and it was clear she did not know on which of us to bestow her favours.

It was as a result of this situation that Jim and I agreed that we would each woo her, ignoring the presence of the other. That is, we would say nothing against our rival and pretend he did not even exist. This seemed the only fair and honourable way to proceed. After all it was up to the lady to decide. Alas, we then agreed to do a despicable thing. We made a pact that whichever of us won Estella would pay the disappointed rival half the lady's fortune.

I am not proud of this arrangement but we were young and in love. And stupid. Regrettably, I was also dishonourable. Instead of our pact to say nothing of my rival I kept dropping hints about him to put him in a bad light, denigrating his character and so on. This gradual dripping turned her away from Jim and closer to me. In short, we were married. Jim was the best man and all our rich young friends attended a lavish ceremony.

After a few weeks Jim started pressing me about our bargain. He was disappointed in love and wanted to assuage his frustration with money. I kept fobbing him off and finally we had a huge row ending in fisticuffs and the police were called. Now in those days Argentina was corrupt and the richest people could buy their way out of anything and use their wealth against others. Jim was thrown into jail.

Estella was eager to visit England and I thought it a good idea to get our wealth out of Argentina and bring it back. Throughout our wanderings I never ceased to think of England as my home. So we settled in the old country and you, my dear, were born.

As you know, your birth was the death of your Mama, my beloved wife. It was a blow from which I have never recovered. I became something of a recluse and tried to shelter you from all the ills of this world. We moved about when you were an infant whilst I sought the most suitable place to bring you up. Eventually we settled here where we are now and I suspect you have forgotten any previous life. I spent my time pleasantly enough walking and reading, and have been proud to see what a beautiful woman you have become."

My reading was interrupted as at this statement Miss Jellicoe said "Tush!" Holmes gestured for me to go on.

"When those odd papers appeared pinned to the door I was not too alarmed as I thought they had no significance. It was only when I saw the picture of the cyclist that I realised they were coming from Jim Wheeler. We had often made jokes in the past about his name and bicycles. Wheeling instead of riding. Then I knew there was some point in those strange letters. They were a message. I soon realised that RLS referred to the writer Robert Louis Stevenson. As you know he is a favourite author of mine. It was a message warning me that Jim was coming to take his revenge. For over twenty years I had forgotten him and now here he was, out of the blue, coming to kill me. I was in no doubt of that. That was the reason for my terror. I knew it was useless to fly. If he had tracked me down to this remote house after all these years he would soon know where I had gone. He was probably watching the house all the time. I feared he would break in. That is why I had the bars put at the windows and the locks on the door increased.

I did not fear for you, my darling, because I knew he would not harm you. You see, I knew Jim like I know myself, and his anger was simply that I had broken our bargain. He probably did not even resent being thrown in jail – he was only there a matter of months. We had both suffered far greater torments in the past. He would be philosophical about not marrying the lady he loved but he would never forget that his own blood brother had severed a solemn pact made between us. I was doomed.

I am doomed. I do not know how my death will strike or how much longer I shall have to suffer the agony of waiting. But if you are reading this you will know that death has struck at last. You will find you are, if not a rich young lady, one who is very comfortably circumstanced. With this letter is the card of my lawyer. He is privy to my will and knows my wishes and is conversant with all the necessary arrangements.

Goodbye my darling and do not think ill of your devoted Papa who has tried his best for you.

It is signed with an affectionate farewell," I concluded as I returned the letter to Miss Jellicoe.

"So there you have it, Mr Holmes," said she.

"A very interesting and moving story, Miss Jellicoe, and you can rest at ease knowing that Jim Wheeler is also dead. You personally have nothing more to fear," replied Holmes.

"I'm sure the lawyer and Dr Gregg will assist you in any formalities," I added.

"My father has already been buried according to his wishes and I find that I am rather more than comfortably off by my standards."

"You will be able to visit art galleries, theatres and museums. Attend concerts and lectures and move in society. Pursue a life more appropriate to a young lady with all her life ahead of her," I suggested.

"No, Dr Watson, I shall use my wealth to do good works. I will detain you no longer. Thank you once again, Mr Holmes."

"Permit me to escort you down the stairs," I said. On opening the door I found the sun was shining and the snow rapidly melting, the roofs dripping. I watched Miss Jellicoe turn the corner and disappear from my view. She was a fine young woman and I admired her firm character. Just as I was about to turn to go back inside, a large icicle broke away from the gutter and fell before me. I picked it up and remarked how strong it was even in its semi-melted state. Whimsically I took it back up with me.

"Look at this Holmes. I was nearly felled by a falling icicle."

There was a long pause as Holmes stared at me. "Watson, in this case you have proved more perceptive than I have. Not only did you hit on the meaning of the cryptic notes you have now explained why there was no sign of a bullet or a bolt in the dead man."

"Have I, Holmes?" I asked quizzically.

"Remember the mysterious sawdust?"

"Yes."

"It is my opinion that Wheeler fashioned a bolt for his crossbow made from sawdust frozen in ice. By doing so he would have added strength to the ice. There would have been no heat involved as there would be by firing from a percussion gun, and the force exuded by a crossbow over the short distance employed would have been immense and inevitably lethal."

"Good Lord, Holmes. How utterly bizarre – death by icicle."

THE ORDEAL OF OSCAR WILDE

One chilly autumn day in 1893 I was having my lunch alone as Holmes ate sparingly, or never, at lunchtime. He had spent the morning pouring over his commonplace books pasting in new material and was totally absorbed, not deigning to break off even for a cup of coffee. I was just helping myself to another cup when Mrs Hudson interrupted our domestic scene by announcing an unexpected visitor. He was a young man clearly distraught, his words tumbling out in an excited incoherent manner as he spoke, and it was some time before we could get him to calm himself sufficiently to explain his business.

"My name is Ross," he said "and I have come to consult you, Mr Holmes, on the most terrible affair. A very close friend has been put under the suspicion of murdering someone. He is totally innocent, of course, but the circumstances are such that, well, I don't know what to do. Then I remembered that you, Mr Holmes, were a friend to people who have been wronged and so may be able to straighten out the matter."

Holmes lifted his hands as if to stop the flow of these tumbling words. "Calm yourself, my dear sir, and we may then understand your business."

"Yes, yes, I am not explaining myself very well. Yes." He paused, gulped, took several deep breaths then continued. "My friend was dining at a hotel last evening, with one other person, in the seclusion of his room. After dinner my friend left, the other person retiring to bed. This morning that person was found dead in his bed."

Holmes stopped Ross by saying "Before we go any further, Mr Ross, in my experience a person who relates something that purports to happen to 'a friend' is actually talking about himself. Perhaps we can drop these vague terms and concentrate on the facts."

"Oh, no, no," cried Ross, horrified, "I am not involved in any way. I say a friend because this horrible affair has happened to a close friend. I cannot reveal his name as he is man of some fame, and any taint of this nature could ruin him. He is totally innocent and must be kept out of it."

Holmes, not a patient man, was beginning to show signs of his wonted asperity. "Mr Ross, I am willing to help you, whatever your problem may be, but I cannot deal with anything without having everything clear cut. It matters not to me who this person is – I regard my clients as cases to be solved, regardless of their standing in society. Dr Watson – my friend and colleague who is the gentleman you have so far ignored – and myself have been consulted by the highest in this land and served several foreign princes and diplomats in our time. Nothing shocks us, nothing we are told leaves these four walls. Now, please answer these questions truthfully before we continue. Who is your friend in such distress?"

"I can't tell, I really can't. He may be accused of murder. He is innocent I tell you," cried Ross.

"How do you know he is innocent?" asked Holmes.

Ross gaped as if any other idea were impossible. "He couldn't, he just couldn't."

"I could tell you of loving husbands killing their wives, bishops and even judges committing murder. Believe me, Mr Ross, anybody is capable of carrying out such a dread deed. Now, I do not want to turn you away but, unless we can have a coherent narrative with names, places and times, I can do nothing."

The poor chap, clearly overwhelmed by the circumstances, and after all not very old, was close to tears but, as we waited, realised that he had to reveal these things if he expected Holmes's assistance.

"Very well. The man I speak of is Oscar Wilde." He paused.

"Yes?" prompted Holmes kindly, "And?"

"Last night he entertained a young man to dinner in the privacy of his bedroom at the Albemarle Hotel. They did not go into the restaurant because the young man was not suitably clad."

"I see. The Albemarle is in Piccadilly, I believe?"

"The corner of Piccadilly and Albemarle Street."

"Continue."

"After dinner, Oscar left the hotel and came to my apartment, arriving at about ten o'clock."

"Yes?"

"That is all there is to it. Then this morning we had a message to say that the young man had been found dead."

"And Mr Wilde is thus under suspicion because he was the last to see this young man alive?"

"Yes, yes, exactly that."

"I presume the police have been called and are investigating?" asked Holmes.

"Yes, yes, that's how we know. A friend who works in the kitchens at the Albemarle sent the message to us."

"Another friend? Your friend or Mr Wilde's friend?"

"My friend."

"I see. And have the police spoken to Mr Wilde?"

"No, no, of course not. He's in hiding. That is why I've come to you! Don't you see? The police will automatically blame him! Oh, you must save him!" Ross buried his face in his hands.

"Mr Ross, I cannot save him if he is guilty of the crime, I can only save him if he is innocent. If he is innocent then the police will not charge him."

"But we can't rely on that! There's no proof of anything! They dined together then Oscar left. They will think he bashed the boy's head in, then fled."

"Ah, now we have a little more in the way of facts. The death was caused by a blow to the head?"

"Yes, yes, so we were told."

"Where is Mr Wilde now?"

"I can't tell you, he's in hiding."

"I will have to speak with him, won't I, if I am to assist?"

"Yes, yes, of course."

"Is he still at your apartment?"

"Yes."

"Very well, do nothing that will make the police find him. He will have to face the police, of course, and that cannot be much longer delayed, but my priority will be to visit the Albemarle Hotel and view the scene of the crime. I fear it will reveal nothing as it is now some hours since the body was discovered and much may have been cleared away. But that I will do immediately. I will then seek to speak to the detective in charge. This I must do before I speak to Mr Wilde. So, rest assured I will look into this case for you, but I warn you, I may find that Mr Wilde is in fact the culprit and, if so, it is my duty to inform the police."

"He is innocent; I know he would not do such an awful thing."

"Now you must give me your address so that I can come and see you. It may well not be until tomorrow. The day is half over and I have much to do. It is essential that you do not contact me again in any way, do you understand?"

"Yes, yes."

"I will see what I can deduce as though I know nothing of Mr Wilde. Then I will introduce him into the affair and things may become clearer than you fear, Mr Ross. You say he came to you at ten o'clock?"

"Yes, I heard the clock strike as he arrived."

"And where do you live, Mr Ross?"

"Kensington. Twenty-four Hornton Street."

I had witnessed this fraught conversation and said nothing. Ross was so overwrought and eager to solicit Holmes's aid I think he was almost oblivious of my presence. It was a sign of his folly that he did so, as he was telling Holmes private matters that he wanted to conceal and, so far as he knew, I could have been anybody, even the police! I was shocked that the person under suspicion of murder should be the well-known author and playwright Oscar Wilde. I could see why his friend was eager to protect him as Wilde was a prominent figure in the high society and popular culture of our city. He had recently had two successful comedies with long runs in the West End and was never out of the newspapers, his own personality apparently as witty and amusing as the plays he wrote. I had never met the man, or even seen him or his plays, but I had read his infamous novel *The Picture of Dorian Grey* which caused a minor sensation and much execration when it was published a few years ago. Now I felt I had to interject. "I believe Mr Wilde is a married man? The police will surely have gone to his home. His wife must be distraught, not knowing where he is or what is happening."

"Yes, sir, you are quite right. I would like to confide in Constance, whom I love dearly, but I dare not go to her as it will put Oscar in jeopardy. As you say, the police will have gone to Tite Street immediately. His safety lies in Constance not knowing where he is."

"Oscar Wilde lives at Tite Street?"

"Yes, in Chelsea. I am often there. Constance, Mrs Wilde, is like a second mother to me. I lived with the Wildes for several months when I was a boy of seventeen and first came to London."

"I see," said I. "Perhaps I could deliver a message?"

"Come, Watson, the police know you as well as they know me, put your gallantry aside for once," said Holmes briskly. "We must be about our business. If the police find Wilde it will not be too unfortunate, but I would prefer to see him first if possible. Goodbye, Mr Ross."

With that Ross was driven out and we ourselves swiftly followed, taking a cab to the Albemarle Hotel.

At the hotel Holmes asked the commissionaire if the police were still here.

"Hush, if you please, sir. We are trying to keep the activities of the police from the guests at the moment."

"Quite right, too. I am Sherlock Holmes, I have been asked to investigate."

"Oh, in that case you want the third floor. A constable is on duty."

"Thank you, my man."

We swept in and up to the third floor, my look of remonstrance at Holmes receiving nothing but a curt "A white lie often saves tedious explanations." On the third floor I witnessed another example of Holmes's guile.

"Is your superior still here, constable?"

"No, Mr Holmes, the investigation was concluded hours ago."

"You know me?"

"Why, yes, sir. You spoke to me when I was on duty during the Limehouse warehouse affair."

"So I did, so I did. How good of you to remember me. Tomkins isn't it?"

"Slingsby, sir."

"Of course. But have you been on guard here for hours?"

"That I have, sir."

"Surely you must wish to relieve yourself?"

"It would be a boon and a blessing if I could leave my post to do so."

"Then you must, we will stand guard until you return."

"It would be a kindness if you could, Mr Holmes."

"Who is in charge of this case?"

"Inspector Lestrade."

"Ah, a good officer, but sometimes neglectful of his men, I fear. Off you go. You will find a w.c. on the floor below. You must be thirsty, too, here buy yourself a bottle and bring it back. We will be on guard for you." Holmes gave the man a coin and the constable hurried away. Holmes opened the door. "We must be quick, Watson. Unless the bar is busy he will be back soon. You wait outside and tap when the constable returns."

I was left outside the closed door and going along the corridor to the staircase, anxiously peered down for the first sight of the returning constable. There was, of course, a facility on the floor we were on but Holmes had cleverly gained extra minutes by the ploy of sending the man to the floor below. It seemed but a few minutes before the constable hove into view as he mounted the stairs. I raced back to the door, knocked urgently and Holmes was out of the door, with it closed behind him, before the constable came round the corner.

"Ah, that's a lot better, thank you, Mr Holmes."

"Do you know anything about the investigation, Slingsby?"

"Not really, sir, I only came on watch after it was all over. An overnight guest was found dead in his bed and murder is suspected because of a great wound on the back of his head."

"I see. So I must go to the Yard and speak with Inspector Lestrade. I would have liked to have seen the room but I suppose you are here to prevent intruders?"

"I am, Mr Holmes, and much as I would like to admit you, it is more than my job's worth."

"I would not dream of asking you, Slingsby. Good bye."

"Good bye, Mr Holmes."

We took a cab to Scotland Yard and on the way I remarked it was fortunate that Holmes had remembered the constable. "I don't, not at all. I took a chance at the name – they're all called things like Tomkins. I don't even remember the Limehouse warehouse affair, or whatever he was on about."

I asked Holmes if he had found any clues during his brief visit to the room.

"Alas, no, Watson. I did not really expect to as the hotel management were sure to have cleared up after the police had left. The bed was stripped to the mattress awaiting making up again, otherwise the room was ready to receive another guest. Although the man's suit was still hanging in the wardrobe."

We were fortunate in finding Inspector Lestrade in his office.

"Why, Mr Holmes! I didn't realise you were a friend of Mr Oscar Wilde."

"Why do you say that, Lestrade? I've never met the man."

"Well, I can't think why else you should come and see me, un-announced, on the day that a body has been found dead in Mr Wilde's hotel bedroom."

"You know me, Lestrade. I am a connoisseur of crime and this case seems to have some interesting features."

"It seems pretty clear cut to me, Mr Holmes. This Oscar Wilde fellow is an invert. He often takes a room at the Albemarle Hotel. He lures young men there and buggers them."

"For God's sake, Lestrade!" I cried. "You cannot go round slandering an eminent person like Oscar Wilde."

"Your outrage does you credit, Doctor, but how else do you explain the circumstances? Would you entertain a man, no more than a youth, in your hotel bedroom? Wilde has disappeared, pushed off leaving a dead man naked in the bed, his head bashed in. He has not returned home, as surely he would have done if he were innocent, but has disappeared. Probably trying to flee the country. I have all the ports and railway stations on alert. He won't get away from me."

"You seem sure Wilde is your man," said Holmes.

"How else can it be? We have only to find him and I'll get the truth out of him."

"Was the door locked?"

"What? How do you mean?"

"A simple enough question, Lestrade," said Holmes patiently. "If, after dining, say at ten o'clock, Wilde left the boy – still alive – and departed the premises, should the door not be locked on the inside anybody could have entered at any time thereafter. Perhaps a hotel employee, or a sneak thief hoping to snatch some jewellery from a rich guest. There are many possibilities."

"Yes, well, there are, but some are more likely than others. Anyway how come you know about it. It hasn't had time to reach the news-papers."

"In this great metropolis there is little in the way of crime that does not come to my ear, Lestrade."

"Well, I hope you are not concealing the whereabouts of the man Wilde, or you could find yourself in serious trouble, Mr Holmes."

"Lestrade, as you know perfectly well, I am and always have been on the side of law and order. How many times have I aided you in your investigations so that you could bring right and justice and the full majesty of the law upon some wretched miscreant?"

"Yes," agreed Lestrade grudgingly, "you have been of help in the past."

"And shall continue to be so in the future, but we cannot jump to conclusions. A man is innocent until proved guilty."

"Are you trying to tell me my job, Mr Holmes?"

"Not at all, but I would appreciate your assistance. Perhaps you could describe how you found the body?"

"There's no secret about it, Mr Holmes, it will be in all the papers tomorrow morning I have no doubt. I was asked to go over to the Albemarle Hotel as the manager had reported a dead body in one of the bedrooms. It seems the occupant had requested to be given a wake-up call at eight o'clock, with a breakfast on a tray. A servant duly gave the call but, as there was no response, knocked again and finally tried the door which, to answer your question, was not locked. The servant saw the man apparently asleep, put the tray down and went to rouse him by shaking him. He could not rouse him, then realising he must be dead, summoned help. Now it's not unknown for people to die in their hotel bed but usually they are older folk. This man was little older than a youth, so a doctor was sent for in particular haste. He soon found that there had been a blow to the back of the head that must have killed the boy instantly."

"Was the boy lying on his back?"

"Yes, the wound was only visible when the doctor moved the body during examination."

"Was there any blood?"

"Very little, a trickle absorbed by the pillow on which the head rested."

"I see. So what did you make of that?"

"I suppose the blow caused internal bleeding, the skull was stove in."

"Yes, but how could he have received such a blow if his head were resting on the pillow?"

"Come, Mr Holmes, surely it is clear. The assailant struck him on the head until dead then lifted him on to the bed and covered him with the bedclothes to simulate the appearance of sleeping."

"Was there any sign of a struggle? Overturned furniture, ruffled carpet and so on?"

"No, Mr Holmes, everything was serene. Even the ashtray had not been disturbed."

"What was in the ashtray?"

"Why, ash, Mr Holmes, ash. That is its purpose."

"Any stubs?"

"Yes, several, some cheroots that I believe Mr Oscar Wilde currently favours, and a cigarette end."

"Does that not seem significant?"

"These two had dinner together, in the room. I expect Wilde puffed away spouting forth frivolous and insidious garbage in his customary manner while the boy sucked on a solitary cigarette."

"Did you come to any conclusion as to the weapon that struck the blow?"

"Nothing was present in the room but that means nothing. Wilde, sorry, the assailant could have carried that away with him."

"True. Now you say the boy was naked under the covers?"

"Yes."

"What significance do you put on that?"

"Well, begging Dr Watson's pardon, I think they were probably up to lewd antics, fell out about something and the blow was struck."

"Some people sleep naked without any night attire, Lestrade," said I.

"Do they?"

"Indeed."

"Did you find the boy's clothes?" asked Holmes.

"Oh yes, his suit was hanging in the wardrobe and his shirt and underclothes were flung on a chair."

"Did you examine them?"

"For what purpose?"

"Clues?"

"They were just clothes – young men's clothes."

"Fashionable?"

"I don't know. I'm not a young man of fashion."

"Where's the body now?"

"In the morgue. Do you want to see it?"

"I would very much like to," said Holmes.

So we all trooped over to the morgue where Lestrade gained permission for us to enter and the attendant led us to where the body rested. When the sheet was pulled away there was the body of a naked youth apparently asleep on his back, no wound visible. However, peering round the side of his head I could see where the doctor had shaved the dark hairs away to gain access to the death wound at the back of the head. Holmes produced a folding rule and made measurements of the feet and other limbs.

"About five feet ten inches, would you say, Lestrade?"

"If you say so."

"And about ten stone, perhaps ten and a half, he tends to the plump."

"Well, he's not Jewish," said Lestrade.

"Thank you," said Holmes to the attendant. "You may replace the sheet."

"Have you learned anything, Mr Holmes?"

"I've simply seen what you have seen."

"I know you have your own special methods," said Lestrade, somewhat condescendingly.

Taking our leave of Scotland Yard we returned home to Baker Street where our dinner awaited.

The following morning after a hearty breakfast, Holmes and I set forth by cab. I was somewhat surprised to hear Holmes order the cabby to drive to Harrods department store in the Brompton Road. Once there we entered the store and Holmes strode out hither and thither, myself following lamely in his wake until we emerged via a different exit from whence we had entered. Holmes hailed a cab and we bundled in.

"Well, what was all that about?" I gasped.

"We were being followed," answered Holmes.

"Followed?"

"Yes. As soon as we left the house. I rather think Lestrade has set a man to shadow us in the hope we would lead him to Oscar Wilde. He clearly suspects that we are in league with him in some way."

"And have we shaken him off?"

"Oh, yes. But we shall alight some way from Ross's address. Should he be traced, I do not want the cabby to be able to inform the police."

"Aren't you being somewhat over-cautious, Holmes?"

"One can never be too cautious in some circumstances, Watson, and never too bold in others."

Ross's rooms were in a building that seemed to comprise entirely of bachelor apartments. I wondered what ties of friendship bound the flamboyant Oscar Wilde to this unpretentious young man. Ross was clearly relieved to see us.

"Thank God, you've come, Mr Holmes. Come in, come in. I haven't slept a wink all night. There has been no sign of the police as yet."

"Is Mr Wilde available to speak to us?"

"Oh, yes. He retreated when the bell sounded in case it was the law. I'll fetch him in."

Although I had often read of Oscar Wilde, seen photographs and caricatures, I had never seen him in the flesh. He turned out to be a large man, well fleshed-out, with a pasty face, bad teeth and a charming manner.

"Thank you so much for coming, Mr Holmes. I presume this is Dr Watson your esteemed amanuensis? Welcome. I am always delighted to meet a fellow author," said Wilde, shaking my hand.

"Perhaps you will tell us exactly what happened and why you are fleeing from the police, Mr Wilde?" asked Holmes.

"Oh, Oscar, please call me Oscar, all my friends do – and many of my enemies."

"I regret it is not my policy to befriend my clients, Mr Wilde, or witnesses, or potential criminals. In this instance my client is Mr Ross. Please explain what happened."

"Well, I must go back to the previous day, Mr Holmes. I had been giving a lecture at the Free Trade Hall in Manchester. There were over a thousand persons present. I was speaking on The House Beautiful. They were delightfully enthusiastic. People think because Manchester is a gloomy manufacturing city that it has no artistic soul. In fact the inhabitants are very musical and appreciative of art and literature in all its manifestations."

"Is this relevant to your story?" asked Holmes, tersely.

"Indeed it is. You see I stayed overnight, departing on the train the following day, Tuesday. On the platform I engaged in conversation with a youth, broad of dialect but delightful of aspect. He put me in mind of Ganymede, Jove's cupbearer. This youth was carrying a violin case and it appeared he was London bound, as was I. So to prolong our pleasant conversation I forewent my first class carriage and sat with the boy in the plebeian part of the train."

"What was the boy's name?" asked Holmes.

"I don't know, Mr Holmes. He said his friends called him Reggie and as I considered myself his new friend I did likewise."

"I see. Proceed."

"The journey passed like lightning. The boy was an enchanting companion, so simple and naïve. I doubt if he had ever left Manchester before, he certainly had never been to London and was full of the wonder of everything. It must be splendid to be young, with everything still to discover. He was clearly a talented boy because he was bound for an audition to gain admittance to a conservatoire. It seems the boy was a brilliant violinist and he had recommendations from his teachers in Manchester for this conservatoire in London. The boy thought it was a great thing, and I'm sure it was. All too soon we were at our destination. Now during our conversation it transpired that his employer, of whom he spoke highly and who seemed to be his sponsor in the enterprise, had arranged overnight accommodation at some squalid premises off Leicester Square, or somewhere equally unmentionable. I had engaged a room at the Albemarle hotel so I suggested he might prefer to sleep there where he would be much more comfortable and far handier for his audition in the morning, which I gather was to be at the unholy hour of ten o'clock."

"Why had you engaged this room, Mr Wilde? As your home is in Tite Street, surely the natural thing would have been to proceed to your own home after the long journey?"

"Yes, one would assume that to be the usual thing. But I am not a man who prides himself on doing the usual. The fact is I am a writer and I find it impossible to write in domestic surroundings with my two boisterous sons and my wife's visiting friends. Therefore, I make a practice of renting rooms both in London and at other places. The fact is, I rely on my pen for my living, Mr Holmes, and it is essential that I am able to turn out work to deadlines. I am sure Dr Watson will appreciate the dilemma."

"Indeed," I assented.

"You see, not only had I been engaged to present my speech at Manchester, but I had been commissioned to write a piece for the *Morning Post* about Manchester and its place in modern society. That is why I took the room at the Albemarle hotel instead of going home."

"But after engaging the hotel room you decided to forego it and still did not go home, did you, Mr Wilde?"

"No, you are quite right. The circumstances are these. When we arrived at the hotel I proposed dinner, but the boy, having only the clothes he travelled in, would not have been admitted to the restaurant, so I elected to have dinner served in my room. As it was getting late and Reggie said he would like to have a practice on his violin before sleeping I said my farewell, leaving instructions that he be woken at eight in the morning with a simple breakfast. I quit the building and, as it was now late, I came here to my dear friend Robbie where I spent the night, writing my piece in the morning."

"I see," said Holmes.

"I would have then returned home to my loving wife but, before I could depart, a message came to say that Reggie had been found dead in my room at the Albemarle. As you can imagine I was horror struck! I had only had a few hours acquaintanceship with the boy and now he was dead. It had nothing to do with me of course, but how could I feel otherwise than responsible? If I had not persuaded him to stay at that hotel he would have been safe and sound in his lodgings in Leicester Square. It was too horrible to contemplate. I was distraught! It was Robbie who pointed out my dangerous position. As I left the hotel late at night after engaging a room, it would be automatically assumed that I was responsible. It would appear that I had murdered the youth and then fled. That is why I asked Robbie to consult you, Mr Holmes. I am completely innocent but I can see how it will appear to others – especially the police."

"There are other possibilities, Mr Wilde. Perhaps Reggie would have met his death at his lodgings in Leicester Square? He could have been followed by someone from Manchester, and your accompanying him thwarted an earlier attempt on the youth's life," said Holmes.

"Do you think so?" Wilde snatched eagerly at the suggestion.

"I merely point out alternatives to what really must have happened. Just as you state your story as an alternative picture, so there will be other possibilities too. As far as you are concerned we have to establish proof that you left the boy alive and were elsewhere at the time of his death."

"Can we do that?" cried Wilde hopefully.

"We can certainly try. You left the Albemarle at what time?"

"9.30 as near as I recall."

"How did you get here?"

"I took a cab from the Albemarle. The commissionaire hailed one from the rank. There is a Hackney Carriage stand just opposite the hotel."

"Excellent! No doubt the commissionaire will recall the incident. We can also find the cab driver who will no doubt recall the journey."

"He should do, I gave him a half-sovereign!"

"Mr Ross can vouch as to your arrival here at, what was it? Ten o'clock?"

"Exactly that, Mr Holmes. I heard a clock striking as I opened the door," said Ross.

"And you have not left these premises since."

"No, no, not at all. I have been too afraid," admitted Wilde.

"Then providing we can prove Reggie was still alive at any time after 9.30 you are in the clear."

"But can we do that?"

"I don't know, Mr Wilde, but I shall now make enquiries. Do you know where Reggie was going for his audition?"

"I've no idea, Mr Holmes. It was a music college. I'm sure he told me but I cannot remember."

"Now there is one important thing, Mr Wilde. So long as you avoid the police you are throwing the greatest suspicion on yourself. An innocent man does not flee. Perhaps you have seen the headlines in this morning's papers? The newspapers are already hinting that you are the guilty man. I suggest you give yourself up to the police immediately and co-operate in every way possible. Inspector Lestrade is in charge of the case. You must tell him everything you have told me. The police cannot put you on trial without evidence, and to find verification they will have to make enquiries. Those investigations will clear you of all suspicion. In this country we do not string people up on hearsay. You may be held in prison for a day or two while enquiries proceed, but I am sure you will be granted bail if such is the case. There is more to this murder than meets the eye and I have my own enquiries to make."

"If Oscar goes to the police may he say that you are defending him?" asked Ross.

"No, I am not defending him, Mr Ross. I am making enquiries on *your* behalf, enquiries that will, I am convinced, show Mr Wilde's innocence. You may tell that to Inspector Lestrade. The decision is yours."

And so we left the two friends wondering how they should act.

Holmes's first action was to go into a music shop to make enquiries about Music Schools. The assistant, unable to answer the questions, summoned her employer from the recesses of the shop. He proved to be a stooping, aged man with a bald head and spectacles as thick as jam-jar bottoms.

"May I be of assistance? My colleague tells me you are seeking a music academy?"

"Yes. A nephew of mine has travelled down from Manchester to audition at one of the London music colleges but he neglected to tell me which one and I have no idea where to go. I agreed to meet him there to take him for lunch."

"Oh dear, that is most awkward. There are many music schools in London. We ourselves run a small music school for woodwind players."

"I think it will be one of the main ones as he has been recommended by his tutors in Manchester."

"I see. Well there are several. There is the Trinity College of Music, that's in Mandeville Place, just off Wigmore Street. Or it could be the Guildhall School of Music."

"At the Guildhall?"

"No, it's situated in John Carpenter Street. What is your nephew's instrument?"

"The violin."

"It could be the London College of Music, that's in Great Marlborough Street. Oh dear, now what's that other one, oh, my memory. Oh, there is the new Royal College of Music – that's a splendid new building in South Kensington, near the Albert Hall, I forget the name of the road. But that's not the one I was trying to remember . . . Ah, yes, of course, the Royal Academy of Music, that's in Hanover Square. I think those are the most distinguished. Actually I believe Sir Charles Hallé has recently opened a College of Music in Manchester, perhaps the boy should try for there?"

"You have been most helpful, thank you."

I had, of course, noted down all these names and addresses and it did not surprise me that Holmes's next suggestion was to visit each in turn to see if we could find out more about Reggie.

"We must divide, Watson. Perhaps you would take Trinity, London College and Royal Academy as they are clustered reasonably together. I will cover Guildhall which is near Blackfriars Bridge if I am not mistaken, and then I will go over to South Kensington to the new Royal College."

"And what is our approach?"

"We need to know if a prospective candidate called Reggie turned up for his audition at ten o'clock yesterday."

"He couldn't if he were dead, Holmes."

"Of course not, but we don't tell them that. We need to find out his full name and address in Manchester."

"Of course! His family will not know. How terrible. They must be wondering why he has not returned home."

"Perhaps you could use that if they are reluctant to give information. I'm sure you will know how to play it, Watson."

"Shall we meet back at Baker Street?"

"Yes. I have also to call in at the National Gallery as well as the colleges."

"The National Gallery?" I repeated in astonishment.

"Ganymede," replied Holmes, leaving me standing outside the music shop.

My first two calls were useless. At one they had not been having auditions at all, and at the other they seemed to think I was trying to enrol my son on a violin course that was over-subscribed. In desperation I abandoned that, thinking if all the others proved to be groundless Holmes could come back to it. However, I struck gold at my last call – the Royal Academy in Tenterden Street off Hanover Square. They had, indeed, held auditions yesterday and were having them each morning throughout the week. I gathered that young hopefuls of both sexes were coming from all over the country to try for places in the new academic year. My enquiry took me to the admissions office where I spun my tale and was able to put my query to the clerk in charge of the auditions.

"Reginald you say?"

"Yes, I do not know his surname."

"And he auditioned here on Tuesday morning at ten o'clock?"

"Yes, yesterday. So I believe."

The clerk opened a ledger and turned the pages. "Ah, yes. Here we have it. But I'm afraid the young man did not actually attend."

"No?"

"No, he was, as you say, expected at 10am to appear before Professor Atkinson. His instrument is the violin."

"Well that is clearly the person I seek. Does it give his surname?"

"Of course. Scutt."

"Scut? S, C, U, T?"

"Double T."

"Is there an address?"

"There is. However, I must ask your interest in these enquiries."

"I thought I had explained? An accident."

"Yes, you said there had been an accident and a young man injured."

"Well, it seems to be this boy Reginald Scutt. His family will have to be informed. They are, I believe, in Manchester."

"Yes, so it would seem. The address I have is 17 Granby Row, Manchester."

"Thank you, I will contact his parents right away."

"What sort of accident would this be?"

"Er, he was knocked down by a brewer's dray."

"Is he badly injured?"

"Oh, yes, quite severely."

"How unfortunate. Such promise destroyed so young."

"Indeed, indeed."

"We were surprised when Reginald did not appear and we received no explanation. Places here are greatly sought after and the auditions are very competitive. Reginald had been highly recommended. An audition once obtained is not to be cast away lightly."

"No, no, indeed."

"Please convey our regrets to Mr and Mrs Scutt."

"Yes, of course. Thank you."

Glowing with pride at my success I hastened back to Baker Street but it was many hours before Holmes returned and I was able to give him my news.

"Excellent, Watson! You have done well. Is there a telegram for me?"

"On the mantelshelf," said I, nodding. Holmes took it up and ripped it open.

"Excellent! All is falling into place. This is from Lestrade in reply to an enquiry I made. It seems there was no violin present when the police searched the room."

"Is that important?"

"It could well be the crux of the matter. I shall have to travel to Manchester tomorrow."

"Do you wish me to accompany you?" I asked.

"That will not be necessary, Watson. However, you would render me a great service if you could follow up the enquiries at the Albemarle Hotel. Find out the truth regarding Wilde's story. See if everything tallies. See if you can find the cabby and so on. Could you do that?"

"Of course, Holmes. I will do my best."

Holmes departed early the next day and I spent a very fruitful time on the enquiries entrusted to me. It proved to be easier than I had feared. Oscar Wilde was a well-known figure in London and a regular guest at the Albemarle hotel. There was little he could do there without it being remarked and the commissionaire not only remembered ordering a cab from the rank, he knew which cabby was driving it. He was, of course, familiar with the regulars on the rank opposite the hotel as he summoned them constantly on behalf of guests. I had to wait awhile before I could speak to the cabby as he was plying his trade and I had to bide my time until he was free to speak to me. He remembered Wilde's taking his cab on the Tuesday night, and the address where he delivered him, as it was one where he had often taken him before. So well, so good. However, I had the nagging thought that Wilde could, in fact, have returned to the hotel later, perhaps after midnight, but the commissionaire cleared that suspicion by stating there was a night porter on duty at all times and nobody would have got past him unbeknownst because after midnight guests have to ring a bell to gain admission. So it seemed as though Holmes had been right and Wilde was in the clear.

These activities, so briefly stated, had taken most of the day, as I had also been able to speak with the manager who told me that Reggie had been heard practicing his violin at 10.30pm. In fact, a guest in a nearby room had complained and a member of staff had been to the room to ask Reggie to desist. The boy was most apologetic and stopped immediately. So he was definitely alone and alive at that time.

I jotted all these facts down for Holmes, not relying on my memory, and spent the rest of the day at my club. Holmes had not returned by evening and I ate a solitary dinner. He had not returned when I retired to bed, but I heard him come in shortly after so had to contain my impatience until the following morning.

When I went down to breakfast I discovered Holmes had already eaten and was looking at the morning paper. He threw it over to me. "It seems Oscar Wilde has taken my advice," he said.

Wilde had indeed gone to the police and the scribe had nothing further to say except that Inspector Lestrade was in charge of the case, several leads were being followed, and Mr Wilde was not a suspect, but a witness in the affair.

"Lestrade must have checked up on Wilde's alibi," I said. "We must have been following each other around as I spent the day as you requested."

"I saw your note, Watson. Well done. It is much as I expected."

"How did you get on in Manchester, Holmes?"

"Very satisfactorily. Do you know if Wilde is back at home?"

"I've no idea."

"I must send some urgent wires, excuse me." And with that I was left alone to eat breakfast while Holmes departed to the telegraph office.

On his return some time later he informed me that we were due at Scotland Yard at ten o'clock so off we set for the appointment.

Lestrade was not pleased to see us. "I got your telegram, Mr Holmes. You must know I cannot dance attendance on you at your whim. I have many duties. I have other cases besides this affair with Wilde."

"Of course, Lestrade, but I am sure you would like to close your book on this one."

"Are you telling me you have solved it?"

"Alas, no. But I have some important and vital information that you must know. The whole aspect of the case is altered."

"Then you had better get on with what you have to say."

"If I may try your patience a little longer I have asked Oscar Wilde to join us."

"I've only just let the fellow go. He was here all day yesterday."

"But you agree he is innocent?"

"He seems to have a cast iron alibi," agreed Lestrade grumpily.

"Is the corpse still in the morgue?"

"I haven't given any order for its discharge yet."

"Has Wilde seen the corpse?"

Lestrade stared. "No, is there any reason why he should?"

"A very cogent reason. Ah, here comes the man himself." At that moment Oscar Wilde entered. He looked worn and haggard and his clothes were less than his usual immaculate turnout.

"What is this? I've been dragged out of bed and summoned here. I thought you had released me?"

"I have, Mr Wilde. We are gathered at the behest of Mr Sherlock Holmes who, I believe, has been counselling you in this affair."

"I see. Well, here I am."

"I would like you to view the corpse," said Holmes.

"My God, must I?" gasped Wilde.

"Indeed you must. Without delay."

"It won't be a pretty sight by now, Mr Holmes."

"Come, less talk. Let's go."

We all made our way to the morgue and Holmes asked the attendant to reveal the head alone. Wilde steeled himself to look. "My God! It's Alfie Craggs!"

"Thank you. Come gentlemen," said Holmes, and we returned to Lestrade's office.

"What's all this about, Mr Holmes? I thought the body was that of a person called Reggie. Now Mr Wilde tells us that it is Alfie Craggs."

Holmes looked at Wilde. "I was convinced some time ago that the body was not that of Reginald Scutt, but I had not bargained on it being a person known to you. Perhaps you can explain?"

"This is all beyond me, Mr Holmes. I am quite bewildered."

"Alfie Craggs is known to us by reputation here at the yard," said Lestrade. "He is a small-time blackmailer. He specialises in targeting men of a certain predilection, manoeuvres them into a compromising situation, then blackmails them."

"Yes, yes," answered Wilde, "That is the man. He has a letter of mine and was attempting to extort money from me for its return."

"A compromising letter?" asked Lestrade.

"Not at all. In fact it is a rather beautiful prose poem. One of the best things I've done. He said he knew a man who would give twenty pounds for it. I told him to take it as it was far more than I would have been paid for publishing it."

"Perhaps we can now arrive at the truth between us. You, Mr Wilde, met an unknown youth on the train from Manchester. You said he reminded you of Ganymede."

"Who's he when he's at home?" asked Lestrade rudely.

"According to Mr Wilde he is Jove's cupbearer. Greek mythology. Now I had the thought in the back of my mind that Ganymede was a beautiful youth with golden tresses. I checked later to see if my memory of the classics be faulty. It was not. When I saw the suit hanging in the wardrobe –"

"I didn't know you had been to the crime scene! How did you get in?" demanded Lestrade.

"With great difficulty, Lestrade. Your man was most efficient and in no way neglectful. Unfortunately, my glimpse was very fleeting but I noticed the suit. It was clearly a cheap provincial sort of suit, one that I believe is called 'off-the-peg' in Manchester, rather than a bespoke tailored suit. I also saw the shoes and other clothes upon a chair. I also observed the bed posts on the bed. Now, Lestrade, when you showed us the body in the morgue you will recall I took measurements. These showed me that the shoes I had seen were undoubtedly of a size to match the feet, but the size and bulk of the body appeared too large for the suit I had seen. However, I was taken aback to see the dead body was that of a commonplace young man with distinctly black hair, when I was expecting a latter day Ganymede. Either Mr Wilde was in error, which knowing his literary reputation and his degree in the classics I doubted, or there was something amiss. Logically, the body should have been of a slighter, fair haired young man. Perhaps, Mr Wilde, you can confirm my deduction?"

"Yes, certainly, Mr Holmes. Reggie was on the small side and distinctly under-nourished and he had fair hair. Not at all like Alfie Craggs."

"So, Lestrade, when you informed me that the violin was missing, it seemed clear that Reggie had taken his violin and fled in Alfie Craggs's suit."

"Why should he do that, Holmes?" I asked.

"Because he had killed Craggs and his aim was to get away and leave the dead body masquerading as himself. Apart from his recent acquaintance Mr Wilde, who had apparently left his life again, nobody in London knew him. He was a provincial youth without any experience of grand hotels. I am sure the death was an accident and the poor lad panicked.

We'll come back to that aspect. He probably intended changing clothes entirely but, realising the discrepancy in size, it was impossible and pointless to change shoes, shirt etc so settled merely for the most obvious – the suit. He was a dedicated musician, he would never dream of abandoning his instrument. Where he went on leaving the Albemarle I do not know. He was due to attend an audition the following morning, but he was now afraid he would be identified so didn't turn up. However, Dr Watson here, tracked down the conservatoire where Reggie was to audition and found out the boy's surname – Scutt – and his home address in Manchester."

"You would have been wiser to tell the police all this, Doctor," glowered Lestrade.

"Mr Holmes is telling you now," I answered.

"With this information I went to Manchester yesterday. The address is a music shop, the proprietor one Amos Leadbetter. Reginald Scutt was his employee. I also met Miss Leadbetter the daughter of Amos. There is an understanding between Scutt and Miss Leadbetter. It was through the urging of Miss Leadbetter that her father put forward Scutt as a candidate for the conservatoire here in London. It seems his talent on the violin is exceptional. As an amateur of the violin myself I regret I have been unable to witness the youth's playing. They were both eagerly awaiting his return and were distressed that he had not come back. Miss Leadbetter, in particular, being acutely worried. This distress was added to when Mr Amos Leadbetter received a letter from the landlady of the lodgings he had engaged, saying she had reserved a room and waited up until late, but nobody had arrived. She demanded payment of Mr Leadbetter who had made these arrangements for the boy. I was obliged to tell them that the matter was in the hands of the police, and they furnished me with a photograph of Reggie Scutt." Holmes took out a *carte de visite* and handed it to Wilde. "Is that Reggie?"

"Yes. That's him."

"I should have that. We will take copies and distribute them. He is a murderer. He cannot be allowed to get away," said Lestrade.

"You shall have it, Lestrade, that was my intention. To prove that the dead man is not Reginald Scutt, and that Mr Wilde is not responsible for his death."

"This is all quite bewildering," said Wilde.

"So now we come to Alfie Craggs; as you say, Lestrade, a known petty crook. How did he get in, why should he attempt to see Mr Wilde and, finding Reggie there instead, why should Reggie kill him?"

"You've told us everything else, are you not going to enlighten us on that too, Mr Holmes?" asked Lestrade sarcastically.

"If I could for certain, I most assuredly would do everything possible to make your case complete, Lestrade, but here I can only surmise, and I prefer certainties. Mr Wilde, you said the news of the death came to you via a friend of Mr Ross's who works in the hotel kitchens?"

"Yes," agreed Wilde.

"Is it likely that this friend was also a friend of Alfie Craggs?"

"Quite likely," answered Wilde.

"There's a group of young fellows – clerks, telegraph boys and so on who prey on older men," said Lestrade. "I'm sure you recall the Cleveland Street affair. My colleague Inspector Abbeline blamed upper-class toffs for corrupting poor lads. The kind of men who are what my mother would have called powder puffs. We have to call them inverts today. But I think the young villains are already evil and see these older men as a meal ticket. I hope you are not mixed up with them, Mr Wilde."

"Certainly not. I told you, Craggs attempted to blackmail me, but failed because all he had was a harmless prose-poem."

"It would appear he gained entry via the kitchens after being tipped off that you would be at the Albemarle hotel that particular night. No doubt he intended to add some form of further persuasion to extort money from you. We cannot tell what happened when he found Scutt there in place of you, but it would seem to me they had some sort of conversation."

"How can you know that, Mr Holmes?"

"There was a cigarette butt in the ashtray I believe? Reggie did not smoke, I ascertained that fact from the Leadbetters. Did he smoke a cigarette while you were with him, Mr Wilde?"

"No. You are correct. He refused my offer of both cheroots and cigarettes."

"I think Craggs smoked that cigarette. The rest were yours, Mr Wilde. Perhaps Craggs made some proposition or suggestion to Scutt that caused offence, and a scuffle ensued. Craggs was clearly of bigger build but I think he was pushed, or fell accidentally, his head striking the brass knob on the bed post. On each is an ornamental brass ball about the size of a tennis ball. I think you will find that one of those exactly fits the wound in the back of Craggs's head. There may even be traces of blood or hair or some tiny indication on the ball itself. I have not been able to examine the room properly."

"Wonderful!" cried Wilde, "You are a veritable genius, Mr Holmes! I am sure you have read the signs aright."

"Well, Mr Holmes, you may have proved that the corpse is not Reginald Scutt but Alfie Craggs, you may have proved Mr Wilde was not the killer, and you may have enough evidence to try the real murderer, but how are we going to find him?"

"You are the police, Lestrade, I'm sure you have your own special methods."

That was all that need be done, as Holmes's task had been to prove Oscar Wilde was not a murderer and in this he had succeeded triumphantly. However, as an author I realise such an ending, whilst satisfactory in itself, would be all the more gratifying if I could actually show that the villain was brought to book. What I did not know at the time was that Holmes had left our address with the Leadbetters in Manchester asking them to get in touch should Scutt return, or if they heard of him.

Thus it was some three months later that Holmes passed a letter to me. It was brief and read as follows:

"Dear Mr Holmes,

I have received the enclosed from Reginald Scutt. It is self-explanatory. After you have read it I would be obliged if you would return it to me as it will be the last memento of one I shall see no more.

Yours sincerely,

Rachel Leadbetter"

The enclosure read as follows:

"My Dearest Rachel,

You will have been wundering what has happened to me. I have gone threw a terrible time. When I went to London to the audition I met a man who perswaded me to stay at his hotel not the place where I was to go. He seemed very kind so I did. He bought me a dinner there. It was a nobby hotel full of nobby people. I had gone to bed and there was a knock at the door. When I unlocked it a man pushed his way in he said where's Oscar who are you and so on. I do not know who he was. He was very angry and he called me vile names which I could not say to you never mind write down. He grabed hold of me and we tuseled and I pushed him away and he fell and hit his head on the bed post and fell to the floor dead. I did not know what to do. I had killed him. So I took the clothes off him and got him on to the bed and I put on his suit. It was a bit big becos he was bigger than me. I hoped peeple would think he was me as I left my suit. I got away without being seen as there was some nobby peeple coming in through the door and the doorman was bothering with them. I did not know what to do. I went to the river and got on a boat in secret and it went to France where I am now and been since. I am fritend the police will find me so I can say no more. Please do not say I am in France or they will find me. I wanted you to know I am safe and all right. It was not my fault I killed that man. I do not know if I will ever see you again, my dearest, I am playing my violin in cafes and bars do not try to find me the police will follow you. All my love Reggie."

"What will you do, Holmes?" I asked.

"Why, return the lady's letter as requested."

THE SURREY MAN-MONKEY

Of my friends Thurston is the jolliest and we meet at our club weekly for a game of billiards. However, I have to confess his sense of humour is rather juvenile and every year he drags me with him to see a pantomime. I would not be telling the truth if I said I did not like these excursions. I enjoy them very much, but I would not attend such shows if Thurston did not demand my company.

This year we went to see *Sindbad the Sailor* at the Surrey which is south of the river. As usual they put on a fine traditional pantomime and we had a jolly time. The star performer, a Monsieur Gouffe, played the part of a great ape. He opened his performance by doing several simple acrobatic stunts such as standing on his hands and turning cartwheels which were rendered amusing by his monkey-like manner. But that was just the preliminary to the hilarious antics that followed as the ape left the stage and ran amok through the audience. Some people screamed, not from fear, because nobody could have believed the creature was a real animal but clearly a man in a costume, but because they entered into the spirit of the charade. Others were laughing and a general hilarious tumult occurred. It was soon clear that M Gouffe was a very clever and skilful acrobat, as he climbed up on the pillars to the dress circle level and actually walked along the front of the circle parapet. All the while pretending to be a monkey, he did amusing things – he picked up a man's hat and stuck it on his own head – and was irresistibly comic as he pranced about.

The man-monkey roamed all over the auditorium; it was a wonder to know where he would appear next – in the gallery one minute, then disappearing to pop-up elsewhere. In the boxes he caused hilarity by picking up a tray of chocolates in one box and offering it to the patrons in the adjoining box. It was all very good natured and the audience loved it, nobody taking the least offence. He stole a lady's handbag and she chased after him brandishing her umbrella.

Finally he returned to the stage by sliding down a rope that had clearly been tied for the purpose because, before finally dropping to the stage, using his feet he pushed himself away from the plaster proscenium so that he was swinging like a pendulum. Then the old lady appeared in the box brandishing her umbrella at the man-monkey, who, now squatting on the stage, had opened her bag, removed the contents and was holding them up for all to see. Ridiculously, the old lady, herself, descended the rope to great gales of laughter as she floundered about. One did not need to be as perceptive as my friend Sherlock Holmes to realise that this 'old lady' was not a genuine member of the audience but a stooge playing a part.

When the old lady gained the stage she started belabouring the man-monkey with her brolly whereupon the ape grabbed her skirt and the 'lady' ran off screaming – without her skirt, which remained in the hands of the ape. As without her skirt the 'lady' was revealed to be wearing ludicrous underwear no offence could be caused, the many children in the audience screaming with delight at this apparent indignity suffered by such a matriarch. However, I, myself, thought the bounds of decency were overstepped somewhat by the crude animal-like manner in which the man-monkey pursued her into the wings. Thurston thought it was hilarious, but, as I have said, he has a juvenile sense of humour.

The curtain fell for the interval after this scene, the hub-hub in the audience making it well-nigh impossible to follow such a wild caper. After the interval, although the clown and harlequin etc were amusing enough in the harlequinade, it is very similar every year and really only entertains the children who have not seen it before. Needless to say, Thurston always thoroughly enjoys the harlequinade. For my part I prefer the jolly choruses and sing-alongs and always buy the book of words so that I can join in. Sindbad, played by a fine strapping girl with long and shapely legs clad in tights, led the choruses splendidly.

After the show we called in at a bar and had a nightcap or two before splitting up to go our separate ways home, arranging to meet up the following week for our regular game of snooker.

When I got in to our rooms at 221b Baker Street I was accosted by a noxious smell and I groaned because this meant Holmes had been up to his scientific experiments again. Sure enough, he was crouched over test tubes and coloured liquids.

"Still looking for the philosopher's stone, Holmes?" I enquired jovially, removing my coat.

"Much more important, Watson. I am trying to evolve a test to tell one man's blood from another, but" he sighed, pushing away from the table and turning to face me, "a failure yet again."

"Bad luck, old chap," said I sympathetically, hanging up my coat.

"And how was the pantomime, Watson?"

"Good Lord, Holmes. How did you know I had been to a panto-mime? I certainly didn't tell you."

"No, you didn't, although I do know your friend Thurston likes to take you. I believe you saw *Harlequin Old King Cole* at Covent Garden last year."

"What a memory, Holmes, you astonish me!"

"But this year you went to the Surrey Theatre and saw *Sindbad the Sailor*."

"I suppose I have mud on my shoes that is unique to the pavement outside the Surrey theatre?" I enquired sarcastically.

"No, my friend, you have the programme of the theatre protruding from your coat pocket!"

I laughed. "It was a damn good show, Holmes. A fine girl flaunting her charms as Sindbad, but best of all, a man-monkey that had the house in uproar. That's why Thurston wanted to go to the Surrey, he had read about the man-monkey in the newspaper reports."

"A man-monkey?"

"Yes, a fellow in a great ape costume. He charged all round the auditorium playing tricks on people."

"How amusing," said Holmes disdainfully. He prefers loftier forms of entertainment such as violin recitals.

"Actually I think I've seen the chap before. I remember seeing something similar when I was a small boy and my parents took me to the pantomime. It can't be the same chap, not the way he carried on; must be dead now the chap I saw then, or very old." I got out the programme and had a look. "Oh yes, that's clever, Holmes. It says Monsieur Gouffe in big letters then, in tiny letters just above, it says 'successor to the famous'."

"I also deduce that after the entertainment you and friend Thurston called at some hostelry to imbibe alcohol," said Holmes.

"Smelled my breath, did you, Holmes?"

"No, Watson, but I notice that the ends of your sentences tend to be a little slurred."

"Yes, we had one or two afterwards. Thurston's such a generous fellow, you know. Wouldn't let me pay for anything." Suddenly coming over rather tired, I bade Holmes goodnight.

A few days after the scene described above, Holmes had a visitor who sought his assistance in a most urgent matter.

"Good of you to see me at such short notice, Mr Holmes."

"You caught me at an opportune time, sir. An expected visitor was obliged to cancel his appointment therefore I am at liberty to give you my full attention," replied Holmes.

"My name is Conquest, perhaps it is not unknown to you? I am the manager of the Surrey Theatre."

"You are currently staging a pantomime called *Sindbad the Sailor* I believe?" said Holmes suavely.

"Why, yes, indeed. Have you been to see it?"

"No, but my colleague, Dr Watson, was there the other night and thoroughly enjoyed himself," replied Holmes.

Conquest turned to look at me. "We are attracting a lot of people from north of the river these days, Doctor. No longer are the transpontine houses considered inferior to the West End. Many people regard our pantomimes to be finer than even Drury Lane and Covent Garden."

"I am sure you are proud of your theatre, Mr Conquest, but I hardly think that you have come especially to discuss its merits with us?" asked Holmes.

"No, no, of course not. But the matter is intimately connected with the pantomime."

"Perhaps you would explain?"

"In the show there is a performer known as Monsieur Gouffe, the man-monkey."

"Successor to the famous Monsieur Gouffe, I believe?" said I cutting in.

"Yes, quite. Gouffe has been dead these many years. But it's such a popular act we revive it every now and then. Gouffe himself was performing seventy years ago. We brought the monkey back and a fellow called Hernshaw did it for a few years. Last time a pot-boy called Sam Todd was persuaded to have a go and he took to it like a duck to water and made a real go of it, better than the original. Now we've got Joe Parsloe who is doing very well. What did you think of the performance, Doctor? Excellent, eh?"

"Very funny, but the monkey's behaviour was rather crude towards the end," I answered.

Conquest sighed. "I know what you mean, Doctor; I've tried to curb his antics but the local audience loves all that and Joe plays up to it. I tell him that the people north of the river are more refined and he must not be so broad."

"So your visit concerns this Joe Parsloe?" asked Holmes.

"Yes, yes. You see last night he was accused of stealing a diamond necklace from one of the patrons and is even now languishing in jail."

"Good Lord," said I. "How did that happen?"

"Well, you know how the monkey comes off the stage and runs about the auditorium?"

"Yes," said I.

"I must explain, Mr Holmes, Joe is dressed in a skin. A costume like a big ape. They are known as skins in the trade. He leaves the stage and runs amok around the audience taking their hats and mixing them up, kissing the tops of men's bald heads, and pinching the children's sweeties. He causes a great riot, I can tell you."

"You are fortunate that Dr Watson saw your show so recently. He has described this artiste to me in the minutest detail so I can easily imagine the scene as if I were there in person. Please proceed to this theft you mentioned."

"At the end of the act, Joe goes into the prompt side stage box –"

"Prompt side?" queried Holmes, interrupting.

"Yes, that's the box nearest the stage on the right side as you face the stage. The stage manager runs the show from the prompt corner which is on the left of the stage, so the right hand side of the stage is known as OP meaning 'opposite prompt'. Of course that's from the performers' view, from the audience they are the other way round. Do you follow?"

"Sufficiently, please continue."

"So Joe goes into the stage box. He always has to end up at that point wherever else he roams because of the rope hanging there by which he makes his way back on to the stage. Well, last night, when he got to the stage, the man in the box started shouting that his wife had lost her bag."

"But isn't that part of the show? The old woman with the brolly?" I asked.

"Of course; this was after she had done her part. That's Mavis who does that, Joe's wife Madame Gouffe. Well, he calls her his wife but it's not the same Madame Gouffe I met when I went to engage him for the pantomime. You see, Mr Holmes, Mavis plays the part of an outraged old lady who has had her bag stolen by the monkey and she climbs down the rope after him to try and get her bag back. Do you follow?"

"Perfectly."

"Well the act ends with the old lady running off minus her skirt with the ape following into the wings."

"Wings?"

"The side of the stage. That's the end of the act and the curtain falls. Well after all that, last night this man in the box stands up and hollers that the ape has taken his wife's handbag. He was getting big laughs because the audience thought it was all part of the show. They thought this man was an actor playing the role of the old lady's husband. But he wasn't at all, he was a genuine patron and was incensed that his wife's bag had been taken by the monkey. Of course, I was soon there, to try and sort things out, but it was awful because the bag had gone. There was the man and his wife, very respectable people, with two children, a boy and a girl. I had to take them to my office out of the way as the rest of the audience were taking notice. They'd stopped buying refreshments.

Eventually I got the full story. The wife had been wearing this diamond necklace, very valuable apparently, but when they got to the theatre they realised it was a bit low-class compared to what they were used to and this man, Cavendish his name is, thought it would be better if his wife took her necklace off as thieves might see it and accost them when they left the theatre. So before the show started she took it off in the privacy of the box and put it in her handbag. Reticule she called it. This she put on a chair. The box takes six people and there were only the four of them so there were two spare chairs. Well Joe comes in, clambers over the box and climbs down his rope, then Mavis follows and she climbs down. They finish the act and as the curtain falls Mrs Cavendish sees her reticule thing had gone and Mr Cavendish starts hollering that the monkey had taken it.

So I thinks the best thing is to take them to see Joe in his dressing room, so we all troop round backstage and catch Joe having a rub down with warm towels. It gets very sweaty in that monkey skin as you can imagine. Joe pops on his dressing gown and in we go and Cavendish is spluttering and accusing so I have to try and calm him down and explain to Joe what it's about. Well then Joe starts hollering that he has been falsely accused and what not, Mavis starts up as well – and she's a right temper when she gets going. Irish you know. The kids then start nattering that they are missing the show so Mrs Cavendish takes the children back and there is a heated argument between Cavendish and Joe. There is no end, it just goes round and round, Cavendish accusing, Joe denying. In the end Cavendish insists on calling the police. So that's what happened. The policeman came, arrested Joe and now he's banged up in jail for something he says he didn't do. Cavendish insists there can be no other explanation as his wife's reticule with the diamond necklace has gone and Joe must have pinched it."

"Have the police carried out any investigations?" asked Holmes.

"There's nothing to investigate. The police have questioned Joe and Cavendish and that's it. One man's word against the other," replied Conquest. "Joe is terrified that he is going to get done for this crime. He was in trouble with the law once before when he had a bit of a scrap in the middle of his act at Windsor. It was his idea to appeal to you. He said 'there's only one bloke who can help me and that's Mr Sherlock Holmes'. Hence my visit to you now."

"Have you considered that Parsloe may be guilty of this theft, Mr Conquest?" asked Holmes.

"I don't know what to think. I've not known him all that long but he always seemed a regular sort of fellow to me. But there seems to be no other credible explanation."

"I think I had better go and see Parsloe immediately."

"Whatever you can do to help, both Joe and I will be grateful for."

"Very well. I cannot, of course, promise anything, but I will do my best to investigate this crime which has, by all accounts, provided a total absence of clues. Before I see Parsloe would it be possible to call at your theatre so that I might see the scene of the crime?"

"Any time of day that you like, Mr Holmes, unless you prefer to come in the evening and see the show," said Conquest.

"That will not be necessary as the part of the show that would interest me is now missing."

"It certainly is. Mavis has stepped in to take Joe's place but it's not the same by any means. She can't do the acrobatics at the start and just runs about the audience aimlessly. We are working on getting somebody to play the old woman, Mavis's usual role, but they will just have to come on to the stage by the steps, we can't expect a newcomer to be able to do all the rope business. But we are keeping faith with our public. We advertise a man-monkey and a man-monkey they are getting, even though it's now actually a woman."

"Perhaps we could return to the theatre with you now? I assume you are on your way there?"

"Indeed. Yes, do pray come along. My carriage is still outside so we can all go together. I take it you, Doctor, will also come?"

"I wouldn't miss it for the world," I replied.

On the journey Conquest kept up an incessant flow of reminiscence about his theatre and his performers, the only item of interest being Parsloe's previous brush with the law. In my limited acquaintance with theatrical people I have remarked how their conversation always turns to themselves and their profession.

At the Surrey, Holmes inspected the stage box. Most people have seen a stage box, even occupied one. This one was typical, a balustrade heavily ornamented with plaster decoration on the front, and a padded cloth top. Above was a swagged curtain arrangement with ornamental cords and tassels depending at the sides. As explained by Conquest there were six chairs in the box, not fastened in any way, thereby giving the occupants some small opportunity to arrange them to their preference.

"Is that the normal arrangement, three at the front and three behind?" asked Holmes.

"Yes, as you see them. Of course, the patrons arrange them to their liking but there is not sufficient room for four in a line," explained Conquest.

"From what you said, I understand that on the night of the theft, the two children were in front and the two parents sitting behind?"

"Yes."

"So the two spare chairs would be empty alongside them?"

"Presumably."

"Tell me, how did Parsloe get through the people to the front of the box?" asked Holmes.

"With difficulty is the answer, Mr Holmes. He had to squeeze past along the side wall. It was a constant moan with him. He kept asking me to make it a four person only box for the duration of the pantomime but, unless he was prepared to have twelve top price admissions deducted from his salary every week to compensate me for the loss of box office takings, I refused."

The rope by which the two acrobats descended to the stage was still hanging there, though no longer used in the show.

"It must have made his job very difficult, I don't know how he did all the wonderful things he did having to see through that mask," I remarked.

"Not just a mask, doctor, a complete head. Do you want to see it, Mr Holmes? The skin's in the dressing room, it's no bother to look."

"Yes, I'll do that, Mr Conquest, I can do nothing here, the carpet has been swept and all is pristine."

"The cleaners are in every morning. You wouldn't believe the rubbish people leave – orange peel, nutshells, paper from bon-bons and chocolate boxes. We have to make it tidy for the next audience."

"Of course. Shall we look at the skin?"

The dressing room was a squalid little room with a dirty cracked window. Apart from a wooden table with a broken piece of mirror propped against the wall, and two bentwood chairs, the only other items of furniture were a gas heater and a wooden clothes horse draped in rough towels.

"Of course Joe doesn't need the mirror and dressing table but Mavis uses it to make up as the old woman. We had the gas heater especially installed for Joe because he is dripping with sweat when he comes off and needs to towel himself down. It's the least I could do for such an outstanding attraction."

The skin was hanging from a hook on the wall. Close up, it was a revolting-looking thing. Like some filthy old rug. Holmes examined it, I wouldn't have gone near it without a pair of tongs. Long-handled tongs. The head was hanging alongside on another hook, and similar hooks carried items of clothing that I recognised as the old lady's wardrobe. To my alarm Holmes placed the ape's head over his own.

"See, Watson," came Holmes's voice, muffled by the head "There is a kind of flap that covers the neck of the body skin."

"Yes, that's to conceal the join," explained Conquest. Some monkey-men put the head on first, then the skin, so that the flap is like a neck, and as it's tucked in there's no fear of the man showing. But it's very constricting doing it that way because there is no air getting in at all, and I think the line made by the neckline of the skin is too obvious. Also the man has to get ready and wait like that. Whereas doing it the way Joe does it he can have the head under his arm to the very last minute before his entrance, and then pop it on just before he enters."

Holmes had removed the head while Conquest gave this lecture on the art of clothing oneself as a monkey and, there being nothing else of interest, we then proceeded to the jail to meet the great actor himself.

After some very troublesome business with the warder in charge – who was most obstructive – I was somewhat surprised when we eventually gained access to Joe Parsloe because he was not at all the type of man I had imagined. After seeing the sort of work that he did in the pantomime I was expecting a young muscular chap, whereas the figure before us was a small spare-looking individual of around forty. He looked up without any interest in his dull eyes until the warder briefly said "Visitors".

"Sherlock Holmes," said my friend, offering his palm. At once Parsloe leapt to his feet.

"Thank God, you've come, Mr Holmes. You've got to help me!"

"I don't have to do anything. Your employer Mr Conquest came to see me and told me of your predicament so I agreed to look into it. I have been to the theatre and examined the scene of the crime and we are fortunate that Dr Watson here actually saw your performance in the show some days ago, so that is of great assistance. But other than that I can do nothing as there appears to be no clue at all as to what actually happened on that night."

"But I am completely innocent, Mr Holmes. This man who accuses me has no right to do so. I didn't take his wife's bag or even touch anything in the box. He admits he never actually saw me do it, he is just guessing that I'm to blame because this bag was missing after I'd passed through."

"Yes, well let us take it step by step and I will understand the actual event more clearly. We have the box with six chairs but only four people occupying them. Do you recall how they were arranged?"

"Clearly; the two children were at the front, leaning on the balustrade, the parents behind."

"Let me stop you. When you face out from the box who was on the left?"

"The little girl at the front, her mother behind, little boy to the right, father behind."

"And the two empty chairs?"

"They were against the right side wall turned with their backs against the wall."

"I see, and when you entered the box it was between the males and the empty chairs?"

"That's right, Mr Holmes."

"So what then happened?"

"I leaned out so that the audience could see me clearly, ruffled the little boy's hair, then sprang up on to the parapet of the box. I used to do a handstand at that point, but one night some years ago a fellow in the box thought it amusing to push me over and I fell into the stalls smashing my collar bone. So I stopped doing that."

"Good God, you might have been killed," I cried.

"I was lucky. It's not an easy profession being an acrobat, Doctor."

"So you stood there in full view?" asked Holmes.

"Yes, then I leaped for the rope and swung around a bit."

"I don't suppose you noticed Mrs Cavendish's bag on the chair as you passed by?" asked Holmes.

"Yes, sir, I did."

"Ah! You saw it on the chair?"

"To be more correct I saw something on the chair. You see I don't have a very good view through the eyeholes in the head but, because my act is to do funny monkey-like things in the audience, I am always glancing round to see what there is at hand to joke around with."

"So you saw something on the chair at the side?"

"Yes, sir. Whether it was a bag, a scarf, the boy's cap, I couldn't say. Whatever it was, I was not going to touch it."

"But you say your act depends on your taking things."

"Yes, indeed, but I have been doing the monkey business for over twenty years and I've learned a thing or two. I never play any tricks with toffs. It's not worth it. Sometimes they take offence very easily and they don't like to be put in a position where the common folk laugh at them. Sometimes if it's a group of men and one has a bald head I might make the monkey kiss him on his dome, but you have to be careful and know what you can get away with and what will give offence."

"I see. So we are agreed that something was on the chair?"

"Yes, sir."

"Well I suggest that you did not ignore it at all but, as is your practice, picked it up."

"I never, sir, I swear it."

"I think you had it when you went down the rope."

"I couldn't have! I need both hands for the rope," protested the little man.

"But you were already carrying a bag, a large capacious bag that was supposed to have been stolen from a lady in the audience, your stooge Mavis."

"That bag is on the crook of my left arm enabling me to have my hands free," explained Parsloe.

"Then you pushed Mrs Cavendish's reticule into the one on your arm. Or possibly, you had chance to hide it in your costume."

"There's no pockets in a skin," protested the man.

"No, but there is quite a wide neck opening concealed by the piece of material depending from the head. It is a simple matter to lift the flap and thrust a small object under your skin via the neck."

"I've worn that costume twenty years and the thought of doing that has never occurred to me!"

"Remarkable, it struck me straight away. The fact remains Mrs Cavendish's bag has gone. This is what really happened. You took the bag almost without thinking, as part of your performance, then, having to get on with the rope business, you automatically pushed it into the bag meaning to return it in the interval which was only a matter of minutes away."

"But I didn't take it!"

"Please let me finish. You ended the act but Mr Cavendish started shouting and making a fuss. This worried you and you were afraid that you would get dismissed. I happen to know that some years ago at Windsor theatre you were taken before the magistrates because you struck a member of the audience during your man-monkey routine."

"That man struck me first and I only gave him back what he gave me."

"The fact remains you have been before the magistrates before."

"I was fined £10 and £10 damages that was the end of it. The chap wasn't hurt, it was just to satisfy his pride."

"As I was saying, you were afraid of the law again so thought to keep quiet about it. It's quite understandable in your peculiar circumstances. Common sense tells us you could not know the contents of Mrs Cavendish's bag. When you got to your dressing room and found the jewels you were most distraught and were not thinking clearly. I don't for a minute consider that you intended to steal the necklace because you could not know of it. You took it almost by habit as part of your performance, then panicked. That's it isn't it?"

"No, Mr Holmes, it is not. I swear on the Holy Book I never

touched the thing at all."

"Come, be sensible, a reasonable magistrate would see that it was all done in error in the heat of the performance and would deal lightly with you."

"I never touched the damned reticule!" shouted Parsloe.

"Well if you insist on that I can do nothing more to help you. Mr Cavendish will demand the utmost rigours of the law, he is a powerful man. The necklace, which is still missing, is worth several hundred pounds."

"Well I'm sorry for them but it's nothing to do with me."

"So you say," said Holmes sarcastically.

The poor little man, slumping back on the hard bench that was the only furnishing in the cell, buried his head in his hands and moaned "Why won't anybody believe me?"

"Because you are not telling the truth," replied Holmes sternly.

The acrobat sat hunched on the bench, tears rolling down his face.

"I give you one last chance. Confess, and I will do all I can to help lighten your punishment."

Holmes stood towering over him but the poor fellow, saying nothing, stared at the floor, tears dripping incongruously off his nose end on to the concrete.

In the long silence the warder who had been on guard throughout spoke up "Have you finished with him now, sir?"

"Yes," said Holmes. "I did my best to help but he is an incorrigible rogue. Let us out."

I had been silent throughout the interview and as we sped back to Baker Street I ventured to accuse Holmes of being unnecessarily vindictive. "I thought you were a bit harsh with the poor fellow, Holmes."

"Did you?"

"I did. It is unlike you not to show some compassion. You have often said how easy it is for the most law-observing man to drift into crime through force of circumstance."

"I still say that."

"But we don't know the personal circumstances of Parsloe, he may have been driven to desperate measures."

"He may. That is not my concern. Conquest has asked me to look into this affair. He wants me to assist his actor. That does not mean that I should save a guilty man from the just measure of the law."

I was getting impatient with Holmes as he peered out of the cab window, not taking much notice of how heated his insouciance was making me. "You ignore my point, Holmes. I am not defending the man. Of course the full might of the law should punish the guilty. That is not the point. Just because the man is guilty does not mean he should be treated with harshness or contempt. It troubles me that you should use the fellow so, even if he is a thief."

"On the contrary, Watson, the man is clearly innocent."

"Innocent?" I gasped.

"Undoubtedly. I suggested to him that it had all been done in haste, almost automatically and in error. If he used that defence he would be let off lightly. You will have noticed I gave him that excellent opportunity to excuse his actions, but he refused to take it. Even when I pressed him severely he maintained his innocence. Our next port of call must be with the family Cavendish."

We arranged to visit the Cavendish home but when we arrived Mr Cavendish himself was absent. "My husband is the largest wine merchant in London and had to be in his office, so he sends his apologies. I trust I can tell you all you wish to know."

"Thank you for seeing us. I am Sherlock Holmes and this is my colleague Dr Watson."

"My husband has told me of you, it appears that he knows of you by reputation. May I ask whom you represent in this affair?"

"I have been asked to investigate by Mr Conquest the manager of the Surrey Theatre."

"I wish we'd never gone to the wretched place. We normally take the children to the Drury Lane pantomime, but for some reason Basil – that's our little boy – wanted to see this monkey-man he had heard about. I shall certainly ignore his pleadings in the future. I had no idea we were venturing into a den of thieves."

"I understand you were wearing the necklace when you entered the theatre?"

"Yes, we went in a private carriage as we do to Drury Lane, and it was only when my husband realised the sort of area the theatre was in, and saw the type of person pushing and jostling to gain admittance, that he suggested that we were perhaps too prominently attired and the jewels may be a temptation for a footpad when we emerged. I removed them from sight as soon as we were safely in our box and placed them in my reticule."

"Which you placed on a spare chair in the box?"

"That is correct."

"Were your little ones enjoying the antics of the man-monkey?" asked Holmes.

"They were, very much so, even though to refined tastes the humour was of a low sort and positively crude from time to time. But I confess mostly it was harmless but childish."

"It was a pantomime, ma'am," I pointed out.

"There are pantomimes and pantomimes, Dr Watson."

"Tell me what happened when the ape entered your box."

"Well my children were watching him down below in the stalls, leaning right out of the box, and I restrained them by holding on to the back of their clothing. Then, turning to me, Basil said 'He's gone.' And almost immediately the monkey himself appeared in our box. He squeezed past my husband and jumped up on to the velvet plush top of the box rail. Oh yes, he ruffled Basil's hair with his filthy paw. He stood waving to the audience then launched himself into space, as it seemed, but he was catching a rope that was hanging there. The next thing is this other person burst in shouting and waving a stick. It appears she was an actress chasing the ape, then she too climbed down the rope until they were both on the stage. And that was it."

"I see. And when did you miss your reticule?"

"Not until Mr Cavendish started shouting about it."

"That was after the curtain had fallen, I believe?"

"Yes. It was rather embarrassing because everybody was looking up, pointing and laughing. So ill-mannered."

"I think the audience thought it was part of the show and your husband was another actor playing a part," I suggested.

"Ridiculous! Mr Cavendish looks nothing like an actor."

"I wonder if I might have a word with Basil and your delightful daughter?" asked Homes.

Mrs Cavendish stared. "My children? I hardly think they can tell you anything."

"I would like to see them if I may," said Holmes with a winning smile.

"Very well." She rang a bell and when the maid answered said "Ask Miss Jones to bring Master Basil and Miss Isabel to the withdrawing room. These gentlemen would like to see them."

"This is a very charming room," said Holmes, gazing in admiration.

"We like it," said Mrs Cavendish simply.

"You say Mr Cavendish is a leading wine merchant?"

"Not *a* leading wine merchant, *the* leading wine merchant in all of London," she corrected.

Further meaningless conversation was spared when the two children entered with their governess.

"Miss Jones, this is Sherlock Holmes and that is Dr Watson, they have come about the jewels."

"Have they been found?" asked Miss Jones excitedly.

"Alas, no," replied Mrs Cavendish, "but apparently investigations are still proceeding."

"What is expected of the children, Mrs Cavendish?"

"To answer questions. Proceed, Mr Holmes."

"Thank you. Now I just want to talk about the night when you all went to the pantomime. I'm sure you remember everything very clearly. Do you know I can still remember things I saw in pantomimes many years ago when I was no older than you." This was Holmes in an unfamiliar mode, he was not a natural uncle. "It's about watching the man-monkey."

"You must think before you speak, children, then answer the questions as honestly and truthfully as you can," said the governess.

"Thank you, Miss Jones," said Holmes with some asperity. "Now Basil first. When the monkey came into your box, did you see him come in through the door, or were you suddenly aware he was there?"

"I didn't see him come in, I saw him down below, then he went out of sight and suddenly he was alongside me."

"You didn't see him actually come in?"

"No," said Basil "I was talking to Isabel, saying the monkey had gone."

"Good. Now Miss Isabel. The same question to you. Did you see the monkey actually enter the box, or was he suddenly there?"

"I saw him come in. He came in very quickly and went straight to the front and jumped up on the wall."

"The wall?"

"Yes, we were sitting behind a wall."

"She means the front of the box, the balustrade or whatever it's called," explained Miss Jones.

"Of course, it is a wall, you are quite right. It stops you falling out, doesn't it? A nice fancy wall with a red cloth top to it. Now think carefully – did you see the monkey look at the spare chair? The one with your mama's reticule on."

"No, he came in and looked at Basil and ruffled his hair then jumped up on the wall."

"Well, that all seems very straightforward," said Holmes.

"Did you expect it not to be?" asked Mrs Cavendish.

"On the contrary there seems to be a remarkable degree of agreement about the whole escapade. The only problem is precisely when the bag was taken."

"I can't see how that makes much difference. The man was only in the box for a minute so it must have been at some time during then."

"Yes. It must," agreed Holmes. "I believe you all went with Mr Conquest so that Mr Cavendish could accost the man-monkey?"

"That was Conquest's idea. First we went to his office, then he took us to where the actors live. It was indescribably awful."

"The actors don't actually live there, Mrs Cavendish. It is simply where they prepare themselves," I explained.

"Yes, I realise that. I don't know what you call it."

"It's usually called backstage, I believe," said I.

"Whatever it's called, it's no fit place for children. We soon left the men to it and returned to watch the rest of the pantomime."

"Did you enjoy it, children?" asked Holmes.

"It wasn't as good as before the interval because the monkey didn't come on again," said Basil.

"Have you any more questions, Mr Holmes?"

"No, you have been most helpful, all of you, including your delightful children. Thank you for seeing us. Good day."

We were shown out and the whole thing seemed icily polite and fruitless to me. Holmes, however, did not seem surprised that no progress had been made. "Everything confirms that what is supposed to have happened did happen, the only point in dispute being did Joe Parsloe take the bag or not. I am convinced he did not."

"Whether he did or not, should this go to a court of law there is no possibility of finding him guilty – there is no evidence of any sort, just a sort of assumption on the part of Cavendish. A man is innocent until proved guilty. How can he be found guilty?"

"Your faith in the law is touching, Watson."

"In this country justice will always be done," said I stoutly.

"Do not confuse justice with the law. And even in Great Britain powerful men can sway the law and poor men be oppressed by it. I would not want this to come to court at all, and I do not believe it will. I wonder if we shall find London's leading wine merchant at his office should we call unexpectedly."

He was, and not very pleased to see us. "I thought you were calling at my home?" asked Cavendish aggressively.

"We have been there and your good lady entertained us most fruitfully."

"What do you mean by that?" demanded Cavendish.

"Simply that she answered a few questions openly and honestly."

"Why should she not? She has nothing to fear."

"Certainly not. Neither, I trust, have you."

"What the devil do you mean by that?"

"Only that I would like to ask you a few similar questions."

"Questions, questions! I've had all this with the police, the insurers, the theatre manager, and now you two. It's time somebody did something to get the jewels back instead of asking all these tomfool questions."

"I would like to ask one or two more tomfool questions if I may," said Holmes.

Cavendish groaned. "If you must."

"It is basically this – did you actually see the ape take up the reticule?"

"Not exactly, no. But I put it on the chair myself, monkey-man comes in, jumps off the balcony, chair empty. What else can one think?"

"Are you prepared to swear to that in a court of law?"

"If necessary."

"You realise that a man will be tried for this crime if you persist."

"So he should be. If he's a thief it will be found out in court."

"Not unless there is more evidence. Even the word of London's leading wine merchant is not enough to condemn a man on that alone."

"If there's no evidence then he will not suffer."

"Do you know the penalty for this crime if he is found guilty?"

"If there is no evidence he will not be found guilty."

"I would not want it on my conscience that an innocent man suffers through my insistence."

"Look, Holmes, or whatever your name is, if the police can't find the fellow guilty he is in the clear. I am the one who suffers. I have lost something precious and valuable, whoever took it gets away scot-free."

"I thought the jewels belonged to your wife."

"Yes, well, I paid for them".

"There is another possibility, of course," said Holmes.

"And that is?"

"The actress who followed the ape into the box. Do you not think she may have been the one to take up the reticule rather than the man-monkey?"

"That's just as likely. One of them must have done it. I don't necessarily differentiate between them. They are both low class entertainers and probably in league with one another," said Cavendish offhandedly.

"I believe the actress playing the old lady is actually Mrs Parsloe, the wife of the man-monkey," said Holmes.

"There you are then, they are both as bad as the other."

"Unless the police can prove a conspiracy between them, only one of them will be found guilty," said Holmes.

"So? What is that to me?"

"Perhaps you don't care if an innocent woman is jailed for seven years?" asked Holmes.

"Are you trying to appeal to my sympathy? Get this straight – I do not give a tinker's cuss whether one or both of them are hanged. My concern is the return of my wife's necklace, that is all."

"Very good. If I can arrange that, then, of course, I would be more than delighted to do so. At present, however, my concern is to prove Joe Parsloe innocent. Good day."

"What a swine, Holmes," said I in amazement as we parted from the wine merchant. "He seems to give a damn for nobody."

"Perhaps he thinks being London's leading wine merchant entitles him to a certain amount of arrogance. I think now is the time to speak to Mrs Parsloe."

Come evening, once more we went south of the river to the Surrey theatre, calling on Conquest who willingly took us backstage to meet Mrs Parsloe. "Two gentlemen to see you, Mavis," he called out after knocking on the dressing room door. "May I bring them in?" The door opened and a buxom young woman stared out at us.

"Yes?" she snapped.

"This is Mr Sherlock Holmes and his colleague Dr Watson. They are trying to get Joe released," explained Conquest.

"You'd better come in," she said, opening the door wide.

"Do you require me to stay?" asked Conquest.

"No," said Mrs Parsloe abruptly, "Clear off!" Conquest shrugged and left us.

"I must explain that I am investigating the theft of jewellery that you know all about and, as yet, I have no information that will free your husband," explained Holmes.

"He ain't my husband," said the woman.

"No? We were under the impression you were married to Mr Parsloe."

"He'd like that, would Joe, he likes to give out that impression. Thinks it makes us look more respectable. We're stage partners that's all. Or were. I can't see it lasting much longer with him banged up and me having to do his job capering about in that stinking thing." She nodded at the skin hanging on its hook.

"All the same," said Holmes, "I'm sure you wish to do your best to get Joe's release."

"It don't matter either way to me, mister. I don't rely on him. I made a living before I took up with him and can still do all right for meself without him."

"On the night the jewels disappeared, you were in the stage box straight after Joe had left it?"

"Yes. What's that supposed to mean?"

"I am simply asking a question. My next question is – did you see anything on the seat of the empty chair during the short time you were in the box?"

"No."

"No?"

"No."

"So you are saying that if there had been something there it had been removed before you entered the box?"

"I don't know anything about it, mister. I'm telling you I saw nothing on any empty chair. That's all I know."

"Well, perhaps, when you returned here, at the end of your perform-ance, Joe said something about it?"

"Gawd! Joe ain't in any fit state to chat, he's gasping for breath for ages before he can talk. He never spoke until Conquest came in with Bunny Cavendish and they started on at him."

"I see. So that would have been the first time you were aware of the theft?" asked Holmes.

"What are you incinerating, mister? I keep telling you I know nothing about it."

"So you do, so you do. Well it seems I can get no help, and poor Joe will get blamed for this theft that he knows nothing about."

The woman shrugged. "That's his problem, ain't it?"

"Well, thank you, Miss –?"

"Riley. Mavis Riley not Parsloe."

"May I leave my card and if you think of anything, or something happens that you think would assist, perhaps you would send me a message?"

We bade her 'good evening', leaving her to prepare for her performance.

"Well, Holmes," I said, "we seem to have found a singular lack of humanity in the people connected with this case. I cannot believe there are people with such a want of morals."

"It does not make my work any easier, I agree, Watson."

And there it would seem the case would end, one of the many inconclusive episodes in which Sherlock Holmes was involved. Poor Joe Parsloe was still languishing in jail without charge as the police dithered whether to take him to court or not. Eventually, they were obliged to release him as the total lack of concrete evidence meant a charge would not stick. Any competent barrister would be able to defend him against such a flimsy case.

However, no sooner was Joe released than he was round at our rooms. It seems his 'wife', as he insisted on calling her, had been attacked by footpads in the street and injured. "She's all bashed about, Mr Holmes, and her arm broken. Vicious thugs attacked her in the street. She says she doesn't know why – she's not worth robbing – but I think they were after her all right. I think she's been seeing some bloke and he's taken against her."

"To be honest, Mr Parsloe, when we spoke to your good lady she bitterly denounced the fact she was your wife as a lie, and was rather dismissive of you," said Holmes.

"Yes, well," mumbled Parsloe shamefaced, "she isn't my wife, strictly speaking, and you're right, she has fallen out with me."

"I am not interested in your or her amorous affairs, Mr Parsloe. You are free again and that is the end of the matter so far as I am concerned."

"But why should she get beaten up?"

"I've no idea, but if she speaks to some short-tempered man as she spoke to me then it is not unlikely to happen."

"She is a sharp woman but I think it may be something to do with those jewels," said Parsloe.

"Why do you think that?"

"Well she won't say anything about it, and ignores the fact I was banged up for a week under suspicion. I may not be her husband but I do know her pretty well by now and she is keeping some secret."

"Do you want me to speak to her?" asked Holmes.

"If you would. She won't listen to me."

"I doubt if she will listen to me. Will you bring her here?"

"I don't think she'll come, Mr Holmes."

"Can you get her to walk out somewhere – Trafalgar Square say?"

"Yes, I could get her to do that."

"Tomorrow at eleven a.m. by the lions; be there. I will contrive to converse with her, but she may not be forthcoming."

"Thank you, Mr Holmes, thank you. We'll be there."

I had no idea what Holmes intended the following morning, but I was slightly alarmed when he asked me if I had some old disreputable clothing I could wear, and produced some excessively hairy side whiskers that he proposed attaching to my face with a special sort of gum. In the end when I left our rooms I had the appearance of an over-indulgent meat-porter. Holmes was completely unrecognisable too, conveying the impression of a rather dashing sporting chap whom your sister might like, but about whom you would be right to be concerned on her behalf.

In these guises we nonchalantly lounged around Trafalgar Square keeping an eye out for our quarry. On the stroke of eleven Parsloe and his lady appeared, arm in arm, she heavily veiled with one arm in a sling. As usual, Holmes had ordered that I left the speaking to him. "Why if it isn't Mr Parsloe and his lady. Buzz off and get yourself a cup of tea, Parsloe, and don't come back until we've left – about ten minutes will be ample."

Parsloe looked bewildered and was about to protest when I mouthed the word "Holmes" and he understood. Blurting "Whatever you say," he hurried away.

"What is this? Who are you?" demanded the veiled woman.

"Nothing to worry about, missy," said Holmes in an assumed voice, "we just want to make sure you are all right after the beating the other night."

She lifted her veil with her good arm. "Have a look, that's how good a shape you left me in." Her face was disfigured with bruising and grazing, but my practiced eye soon showed me that with any luck there would be no lasting damage to her looks, which was a blessing for she was a handsome woman.

"We are not the men, missy. Neither of us would raise a fist to a woman. Surely you can see we are not thugs."

"All right, I agree you are not the same men. What are you after? Why have you sent Joe away?"

"Relax, missy. I think you have been trying to consume more high class wine that you are entitled to, if you get my meaning."

The woman stared at Holmes. "What do you know? Who are you?" She was certainly a more chastened person than on our previous meeting when she flaunted her contempt.

"I know everything, lady, except why you double-crossed your lover."

Her eyes blazed and she spat out: "He was the one who double-crossed me! The low-life turd! Then when I protested he set his bully-boys on to me!"

"How did you two come together?" asked Holmes.

"He picked me up in the National Gallery."

"Very high class."

"I'm not a common prostitute, whatever you might think," said she.

Holmes raised his hands. "I don't suggest that for the world, missy," he protested.

"A girl likes a good time with a gent. I thought he was a toff and I could tell he liked me so we met again and, well, I realise now he was just using me, but I thought he really loved me."

"Where do the jewels come in?"

"I knew he was married, of course, I'm not that green, and he said he had given his wife a diamond necklace that cost a fortune and he would much rather that he had given it to me because his wife was a stuck-up bitch. That's what he said. So I said in that case get it back and give it to me. 'If only I could' says he. So I thought about it a bit and as you seem to know so much about it you must know I work at the Surrey."

"Playing an old lady chasing an ape."

"I don't know who you are but you seem to know a lot about me that's not your business."

"So you came up with the idea of getting the ape to pinch the gems."

"It was better than that. To make it look as though the man-monkey had done it."

"Whereas you, yourself, were the thief," said Holmes.

Miss Riley laughed scornfully, "I thought you knew all? Of course I didn't nick the jewels! I didn't want to go to Tasmania for seven years. They were never stolen at all."

"Ah, it was an insurance scam."

"That was my idea. He pretended the necklace had been stolen, his wife's distraught – she didn't know anything about it of course – he claims on the insurance, when all's died down he gives me the necklace as he promised."

"Very clever. So what went wrong?"

"Nothing. It worked perfectly. Even Joe wasn't banged up, so that was all right. It all went fine except Cavendish wouldn't tip up the diamonds. When I asked him he just laughed in my face. I realised that he had no intention of giving me anything. I saw I had been a fool and been used just to help him commit a fraud. That might have been it, I might just have gone like he wanted, like he thought I would, but when he laughed again and said did I really think he would give a diamond necklace worth thousands to a tup'ny-ha'p'ny whore, I lost my rag. Nobody calls me that! So that was it. All over. I told him I would go to the police and tell them everything. He didn't like that. And it was after that he set his bully-boys on to me. They said who they were from and after beating me up they said that was just a taster and if I went to the police they would come and finish me off. I can't cope with all that, mister. I'm leaving town. I'm trying to get Joe to take us up north for a bit."

"Don't you want to see Cavendish get his come-uppance?" asked

Holmes.

"Nothing would please me more, but I value my own life and I don't want dragging into a court case. If the law does for him they'll get me as well. He'll make sure of that."

"You're probably right, missy. You've got yourself into a right mess, haven't you?"

"And what can you do about it, whoever you are?"

"I am going to try and nail Cavendish, missy, but you are right, you had better do a runner soonest. Watson, call Joe, I see him hovering."

"'Ere, you're the two blokes who came to see me at the Surrey!"

When Parsloe joined at my beckoning, Holmes handed him an envelope. "Here, there's money in there, enough to buy passages to America. Get away as soon as you can. If I nail Cavendish as I hope, then you need to be out of the country. Miss Riley will inevitably be involved and jailed as an accessory. Get off immediately. Start a new life. I believe they like English performers in the United States. You will find a form of popular entertainment called the burlesque that relies on exactly your sort of act. Come, Watson."

And we walked away.

"I say, Holmes, this is all getting bewildering. Cavendish and Miss Riley?"

"Yes. Miss Riley, as you will have gathered, is, I'm afraid, very free with her affections."

"But Cavendish – he's a respectable family man. The biggest wine merchant in London. What's he doing with a low-life music hall turn?"

"Many a respectable married man has a mistress, Watson, others frequent prostitutes. I rather think Cavendish is the sort of man who wants more than his respectable wife provides."

"But how did you know all this?"

"I didn't. It was only the fact that Miss Riley referred to Cavendish as Bunny. A term of endearment, I assume, as my enquiries turned up nobody who referred to him by that nickname. When we met, I made the obvious double-entendre about wine which she picked up instantly. She may be low-life, Watson, but she is not witless. Up to that point all I had was the faintest of suspicions of a link between them. From then on she told us everything."

Holmes waited until the Sunday morning and asked me to accompany him to the Cavendish residence where we lurked until we saw the family return from church. After half-an-hour, Holmes knocked on the door.

"May I see Mr Cavendish, please? My card, he does know me," said Holmes proffering his card.

"Be so good as to wait here, sir," replied the servant haughtily, and disappeared through a large oaken door, bearing Holmes's card on a silver salver. He was but a brief time.

"Mr Cavendish is not at home."

Holmes took up the card that was being clearly presented to him as a reject and whipping out a pencil scribbled a couple of words on the reverse. "Please present my card again; I am sure your master will be very interested in what I have to say." The servant inclined his head slightly in a manner that indicated strong disapproval rather than acquiescence. It is amazing how these fellows manage to convey their meaning without overtly insulting you, yet subtly doing so in some way. Whatever Holmes had written had the desired effect as Cavendish himself appeared, "What do you mean coming here on a Sunday disturbing my family life by sending in your card with that name inscribed?" he demanded.

"I thought you would like to know that Mavis Riley has been apprehended for the crime of stealing your jewels," explained Holmes placidly.

"Indeed?" replied Cavendish, "well that's no surprise. I said they were as bad as each other, didn't I?"

"Well, that is, of course, not so. Joe Parsloe was, and is, completely innocent. It seems Mavis Riley is not married to him at all, they are merely theatrical partners."

"So what is all this to me?"

"Unfortunately, this means that the investigations have to start anew. All the evidence that is used for and against one person cannot simply be assumed to be the same in the case against another. Surely a man of your standing and intelligence will realise that?"

"Yes, yes, of course. How all very tiresome this is," agreed Cavendish snappily.

"I wonder, seeing as we have disturbed you already, you would be prepared to permit my asking a few questions of you and your family again? I know it's a trouble but I shall be very brief."

"Oh, very well, come inside. But do be brief, we will be lunching soon."

We followed Cavendish into the same pleasant room where we had interviewed his wife and children and, sure enough, they were there again in much the same places as before.

"It's Holmes and his colleague once more, I'm afraid, Laura. They want to ask again about the theft of your necklace."

"Again?" Mrs Cavendish queried with deep dismay.

"Yes, it seems the chap they thought had done it hadn't, and now they've caught somebody else, a woman," explained her husband.

"Yes, the suspicion now falls on Miss Riley, the actress playing the part of the old lady in the pantomime, the one who chases the man-monkey. I am sure you recall how she entered your box hot on the heels of the ape and followed him down his rope."

"I remember," cried out Isabel the little girl, "she was so funny waving her umbrella and shouting."

"That's right," said Holmes, beaming in what he imagined was an avuncular manner. "Now I wonder if you remember that your Papa placed a little purse on the spare chair in your box at the theatre?"

"Of course, that was Mama's reticule with her jewels that have been stolen," said Isobel pertly.

"Well remembered!" cried Holmes. "But do you remember if the purse had gone before the funny lady came in, or after she had slid down her rope?"

"I don't know. I saw Papa put it on the chair at the start of the show and I never looked again until Papa said it had gone."

"Yes, that seems to be it. Thank you, young lady, you have been most helpful again. Now Basil, let us see what you remember. When the monkey came into your box, did you see him come in through the door, or were you suddenly aware he was there?"

"I didn't see him come in, suddenly he was alongside me."

"The children have told you all this previously, Mr Holmes," protested Mrs Cavendish.

Holmes, ignoring her, carried on questioning. "You didn't see him actually come in?"

"No," said Basil.

"And did you see him pick up anything from the chair?"

"No."

"Did you see him carry anything, other than the large bag on his arm."

"No."

"Right, forget the monkey now. I want you to remember when the funny lady came into your box, you remember that?"

"Yes."

"Did you see her look at the reticule on the chair?"

"I don't know."

"You mean you don't know if she looked, or you don't know if you saw her look?"

"I was not watching her, I was looking at the ape man swinging on his rope," explained Basil.

"Of course, and you were first aware of the funny lady when?"

"When she stood alongside me and started shouting."

"I see. So you did not see the monkey-man touch the reticule and you did not see the funny lady touch the reticule?"

"No," said Basil. Holmes rose to his feet. I do not know what he hoped to achieve by this repetitious questioning of the two children but it had been fruitless again.

"Did you see anybody else touch the reticule?" he softly asked.

"I saw Papa," said Basil. Holmes spun round.

"Yes, Basil, you saw me put it on the chair before the show. Mr Holmes means later whilst the pantomime was on," blustered Cavendish.

"Yes, Papa, I know. I saw you put it in your pocket when the funny lady leapt on to the rope. I turned round to see if you were laughing."

"You really do not know what you are saying, Basil. It's so long ago now, you cannot possibly remember!" Cavendish was getting remarkably heated and raised his voice. "How dare you talk such nonsense!" This loud and sharp rebuke from her Papa set Isabel in a wail causing her mother to leap up to comfort her.

"I'm sorry to have caused a disturbance," said Holmes calmly, "perhaps we had better finish our discussion elsewhere?"

"I've nothing further to say to you, Holmes! Except get out of my house!" shouted Cavendish.

"It really would be wiser if you heard me out, Mr Cavendish. Your next unexpected visitors may well be the police."

"Don't you threaten me, Holmes!"

Holmes shrugged and turned to leave. "I believe Miss Riley may be suing you for grievous bodily harm, Mr Parsloe may sue for slander and, of course, the insurance company will want its money back. In addition, the law does not look kindly on perjury, and," Holmes paused, "I believe you are also likely not only to lose your position of London's largest wine merchant, but in danger of going out of business altogether. Good morning."

As we journeyed homewards Holmes did not seem at all downcast and I ventured to say that Cavendish was a thoroughly unpleasant sort of character.

"Well, Watson, I do not suppose you, yourself, would enjoy your small son accusing you of theft before strangers."

"At least the boy has been brought up to tell the truth."

"As we speak I have no doubt Master Basil is suffering quite a hefty beating."

"Poor little lad. What will you do now, Holmes?"

"About what?"

"Bringing Cavendish to book. Once again you have brought light to what was dark and caught the fraudster."

"I cannot do anything."

"Of course you can! You said yourself – Miss Riley could sue him for common assault, for one thing."

"Oh, Watson, is that likely? The woman was terrified of him. And as I said before, if she came forward she would only be giving herself up as an accessory. Do you think a court would be sympathetic to a loud-mouthed prostitute? Cavendish knows that is no possibility."

"What about your saying Parsloe could sue him for wrongful imprisonment?"

"Bluff, Watson, pure bluff, and Cavendish knows it. If Parsloe sued, it could only be the police and court, Cavendish didn't imprison him. Declaring Parsloe is innocent does not make Cavendish guilty."

"But the blighter has virtually confessed!" I expostulated.

"Nonsense. Nothing of the sort."

"Come on, Holmes, we were as near as damn it thrown out of his house. He was in a towering rage, do you think he would have done that if he had not been guilty?"

"You, my dear Watson, as a totally innocent man, would be extremely angry if you were accused of a crime in front of other people."

"Well, of course, but he is as guilty as hell."

"We may know that, but once again it all boils down to a difference of opinion; which of two people one believes. If you were a juryman would you believe a pillar of society, London's leading wine merchant, or an eight-year-old boy?"

Holmes, was, of course, right. No further evidence had been produced and one could hardly expect a child to testify against his own father. No adult would take the word of a small boy, especially one such as Basil who did not strike me as being the sharpest knife in the box. We were no further to the satisfactory conclusion of this case. It looked very much as though it were one of those adventures that would merely peter out, my readers being cheated of a resolution. Holmes has many unsolved cases in his files.

So that seemed to be that.

Several weeks later we were surprised by Mrs Hudson announcing an unexpected visitor. The young woman looked familiar but I did not instantly place her face and I was slow even when Mrs Hudson stated her name as Miss Jones.

"Perhaps you will not remember me, Mr Holmes," said she after Mrs

Hudson had left.

"Of course I remember you, Miss Jones. How are Miss Isabel and Master Basil. Well I trust?"

"Quite well, thank you. Actually it is in connection with Basil that I have come to see you. The truth is, Mr Holmes, I am in a total quandary as to how to proceed. I have been unable to sleep for worry and have no father or brother to turn to. I really did not know what to do, then thought of you and Dr Watson. I know you are both gentlemen of rectitude and wisdom and would be able to advise me."

"Perhaps you would explain your dilemma?"

"Two days ago, one of the books that we use for our lessons went astray. It was most aggravating as it contained material I particularly wanted to use for the next few lessons. Both the children and I searched everywhere but to no avail. I could not think where it might have gone. Then later in the day Mrs Cavendish took the children out on a visit for which I was not required. So I took the opportunity to search the children's rooms. Something I would never normally dream of doing, of course, but I was considerably vexed at the loss of the book. Under Basil's bed he keeps a small hamper where he puts his little treasures – seashells he has taken a fancy to, trinkets given by relatives, all those kinds of things. Within the hamper I found the missing book. I strongly suspect he had taken it and hidden it deliberately so that we could not embark on our first steps into the language of France."

During this recital Holmes had sat with apparent rapt attention but as Miss Jones paused he interjected: "That must have been gratifying for you, Miss Jones, but I am puzzled as to why you should take the trouble to come here to tell me this."

"Because, Mr Holmes, also in the hamper I found this." Miss Jones produced an elegant small purse with a drawstring. "Look inside." Holmes loosed the string and produced a jumble of silver and diamonds that, when laid out on the table, resolved itself into the long-missing necklace.

"The missing reticule, Mr Holmes. It must have been in Basil's hamper all the while."

"Very, very interesting," mused Holmes. "But what is your dilemma? The jewels are found, your employer will be excessively grateful."

"Basil must have taken them. The boy clearly lied. He knew where the necklace was all the time the police and you were searching for it. A man was locked up in prison under the greatest suspicion."

"He's only a small boy, he would not have realised the distress he was causing," I said gently.

"Dr Watson, I am a governess, Basil's governess. I am employed to teach children not only the three Rs, but right from wrong. It is my duty to inculcate manners and morals. I have plainly failed to do so. I am a professional failure and I can no longer stay in the house knowing that fact. Neither can I merely hand the necklace back without explaining the circumstances. You saw how berserk Mr Cavendish behaved when Basil said he had seen him place the reticule in his pocket. You were not there when he punished the boy. It was horrible. As you say, he is only a little boy. It was some time before he recovered from his father's brutal assault."

There was silence in the room until broken by Holmes. "I can assist you in the returning of the necklace, Miss Jones. If you will be guided by me, I suggest you leave it with me. I undertake to return it without you or Basil being implicated in any way."

"Oh, Mr Holmes, if you could, I would be infinitely grateful."

"I cannot, however, decide your dilemma for you. That you must do yourself."

"Of course. I am resolved to give in my notice. The agency has a high opinion of me, I know, and I do not anticipate any difficulty in finding a new situation. I think one far away from London would be best. I am confident that I could explain that my mother has become a permanent invalid and I must resign my post and try to obtain one nearer to her. Under those circumstances I feel Mrs Cavendish would furnish me with a satisfactory testimonial."

I had to admire this staunch young woman, who had clearly had a difficult time and thought out all the aspects of her quandary.

"That would seem to be an ideal solution. Will you do this immediately? I ask because the timing of the return of the necklace must be quite independent," said Holmes.

"I have to give one month's notice."

"Excellent. If you do that immediately, I will see the necklace is returned one week after you have given notice. You will then have three weeks before you leave. You will have to have no knowledge of anything. And, of course, should Basil have anything to say when the necklace reappears you must act your part. At all times you must be innocent and unknowing. Is that clear?"

"Perfectly."

"Then I think you may rest assured that all will be well. You have done the wisest thing in bringing the necklace to me."

"I was sure I could rely on you, Mr Holmes. I presume it would also be wise that we do not communicate with each other again?"

"It is essential, though you are in no way involved in this messy affair, you could be dragged in if it were known you had even spoken to me. This is not *au revoir* but *adieu* as I am sure your missing text book will confirm," said Holmes with a smile.

"Then good bye, Mr Holmes, Dr Watson." The young woman held out her hand and thus we bade our final farewell.

"Well, that's a surprise, Holmes," said I after the door had closed. "Master Basil was the thief all along. Just think, through his childish prank, poor Parsloe could be languishing in jail."

"Perhaps you are less sympathetic about his father beating him, now, eh, Watson?" said Holmes with a smile.

"The thing that amazes me is that Cavendish is *not* responsible. Mavis Riley told us she had devised the plot to defraud the insurance company and we assumed he had double-crossed her. How can that awful man be innocent – consorts with prostitutes, vicious temper, employs thugs to beat-up women and I don't know what else."

"None of those things makes him a thief, Watson. In my experience no man is wholly bad just as no man is wholly good. No doubt Moriarty was very good to his mother. Cavendish will have, as most of us, his own personal moral code with a boundary over which he will not step. We all have one, and the boundary varies from person to person. Because he is such a repellent fellow we fell into the trap of assuming he could not possibly be innocent."

Exactly seven days later we had a visit from an excitable Mr Conquest, the manager of the Surrey Theatre. "It's been found, Mr Holmes! The missing necklace has turned up after all this time!"

"Indeed? How astonishing," said Holmes with a straight face.

"Look at that!" Conquest thrust a sheet of paper at Holmes. It was a message created by crudely cutting words from a newspaper.

"A commonplace ruse to prevent the possibility of the sender's hand-writing giving a clue. The words, if I mistake not, are cut from a copy of the *Morning Post*, the type-face is quite distinctive. Have you the envelope?"

"No, it was not sent via the post but handed in at the stage door of the theatre. It simply said 'Mr Conquest' in cut-out letters."

"What was the person like who handed it in?" asked Holmes.

"Well, to say truth, handed in is a misnomer, it was pushed under the door last night after the place was locked up. The stage-door keeper found it when he opened up this morning."

"Ah, so we have no clues at all. The person who did this was clearly very clever," said Holmes. "It says 'Look in the drapes of Box B'. Did you do so?"

"Immediately. Box B is the one that the Cavendishes occupied."

"A moment please, what are these drapes that are mentioned?" asked Holmes.

"All the boxes have a swagged pelmet with ornamental cords. This is normally too high to reach and, quite frankly, gets neglected. The drapery is only cleaned once a year in our summer recess, otherwise it is allowed to gather dust. To reach it I had to stand on the padded ledge of the box front."

"Most enterprising of you, and what did you find?"

"Why the reticule thing itself with the necklace inside! It was simply tucked within the scoop of the folds. Filthy dirty up there actually."

"So all ends happily."

"But don't you see what this means? The only way it could have got there is by being placed by someone standing, as I did, on the box front. And who did that? Parsloe the Man-monkey!"

"So you mean, he was, after all, the thief?" I asked.

"Of course! He obviously swept up the reticule as he leapt on to the parapet, instantly popped it into the folds and carried on with his act. He clearly intended to retrieve it after the show unknown to anybody, but was both scared off by the hullabulloo and the fact he was promptly arrested."

"There is one flaw in your excellent summing-up, Mr Conquest," said Holmes.

"Flaw? What do you mean?"

"Miss Riley – known as Mrs Parsloe – also leapt on to the parapet, she was just as able to proceed as you have described."

Conquest looked a little dashed. "Well, yes, I suppose you are right."

"Perhaps, after all, they were in it together. I understand they fled the country some weeks ago. Guilty or not, they obviously did not get away with the booty. Now they are untraceable and Mrs Cavendish has her property returned. I take it you have done that?"

"Yes, yes, I have just come from their house. I was so elated at finding the jewellery I hastened there at once. I must tell you, I have felt this affair reflected very badly on my theatre and I am relieved to have it all cleared up. It was Mr Cavendish that said you must be told. I think he was under the impression that you suspected he, himself, was the thief!"

Holmes held up his palms in protest. "Not at all, not at all. He must have misunderstood when I said nobody, whomsoever they be, can be ruled out of my investigation."

"Well he is certainly a happy man now."

"Thank you for bringing me the joyful tidings. I regret my services to you were not sufficient to find either thief or property."

"Oh, do not trouble yourself, Mr Holmes, you are only human. We all fail sometimes, don't we? Well, I must away." With that Conquest breezed out.

I looked at Holmes who nonchalantly took up the newspaper he had laid aside when Conquest had entered. "Holmes," I said in a tone of voice that could not be mistaken.

"It is a singular fact that Mr Conquest and Joe Parsloe are both small men, no taller than Miss Riley. I do believe that I, myself, may be as much as ten inches taller. Not that small men are at a disadvantage; by no means. A couple of nights ago I saw a small man called Dan Leno, a very humorous fellow whose personality was so magnetic that while he was on stage all eyes were glued to his very entertaining performance. I'm sure you would enjoy his act, Watson, I believe he is still at the Surrey until the end of the week. Should you choose to write up this case in one of your admirable, though somewhat embroidered tales, an excellent appropriate title has, alas, been taken already by one Mr Shakespeare – *Much Ado About Nothing*."

THE BLACK PEARL OF RAJASTHAN

In recounting the adventures of my friend Mr Sherlock Holmes I try to show different facets of his deductive genius. In most cases Holmes's work is careful and painstaking but, inevitably, slow. Thus some cases occupy many weeks or even months before providing a satisfactory conclusion, indeed on occasion it is a period of years before a matter can be truly closed. Also, of course, there are many cases which are never closed because Holmes did not succeed in solving them. The event I am about to relate, however, is singular in that Holmes provided the solution in a matter of hours thus making it the most swiftly-solved case on his books.

Mrs Hudson is not a woman to get easily flustered but even she was discombobulated one autumn morning when we had an unexpected visitor. It is not an every day event, even in the elevated circles that Holmes occasionally finds himself, to open the door to Robert Gascoyne-Cecil, Lord Salisbury, the prime minister of our country. We were, indeed, unexpectedly honoured by such a visit by that august personage. It needed no clever deduction on my part to conclude that a sudden unannounced visit by our leading statesman at eleven o'clock in the morning presaged the dire necessity of Holmes's immediate assistance on a matter of national importance.

"I am sorry to arrive unannounced, Mr Holmes, but my mission is of the utmost secrecy, the fate of the nation is at stake," said the prime minister in tones weighty with dread.

"You have my immediate attention, prime minister, I am entirely at your disposal. Please say in what manner I can be of assistance," replied Holmes.

"Perhaps you have heard of the famous Black Pearl of Rajasthan?"

"Indeed. I understand that it is a recent gift from the Maharajah of Jaipur, to our monarch."

"A unique pearl beyond price, Mr Holmes. Most so-called black pearls are not truly black but dark shades of other colours. The Black Pearl of Rajasthan is jet black and a perfect sphere almost one inch in diameter. Its monetary value exceeds the rarest diamonds. The pearl has been presented by the Maharajah as a token of esteem and friendship. I have had it in my safe for several weeks whilst discussions have taken place as to how it can be shown to the greatest advantage. You may also know that the Maharajah himself is coming on a state visit next month."

Holmes inclined his head. "I am aware of these facts, the newspapers are full of the news."

"It was decided that a tiara would be made for Princess Alexandra which would feature the Black Pearl. An eminent artist has designed the tiara, and goldsmiths, silversmiths and jewellers are waiting to begin work on making the piece. They were due to start this very morning."

"Were due?"

"Yes. Alas, they cannot! For the Black Pearl was stolen as soon as the messenger carrying it left my office."

"Great heavens!" I cried.

"Please relate the circumstances in as much detail as possible, sir," said Holmes crisply.

"The circumstances, appalling as they be, are simple," said the prime minister sadly. "I thought the matter would best be done in an uncomplicated manner by keeping the knowledge to a close group of trusted people and using commonplace methods. The lack of ceremony would provide the best form of protection. As I say, I had the pearl in my safe. It was housed in an ornate jewelled box – a cube of about two inches every way. I decided that there was no need for the box to leave the office, so I ordered an ordinary small wooden box lined with cotton wool for the transportation. I asked my chief clerk to propose a suitable messenger from our staff to take the little wooden box containing the pearl to Asprey's premises in a government carriage. He put forward a man by the name of Mackenzie, a very reliable fellow."

"Did you personally know this Mackenzie?"

"Oh yes, he is a senior clerk, been at the office for years. Totally reliable. Dedicated to the Government."

"I see. Pray continue."

"Mackenzie came to my office at the appointed time of nine o'clock this morning bringing a leather handbag as arranged. I took the pearl from the jewelled box, placed it in the wooden one and Mackenzie put it into his bag."

"You saw it go into the bag?"

"Oh yes, there's no doubt about that. He locked the bag with a key. The theft was outside in the street."

"Pray continue."

"Mackenzie left my office, went down the steps to the hall where a commissionaire is always on duty, and he opened the door for Mackenzie. The carriage was drawn up immediately outside, and as Mackenzie crossed the pavement to the carriage, a man, or perhaps a youth, reports are varied, rushed past and, grabbing the bag, raced off down the street. Mackenzie was left sprawling on the floor, the coach driver, seeing everything from his seat aloft, immediately shouted and started up his horses, but the youth was very quick, darting in and out of the few people around. Fortuitously, there was a policeman at the end of the street and he attempted to stop the thief, grappling with him, but the man made off down an alleyway to disappear from sight. The constable, who had been thrown to the ground, followed with all due speed, but the man had got away. However, a brief search of the alley found the bag, which had been cut open with a knife. The wooden box was open, thrown to one side and the pearl abstracted."

"So the bag and box were retrieved?"

"They were. I must add that the commissionaire flew up to me as soon as the incident occurred and I, along with Collins the head clerk, were out on the pavement before the man had disappeared from sight."

"So you saw him evade the policeman?"

"Yes."

"And the policeman brought the bag back to you?"

"That's correct, Mr Holmes. Collins and I took control of the bag and went back up to my office. Mackenzie was helped by the commissionaire and was seated in the hallway. The policeman remained there too. Collins and I, upon examining the bag and box, found a slit along the side of the bag. The thief must have carried a knife so he could cut the bag open and abstract the pearl. He must have considered he would be hindered by the bag and could throw it away."

"So what steps did you then take, having found the pearl missing?"

"I summoned the police commissioner and he is, as I speak, alerting his entire force to seek out the criminal. But I cannot let this matter become public knowledge. Although providing a description of the thief, I must be circumspect. Unable to fully confide in the police, they are now handicapped by searching for an item that I am not at liberty to completely describe. I am aware, Mr Holmes, of your previous efforts to assist the crown so I immediately thought you were the man to whom I must turn."

"Where is Mackenzie now?"

"He is still at the office. The poor man was so shaken and distraught I urged him to go home, but the stout fellow insisted he was not harmed and would stay at his post."

"Indeed? This case has remarkable features and I will of course assist you in every way I can. May we return with you?"

"I was expecting you to do so, Mr Holmes; my carriage awaits."

As we made our way to Downing Street, Holmes went over the facts yet again to make sure he understood the sequence of events. Finally he said "You must arrest Mackenzie, put him in solitary confinement and strip search him."

"Mackenzie?" asked Lord Salisbury in bewilderment. "Surely he cannot be held responsible? We know the thief was a low-class youth. He was seen committing the crime by several people."

"We must start somewhere, prime minister."

I felt that I had to interject. "But Holmes, the man is the victim and surely, if he had the pearl he would have immediately taken the chance to leg it off home, not insist that he stayed."

"Exactly, Dr Watson; my thoughts too. I don't think any blame can be attached to Mackenzie, Mr Holmes."

"I do not for a minute think Mackenzie has the pearl, but we must explore every avenue, eliminate every possibility. There are so few persons involved in the affair. I urge you to do as I say."

"Oh, whatever you suggest shall be done," agreed the prime minister.

"As I understand it, the number of people with knowledge of the intention to move the Black Pearl is limited to the following: Collins your head clerk, Mackenzie, the craftsman or men who were to receive the pearl at Asprey's, and you yourself. Were there any others? What about the coachman and the commissionaire?"

"The coachman's instructions were to take Mackenzie where he asked to go. He did not even have an address given to him in advance; neither did Mackenzie until I gave it to him immediately prior to departure."

"Excellent. But the coachman could have gleaned knowledge of the package he was to carry."

"Totally impossible. Everybody concerned was sworn to secrecy and is of the highest calibre of trustworthiness."

"And the commissionaire?"

"A totally reliable man. But in any case he knows nothing. His job is merely to assist people in and out of the building."

It seemed to me to be an impossible case to solve, there was so little to go on. Basically, it was a matter of a simple bag snatch and the thief had got away. I voiced my opinion. "Surely this is merely an opportunist bag snatcher, Holmes. It is, unfortunately, commonplace in the capital for rogues to pick pockets, grab bags and so on. No doubt this lad lingers about where he sees a coach, looking for opportunities to run by, stealing a bag as he goes."

"In that case he would not know the bag contained the Black Pearl, Watson."

"He won't care what it contains; these fellows steal whatever is to hand. If the bag has money or valuables so much the better. I should think most times they end up with some lawyer's boring papers or similar. Or perhaps some poor fellow's lunch."

"If that were the case, Watson, the thief would hardly have paused in his flight to slit open and examine the contents. He would either have fled, clinging on to the case to examine his booty later at leisure, or jettison it to halt the chase and wait to steal another bag from someone else at another time. He must have had knowledge of the contents to take the risk of pausing in flight to open the bag and take out the pearl. As long as he kept hold of the bag he might be recognised but, once he had rid himself of it, he could blend away into the crowds, the pearl alone in his pocket. A normal petty thief snatching a bag would simply throw it back at his pursuers to make his escape. Regaining the bag would be more paramount than catching the thief." Holmes then lapsed into silence and the prime minister stared ahead, his face a picture of dejection. This great man, Lord Salisbury, descended from the famous Cecil, Queen Elizabeth's chief minister, was powerless in circumstances such as these. It was alarming to be at such close quarters to the leader of our country and realise that he was but a man with all the fears and inadequacies of the ordinary man, but all the responsibilities of running the greatest empire in the world on his shoulders. It is not a pleasant sight to see one's leaders helpless.

On arrival at Downing Street we immediately went to the prime minister's office. Collins was sent for and the order given to arrest Mackenzie. Collins looked shocked, but said nothing before hastening out to obey. I was quite astonished to find that in the office, whilst there was a large business-like desk in the centre of the room with book-shelves behind, against one wall were ranged several chairs, presumably on hand for meetings with colleagues. At the left was a table with a splendid array of cut blooms expertly arranged, and against the right wall a sideboard with a lavish bowl of fruit and several pieces of plate. It was to this sideboard that the prime minister drew our attention.

"This is the safe," said he, opening one of the low doors.

"Can you stand exactly where you were, sir?" asked Holmes. The prime minister obeyed. "And where was Mackenzie at that point?"

"He was standing just here alongside."

"Watson, can you stand in for the clerk, please?" I did so. "When you removed the jewelled box where did you put it?"

"Oh, just here on the top. The wooden box was also in the safe so I removed that too and they were side by side."

"I see. Then what did you do?"

"Why, simply took out the pearl from the jewelled box and placed it in the wooden one."

"And Mackenzie watched you do it?"

"Oh yes. We both admired it before closing the lid."

"And this is the box, you say?" It was a simple cube made from some light wood such as cigar boxes are made from. Inside was cotton wool padding. "I note there is no catch of any sort."

"No, the lid was held closed with a rubber band."

"Then did you, or Mackenzie, place the box in the bag?"

"He put it in, closed the clasp and turned the key."

"Then what happened?"

"We both walked to the door, I opened it and stood aside to permit him to exit. Closed the door after him and went to sit at my desk to work. I had been there but a minute when the commissionaire burst in and announced the dread news."

"Whereupon you rushed downstairs?"

"Yes, calling to the commissionaire to rouse Collins, who followed us immediately."

"Could you ask Collins to join us downstairs?"

The next stage of Holmes's investigation centred around the pavement, and how Mackenzie had just been about to open the door of the carriage when a youth, appearing from nowhere at speed, knocked the man down and sped off with his bag. Everybody concerned with the incident seemed to agree the salient features which were as we had initially been told. The only points of dissension were the age of the assailant, whether a man or a youth, and whether he was wearing gloves, most maintaining he did not, but the policeman adamant that he did. I must say that Holmes had very little in the way of evidence, and crawling about on the pavement with his lens proved a fruitless exercise.

Holmes asked Collins, the head clerk, if he had Mackenzie's address.

"Of course, but he is not at home. Lord Salisbury has had him arrested and taken away to jail," replied the man.

"I am aware of that, Mr Collins. It is not he to whom I wish to speak."

"I must say I think Mackenzie has been treated most unjustly. The idea of such a loyal servant of the Crown being placed in a common jail is abhorrent," said Collins.

"It is merely a necessary precaution, Mr Collins. He will come to no harm," assured Holmes.

"But the indignity of it! Mackenzie is a very proud man."

"His address, if you please."

Holmes ordered a cab and on our journey I ventured to say "Well, as I see it, the number of men who knew about the arrangement to deliver the Black Pearl is very small – apart from Mackenzie there are only his boss Collins, the prime minister at Downing Street, and whoever was expecting it at Asprey's at the other end. Perhaps you should investigate there?"

"We are going to New Bond Street now."

However, at Asprey's we drew a total blank. This high class jeweller, by appointment to several royal personages over the years, was of such standing any nefarious activity on its part was unthinkable. We were welcomed by Mr Charles Asprey himself and he confided that he alone knew that the Black Pearl was coming that day, but even he had not been told the time, from whence it was coming, or how it would be delivered. The visit was, in fact, fruitless but, as Holmes pointed out, everything he could eliminate from suspicion helped target the true position.

Thereafter, we sped instantly to Mackenzie's address which was in Holloway. It was a neat house in a very respectable street, but there was no reply to our knocking.

"It seems nobody is at home, Holmes," I said.

"On the contrary, Watson, we have been observed from an upstairs window. Did you not see the movement of the curtains as we approached? There is somebody in and that person is deliberately refusing to answer the door."

We hammered a few more times with no better result.

"This is annoying, Watson, we cannot break in. We shall have to wait while I ponder our next move."

We moved across the road out of direct sight of any person in the house. We discussed the situation and Holmes had just decided that we would make some enquires at the next house, when a woman coming up the street passed us and then turned in at the gate of the very house we were watching.

"Quick, after her!" said Holmes dashing off. We were there before the woman had time to withdraw the key from her pocket.

"Mrs Mackenzie?" asked Holmes.

"Oh, no!" she cried in alarm. "Not again! We've told you that you'll get your money. We cannot pay it all at once, you know that. It was agreed we would pay in instalments. We are not evading payment. But we must have time. We cannot have you coming here and bothering us like this. We don't want any trouble. If you keep on and on at us I will call the police."

"We are the police, madam," said Holmes.

"Oh, no!" cried the woman again, falling in a faint on the doorstep.

I dropped to my knees to attend to her. Of course, I did not have my medical bag with me, but I had my brandy flask. "We must get her inside, Holmes," I said.

"Permit me, madam," said Holmes to the insensible woman, as he slipped his hand into her coat pocket and withdrew the key. The door was soon open and I carried the woman bodily into the house, laying her on a chaise-longue that was conveniently to hand. I raised her legs on some cushions and she soon stirred, whereupon I forced some brandy between her lips which set her coughing and she attempted to sit up.

"Lie still, Mrs Mackenzie, I am a doctor. You are in no danger. You have fainted but will soon be yourself." My calm bedside manner seemed to reassure the poor woman who consented to lie still.

While I was attending to my patient, Holmes had gone upstairs and he now returned with the news that there was somebody in one of the upstairs rooms, but the door was wedged fast closed.

"We can attend to that later, Watson. How is your patient?"

Mrs Mackenzie now sat up and stared at us. "I am quite well now, thank you. But I do not understand what is happening. I thought you were the men come to threaten us again. But you say you are the police. You are not in uniforms. How do I know you are who you say you are?"

"Forgive me, madam. It is true we are not the police but we represent law and order. My name is Sherlock Holmes and this is my colleague Dr Watson."

"A doctor? Oh, could you look at Jim's poor hand before you go?"

"I am at your service, Mrs Mackenzie," I assented.

"We have been engaged by Lord Salisbury the prime minister to investigate a crime. The purpose of our visit is simply to ask a few questions," said Holmes sternly.

"Questions?"

"Yes. Firstly, you mistook us for some men who require you to pay them some money. Would you please explain what that is about?"

"Oh, I couldn't. Henry was very strict about it. He said not only was it embarrassing, if his employers heard of it he might lose his job."

"Henry being your husband Mr Mackenzie who has a civil service position with the prime minister's office staff."

"Yes, you know about Henry?" she said in wonderment.

"I have said we are employed by the prime minister on a work of great but secret importance. Anything you say to us will remain secret. Nothing you say will harm your husband and may well help to solve your problem with these men who are plaguing you," explained Holmes.

"I can see you have been under a great weight of trouble for some time, Mrs Mackenzie," said I. "You can only benefit your health and mind by telling Mr Holmes your troubles."

"You promise to keep it secret? I couldn't bear to get Henry into trouble as well as Jim," replied the fearful woman. "You will look at Jim's hand won't you, Doctor?"

"Of course. I have said."

"Is Jim your son, Mrs Mackenzie?" asked Holmes.

"Yes. He's a good boy but he got into bad company. He was always a bit wayward."

We both waited, saying nothing. Eventually, Mrs Mackenzie started to tell her tale and all tumbled out. It was obvious that the poor woman had been trying to cope with matters far beyond her competence, and my friendly manner and care encouraged her to confide matters that she had kept bottled up inside her for some time. The matter was common-place enough but the result devastating to a respectable family.

Mr and Mrs Mackenzie had two children, the elder a daughter, now married and living at Sutton. The poor lady was insistent that she had 'married well' and that the husband was a man of some substance. She seemed to be in awe of this son-in-law and part of the problem was that she was terrified that they would bring disgrace upon him. The Mackenzies also had a son, James known as Jim. He was the cause of their woes. He was twenty years of age, had no settled profession or training, drifting from job to job unable to hold anything down for long. His father, the ultra respectable Henry, had done his best for his son, and a year ago had managed to get him the position of junior clerk in a government department. According to his mother, the boy was not stupid, he was good with figures and when he buckled down to things he was quite capable of the duties of a lowly clerk. Unfortunately, Jim's temperament was not suited to such a position. He was unlike his father who believed in doing one's best for one's employer, so becoming esteemed; progressing through diligence and assiduity. Jim found his employment tedious and boring, his work soon became slipshod, mistakes were made too often and his time-keeping became erratic. He was also addicted to gambling. While his superiors put up with much of the young man's incompetence in respect for his father, they could not turn a blind eye to his taking money from the petty cash. So Jim was dismissed in ignominy. Again his father's respectable position saved him and he avoided prosecution, but Henry, now thoroughly ashamed of his son, felt that all his own hard-won prestige was blighted.

The son was now at home living in fear because he owed money to bookmakers, and these men were hounding him for repayment. Henry claimed to have washed his hands of his scapegrace son but, of course, he loved him still and could not in conscience cast him off. Thus the entire family were drawn in. They had to dismiss their servant to save money, Mrs Mackenzie had taken paid employment herself to earn extra. She now, for the first time in her life, worked in a general store.

"It's a respectable shop and the work not too arduous. I am the only assistant permitted to handle money, I am the cashier. The salary is modest but we can live off Henry's pay so all I earn goes to pay Jim's debts. We agreed with the men to pay in instalments after last time. That's why I was so frightened when I saw you and Dr Watson here today. I thought you were the men come back again. Will you look at Jim's hand now, Doctor?"

"If you can call him down, Mrs Mackenzie. He seems to have barricaded himself in his room," said Holmes.

We had great trouble persuading the fellow to emerge. It was only when I pushed my card through the slit at the side of the door that he removed the obstacles wedging the door closed, and came out. As Holmes has remarked more than once, it is amazing how people will disbelieve a name when announced, yet accept the same name simply because it is printed on a card.

Jim's left hand was bandaged, over which he wore a woollen glove. When I had removed the dressing I was astonished to see that his little finger was missing.

"Good heavens, how did this happen?" I asked.

"Those wicked men chopped it off, Doctor!" cried Mrs Mackenzie.

"Hush, mother!" snapped Jim. It was the first words he had uttered.

"You look a healthy young chap," said Holmes heartily. "I'm sure you will survive."

"The wound has been efficiently tended. It is healing well," I said.

"I did it myself; we could not afford to call in the doctor. I staunched the bleeding and treated it with disinfectant and bandaged it up. But I was afraid I may not have done it properly," explained Mrs Mackenzie.

"You could not have done better if you had been a trained nurse," I reassured her. "But I must now redress it. Have you another bandage?"

"There is a medicine chest in the kitchen cupboard."

"Excellent. Come, Jim, we will need some water too."

Once we were in the privacy of the kitchen I was able to draw Jim out a little. "It seems your pals have a vicious turn of mind. Perhaps you should choose different friends."

"Pah! They're no friends of mine. Just because I owe them a bit of money they revenge themselves like butchers," said Jim contemptuously.

"Fortunately it is the little finger, which, to be honest, unless you are a musician, you can cope with without too much trouble. You're not left-handed are you?"

"No, thank God!"

"Well, there we are. Be careful you don't lose any more fingers."

"That's what I'm afraid of. If I don't pay up they say they will come back and hack one off each time."

I was aghast, and hurried back into the room where the others awaited us.

"This is horrible, Holmes, those villains have threatened to chop the poor lad's fingers off, one by one, until the debt is cleared," I said.

"How much do you owe, Jim?" asked Holmes.

"Two hundred pounds," answered Jim sulkily.

Mrs Mackenzie gave a cry. "You told me it was fifty pounds!"

"I didn't want to worry you," replied Jim.

"But this is impossible. I have told the men we will clear the debt within six months. I thought it was fifty pounds! There is no way I can earn two hundred pounds with my wages!"

The poor mother dissolved into tears.

Holmes, who was never at his best with women, especially weeping ones, rose to his feet.

"Do you know Downing Street?" asked Holmes.

"Why do you ask that?" demanded Jim belligerently.

"Simply that your father is employed there, isn't he?"

"What is this? Who are you?" demanded the young man.

"Now, Jim, don't be aggressive to these gentlemen," said his mother between her sobs.

"I don't trust them, nosing around here asking about Downing Street."

"We will soon take ourselves off and no more be a nuisance to you. Watson, a word," said Holmes stalking off into the kitchen. "Have you any great amount of money on you?"

"I have two five pound notes that I keep in a secret place for emergency."

"Excellent. I'll send Mrs Mackenzie in. Give her the money and impress upon her she must keep it hidden from Jim. Then if the men return she may be able to fob them off a while. Get her to take you upstairs to show you some hiding place in the bedroom. Detain her as long as possible."

Holmes always has a reason for his actions so I did not hesitate to obey. I asked to speak to the woman confidentially and disclosed the banknotes. Suggesting that the best place to hide them would be in her bedroom, the two of us went up together to find a suitable location.

"This is so good of you, Doctor. I cannot believe there are such kind people in the world who would help a stranger in this way. After dealing with those wicked men, you seem like a saint, Doctor." The good woman prattled on in this way for some time, so much so that I felt much embarrassed, as I was not a saint at all, but carrying out Holmes's mysterious orders.

When we returned downstairs the two men were sitting in silence. Holmes rose. "Thank you for seeing us, Mrs Mackenzie. Good day."

Returning in the cab, Holmes mused "I wonder how many small tragedies are being enacted at the very moment in this great city? The Mackenzies may not rank with Oedipus and Jocasta but to them their fate is just as terrible. People like the Mackenzies have very little to support them except their position in society. Their dignity and respectability is all-powerful. Without those they have nothing. How soon a respected man will fall from grace through one single flaw. Whilst the aristocracy of our land may indulge themselves in illicit romances, our crown princes coveting other men's wives without fear or condemnation, such conduct would be the ruination of a man like Henry Mackenzie. His life is ruled by probity, integrity, veracity. These virtues are his badge of honour, without them he is nothing."

"Very true, Holmes. But whilst I have the utmost sympathy for the Mackenzies and people in similar distress, I cannot give ten pounds to them all."

Holmes laughed. "You will be reimbursed, Watson. It is all in the cause of finding the Black Pearl."

I really could not see what this visit had accomplished and tasked Holmes with the point of it.

"We have established that, in spite of a good salary, Mackenzie is in want. His son is a gambling man and has run up debts. Is that not a temptation for him to steal?"

"You suspect Mackenzie of being the thief?"

"It is a possible motive why he might be. We have also met a sparkish young man who could conceivably be the same one who grappled with the constable."

"Come off it, Holmes, London is full of youths like Jim – thousands of them. It could be any one of them. As you know, many a young man prefers thieving to working for a living."

"Watson, I have been called in by the prime minister – the highest in the land. He expects results from me. You, through your incessant writings having inflated my prowess to magical proportions, I have to provide an answer to this theft. I must follow every lead I can in the hope that something matches up somewhere."

On our return to Downing Street we were shown once more into the prime minister's gracious office.

"Time is of the essence, Mr Holmes. Princess Alexandra is to wear the tiara at a dinner to welcome the Maharajah of Jaipur. If he does not see the Black Pearl that he has graciously bestowed on the future Queen of England the insult will lead to an international incident of terrible proportions."

"Which is more important – to catch the thief or retrieve the jewel?"

"Surely if we catch the thief then we will also have the jewel?"

"The thief no longer has the jewel."

"You have discovered the thief?" asked the prime minister in amazement.

"I was never in doubt about that, but I confess I am still unsure of what actually happened."

"But that is surely clear – there were witnesses to the whole thing – the coachman for one, the constable, and latterly even Collins and myself, the commissionaire too was partly present."

"They saw the bag being snatched, they saw a youth run up the street, the policeman found the bag and box thrown away."

"Yes, yes, all of that."

"Did they see the youth slit the bag? Did they see him open the wooden box? Did they see him abstract the Black Pearl and thrust it into his pocket?"

"Well, no, but he must have done," said the prime minister.

"You are correct in all your assumptions but one, prime minister. I know the youth slit the bag, I know he took out the wooden box, I know he opened it. But the box was empty."

"Empty?" repeated the incredulous prime minister. "How could that be?"

"The Black Pearl was never in the box in the bag."

"That is incredible! I placed it in the box myself. I saw it enter the bag with my own eyes!" protested the prime minister.

"I beg to differ, sir. You thought you saw it done. Tell me, when you had admired the pearl with Mackenzie here in your office, what actually happened then? Please be as precise as possible."

"As I told you previously – I placed it in the box, Mackenzie closed the lid, put the rubber band around it and placed it in his bag and, closing the clasp, turned the key."

"And at what point did you return to your safe the jewelled box that had previously contained the pearl?"

The change of the prime minister's appearance was ghastly to behold. He lurched and stumbled against the sideboard, dislodging an ornamental plate. His voice was reduced to a hoarse whisper. "I replaced it in the safe, locked the door. I had my back to Mackenzie while I did it.

I had put the pearl in the wooden box and he closed the lid. When I straightened up he still held it with the rubber band he had wrapped round it and I saw him put it in the bag."

"Thus you didn't see him take the pearl out again before closing the box lid. You had your back to him for a long time?"

"No, no, it was but the action of less than half a minute. The door was open, I put the casket in and closed the safe up."

"To take the pearl out and conceal it elsewhere did not take half a minute, it was an action performed in five seconds," said Holmes.

"How blind I've been! It was Mackenzie all the time," groaned the PM.

"Mackenzie is both a clever man and an unfortunate one," said Holmes. "He is unfortunate because he cannot control his son's extravagant betting habits that are running his very pleasant family into penury. He is doubly unfortunate that he loves his son too well. He is a clever man because he purloined the pearl to prevent an audacious robbery."

"He could hang for this," blustered the PM.

"I don't understand, Holmes," I protested. "How could stealing the pearl prevent a robbery? It *was* a robbery."

"Mackenzie thought it was essential that the pearl did not go in the bag, so he made sure by taking it himself."

"I see – the footpad who snatched the bag was Jim, his son!" I exclaimed.

"Exactly. Jim was desperate. He had already been mutilated by felons who threatened him further. His father, who is a man of the utmost probity, was appalled by his son's behaviour. He tried to impress upon the youth how diligence and hard work brought their own reward. Unfortunately, his error was in choosing the example for this precept. He told Jim that his father was so respected that he was being entrusted with one of the world's most magnificent jewels. Once the boy knew this he boasted that he could steal it and solve all his money troubles. All he had to do was lurk in Downing Street until he saw his father leave with the bag. As Jim taunted him, boasting of his plans, Henry realised at once how foolish he had been to give away this top-secret information."

"And Mackenzie's son duly snatched the bag," stated Lord Salisbury.

"Indeed, exactly as he boasted his would."

"But it was Mackenzie's duty to report his suspicions. Our plan could have been easily changed. Somebody else could have been substituted for Mackenzie, with a different time and mode of transport."

"Of course, but Mackenzie had his code of honour to his masters. It was inconceivable for him not to obey orders. He never even considered asking for them to be changed. Also, he loved his son but, knowing he was reckless, feared he would most likely be caught in the act. If the pearl were not in the bag, his son's crime would not be the great matter of stealing a royal jewel, but be the much lesser one of stealing an empty bag. In fact Jim did get away with it, he pushed his father to the ground and sped off with the bag."

"What an ungrateful wretch! To treat his father such when you know what his parents have done and are doing for him!" I expostulated.

"I have spoken with Jim and he has confessed all. Having shaken off the policeman, he ventured to cut open the bag with a pocket knife. Eagerly taking out the box, he was stupefied when he found it was empty," said Holmes.

"Of course, you learned this when we were at the house and I took the mother upstairs."

"As soon as I saw the glove on Jim's hand, everything fell into place. The reason there was doubt over whether the thief wore gloves was the fact that he wore one only, some seeing one side of the man, some seeing the other. I was in a position to tell Jim exactly what he had done as though I had been a witness to it all myself."

"You are amazing, Mr Holmes!" said Lord Salisbury in admiration.

"Mackenzie, fearing his son had a good chance of being caught, took the pearl himself."

"So where is it, Mr Holmes?" asked Salisbury.

"I presume Mackenzie has been searched and found to be clean?"

"He has and nothing was found."

"Perhaps he swallowed it!" I cried.

"Excellent, Watson!" replied Holmes. "You may well be right."

"Swallowed it? By God, the man's a cunning devil," said the prime minister.

"Cleverer than you can imagine, Lord Salisbury. The whole essence of Mackenzie's scheme was not to steal but merely temporarily remove the pearl so that it would not be stolen. He fully intended to replace it."

"I don't follow you, Mr Holmes," said the baffled prime minister.

"Before I explain, sir, may I point out that we have not discussed the fee for my services. Whilst I am always willing to help my country, I regret that on this occasion I have been to some particularly peculiar expenses."

"Already?"

"I'm afraid so. I must ask you to agree a payment of two hundred and ten pounds."

"Good heavens!" exclaimed the prime minister.

"I'm sure you will agree it is a modest amount to guarantee having the pearl returned."

"I cannot condone treating with thieves, Mr Holmes."

"That is not in question, sir, I assure you."

"Very well. That sum will be paid to you. I await your explanation."

"Mackenzie did not swallow the pearl. The most telling clue from the start was the fact that he was reluctant to go home. Why would any employee given leave by his employer to go home, nay, commanded to do so, insist on staying at his post? Any man having suffered such an event as being assaulted and thrown to the ground would clearly take the opportunity to quit the scene of the crime if he were innocent; similarly if he had swallowed it he would be eager to go home to purge himself. But no, he insisted on staying here at his desk. Why? Because the pearl is still here. He did not have it on him, otherwise he would have been a thief. It was not in the bag, it was not on his person, so he must have placed it somewhere where he could retrieve it later."

"He had to hide it!" exclaimed Lord Salisbury.

"Not only hide it, but put it somewhere where the chance of some-body else finding it was remote. His plan would be well and truly scotched if it were to be found before he could retrieve it, that is why he dare not leave his post. He sought some opportunity to bring it back to light. However, he did not bargain for being arrested and confined. That thwarted any opportunity of returning the pearl as he had hoped."

"But he would hardly have had time to hide the jewel, Holmes," I pointed out. "You talked of five seconds, but even allowing the prime minister's half a minute, where could he have found a safe hiding place in such a short time without arousing suspicion?"

"He found a very convenient place without stirring a step."

"You mean here in this room?" gasped the prime minister.

"Yes, sir. While you have sent constables searching all over London, the missing jewel was never at any time very far from your elbow."

"You have me baffled, Mr Holmes."

Holmes smiled and sauntered over to the sideboard. From the bowl of fruit he gently lifted out a bunch of grapes. "May I offer you one of these excellent grapes? Pray avoid the one on top, you will find it exceedingly hard and may break a tooth."

THE DEMISE OF THE FAVOURITE SON

"What do you make of that, Watson?" asked Sherlock Holmes, tossing a letter over to me. It was a late autumn day, the weather hinting at the rigours of winter to come, and we were grateful for the coal fire that was burning cheerfully in the grate.

The letter was headed Dutton, Penrose and Whittaker, a firm of solicitors, and the signature was that of Mr Gordon Penrose himself. *Dear Mr Holmes*, I read, *I am writing to you at the suggestion of Inspector Lestrade of Scotland Yard who said that the matter was "more in your line than the official police". I fear that in the not too distant future a crime may be committed and I would, naturally, wish to prevent it. I would be obliged if I could call on you and explain the matter more fully.*

"How intriguing," said I, handing the letter back.

"I have invited him to call, he should be with us shortly," replied Holmes.

"But what can it mean?" I asked.

"I have no idea, Watson, but we shall in a moment as I hear a tread outside." And sure enough, Mrs Hudson showed in the solicitor. He could not have been anything else, his appearance being exactly that of a family solicitor of the old-fashioned sort, dressed entirely in black clothes of a previous generation, a head of white hair, bald at the crown, and a pair of rather thick spectacles perched on a pointed nose.

"Pray take a seat, Mr Penrose. I trust the omnibus was not too crowded?"

"Oh, no, not at all," replied Penrose, then staring, "How on earth did you know I took an omnibus?"

"You have tucked the ticket into the cuff of your glove," replied Holmes pleasantly. "Now how may I assist you?"

Penrose glanced at me. "It is rather a delicate matter, Mr Holmes, the fewer people involved the better."

"Of course," agreed Holmes. "May I introduce my friend and confidant, Dr Watson. He is conversant with all my work. He served in the Indian Army, is a valued assistant, and secrets are as safe with him as anything placed within the vaults of the Bank of England. Have no fear. Please state your business."

"Oh, yes, yes, of course. Well, it is this way. I have been placed in the most peculiar position that has ever occurred in all my years of practising law. If I may give you some family background before I come to main point I think it will assist your comprehension."

"I am at your disposal, Mr Penrose," smiled Holmes, "tell your tale how you will."

"Firstly, you must know that I represent a family of the most notable and long lineage. The head of the family died some months ago leaving a large fortune. The man was a widower with three sons, his wife dying many years ago while failing to give birth to what would have been a fourth child."

"Poor lady," I murmured sympathetically.

"Yes, Doctor, it hit the husband very hard, losing his wife so young and, as a result, he devoted extra care and attention to his three boys. To simplify the rather complex nature of my narrative I propose using the nomenclature of Tom, Dick and Harry for these sons. Tom being the eldest and Harry the youngest. They are very close in age with only one or two years between them. They married young and even now are only in their early thirties, though grown men with wives and children of their own. Do I make myself clear?" asked Penrose anxiously.

"Perfectly," replied Holmes, "please continue." He sat with his hands together, forefingers extended touching his lips in a pose I had often been accustomed to see.

"Well, as boys these three were always ragging each other, as boys do. There was no harm in them, but they used to claim that one of the others was their father's favourite son. If, say, Harry wanted a horse and his father bought him one, Tom and Dick would claim that he was the favourite because they had not been given horses. Should Dick be given a rowing boat so he could go fishing on the lake, then Tom and Harry would say Dick was being favoured and so on. It was just boyish fun, of course, because the old man was very scrupulous and tried to treat his sons equally and impartially. Since they had separate interests, it was no point in buying a rowing boat for a boy who did not require one, and that boy in his turn would, at another time, perhaps be given a watch or something. Do you understand what I mean, gentlemen?"

"Of course. Both Dr Watson and I have brothers."

"Yes, yes, I just wanted you to be sure that there was no real malice in these statements. It was all boyish banter. You must understand that the family is one of some, but not great, wealth, and the loss of their mother when all three boys were still very young was a bitter blow. The father had an unmarried sister and she lived with them, acting as a substitute mother while the sons were small, but once they went off to school she was not really so important any more. Even so, she stayed on with her brother in the house. It is a large comfortable place of many rooms. However, sad to relate, the brother and sister fell out, I do not know the cause. A great rift arose and the sister, leaving the house, went to live out in the country on her own in a simple cottage with only a companion to minister to her wants. When the boys returned from school for the holidays they found their aunt was no longer there and although their father did not forbid them to see or write to their aunt, none of them was inclined to do so and the relationship lapsed. Tom, Dick and Harry have not seen their aunt for many years. She is still alive, I am her solicitor too and am regularly in touch with her because her brother arranged for an annuity that provides a modest stipend."

Penrose paused and Holmes said "This is all most interesting, Mr Penrose, but it gives no indication to the purpose of your visit."

"I am now coming to that, Mr Holmes, but it was necessary you should know that history. The old man died and his will, though very short and simple, has caused, and continues to cause, complications of the most complex nature. I, myself, was totally at a loss as to how to proceed, but fortunately there are better brains than mine that I have been able to consult. I have spoken with lawyers of far more distinction than I could ever have achieved. But it seems the will is valid."

Penrose, taking out a handkerchief the size of a small tablecloth, mopped the gleaming top of his head. Holmes, not a man of infinite patience, urged him on: "Pray continue, I have as yet no idea what you are talking about."

"No, no. The will. The will of which I speak had one simple clause. It read *I leave everything I possess to my favourite son.* Just that."

"I should have thought you, as a lawyer, would value the simplicity," said Holmes.

Penrose groaned audibly. "Oh, no, no. Do you not see? The man had three sons. How is one to tell which one is the favourite?"

"You mean no name was given?" I asked incredulously.

"Exactly, Doctor, no name at all, no hint, no clue."

Holmes chuckled and rubbed his hands, "Indeed, a pretty problem."

"But surely, the will can't be legal?" said I.

"That was the first difficulty I faced. I assumed that it would not be legal and that I should have to deal with the matter as though the will did not exist and treat the deceased as intestate. But, after seeking the advice I mentioned, I was instructed that the will had been signed and witnessed correctly and was legal. I was told that I must identify which of the sons was intended, then proceed to prove the will as customary."

"Did you draw up the will, Mr Penrose?" asked Holmes.

"Certainly not!" said Penrose affronted. "I would have refused to take part in anything so ambiguous and, I may say, so highly dubious."

"What did you do on receiving this advice?"

"Well, firstly I sought to ask Tom, Dick and Harry themselves, as there could well be a common understanding which son was the father's favourite."

"And did they provide agreement?"

"Not at all, Mr Holmes. If I were not intimately concerned and puzzled to death about the affair, I would be amused. After years of protesting that they were badly done to and one of the other brothers was their father's favourite, now they each claim that he himself was the preferred son."

"Each trying to claim the money," I stated.

"Exactly so. Each man loudly claiming he was the favourite. It disgusts me as much as it depresses me. I thought they were made of sterner stuff."

"But I don't see that it need be a problem," I said. "If all the brothers agree on one as the favourite, say Tom, he could inherit everything and then share it out equally, a third each."

"Alas no. That, of course, was the next approach I made, thinking I had found the fairest solution."

"But why not?" I persisted.

"Greed."

"Greed?" I repeated in astonishment.

"Certainly, Watson," said Holmes. "If you were offered the whole, would you accept thirty-three per cent?"

"Should I be offered a large amount of money for nothing, I think I would be prepared to share it with total strangers, much less my own brothers," said I hotly.

"May I ask what kind of amount we are talking about, Mr Penrose?"

"With the house, stocks and cash, about £250,000."

"Great heavens!" cried I in astonishment.

"See, Watson, would you settle for a mere £83,000?"

"It is tragic how money corrupts the best of men," said Penrose, shaking his head.

"Although I gather you do not regard Tom, Dick and Harry as the best of men?" asked Holmes.

"Oh, I suppose they are no better or worse than the general run of mankind, but having known them from when they were young, and watched them grow over the years, I had hoped they possessed a higher sense of morality, or at least, duty. The fact remains they are squabbling for a single inheritance and I see no way out of that."

"Are there no other relatives whom you may consult? It may be clear to other members in the greater family which son was favoured by his father," suggested Holmes.

"I have anticipated you there, Mr Holmes, yes indeed. It was one of the first things I thought of. But, alas, there is only one such person – Miss Harling, the aunt who is now of a venerable age. She lives out in the country beyond Esher and I made it my business to visit her to solicit her opinion."

"Which was?"

Penrose sighed. "That her brother was a loony to write such a vague will in the first place. She had no idea which son may have been favoured, but she expressed her own opinion that was totally unhelpful since she had not seen the sons since childhood. She did not even attend her brother's funeral, being now too infirm to travel. It seems Tom always had his nose in a book, while Harry was a villain who pulled the wings off butterflies."

"Nothing on Dick, then?" I interjected.

"He would not eat spinach," replied Penrose with another sigh. "Miss Harling is very old, and I fear not totally in her right mind. She spends her days pottering in her garden, making elderberry wine, bottling plums and so on. She has one servant, well, a companion lady really. A lady called Matilda was with her for years. Unfortunately, she died about two years ago and I was under the necessity of finding a replacement for her. She now has a much younger woman to attend to her wants, but as I said, she could provide no guidance to me."

"Well, sir," said Holmes rising, "this story is very interesting but I fail to see why you have come to me. I am not a lawyer. Your letter mentioned the possibility of some crime being committed?"

"That is so. Events have taken a most sinister turn which is why I have come to consult you."

"Then," said Holmes, as he loomed over the rather abject solicitor, "pray explain the point of your visit."

"A few days ago Harry, the youngest son, came to me to request that I draw up his will. He wished to leave everything in which he was possessed on his demise, equally between his brothers."

"That doesn't seem so terrible, only to be expected, I should have thought," I said.

"Harry is a married man with a wife and three tiny children. He has made no provision for them at all," protested Penrose.

"Did you challenge him on that point?" asked Holmes.

"Most certainly. He merely said his brothers would see her all right."

"I'm sure they will," assured Holmes smoothly.

I am sorry to say the words "Callous swine," passed my lips.

"The poor woman could be left destitute should the will be written in that form," said Penrose, twisting his handkerchief in anguish.

"You say 'if'. I take it you refused to write the will as asked?" enquired Holmes.

"Most certainly! Do you not see the implications?"

"Please elucidate."

"The three brothers came as a body to me stating that they now agreed that Harry was their father's favourite son. It was right that he should inherit everything under their father's will."

"Aha!" exulted Holmes. "All now becomes clear!"

"Not to me, it doesn't," I complained.

"The money goes to Harry. He dies, his brothers get half each – £125,000 instead of £83,000."

"Exactly, Mr Holmes."

Holmes smiled and threw himself back into his chair. Both men seemed to ignore the many variables that could happen in the men's lifetime, as I pointed out. "You are assuming that all this would happen if Harry died tomorrow. He could live to a ripe old age. He could have spent or lost all the money before then. He might have increased it. How old is Harry? Early thirties you said; he could live another forty or even fifty years. His brothers could die before him."

"There is a clause that, should one of the brothers pre-decease Harry, then the other brother would inherit entirely," explained Penrose. "The brothers have given sworn affidavits all agreeing that Harry should inherit as he was clearly their father's favourite son. Harry is at this moment moving his wife and family into the ancestral home. He has given up his business – he operated a small import and export firm – and is preparing himself for a life as a gentleman."

"I must say, that seems to be what most men might do. He can't be blamed for that if his brothers have agreed," said I.

"Harry is a heavy gambler, I am sorry to say," said Penrose. "I fear some evil is planned, Doctor."

"Evil?"

"Most certainly, Watson. I follow you exactly, Mr Penrose. You fear that now Harry has all their father's wealth, his brothers may be tempted to expedite his death so they can inherit sooner, rather than take their chances much later."

"Indeed, that is what I fear," said the old man, shaking his head at the very idea.

"You mean Dick and Tom will conspire to murder their brother?" I gasped. "Such a thought should be unthinkable!"

"Oh, Watson, in spite of all you have seen, you still have faith in the decency of mankind."

I was at a loss for words. If such things are accepted in our society as only to be expected, we are nothing more than brute beasts, no better than the ancient caveman.

Penrose spoke: "In the Holy Bible was it not Joseph's brothers who conspired to kill him? Did not our ancient kings pit father against son, brother against brother in our civil wars? Did not Richard III murder his brother and nephews to obtain the crown?"

I could not gainsay the solicitor's statements. They were facts, but I could not credit that, in our modern civilised age, a respectable old gentleman, not saturated in the worst of men's sins and crimes like my friend Sherlock Holmes, should even think on those lines.

Holmes who, as so often, seemed to have the ability to read my mind, said "Men have been murdered simply for the clothes on their back, Watson. I have found your narrative most interesting, indeed, quite fascinating, but I fail to see what you expect me to do, Mr Penrose."

"I went to the police about this but they were not interested. They said they had enough to do dealing with crimes that had happened without trying to find people who were merely thinking about committing one."

"I do see their point of view," agreed Holmes.

"The man there, Lestrade, said you were the man I should consult. You would help me as you could do miraculous things."

Holmes laughed. "See, Watson, your romances have inflated my modest successes into miracles."

Penrose, dropping his voice, spoke in a confidential manner as though afraid of being overheard, "Lestrade did remark that you were somewhat unorthodox in your methods, but your colleague Dr Watson was very level headed and, er –" he gave a little cough, "kept you under control."

Holmes, looking across at me, gave a smirk, "Oh, yes. Watson curbs my more outlandish proclivities."

"Surely these men are committing conspiracy to murder?" protested Penrose.

"Hardly that, Mr Penrose. The whole idea is simply a surmise on your part. An unkind person may even suggest you possessed an overheated imagination. There is no proof of any such conspiracy, something very necessary to bring an accusation."

"No proof, sir, but would any gentleman leave all his wealth to others without providing for his own wife and family?"

"You say the brothers have assured you they will see to their wants."

"You must be very naïve, sir, if you put your trust in mere words," said Penrose hotly.

Holmes inclined his head slightly and smiled. "I'm sure that Dr Watson here has been infuriated with me on many occasions and felt like murdering me, but fortunately he has not, as yet, carried out the dread deed."

The solicitor rose to his feet, stuffing his handkerchief into his pocket and clutching the briefcase that had accompanied him throughout our interview. "I can see my concerns are taken no more seriously here than at Scotland Yard. Pray send me your account for the consultation to my office."

Holmes smiled his thin smile. "Unlike some professional men I do not charge a client for telling him that I am unable to help."

The lawyer stalked to the door. "Then I thank you for your time. But I warn you, Mr Holmes, you may come to regret your flippancy when a man is dead, a woman widowed and innocent babes left fatherless. Good day!" The door was closed with more force than was necessary.

There were some minutes silence after our guest had gone and I felt I must protest to Holmes. "I am astonished, Holmes, that you were unable to offer any form of succour to the poor man. He is very clearly worried out of his mind."

"What would you have me do, Watson? Seek out Tom and Dick and say 'I understand you are thinking of murdering your little brother Harry. Now you know that's naughty. Don't do it.' Be sensible man, we cannot arrest people for their unspoken thoughts. Who in the world could claim their thoughts were all entirely innocent?"

Of course I understood the difficulty, but thought that something must be done. "Surely the men could be told that their plot has been rumbled and that you are on to them? That would certainly make them abandon their plans?"

"These men are respectable citizens, not tuppeny-ha'penny footpads that I can browbeat. They would have me arrested for slander."

It really was a difficult position. There was no logical answer. Neither Holmes nor the police could act until a crime had been committed. Then it would be too late. When Peel set up the police force one of its tenets was the prevention of crime. But how could we prevent what we did not know?

"Come, Watson, don't look so gloomy. Nothing may happen at all. Mr Penrose may be completely mistaken in his surmise and the whole thing a figment of his imagination."

And, alas, with that I had to be content.

It was fully nine months later when reading my post-breakfast news-paper while Holmes attended to his normal voluminous correspondence that I suddenly spotted this paragraph:

> That well-known sportsman Harry Harling had an even broader grin on his usual genial countenance yesterday when, for a trivial stake, he walked away from Ascot 500 guineas to the better. It is rumoured this followed swiftly on from a much larger windfall which he received from a deceased benefactor. It is thought that Mr Harling's gain was detrimental to close relatives.

"Holmes!" I cried, "I have found Tom, Dick and Harry!"

"Really, Watson, do not excite yourself so; it can do your digestion no good so soon after breakfast," replied Holmes in his infuriating calm manner.

"You remember Penrose the solicitor? Consulting you about three brothers he called Tom, Dick and Harry? This must be the Harry that benefitted. The favourite son!"

"Indeed, you're probably right," Holmes replied, imperturbably per-using his letters.

"Is that all you have to say?" I asked incredulously.

Holmes sighed, picked up a slip of paper and read "Thomas Seymour Harling, aged 37, 19 Jermyn Street; Richard Duncombe Harling, 35, 8 Tite Street; Milton Harold Harling, 34, Harling Manor, Epping."

"Good Lord, you know about these men?"

"Certainly. I also know that Mrs Harold Harling travels up to town each Friday morning to have her coiffure attended to. I know Mr Harold Harling rides out each morning from ten-thirty until lunch time; and whilst Mr Harold Harling, commonly known as Harry, loves his wife dearly, unbeknownst to him she is having a romantic *affaire* with his brother Mr Thomas Harling."

I gaped in astonishment at this revelation. "How can you know that? Is it common knowledge?"

"Certainly not, Watson. It is known to very few and was told to me in the strictest confidence."

"By whom?"

"My fiancée."

"Holmes!" I gasped, "What have you done? Engaged? Congratula-tions!" I went over to him and proffered my hand. "Who is the lucky woman?"

Holmes yawned. "A rather plump girl called Susan, with a dreadful complexion, who happens to be the personal maid of Mrs Thomas

Harling."

I dropped my hand. "Holmes, what have you been up to? There is obviously some devious purpose in this?"

"Of course. I am also engaged to a more delightful little body called Amelia who has the most charming giggle. She is a kitchen maid at Harling Manor, the former home of the late lamented Percival Preston Harling of Harling and Groots Bank."

"Holmes, how could you? Trifling with these innocent girls! You're a bounder, sir!" I declared.

"Come, come, Watson, when they find out I am a cad who has deceived them, they will think they are well out of it, and it will be a lesson for them in the future to be on their guard against unscrupulous men."

"You are surely taking a risk, the two households presumably being well acquainted with each other," said I.

"I am not the same man to both young ladies, Watson. Susan, on her evenings off, has fallen for a sailor, whereas Amelia is more taken with the manly breast of the soldier's uniform. It is inevitable that when duty calls, a soldier or sailor must leave a broken heart behind. Enough of this! It all serves a greater purpose."

"But how did you know these Harling brothers were the Tom, Dick and Harry of Penrose's story?"

"He, himself, revealed the fact. He said he had consulted the boys' aunt Miss Harling. Harling and Groots is a well-known name in the City, we knew the men were scrapping over wealth. Elementary."

"What's going on, Holmes, what is this all about?" I asked.

"Murder, Watson, murder. Just as friend Penrose feared. I have not been idle since he left us months ago. I have been making enquiries. The local pub is the place to find things out. There, and from the gossiping servants who frequent it. I told Penrose I could do nothing unless a crime is committed. That is true, but if I can anticipate it, of course I will. But there is no way a defence can be planned as I have no idea when, how and in what form the attempt to murder will be made."

With that I had to be content. It is useless to press Holmes, he will only tell you things when he is ready to do so, that usually being when the case is solved. However, a few days later we were taking a walk in the park as the sun was at its cheeriest and a gentle breeze fanned the trees as we strolled along. To my joy Holmes had not spurned Mr Penrose as he appeared to do, but had actively spent much time on the case, preparing himself to be in a position to act should it be necessary. To that end he had ingratiated himself with the servant girls in two houses. He protested that he would have included the third but did not have the time at his leisure. Holmes is a consummate actor and when he chooses he can project a quite charming manner that many females find captivating. I would wish that he did it more often, but it is simply play-acting with him.

It seemed that Thomas Harling was something of a ladies' man with a history of old flames. Unknown to his wife, however, there had been several dalliances since his marriage too. Now he was enamoured of his brother Harry's wife and she with him. Neither spouse, of course, being aware of this, but servants are the ones who know all the secrets of a house, and they often have loose tongues. Holmes was in no doubt the adulterous *affaire* was in earnest. Harry was a 'hale fellow well met' sort of chap and, whilst loving his wife dearly, very neglectful of her while he swanned around the town with his masculine chums.

As we walked around the lake, Holmes said "Nothing is happening, or due to happen that I know of. Now the world is aware that Harry was the favourite son as the will has been proved and he is lording it up in the ancestral home. However, the knowledge that Harry has made his own will in favour of his brothers is known to few."

"What's going to happen, Holmes?"

"I don't know, Watson. I can get no further in this until something out of the ordinary occurs."

What happened next is almost too horrible to relate. Holmes received a telegram urging him to come out to Harling Manor without delay. It spoke only of a dreadful accident. We took a fast train out to Epping, and hence to the manor, where we were greeted on the step by Penrose, who seemed considerably older than when he had left our rooms in anger all those months ago.

"Thank God you've come, Mr Holmes. It's happened, just as I feared. Harry Harling is dead."

"Where is the body?" snapped Holmes.

"In the billiard room, follow me. He was out on his morning ride. He rides most mornings. When he did not return for lunch a groom went out to look for him. He found Harry dead on the ground. He was brought back here to the house, and a doctor sent for. Here we are."

The body was lying on the billiard table. The stiff cover used to protect the baize surface was still in place and over that had been thrown several layers of bed sheets. These were covered in blood and mud. It was a gruesome sight even for me, an experienced army doctor who had tended the wounded in the Afghan war. It was no wonder Penrose looked ill. The skull was smashed in and the face full of bruises and gashes. The doctor, who had only recently left, had tried to clean up the wounds to examine the damage, and stripped the body of its clothing, where we saw many bruises and damaged flesh.

Holmes was examining the head and body with his lens. At certain points he made a sketch, and with his miniature ruler took measurements. He stood up. "Were you here with the doctor, Mr Penrose?"

"Yes, yes. Not immediately of course, but I came as soon as I could, and the doctor was still here."

"Who sent for you, and why?" asked Holmes.

"I have not thought to enquire. I assume Mrs Harling gave the order or perhaps one of the senior staff took it upon himself. Does it matter?" asked Penrose.

"Of course not," said Holmes. "I wondered why you should have been summoned. This kind of emergency is not, I fancy, part of your usual stock in trade."

"Fortunately, no. To answer your question, I am more than a solicitor to this family. I am an old and valued friend."

"What comments did the doctor make?"

"He said that there was nothing he could do as Harry was obviously dead."

"Did he give a cause of death?"

"I think that is clear to all. He had been thrown from his horse which had then trampled on him."

"Some of those marks have certainly been caused by horseshoes, Holmes," I indicated.

"Of course. There will have to be a post mortem. Is the doctor arranging that?" asked Holmes.

"Yes. We are awaiting the undertakers' men."

"Where is Mrs Harling?"

"She is in her room, sedated by the doctor."

"Very wise," said I.

"Where is the horse now?" asked Holmes.

"The groom returned it to the stable."

"I would like to see both horse and groom, if you please."

"So you shall. Follow me."

We were all pleased to leave that poor ravaged body which Holmes recovered with a sheet. Penrose led the way through the house and out of a rear door into a cobbled yard. Across the yard we could see the stable, and outside the groom pottering about with something. He looked up as we approached.

"Ah, Junkins, these gentlemen are Mr Holmes and Dr Watson. They would like to ask you a few questions about the accident."

"Did Mr Harling often go riding in the mornings?" asked Holmes.

"Oh, yes, sir. He was very regular in his habits since he and his lady moved in. Half-past ten o'clock every morning after breakfast he would take a gallop."

"Always on the same horse?"

"Oh, yes, sir. Brutus is our only riding horse. All the others are carriage horses. Brutus belonged to old Mr Harling. As you can see, he's a fine black stallion." The groom stood aside so we could peer into the stable. As it approached the door, on seeing us, the horse placed its head over the top.

"Is he reliable?" asked Holmes, patting the horse's nose.

"Oh, yes, sir. He's big and fast but old Mr Harling never had a moment's trouble with him, even when the master got so aged it was an effort to get in the saddle. I've never heard young Mr Harling complain either. If he threw the master something very unexpected must have scared Brutus."

"You found Mr Harling, I believe?"

"Yes, sir. And a nasty sight it was. I'm not ashamed to say I threw up at it."

"What was Brutus doing when you arrived?"

"Why nothing, sir. He was standing there as docile as a lamb."

"Over the body?"

"Oh, no, sir. Quite a way away. Over by the hedgerow."

"I see. Could you lead us to the spot?" asked Holmes.

"Yes, sir. It's not far, we can soon walk there. Mr Harling must have been well on his way back when the accident happened."

The solicitor excused himself, saying he would await our return, as he thought he should be present when the undertakers arrived. Walking to the site of the tragedy over some very pleasant parkland, we soon reached the spot.

"Mr Harling was lying just here where all the grass is trampled. All that's blood; the horse was over by that hedge," said Junkins, indicating.

Holmes dropped to his knees and with his lens scoured the trampled grass. It was not very churned up as the ground was fairly firm. As is his wont, Holmes then strode about taking sightings in various directions. He stooped and picked up one or two things scattered on the ground, slipping them into one of the envelopes which he always carried.

"There are few trees here, Junkins, apart from that copse over there, so it is hardly likely Mr Harling was knocked to the ground by a branch. I see no jumps either that might cause Brutus to stumble or unseat Mr Harling in flight."

"No, sir. It's strange. Mr Harling was a very experience horseman. He'd been riding since the age of seven, I believe. Brutus must have thrown him for some reason, it's all open ground round here."

"I see a little copse over there." Holmes indicated.

"Charcoal Wood we call that, sir. 'Tis not much of a thing. In the olden days a charcoal burner used to make his camp there."

Holmes strode towards the wood. Junkins, looking at me with a puzzled frown, said "Why should he want to see that, sir?"

"Come, let us follow. Mr Holmes does nothing without a purpose."

"Is he a policeman?"

"No. Mr Holmes is this country's leading detective."

We arrived at the copse to find Holmes on hands and knees, lens in hand, examining the ground. The copse was, in truth, nothing larger than a clump of trees on a slight elevation. Holmes rose and faced Junkins. "Did your master smoke Turkish cigarettes?" he asked.

"I couldn't say, sir. He certainly did smoke cigarettes, but I do not know the type. No doubt one of the indoor staff would know. Is it important, sir?"

"Probably not," said Holmes dismissively. "Let us return to the stable."

Back at the stable Holmes examined Brutus's hooves, the groom lifting each leg of the horse in turn. The great horse stood patiently while all this was going on.

"Have you washed the horse's legs or hooves?"

"No, sir, I have not yet got round to it," replied the groom.

"Thank you, Junkins, you have been most helpful," said Holmes, giving the man a coin.

"It's my duty, sir, and a great honour to assist the country's leading detective," replied the honest fellow. Holmes looked at me; then smiled.

On regaining the billiard room we found the undertakers had been and gone, the domestic staff had removed all trace of the bloody sheets and the room was restored to normal. Penrose awaited us and immediately said "Perhaps you will give more credence to my apprehensions now, Mr Holmes?"

Holmes smiled. "Are you implying Mr Harry Harling's death was not an accident, Mr Penrose?"

Penrose shrugged. "You are the expert, Mr Holmes. Do you think it was?"

"If, as you think, Mr Thomas Harling and Mr Richard Harling are in some way responsible, we must interview them to see where they were earlier today. I take it they have been informed of their brother's death?"

"Not as yet."

"No? Why is that?"

"I should correct that statement, Mr Holmes. Neither I, nor anybody else has officially notified them. Though news of this nature seems to spread like wildfire. Heaven knows how. But I thought you may like to accompany me when I go to inform them. With your intimate knowledge of criminal behaviour you may detect that the men do not respond in an expected manner."

Holmes laughed. "Oh, Mr Penrose, you have hidden depths! I know lawyers are often devious, but you excel yourself. An excellent suggestion. Perhaps Dr Watson may be permitted to accompany us?"

The aged lawyer made a slight bow and said: "Of course."

Both brothers lived in town. Thomas Harling was a director of Harling and Groots Bank. As Penrose expected that he would be at his office, we elected to go there first. Mr Thomas was a very self-assured man who seemed to run his bank like a military operation. Such members of staff that we saw seemed to be in awe, if not fear, of him. On receiving our message he emerged from his office to meet us.

"What is it, Penrose? Who are these gentlemen?" he demanded.

"It is rather public here, Mr Harling, may we be more private?" asked the lawyer.

"Certainly, follow me." He strode off, leaving us to hurry in his wake. We were ushered through an outer office where a clerk sat at a desk. "Clear off, Hopkinson. See that I am not disturbed by anyone for any reason during the next half-hour." Harling then ushered us into his inner sanctum. It was not a very big room, a large desk being the main feature. There were also some wooden cabinets with deep drawers against one wall, and some open shelves with books, ledgers and stacks of miscellaneous papers. Light came from a tall window which was strongly protected with thick iron bar work arranged in scrolls.

"Right. Sit down all of you." As there were only two chairs in front of the desk and Holmes and Penrose took those, I was obliged to stand.

"I'll get another chair," said Harling, semi-rising.

"Please don't trouble, I'll perch on these," I said, spying a small set of library steps in the corner.

"Good man! Now what is it?" asked Harling.

"I have some terrible news to impart," said Penrose hesitantly.

"Then impart it," said Harling.

"There has been a most dreadful accident. Your brother, Mr Harry Harling."

"Injured?" barked Harling.

"Dead," said Holmes.

"And who are you, sir?" asked Harling.

"I am Sherlock Holmes and the gentleman in the corner is Dr

Watson."

"I see. You, I take it, Mr Holmes, were responsible for my brother's death and he is your medical man that you have brought to make your excuses."

"No, no, not at all," spluttered Penrose. "Mr Holmes is a detective."

"A detective? Explain yourself, Penrose. Why have you brought a detective?"

Holmes spoke up. "Mr Penrose is very upset and has spent a most trying day. May I be permitted to explain?"

"Please do, sir."

"Your brother was out riding this morning upon his own land – "

"Our dead father's land, I presume you mean; our ancestral home," interrupted Harling.

"His horse threw him to the ground and trampled him," said Holmes.

"My God!" gasped Harling. "Were there any witnesses to this?"

"Alas, no. But, as it is known that both horse and rider were totally capable, there is a suggestion that perhaps your brother was attacked by footpads."

"Attacked?"

"Yes. I think he may have been stopped, probably someone pretending to beg assistance. When he reined in, this person or persons dragged him to the ground."

"Where he was trampled by the horse?"

"That is what all the signs indicate," said Holmes.

"We shall, of course, make every enquiry, Mr Harling, but I sought to bring the news as swiftly as possible," said Penrose.

"You were quite right. How is Constance taking it?"

"Naturally Mrs Harling is totally distraught and the doctor put her under sedation. She was sleeping when we left."

"Thank you, Doctor, that would seem to have been the best thing to do," said Harling, addressing me.

"I was neither the doctor summoned, nor who officiated," I explained. "I am a colleague of Mr Holmes."

"It all sounds very complicated. Perhaps I had better get out there and take my wife to offer some comfort to Constance while I deal with matters," said Harling.

Penrose stood up "If you have nothing more you wish to ask, we beg your leave to call on your brother Mr Richard, as he too, must be informed."

"Of course. Would you prefer I broke the news to him, Penrose?"

"I think it more important that you take charge up at the Manor. The police will have to be informed and the post mortem arranged," said Penrose.

"Police? Do they need to be dragged into this?" demanded Harling.

"It's imperative we catch these footpads, sir," said Holmes.

"Yes, yes, of course. Leave it all to me. I will take charge of things. I am the head of the family. Though perhaps you could speak to my brother and explain I am at the Manor. He could join me there," said Harling, then added, "though I am not sure if he will be at home. I believe he was going to visit our aunt at Esher today."

As we rose to leave, Holmes said: "What delightful flowers," and stooped to smell the small vase of blooms that brought the only cheer to a very austere desk. "Pray accept our condolences on the death of your brother."

I made a slight bow before taking our leave. Somehow it seemed natural to do so as one felt automatically one was in the presence of a leader of men.

The three of us then called on Mr Richard Harling at his home.

"I hope Mr Richard is back," said Penrose, "I do so hate breaking this sort of news to women. They do take on so."

Richard Harling was indeed at home. "Why, Mr Penrose, what brings you here?" he asked. "You are lucky to find me in, I have not long returned from visiting my aunt at Esher."

"I was not aware you were accustomed to visit her," said Penrose in surprise. "How is the old lady?"

"As dotty as usual. She's getting very frail, I'm afraid."

"Well, she is of a great age, she is somewhat older than your late father."

"What can I do for you?" asked Harling, seeing our grim faces.

"I have some rather bad news," said Penrose.

"It's not about Harry, is it?"

"I'm afraid it is – " began Penrose.

"He's dead," jumped in Holmes with shocking brusqueness.

"Dead?" gaped Harling.

"He had an accident this morning. Killed falling from his horse," added Penrose.

"Good God, poor Harry dead. Does Tom know?"

"We have just left him. He is on his way to the Manor now. He would like you to join him there."

"In what he terms his ancestral home," interjected Holmes.

"Aye, he does call it that. It really sticks in his craw that Harry now lives there. As he's the eldest, Tom thinks it should have been left to him."

"Yes, well, my opinion of your father's will is known to you. It is hardly seemly to enter into the matter now," said Penrose.

"Of course not. Poor Harry dead. I can scarcely believe it. He was always so jolly and full of life."

"Perhaps I can leave you to break the news to your wife?" asked Penrose.

"Of course. I think I had better get out to Epping. It's quite a way, isn't it? We will both go. Harry's wife must want some female company."

"Yes. I am at your disposal at any time. If you need me for anything send a message to the office and I will drop everything to be with you and your brother."

"Thank you. You're very kind. This has been such a shock. I was angry at losing my hat earlier on. This shows how trivial that matter was," said Harling, shaking his head.

"You lost your hat?" queried Holmes.

"Yes, yes. Just a petty annoyance but I had toffed myself up for Aunt Phoebe's benefit, so it was my best one. Still that's life isn't it? But this – poor Harry gone at his age. You must excuse me, I can hardly take it in. I'm sure you understand."

"Do you mind if I smoke?" asked Holmes.

"What? Oh, no, please do," replied Harling.

"I see there is an ashtray and matches on the side table, may I help myself?" said Holmes, walking over to where those items were.

"Yes, yes."

"We will leave you now, Mr Richard, unless we can do anything else for you," said Penrose.

"No, I shall be all right," said he, smoothing his moustache. "I'm just shaken up by your news."

So the three of us bade our farewells, leaving the poor chap to tell his wife the bad news. As we stood outside waiting for a cab, Penrose said "Well, Mr Holmes, I do not know what impression you have gained of those two men and this so-called accident?"

"Very little at the moment. I quite agree with you that this is no accident, but what exactly has taken place I am, as yet, unable to say. On one point, however, I am very sure – Brutus is innocent."

"Surely we must ascertain where the two brothers were at the time of the accident? If they should provide an alibi then that puts them beyond suspicion," I blurted out.

"As usual, Watson, you home in on the nub of the problem. That shall be my next step. I could hardly question the men today when they have just been given the news, but I shall return to them, have no fear," said Holmes.

"I do not think an alibi would necessarily render the brothers blameless, Doctor. They could easily have employed some ruffians to do the deed in return for a cash payment. As Mr Holmes has said, footpads may have done this wicked thing," said Penrose.

I was forced to agree that this was most likely, though Holmes pointed out the dangers of respectable men employing petty crooks to do their dirty work for them. They leave themselves wide open to the possibility of blackmail. A scoundrel may commit murder for five pounds, but then extort thousands while his principal tries to keep it quiet. To employ more than one such fellow more than doubles the risk since either could play his partner off against the schemer. "I feel sure two intelligent men like Messrs Harling would not have risked that."

We allowed Penrose to take the first cab as he hurried off to deal with the family affairs of police investigation, post mortem and funeral.

"Did you not find Mr Richard Harling's attitude to you and me rather strange?"

"Strange? Not at all. I thought he welcomed us in a friendly enough manner."

"That is what is strange."

As we strolled on, Holmes remarked that it was singularly fortunate that he had been called in so early in the investigation, so often he could only visit a crime scene long after the police had been. "It would have been perfect if the body had been left in place, Watson, but that was too much to hope for. At least the location was not ruined by hordes of trampling policemen's boots. And the chance to inspect the body much as it had been found was indeed fortunate."

"It will be interesting to hear the result of the post mortem," I ventured.

"I fear that will not tell us anything. I expect we will be told that Harling was thrown from his horse, which then trampled upon him."

"Have you gained any clues, Holmes?"

"The greatest clue we were given months ago when Penrose warned us that there was a likelihood of murder. As it has fallen out much as he suspected, the motive seems to be the extraordinary wills that the Harling family chooses to make. But we cannot jump to conclusions. Harry Harling may have had other enemies, popular men often do."

"Could Mrs Harry Harling be involved? You said she was conducting an illicit liaison with Tom Harling."

As a cab came into view Holmes hailed it and my question remained unanswered.

Some days later after the post mortem had returned a verdict exactly as Holmes predicted, a rather grandiloquent funeral had been held, attended by a great many men of the Turf and Fancy. Holmes had arranged with Penrose that we should all visit Mr Thomas Harling at his home. Penrose informed us that Mr Thomas was unwell, had been confined to his bed since we had last interviewed him, had risen and struggled to his brother's funeral in great pain, then promptly returned after the ceremony, excusing himself from the lavish funeral tea. Thus we were shown into his bedroom where the man was a shadow of his former self, the efficient military-style manner totally gone and a feeble valetudinarian left in its place.

"Come in, gentlemen. I am not in a fit state for receiving and only agreed because of Penrose's insistence. I would like you to be brief."

"It has clearly been a distressing time," said Holmes soothingly, "and I would not wish to add to your obvious discomfort or prolong your agony, but may I ask a few questions of you?"

"You may recall, Mr Holmes is a detective whom I have engaged on behalf of the family," explained Penrose.

"What the devil for? What is there to detect?" This outburst precipitated a bout of coughing and gasping that was distressing to witness as he fell back against his pillows. Penrose then gave the explanation that he and Holmes had cooked up between them to account for our presence and questions. We were from Harry Harling's life insurance company and needed to make enquiries before paying out the large sum for which his life was insured.

"Oh, very well," said the invalid resignedly.

"When your brother was out riding, do you recall where you were?" asked Holmes.

"Very clearly. I am a man of regular habits. It was a working day and if poor Harry was riding between ten in the morning until one o'clock lunchtime then I was in my office."

"Were you there throughout the entire morning?"

"Of course I was. What is this? What is your meaning, sir?" said Thomas Harling, rousing himself towards his former manner.

"It's a mere formality, sir; my company's form that Mr Penrose has to complete to release the funds requires to know the whereabouts of each member of the family at the time of the accident."

"A lot of stuff and nonsense. These companies take your premiums readily enough then don't want to pay out. Do their damnedest to obstruct and prevaricate!" This last word led to a further bout of coughing while Holmes, in his blandest manner, said "I quite agree with you, sir, but it keeps fellows like me in employment. I will disturb you no longer. I wish you an early recovery."

Harling flapped feebly. "This agony has gone on a long time, my insides were wretched, but I confess that today I do feel somewhat improved."

Leaving the invalid under that impression we made straight for the bank, where everybody agreed he had been there from ten until one, as he had stated. At lunchtime he had gone to a restaurant to meet a client. Thomas Harling's office was in the City, Harry Harling's home was at Epping, there was no possibility that Thomas could have been personally involved.

We pressed on to Jermyn Street where we were given an effusively warm welcome by Mr Richard Harling. "Come in, gentlemen, I'm glad to see you again. When we last met I felt I was most unwelcoming, but the shock quite unsettled me as you can imagine."

"Very understandable, Mr Richard. Of course we all realised that. It was our misfortune to be the ones who had to bear the dreadful tidings to you. I trust you are sufficiently recovered to be able to answer a few questions from Mr Holmes." Penrose lowered his voice. "He is from your brother's insurance company."

"I see, fire away!"

"Can you recall where you were on the morning of the accident?"

"Indeed I can. I had chosen that very morning to visit our Aunt Phoebe who lives beyond Esher. You know Aunt Phoebe, don't you, Penrose?"

"Of course. I still deal with her legal affairs, not that they amount to much these days. How was the old lady?"

"Very frail, but game. She still potters round her garden, bakes bread for the village poor and so on, just as she always has. I fear her memory is slipping; still she's always pleased to see her nephew and chat about the old days."

"Is her new help competent?" asked Penrose.

"Thinks the world of her, you did well finding her. She was a bit dubious at first with – Lydia, is it? Being so young compared to old Matilda." He turned to us. "Matilda was as old as Aunt Phoebe and they had been together since she moved to Esher. Phoebe was distraught when she died, but good old Penrose here found a suitable replacement."

"Were you with your aunt all morning?" asked Holmes.

"Most of it. I caught the 10.13 from Waterloo then took a trap from the station out to her place. I suppose it would be about 10.45 when I arrived. I was a bit delayed messing about over my hat."

"Oh, yes, remind me what that was about," said Holmes.

"It was a bit embarrassing. On the station at Esher it got knocked off when I was looking down at the rails. I suspect some lout did it on purpose. Some oafs think that kind of thing amusing. Anyway it fell on to the rails so I reported it to the stationmaster. He said he couldn't get it immediately, but would rescue it in time for my return journey. I left my card just in case there was a problem. All very annoying as it was new and Aunt Phoebe does demand a smart turn-out. If I go in anything less she moans on that she isn't worth coming all that way for, not worth dressing up to visit and so on. You know what she's like, Penrose."

"Indeed, though I may say not as cantankerous as some of my other older clients," said Penrose, with a small chuckle.

"How long were you there, sir, with your aunt?" asked Holmes.

"Oh, not long, about an hour I suppose, just long enough for a glass of her elderberry wine and a piece of cake. She can't really put up with visitors for any length of time. To be honest it's a bit of a fag trailing all that way every week, but the old dear does like to see me, she was always good to me as a boy."

"Did your late brother Harry visit her too?"

"I'm afraid not. Harry was always a bit slapdash about his social obligations. He had his own pals and was not very family bound. Tom's the same. Never thinks of going, so I feel it's even more up to me to keep the family ties. Penrose will tell you I've always been the dutiful son."

"Did you get your hat back at the station?" asked Holmes.

"I did, yes, thank you for asking."

"And which train back to town did you take?"

"The 11.45. I had a committee meeting at my club, then had lunch with some of the chaps. There was another annoyance on the return journey which made me a little late getting to the club. I'd tucked my return ticket in the ribbon of my hat and it must have fallen out, so when the inspector came to check the tickets I couldn't find it."

"So what did you do?"

"All a bit embarrassing really. It seems that one may be fined for travelling without a valid ticket, even taken to court. But the inspector could see I was a respectable sort of chap and had heard the saga of my missing topper. He said when we arrived at Waterloo he would escort me to the ticket office and I would be permitted to buy a single ticket for the journey. So that's what he did, thus my wife was spared the ignominy of seeing her husband up in court as a fare dodger," laughed Harling.

"And you were back at Waterloo at what time?" persisted Holmes.

"Just gone noon. With messing about at the station I didn't get to the club until about 12.30 and the meeting had just started."

"You say you lunched at your club. Did you then go straight home?"

"No, I didn't. I had a game of billiards after lunch."

"With whom did you play?"

"Oh, some fellow at the club, can't remember his name. I say, this is all getting personal isn't it? I'm beginning to resent all this probing."

"Then I shall bother you no more," said a smiling Holmes. "Thank you for giving up your time."

"A pleasure, gentlemen. Oh, Penrose, I suppose we will have to get together with my brother and discuss you know what."

"Indeed. I will communicate with you in due course."

"Fine. Good day."

Thus we three left the smiling Harling on the step.

"Have you learned anything from your questioning, Mr Holmes?"

"Possibly. I have further enquiries to make. They do not concern the family so I shall not require you to accompany me, Mr Penrose. Are you still convinced one of the brothers was responsible for Harry Harling's death?"

Penrose had the grace to look chastened. "Well, after what we have heard it does seem very unlikely I must say. Perhaps I have totally misread the situation."

"Where does Aunt Phoebe live?"

"Esher. Honeysuckle Cottage. It's down a lane off the High Street."

"Thank you, Mr Penrose. I cannot promise what kind of outcome there will be to all this but, rest assured, if there is knavery afoot I shall find it out."

As we returned to Baker Street I ventured to remark that Mr Richard had been most helpful. "Yes, indeed. The last time we visited him we were never introduced. He had no idea who we were yet he spoke openly and freely. This time he is told we are insurance company investigators and again he is most forthcoming."

"Surely that just shows he has nothing to hide?"

"Wouldn't you, on being told of a brother's death, wonder why an insurance man was on the scene so swiftly and why he was the one to announce your brother's death?"

"Shock, Holmes. People react in very many strange ways when greeted with sudden death. You must admit that you did announce it rather brutally that first time."

"As you know, Watson, I do nothing without a reason."

It was two days before I saw Holmes again. His absences coinciding with my periods of occupation at 221b, I presumed he was there while I was out and about my own affairs.

"Have you made any progress on the favourite son business," I asked?

"Some progress but no help. I have checked the two brothers' alibis and there is no doubt that Thomas Harling was in his office in the City all the morning of the murder at Epping. Then he was the guest of a Mr Gravison who had a table for four gentlemen at lunch at the Savoy Hotel. I checked with the head waiter there."

"So it can't be Tom who murdered Harry, then," said I with some satisfaction, as having seen the men I had grave doubts that either could have carried out such a heinous crime as fratricide.

"It would seem not. But why, at the scene of the crime, were there cigarette stubs of a Turkish cigarette of the kind Thomas smokes?" mused Holmes.

"Perhaps Harry also smoked them?"

"No, not at all. Harry smoked cigars. I ascertained from the staff at the Manor that Mr Harry had never been seen with a cigarette in his mouth, although he kept a box of cigarettes for guests. Virginia."

"How do you know Tom smokes Turkish cigarettes anyway?" I asked.

"I saw stubs of them in his office ashtray and smelt them. They are quite distinctive, as is the ash they leave. I have no doubt the cigarettes are identical."

"Oh, when you suddenly seemed to have a penchant for horticulture in Tom's office the other day. What about Dick? Did Richard Harling's alibi stand up to scrutiny?"

"The porter at Esher remembers the hat business as he had to jump down on to the line to retrieve it. He also still had Mr Richard Harling's card. I enquired at Waterloo station ticket office if anybody remembered letting off a gentleman who had travelled without paying for his ticket. It was clearly recalled by a clerk there, as it was most unusual. It was entered in the accounts. As the inspector is not allowed to collect money on the train, if anybody travels without a ticket they are asked their name and address and given a penalty form which carries a fine. The inspector was exceeding his authority by marching Harling to the ticket kiosk and allowing him to buy a ticket. As the clerk said, it was out of order and Harling left his card in case there were any repercussions on the railway employees. It was still tucked away on a notice board. They all knew about Harling losing his ticket when his hat fell off, it was considered quite a joke with the staff there. Dick was due at his club as you know, and he showed up for his committee meeting just a few minutes late, had lunch, played billiards and went home where, shortly afterwards, the three of us arrived to break the news of his brother's death."

"So that's the other brother in the clear, then?" I affirmed. "Esher is completely the opposite direction to Epping. A train to Epping would take the best part of an hour from London. Esher is a twenty minute journey in the opposite direction. Neither men could have done it."

"So it would seem, Watson. But there is something that is not right about this case. I wonder if Penrose is as innocent as he seems?"

"You surely can't suspect the family's solicitor," I protested. "Anyway he's an old man, he could never have got the better of a sportsman like Harry Harling."

"I suspect everybody, Watson, until definitely disproved. It was Penrose who came to us in the first place with his tale of the bizarre will without a name. Then he spoke of a second unusual will. We have only his word for all this!"

"But surely, there is proof in the fact that Harry moved into the Manor?" I said.

"I said I suspect everybody, Watson. I even suspect myself of letting my imagination intrude in place of facts. Facts, Watson! We do not have them all. There is something missing. It is like a map of the British Isles without Warwickshire, there is a hole somewhere in my assembled facts. But I'll get there, I shall get there."

I can always tell when Holmes is baffled by a case. He takes it out on his violin. Sometimes, when thinking deeply he has the instrument on his lap and he drags the bow slowly and tunelessly across the catgut, but when, as now, he cannot ascertain what he needs to know, he plays as in a frenzy, ignoring wrong notes, and losing any tune that may be recognisable at the start. No wonder people said that Paganini was in league with the devil if he played like that.

Finally, to my relief, and a blessing to my eardrums, he ceased and enquired if I would be prepared to go with him after lunch to Esher.

"I would be delighted," I replied. So we went to visit Aunt Phoebe.

At Esher, as we handed in our tickets, Holmes said "Lovely afternoon, Cornwell," to the ticket collector. He looked startled and mumbled "Yes, sir."

"The fellow clearly does not remember he directed me to the station master only yesterday," said Holmes as we walked out of the station. Outside we asked about a pony trap out to Honeysuckle Cottage, but were told it was only a short walk, down a lane off the High Street by the general stores. So we strolled round there to find a dusty country lane with simple rustic cottages dotted along both sides to no kind of order or pattern. Honeysuckle Cottage was the third or fourth on the left, a picturesque affair with a front garden full of roses, larkspur, lupins and other typical cottage-garden flowers within a rambling and over-grown hedge of privet and laurel bushes.

Our knock was answered by a pleasant looking woman of, I judged, about thirty years.

"Good afternoon. Miss Bonneville, I presume?" said Holmes, raising his hat.

"Yes," she relied cautiously.

"My name is Goldborough," said Holmes, proffering a card with that name proclaiming he represented the Marine & General Insurance Company. Holmes kept a large collection of cards, both genuine and specially printed to his specifications. He found these useful on many occasions when he wished to masquerade under a pseudonym. Holmes maintained that a card with a name printed on it was much more persuasive than merely stating a name. For myself, I was relieved to be introduced as Dr Flegg. In the past when we have had to assume roles, Holmes has saddled me with some ludicrous nomenclature because of his misplaced sense of humour.

"Perhaps you've had a letter from Mr Penrose about our calling?" asked Holmes.

"No."

"Ah, no wonder you are surprised. You do know Mr Penrose, the solicitor, who looks over Miss Phoebe Harling's affairs?"

"Yes, of course," replied Miss Bonneville. Holmes proffered an envelope saying "I thought Mr Penrose would have written to warn you, but please read this note from the man himself." Holmes, conspiring with Penrose, had come armed with a note from the lawyer backing up our impersonation.

"You had better come in," said the handsome young lady after reading the note, and we followed her into the interior. The cottage was an old low-ceilinged affair and, whilst the front windows that looked out on to the road were small, the rear windows had, at some point, been enlarged and the cottage was filled with sunlight. These windows gave out on to a rear garden that was even more magnificent then the front. Though not large it was of a size greater than one would expect an old lady to need.

"Miss Harling is out in the garden as usual. She spends a great deal of her time there, please come through. I must warn you, Miss Harling is rather vague and does not always comprehend things."

"We quite understand, Miss Bonneville. Our duties often take us to elderly people and Dr Flegg is a specialist in mental problems," said Holmes in a sympathetic manner.

Miss Phoebe Harling was a small bird-like lady who, at that moment, was wielding a pair of secateurs on some sort of rose bush.

"Phoebe, these gentlemen are from an insurance company," said Miss Bonneville.

"How nice, how do you do? These roses don't last anytime, I'm for ever dead-heading them. I thought next year I'd get rid of these floribundas and train an espalier up the wall, what do you think?"

"The men have come to talk to you about Harry's death," said Miss Bonneville.

"Oh, has somebody died?" asked Miss Harling, her eyes widening as she gazed at Holmes.

"Your nephew Harry had an accident and now he is dead," said Holmes gently.

"Oh, yes, he fell off a horse. I remember now. He shouldn't have been allowed. He's too young to ride out on his own. I've told Fergus many times."

"He was a grown man, Phoebe. He was married with children. You still keep thinking of your nephews as young boys. That was a long time ago," said Miss Bonneville.

"Oh, yes, I am a silly woman. I know I'm getting old, but I forget so is everybody else."

"Your other nephew Richard, the one who comes to see you, he's a grown man, isn't he?" asked Miss Bonneville.

"Of course he is, how silly." Turning to me she said: "Richard comes and sees me every week, he's very good, you know." She dropped her voice to a whisper, "He brings me chocolates, you know. I love chocolates. We were never allowed them at school."

"Mr Goldborough wants to ask you some questions, Phoebe, do try to concentrate."

"Is it an examination? I love examinations. We used to have them at school at the end of term. You could show off everything you'd learned during the term. I went to school, you know. It was most unusual in those days for girls to go to school. Only boys went to school."

Holmes, never a patient man, was becoming anxious to ask his questions. "Shall we sit down together on that bench and I will ask questions and you try to answer them?"

"Yes, let's do that, come this way." Miss Harling took Holmes by the hand and led him to the bench. "Now first question," she said beaming expectantly. Miss Bonneville and I stood to the side.

"Do you remember your nephew Richard coming to see you last week?" asked Holmes.

"Yes, yes, I remember that. We sat on this bench like this and chatted. We had elderberry wine and a piece of cake," said Miss Harling with a note of triumph.

"Good. Well that same day was when your other nephew Harry was killed in his riding accident," said Holmes.

"That was a shame. Poor Harry. I never liked him, he was a cruel boy. He used to collect butterflies and stick pins into them. He was always Fergus's favourite, you know, he loved that boy, said he reminded him of his wife. He did have a look of Caroline. I liked Caroline, we used to have such jolly times together when we were young. She died, you know. Everybody's dead now, except me. Matilda died and left me all alone." She started to weep.

"Now, Phoebe, you mustn't think about the past. You have lost your friends because they were old. You should be pleased and proud that you are still alive and that your nephew Richard loves you and comes to visit you and, whilst I can never replace Matilda, I am here, as your friend and companion," said Miss Bonneville.

I admired the way this young woman dealt with her vague, elderly employer, it must be very trying on the patience. The mention of Richard must have sparked a memory because she suddenly said "He lost his hat at the railway station."

Holmes seized upon this shaft of lucidity. "Really? What did he do?"

"It blew off his head in the wind on to the line. A railway man had to go on the lines to get it back. Imagine if a train had come and knocked the man over." She started laughing at the thought. "Bump! The train knocks the man over!"

"It's very difficult, Dr Flegg, as you will know, she does ramble so." I was suddenly startled to be thus addressed, having momentarily forgotten whom I was supposed to be.

"Yes, it's usually the recent memory that fails first. One can still remember things of long ago, but not what happened yesterday." I turned reluctantly from this handsome woman, as Miss Harling was speaking again.

"He lost his ticket as well and had to pay again. It was funny wasn't it, Lydia?" Of course, I recalled that was Miss Bonneville's name; Lydia suited her very well I thought.

"Yes, we had a good laugh about it, didn't we Phoebe? Have you any more questions, Mr Goldborough? It is rather hopeless, as I'm sure you realise. Can I assist in the matter?" asked Miss Bonneville.

"I don't think so, Miss Bonneville," said Holmes and rose to speak more intimately, dropping his voice. "The true purpose of my visit, and bringing a specialist doctor with me, is simply to ascertain that the beneficiaries of the late Mr Harold Harling's policy are still alive. My company has to be on the guard for fraudulent claims, as I am sure you will understand. Some unscrupulous persons sometimes claim beneficiaries are still alive when in fact they have passed on. They hope to gain pecuniary advantage for themselves, you see."

"I understand. And is Miss Harling a beneficiary in Mr Harold Harling's insurance policy?"

"Oh yes, to the tune of several hundred pounds. Discretion forbids me to say more."

"Are you sure?" asked Miss Bonneville.

"My superior tells me so. Why do you question it?" asked Holmes.

"Oh, nothing really. I am a little surprised because, whilst Mr Richard is a regular visitor, so far as I know Miss Harling has had no connection with Mr Harold and Mr Thomas since she was driven out of the manor by her brother Fergus. I am surprised, that is all. It will be a great help, I am sure. Her allowance is quite modest considering her brother was a wealthy man. I do feel that throughout her life she has been badly treated by the family."

"Driven out?"

"So she says. It was many years ago and I have no idea of the cause. Some family dispute I presume. How thrilling that some benefit should arise from such a tragedy."

"Indeed, we insurers are often criticised, but we perform a valuable function. Mr Harold's wife and family could be destitute if he had not provided for them via a life insurance policy," said Holmes smoothly. He then coughed and murmured "May I have use of your facility before we leave?"

"Come with me," commanded Miss Bonneville, and led Holmes round to the side of the house. I was left with the old woman. I uttered a few platitudes about the delights of her garden by way of conversation.

"All the countryside is beautiful round here, Dr Begg, my garden is a bonus. I don't really need it. I can roam for miles around here. I loved picking wild fruit as a girl. I still do. I love the autumn with the berries. I make apple pies and blackberry pies for the poor people. We have a lot of poor people round here, you know. The vicar keeps asking for money for the poor heathen Africans but I tell him there are lots of poor people here on his doorstep." During this rambling speech Miss Bonneville had returned from conducting Holmes to the privy. She smiled – a very charming smile I may say – as she caught the end of it.

"A bit of a hobby horse, Doctor, she doesn't like the vicar. 'Our new vicar' she calls him though he's been here at least five years to my knowledge."

Miss Harling had now wandered off in search of something.

"Have you been Miss Harling's companion very long?" I asked.

"Two years. I succeeded a lady who had been with her for over thirty years. Before I was born, in fact," said she blushing prettily.

"You seem to deal with her remarkably well."

"Oh, she can be quite a handful sometimes. Mainly in the winter when she can't get out as much. She's a real outdoor body. I suppose your duties take you all over the place, Dr Flegg?"

"Oh, yes, yes. Mainly in and around the capital but sometimes further afield. Do you, by any chance get up to Town at all, Miss Bonneville? You have a very good train service, here, don't you? It only took us about twenty minutes to get here." I enquired.

"It would be lovely. Unfortunately, pleasant as this position is, time off is not possible. Miss Harling cannot be left. I am tied very strictly; even a visit to the High Street is an expedition as I either have to take her with me, which is, truth to tell a chore as, though she can walk ably enough, she wanders away. I can hardly keep her on reins like a horse or a small child. If I go out on my own I have to arrange for someone to sit in for me, even for such a short time as a visit to the shops."

"It must be very tying as well as trying," said I, hoping to bring a little levity to the young woman's parlous situation.

"Once, early in my position here, I returned to find her attempting to light a paraffin lamp, fiddling with matches. She had lit a candle and burnt the table cloth in the short time I was away. It is too much of a risk."

"I do see the difficulty," I agreed. "It's a great pity you cannot arrange the occasional trip up to London, you must miss lots by way of concerts, exhibitions, theatres and, of course, the shops."

"Quite; so tantalisingly near yet out of reach," said the charming Miss Bonneville.

"Perhaps I may be permitted to see if I could arrange for a trained nurse to come for an evening so that I might have the honour of escorting you to some pleasant diversion in Town?" I ventured.

"Your colleague seems to be taking a long time; should you see if he is all right?" Just at that moment Holmes came into view, preventing any further conversation.

"Thank you, very much, Miss Bonneville, we will take up no more of your time. Come, Dr Flegg," said Holmes heartily.

As Miss Harling was now at the end of the garden pottering about with a watering can, Miss Bonneville said not to trouble to say farewell, the likelihood being that she had already forgotten all about us. "Just slip away round this side of the house; that will take you to the gate, there is no need to go through the house. Good bye."

"Good bye," said I and ventured to take her hand, bestowing a light kiss upon it.

In the train Holmes was slumped in thought. "Fine woman, Miss Bonneville," said I. Holmes merely grunted. "Have you gained anything from our visit?"

"Have you, Watson?" said Holmes smirking.

"I meant any clues."

"Dick's alibi is invincible. He left on the 10.13 from Waterloo. He arrived at Esher 10.35. At that time he lost his hat on the line. The stationmaster and the porter were involved in retrieving it. While they did so, Dick visited his aunt Phoebe. Both the Aunt and Miss Bonneville recall the visit. The Aunt, feeble though she is by intellect, recalls laughing over the hat business. Dick returns to the station, retrieves his hat, gets on the 11.45. On the train he has problems with his ticket, again the inspector recalls it well. He buys another at the station, the clerk recalls it clearly as he had awkwardness accounting for it in his ledger. Dick arrives at his club about 12.30 and promptly attends a committee meeting with seven other fellows. At the end of the meeting, he lunches with some of these men, plays billiards with another, then leaving his club about 3pm goes straight home."

"As you say, Holmes, invincible. He could not possibly have been at Epping. If one of the brothers is involved it must have been Tom."

When we got back to Baker Street there was shocking news. Thomas Harling had died. A telegram urged us to go to his house as soon as possible. The police had been called and Penrose awaited us. Without delay we shot round to Jermyn Street to find Penrose and our old friend Inspector Lestrade.

"Mr Holmes and Dr Watson, how nice to see you again. Mr Penrose here has been telling me of your involvement in this affair. It would serve the fight against crime better if people came to the police in the first instance instead of paying good money for the services of ill-informed amateurs," said Lestrade.

"Good afternoon, Lestrade," said Holmes. "In your one sentence you have uttered two contradictions. If a man is paid for his services he is a professional and not an amateur, but more to the point Mr Penrose came to you some months ago with his suspicions that a murder was likely amongst the three brothers, and you said the police could do nothing, recommending that he should consult me. Which he did, on your advice."

Lestrade, ignoring this sally, merely said "This man died in bed. He had been ill for days. We do not as yet know how he died. It may be natural causes. It seems he had stomach pains for some time, but did not summon a doctor until lately. The doctor prescribed some form of relief which seemed to alleviate the condition, but suddenly the man took a turn for the worst and when Mrs Harling sent for the doctor again he arrived to find his patient dead. There will be a post mortem of course but the doctor now seems convinced that somehow Harling died of poisoning."

"Poison?" I said incredulously.

"Is the body still here?" asked Holmes.

"No, it's been taken away," replied Lestrade.

"May I examine the bedroom?"

"By all means. I've had a look round. There's nothing suspicious. The doctor looked through the medicines and stuff with me and all seemed innocent enough."

"Excuse me, gentlemen," said Holmes, disappearing up the stairs.

"Well, Doctor, you've just arrived, I've been here some time and there's nothing further I can do. The post mortem will reveal all. If the man's been poisoned, I shall have work to do then, and no doubt I shall be seeing you and Mr Holmes again. Good afternoon, Doctor, Mr Penrose," said Lestrade, and ambled away.

Penrose glowered after him. "I do not like that man. Why did they send him, of all people? He was the one who scoffed at me in the first place."

"He's their top man, Mr Penrose."

"Then the Lord help us!" he exclaimed. "I really do not know where to turn next. The entire Harling family seems to be dropping down dead around me."

"If your original surmise is correct, there will be no more. When you originally consulted Mr Holmes your fear was that Tom and Dick would kill Harry, which has come to pass. With Harry and Tom now dead, only Dick remains. Where is Mr Richard?"

"Abroad."

"Abroad?" I could hardly believe it.

"Yes, he took his wife and Mr Harry's widow and all their children to Deauville yesterday. He thought they all ought to get away from the troubles of the past days."

"So they will not know about Tom's demise?"

"No. I have sent a telegram to Deauville, but as I do not know which hotel they are staying at it may be some time before it reaches them."

"How is Mrs Thomas taking her husband's death?"

"Very badly, as you can imagine; she thought he was on the mend, then suddenly this turn for the worse, and within a short time he was gone."

Holmes returned to us. "Where is Lestrade?"

"He said he could do nothing until after the post mortem."

"Where is Mrs Harling?" asked Holmes.

"Do you wish to see her?" asked Penrose.

"If it is convenient."

"I will ask if she is available." Penrose left the room to enquire.

"This is a surprise, Holmes, another death. It would seem to rule out Tom as a suspect."

"Does it?"

"Well it is all getting very complicated, another death to be account-ed for, and poison suspected."

"On the contrary, Watson, this death clarifies matters. At last I begin to see daylight."

"Well it's still midnight as far as I'm concerned. By the way, Dick has taken his family to Deauville."

"Deauville? When?"

"Yesterday, according to Penrose."

"So he knows nothing of his brother's death?" asked Holmes.

"Not unless he caused it. If Tom's been poisoned I can see no other possibility."

"Oh, madam, thank you for coming down." We turned as Penrose came in with Mrs Harling. She was not a very striking lady, but one could not expect her to be at her best having lost her husband a few short hours ago. She bore herself very bravely, but my practiced eye could see the effort she was making. "I am Sherlock Holmes, this is my colleague Dr Watson. We both offer you our deepest sympathy."

"Thank you, Mr Holmes. Mr Penrose tells me you are a detective." Holmes gave a slight bow of acknowledgment. "I have told Inspector Lestrade all I know about this illness. Now you are here, and you all appear so interested, I fear it was not an illness at all."

"I am afraid your husband's death is suspicious, Mrs Harling, hence our interest," said Holmes.

"First Harry, my brother-in-law, now my husband. Is some lunatic at large?" asked the good lady in bewilderment.

"Rest assured, Mr Holmes will get to the bottom of it all if anybody can," said I.

"May I ask you two or three questions? I fear they may cause you some distress."

"If it assists in explaining the inexplicable then I shall be pleased to do so."

"I understand your husband was taken ill on the day of Harry's accident?"

"Yes, in the evening. He had dined at the Savoy with his old friend Mr Gravison and some other gentlemen. He said he had eaten oysters and feared they may have been off. I know the hotel is famous for its electric lights and lifts, but one never knows about hygiene, does one? After all, I believe both the manager and the chef are foreigners," replied Mrs Harling.

"He had stomach pains?"

"Yes, he took an indigestion remedy but it was no good."

"He was thereafter confined to his bed?"

"Yes, I've never seen him so bad. He loathes missing his morning at the bank so I knew he was bad as he didn't attempt to rise; he found difficulty in swallowing and speaking, and said he couldn't see clearly, then he started vomiting and became agitated."

"But he did go to Mr Harry's funeral?"

"Yes, but he looked awful. I begged him not to go in that state, but he was adamant he must make the effort in case people got the wrong idea?"

"Wrong idea?"

"Well, yes. If he were absent it might look as though he did not care about his brother. On the other hand, if people thought he was so upset by his death that he was unfit to attend they would think him a weakling. Tom was never that and he would hate to be in such a position. But he was clearly ill. He did not seem to know where he was half the time, and when people spoke to him his speech was slurred. Somebody told me he must have had a stroke and we should get him to a doctor. "

"But you didn't?"

"No, not at that time. When we got home he seemed a little better. He was very sleepy and that seemed to help matters."

"I see. Do you have a photograph of your husband?" asked Holmes.

"Why, yes, of course. Several."

"I wonder if you have a recent portrait of him?"

"I have the very thing. All the directors of the bank had one taken to illustrate the year-end report for the shareholders."

"That would be most kind. I believe when we visited him last time he said he was feeling a little better?"

"Yes, he rallied. We both thought he'd turned the corner. In fact he said he felt like a glass of wine and some thin-sliced cold beef, but it did no good. In the night he was vomiting again and becoming agitated. He couldn't keep still. After being sleepy he was now thrashing about, so I called the doctor as soon as morning came."

"You had not summoned him previous to that. Why was that?" asked Holmes.

"I pleaded with Tom but he was adamant. He did not want it to get out that he was ill. He was always concerned about the shares at the bank. The slightest thing can send them tumbling it seems. When at last I sent for Dr McIntyre and he did not protest, then I knew it was really bad."

"Have you the bottle of wine he drank from?"

"I have really no idea. There wasn't much left in it and he finished it. You could enquire of the kitchen staff." She suddenly gave a gasp. "You don't think the wine was responsible, do you?"

"I have to consider the possibility that it may have been contaminated, but it was probably quite innocent," assured Holmes.

"Should the wine be the cause then he has killed himself; and I helped him do it!" The poor lady could contain her grief no longer and flung herself weeping on to the sofa. Holmes nodded to me and I, of course, went to her aid. I did not see Holmes slip out of the room.

On our way back I was cast down with the misery we had just witnessed. This poor family seemed cursed with tragedy. Holmes, on the contrary, was in a cheerful mood which I must admit I found unseemly in the circumstances. He asked the cabby to stop at the first telegraph office, and I waited whilst he conducted his business.

"Telegrams, Holmes?" I enquired as we travelled on.

"Yes. I have asked Lestrade to meet us outside the bank at eleven o'clock in the morning. He can be a dullard at times, but he is the official police and is able to command where Sherlock Holmes may only request. He has his uses. You are an intelligent fellow, Watson. Can you answer these questions. One – why should Richard Harling, after losing his hat, not wait for it to be retrieved?"

"It was retrieved."

"Yes, but not until an hour later when he boarded the return train to London. If Aunt Phoebe was such a stickler for formality would he not have waited the five minutes or so until the hat was restored to him?"

"Perhaps Aunt Phoebe was also a stickler for punctuality and he did not wish to be late?"

"Two – why did he take a pony trap for the distance which we found to be a short walk only?"

"Same reason – punctuality."

"Three – why did he make such a fuss of paying his fare at Waterloo?"

"He didn't want to be accused of dodging paying his due fare."

"Most importantly – how did Aunt Phoebe know he had lost his ticket for the return journey?"

"Did she know?"

"Yes, Watson; she laughed immoderately at the whole incident and said he had to buy another ticket."

"Richard must have told her that he had lost his ticket and that was what he would have to do."

"Richard told us he only realised the ticket was lost when the inspector on the train came to clip it."

"She is a very confused lady. Perhaps she was told after the event?"

"By whom?"

"Miss Bonneville, perhaps?"

"Possibly; but equally how would she know?"

"Penrose? He is in communication more than anybody, perhaps he wrote about it in a letter?"

"You have said 'perhaps' three times, Watson. I am not happy with 'perhapses'. I need certainties and the one certainty I am sure of is that this visit was planned entirely to set up an alibi. The hat nonsense was a way to be noticed. To make sure his arrival and departure in Esher was marked by witnesses. He also took the opportunity to leave his card as further evidence. He took a trap so that yet another person would know he was there. The elaborate charade over the ticket was to call attention to himself again at Waterloo, again leaving his card.

"You saw, yourself, Watson, how the ticket collector at Esher clearly did not remember me from only the day before when I had conversed with him."

"These fellows must have hundreds of passengers pass through their gates, Holmes, they can't be expected to remember them all." I protested.

"You prove my point, Watson."

"So you say all that was to make sure Richard was seen by as many people as possible at Esher, and remembered?"

"It was essential that as many people as possible were aware of where he was, and at what time."

Promptly at eleven o'clock the next morning we met Lestrade outside the bank.

"This better be good, Mr Holmes, I have had to alter plans to meet you here."

"Lestrade, if this works out as I expect, it will be the biggest coup of your career. You will solve an impossible murder."

"Killing a man with a poisoned bottle of wine doesn't seem very impossible, Mr Holmes."

"I am not referring to that, Lestrade. I think you will find that was an unfortunate accident. Now I need to inspect the office of Mr Thomas Harling. You know he was a director of the bank?"

"Yes, Mr Holmes, I am conversant with the facts. Mr Penrose told me in great detail what this was all about, and claimed that Mr Harold Harling had been murdered by one or both of his brothers. The police investigated that accident at the request of Mr Thomas Harling and it was found to be an accident. The coroner's verdict was death by trampling of the horse, and recommended that it should be shot."

"The horse was innocent, I hope it still lives."

"I wouldn't know. It was not my case. I think Penrose is a bit round the twist, he has been harping on about this for months. Long before it happened."

"Yes, Lestrade, you sent him on to me, but at the end of it all you will get the credit as usual."

"Oh, I know you only do this sort of thing for the fun of it, Mr Holmes."

"Hardly 'fun', Lestrade. For the intellectual satisfaction of pitting my mind against the criminal."

"And bringing villains to trial, Holmes," I added.

"Oh, yes, and that."

"Shall we go in?" asked Lestrade.

Inside the bank Lestrade showed his credentials, asking to see the most senior person on the premises. This turned out to be one of the other directors of Harling & Groots, a Mr Whitehead, a nephew of the Groots family. We were shown into Harling's office, it having remained empty and unused during his illness.

"Before we go any further may I clear something with Hopkinson, the secretary."

"Certainly, I will ask him to join us," Whitehead went to the door. "Come in, please, Hopkinson, these gentlemen would like a word."

Hopkinson was a thin pasty-faced young man with a feeble attempt at a moustache under a rather prominent nose. I remembered him from our previous visit as a down-trodden individual very much put-upon by his employer.

"Ah, Hopkinson," said Holmes genially, "you recall when I came previously and questioned you, you said that Mr Harling entered his office at just after ten o'clock and did not emerge until one o'clock."

"Yes, that's correct, Mr Holmes, he said he did not wish to be disturbed," agreed Hopkinson.

"And you were in the outer office all the time?"

"Yes."

"You are convinced he was in the office the whole time?"

"Oh yes, I kept hearing him. There is that filing cabinet there – "

"The set of wooden drawers?"

"Yes, you can clearly hear them. Mr Harling bangs – er, used to bang them on closing."

Holmes walked over to the drawers and opened and closed them in turn several times. They were noisy.

"He also has a private water closet behind that door, as you saw before, Mr Holmes, and you can hear that flush from the outer office."

"Watson, go out and close the door," commanded Holmes. I did as ordered, and waited. I distinctly heard the flush of water through the walls. The door opened and I returned. "Did you hear anything, Watson?"

"Clearly. The flushing of a water closet."

"Thank you, Hopkinson, you have been most helpful, you may go."

"Thank you, sir."

"So Mr Harling was here as he claimed. So what have you proved, Mr Holmes?" asked Lestrade.

"Please observe the window." We all looked at the window. "It is covered with a pattern of iron bars arranged in loops and scrolls. Would you like to explain that, Mr Whitehead?"

"Explain? There is nothing to explain. This building is a bank, with large amounts of cash and securities on the premises. We have underground strong-rooms and internal barred rooms just as other banks. The rooms on this side of the building open on to what is little more than an alley-way. So the windows must be protected. Hence the ironwork."

"Whose idea was it to have the fancy scroll work rather than conventional bars?" asked Holmes.

"Mr Harling's. He often sees clients in this office and we all thought conventional bars would give a prison-like appearance. We commissioned the grill you see. My office has a similar one, as do one or two more rooms."

"Now we come to the crux. As you say, the bars are assembled in the form of a large grill which I observe for the first time is hinged at one side and padlocked at the other." Holmes pushed the curtain hanging at either side away, so that we could all see.

"We had the grill made to open for the purposes of cleaning the windows, and sometimes in the heat of summer it would be possible to open the window to admit cooling air," explained Whitehead.

"Of course," assented Holmes. "Who has the key? Mr Harling?"

"The caretaker has keys for every ordinary lock in the building. Of course the secure areas are treated more strictly. But there should be a key for the grill near to hand. It was considered essential in case of fire, or similar emergency, that an exit via the window should be possible."

Holmes, who was peering round, pounced on the key in the door of the closet which had further keys on the ring. Quickly finding one to fit the padlock, he pulled the grill open. "Very smooth, everything has been recently oiled." He slid up the bottom part of the sash window and leaned out. Lestrade and I joined him and we took turns to peer out into the alley. The level on the outside was only a few inches below the level of the floor inside. The alley, a rather dismal little-used affair, looked as though it were rarely cleaned.

"Do either of you see those marks on the ground?" asked Holmes.

Lestrade looked again. "What is the significance?"

Holmes looked around and gave a cry of exultation. "Of course! I have been stupid, Lestrade." He pointed to the little set of library steps that I had perched upon on our previous visit. "Why are they in the room?"

"We have several such steps in the building, Mr Holmes," said Whitehead. "They are commonplace in offices as well as libraries. People often have to reach high shelves."

"But not in this room. There is nothing in here that an average man cannot easily reach."

Staring round we all agreed the point, while Holmes picked up the steps and lowered them out of the window. They exactly fitted the marks perceived on the ground.

"What does all this mean, Mr Holmes?"

"It means, if I am correct, that rather than being in this room for three hours, Harling climbed out of the window and was away for as much as three hours, returning just before one o'clock."

"That won't do, Mr Holmes. Hopkinson swears he heard drawers closing and the closet flush."

"Perhaps I must explain further. The steps are not for the purpose of climbing out. As you see, any able-bodied man could swing his leg over the sill and drop down the very short distance to the ground. The steps are to assist a person climbing in."

"Unnecessary, Mr Holmes; a man who could climb out could just as easily climb in. I'm not particularly agile, but I could soon scramble in," said Lestrade.

"What if you were a woman in a dress?" asked Holmes.

"A woman?" cried I incredulously.

"Just so. I must trust to your discretion here because a lady is involved and as yet I am not clear of her part in the proceedings. Do I have your word as gentlemen you will say nothing unless the lady is proved to be an accessory to this crime?"

We all gave our promise and waited for Holmes to expound. First, going to the door he spoke to Hopkinson, who went away. "We know friend Hopkinson has acute hearing," smiled Holmes. "I have the advantage of knowing that Mrs Harry Harling and the late Mr Tom Harling have been conducting an illicit liaison." Whitehead gasped, Lestrade was unperturbed as the fact meant little to him and I, of course, already knew, Holmes having confided the fact to me months ago before the death of Harry. He had learned of it from the gossip of servants.

"Every week on Friday, Mrs Harry Harling came into town to have her hair done. She came alone and took the opportunity to come here. As I now believe, she tapped on the window, a signal that Thomas was expecting. He opened the grill, raised the sash and put the steps out exactly as you saw me do a moment ago. With Mrs Harry Harling safely inside, he retrieved the steps and closed up again. The couple had their *tête-à-tête* and he then let her out the same way. A regular arrangement that seemed to suit both parties. I should imagine being related by marriage there were other opportunities too, but probably other family members, including their respective spouses, were always at hand."

"This Thomas Harling seems to have been a bit of a cad," remarked Lestrade sourly.

"Yes, as I suspect that Mrs Harling may not have been the only lady he entertained in this manner."

"That's all very well, Holmes, but on the day of the murder he must have been away three hours, going to Epping and back by train, and committing the murder in the middle of it." I said.

"Murder?" gasped Whitehead.

"It's a bit complicated, Mr Whitehead, but rely on Mr Holmes to sort it out for us. I shall. I think we are entering the realms of fantasy here," said Lestrade.

"Mrs Harling was so used to entering via the window, her brother-in-law prevailed upon her to assist him on the fateful day for a much longer period of time. He left, she lifted the steps in and closed the window. The door to the office was locked, Harling had given orders he was not to be disturbed. He had instructed her to noisily bang the drawers now and then and mid-way through, flush the water closet. This was all heard by Hopkinson outside who naturally assumed the noises were made by his chief. When Thomas returned, the entry was effected, Mrs Harling was permitted to go and get back home to be told her husband was dead."

"And Thomas unlocked the door as though he had been there throughout. The devil," I breathed. I suddenly remembered. "The cigarette stubs!"

Holmes took out an envelope and handed it to Lestrade "These were found by me at the scene of the so-called accident. There were four, I took one only, so that your detectives would find the others. There were also six in the little copse near the scene of the trampling, and I took one from there. The two are identical."

"Yes, and they are the same type as Thomas smoked and Holmes found identical ones here in this office in the ashtray!" I cried.

"This is incredible," muttered Whitehead, "our principal director, a lecher and a murderer."

"We do not know he was the murderer, Mr Whitehead. I merely point out how he could have been. It will be up to the police to prove it."

"It doesn't matter, does it. The man's dead. Poisoned. Probably self-administered. He kills his lover's husband and, filled with remorse, kills himself."

"Straight from the *Police Gazette*, eh, Lestrade?" smiled Holmes.

"Well, saves us the job of trying to hang him. Just a minute, perhaps Mrs Harry Harling did not want her husband killed and she revenged herself by poisoning Thomas."

"No, she did not poison him. Which reminds me, we must find out the result of the post mortem. We can do no more here. Thank you for your co-operation Mr Whitehead. I would just like another word with Hopkinson on the way out."

Leaving the director agape at the nefarious activities that had taken place behind the respectable doors of his bank, we stopped to talk to Hopkinson.

"Just one thing, Hopkinson. Mr Harling was a creature of habit, do you agree?"

"Oh yes, sir, each morning was the same. Prompt at ten he came in, hung up his coat and hat in my office. At 11.30 tea was brought to us both and I took his into him. Then at 1 o'clock he donned coat and hat and left."

"Was there not one day in the week that varied?" asked Holmes.

"Yes, actually there was," said Hopkinson.

"Fridays were a little different I fancy," said Holmes.

"Yes, yes they were! How on earth did you know?" Holmes waved his hand airily. "On Fridays he always had his tea at noon, and for some reason they always supplied a larger pot, I never knew why."

"Did you take it in to him as usual?"

"Sometimes, but more often he came out for the tray himself."

"Thank you, Hopkinson. As I said before, you have been most helpful. Good day."

We accompanied Lestrade back to Scotland Yard where the report of the post mortem revealed that Tom had indeed been poisoned by atropine. "What's that when it's at home?" growled Lestrade.

"A poisonous alkaloid commonly known as deadly nightshade," I explained. "It causes vomiting, excessive stimulation of the heart, slurred speech, hallucinations, disorientation, delirium, and agitation. Convulsions often precede death."

"How did he come to take that then?"

"It is most commonly found in the form of black berries on a plant. Animals seem to eat the berries without ill effect, but they are fatal to man."

"They were certainly fatal to this man," agreed Lestrade. "What do we do now?"

"I suggest you prepare yourself to arrest Mr Richard Harling on his return from Deauville," said Holmes.

"Why, did he poison his big brother?"

"No, Lestrade, that was an accident. Richard Harling killed his younger brother."

"I don't follow any of this," complained Lestrade, and I was forced to agree with him.

"Will you humour me in this? I have some enquiries still to make which will make your case complete. Will you call in at Baker Street this evening about six o'clock, Lestrade, and I shall explain all. Dr Watson, too, is owed an explanation as he has manfully assisted me in this."

"Very well, Mr Holmes. But I hope you are right. If I arrest Richard Harling I will need to know why!"

"You shall be satisfied. Until six! Come, Watson!"

Holmes hurried me away. "There is one more duty you can perform for me. I need you to go to Esher again."

"I will be delighted to do so."

"I thought you might. I sent a telegram to Miss Bonneville informing her that the elderberry wine had been contaminated and that she must not touch it until you saw her again."

"You mean the wine that killed Tom was from Aunt Phoebe?" I gasped.

"Yes."

"But I don't understand, how did he imbibe it?"

"With a piece of cake I believe. It would seem that Aunt Phoebe is so far gone in her faculties that she cannot tell elderberries from deadly nightshade berries. She made her latest supply from the deadliest wild berries known in this country."

"Good God, I must get out there before somebody else drinks it."

"Oh, and by the way, take a close look at the photograph reposing on Aunt Phoebe's mantelpiece."

I hastened away on my errand of mercy and it was with great relief that my frantic knock was instantly answered. However, to my distress it was Aunt Phoebe herself who opened the door, thus catching me off balance.

"Oh, hello. I think I know you, don't I?" she said, peering up at me.

"Yes, yes, I was here with my colleague Sherlock Holmes yesterday," I spluttered, momentarily forgetting who I was supposed to be. At that moment Miss Bonneville appeared.

"This man is Sherlock Holmes, he said he came yesterday," said Aunt Phoebe turning.

"It's Dr Flegg, I believe, Phoebe, you are getting muddled again. Come in, Doctor. I received Mr Penrose's telegram telling me you would come."

I entered the cottage which I had seen so little of yesterday, as we had spent most of the time in the garden.

"I was rather puzzled by the message. Mr Penrose said the elderberry wine was contaminated and that we must not touch it until you had been. Perhaps you could explain what the message means?"

I had spent the journey on the train thinking out how I could explain without alarming the two ladies, and now was the time to see if my approach worked. "It seems that the elderberry wine that Miss Harling's nephew drank here was not as it should have been. I believe he took the rest of the bottle home with him, is that correct?"

"Why yes, he said he found it so pleasant and to his liking that Miss Harling pressed him to take the bottle. We, ourselves, don't drink it, and in any case it was the end bottle, there are no more."

"No more?"

"No, Miss Harling only made a dozen last autumn and they have all gone now."

"But where?" I thought frantically, if these bottles had been dispersed there could be other deaths. "Who had the other bottles?"

"I've really no idea, Doctor. Is it important?"

"Very important. I must trace those bottles."

"Oh, dear. Phoebe, you know the elderberry wine you made in the autumn? Who did you give it to?"

"Elderberry wine? Oh, I must make some more. It's all gone. I can't make any more until the autumn when the berries arrive."

"Yes, Phoebe, but who took the ones you made last year?" asked Miss Bonneville patiently.

"Oh, I don't know. I gave them to the vicar for the poor people."

"The vicar? Where can I find him? It's most urgent," I said.

"Our vicar is Mr Tooley. The vicarage is right next to the church. If you return to the High Street and look to your left you will see the spire."

After gaining directions to the vicarage and promising I would be back, I hurried round to see the clergyman. Fortunately he was in and agreed to see me at once.

"My name is Dr Watson," I explained, concealment now being unnecessary. "I believe that Miss Phoebe Harling gave some bottles of elderberry wine to you last autumn."

"Yes, yes, she did. She's a good soul, always making small comforts for the poor of the village. Actually she doesn't like me, you know, because I'm a newcomer and raise money for our missionary work in Africa." He laughed. "I've been here for seven years and this parish has a link with a church in Africa, so we pray for each other, and from time to time send money to help in social projects such as digging fresh water wells. I don't mind Miss Harling, she's very old, can be cantankerous, but she is a good God-fearing Christian of the old school and I rather like her."

I endured this speech impatiently before I could butt in with the point of my visit. "I am very troubled about the bottles of elderberry wine. What did you do with them?"

"As I always do, distribute them to the most deserving, along with other comforts."

"When did you do that?"

"Oh, normally at Christmas time; that is when the poor folk feel it the hardest, when richer people tuck into their goose and plum pudding." He gave a merry chuckle.

"So these bottles of wine have been with various households for five months?"

"Since Christmas, yes."

"Have there been no reports of illness?" I asked in astonishment.

"I do not follow you, Doctor."

"People did not find the wine made them ill?"

"Apparently not. Should it have done? How silly of me, of course it should not have done, but you seemed to expect that it would."

"I have reason to believe that instead of elderberries Miss Harling, in error, used berries from the deadly nightshade plant."

"Oh, my goodness. I do see why you are worried. But nothing has been reported to me. Our local doctor has not spoken to me about strange illness or sudden death, so perhaps you are mistaken?"

"Mr Tooley, is it possible to trace the people who received the bottles?"

"I could try. It will take some time. We do have a record of the deserving poor. Miss Marley keeps it, and I believe she makes notes of who receives what. She likes to be as fair as possible from year to year in allocating the gifts."

"Can you see Miss Marley and retrieve the bottles?"

"Well, yes, but I fear most, if not all, will have been consumed at Christmas. That is, after all, when wine is usually drunk by those accustomed to ale. There will be a delay, doctor, as Miss Marley is away at present."

I groaned, but realised this was going to be all I could do. Pressing the urgency of the matter, I asked him to get back what bottles he could, then telegraph the information to Sherlock Holmes. With that I had to be content and trudge back to Honeysuckle Cottage.

"Did you find the vicar, Dr Flegg?" asked Miss Bonneville.

Here they still thought of me as Dr Flegg. I was finding it difficult to keep these impersonations going. It made me realise what an achievement planning and carrying out the alibis had been for Richard and Thomas Harling. A pity such acumen could not be turned to an honest purpose. "Yes, yes. He will try and retrieve any bottles that have not been drunk." I was depressed because I had failed my friend Sherlock Holmes. He wanted me to return with a bottle for analysis and I would not be able to do that. But I soon bucked up when assured that Miss Bonneville was in no danger, and when she suggested a cup of tea before I returned I gratefully accepted. The three of us sat by the fireplace, which had no fire blazing as it was summer.

"Have you thought any more about my suggestion of getting a trained nurse in to enable you to have a day off now and then?" I enquired. Miss Bonneville frowning, made a gesture with her head towards Miss Harling which I, clumsy fool that I was, realised was a warning not to speak of such things before her employer. Thus we spoke of the weather and similar meaningless topics, when all the time I wished to get to know this fascinating woman more closely. Then glancing at the clock, I recognised I must leave if I were to be in Baker

Street by six. Something I could not possibly miss if Holmes revealed the mystery of the favourite son to Lestrade. As I rose, saying that time waits for no man and nodded at the clock, I noticed the photograph on the mantelpiece and recalled Holmes had told me to have a look at it. "What a striking photograph," said I.

"That's my nephew," said Miss Harling proudly. He comes to see me every week. See he has signed it. It says 'to my beloved Aunt Phoebe from her nephew Richard.' isn't that nice?"

I agreed it was nice, and parted reluctantly from Miss Bonneville, promising I would return when I heard from the vicar.

As the train took me back to town, I pondered why a signed photograph from Richard Harling should be one of his brother Tom.

As arranged, we three promptly assembled in our rooms.

"Sit down, Lestrade. Do you care for a drink?"

"A whisky and soda would be welcome, Mr Holmes." I hurried to execute the request. "Now you promised to explain what this was all about."

"So I shall. For clarity I will follow Penrose in calling the brothers Tom, Dick and Harry. As Mr Penrose suspected from the start, the two brothers Tom and Dick conspired to murder their young brother Harry. They could only get at the money with his death, when it would be left to them equally. They decided one of them should do the deed while the other provided an alibi. Dick was to do the murder. Once the plan was agreed Tom set about preparing for the alibi. He started visiting his aunt who lived at Esher in completely the opposite direction to Epping. The Aunt, Phoebe by name, had had no dealings with her nephews since they were boys so, when this strange man arrived bearing chocolates saying he was her nephew Richard, she had no reason to doubt it. Her companion was a young woman."

"Miss Bonneville," I interjected.

"A Miss Bonneville, who had only been with Aunt Phoebe for two years. She had barely heard of the three brothers so she, too, had no reason to think anything untoward about this nephew who had, somewhat late in his aunt's life, thought he should visit her. When the nephew said he was Richard, why should they doubt it?"

"So Tom pretended to be Dick, right?" confirmed Lestrade.

"Correct. He came for an hour, brought chocolates or similar trifles, chatted amiably then left. He did this for several weeks. All this was to prepare an alibi for the big day. Timing was of the essence as Tom had to provide two separate alibis for the same time span. He had to have his own alibi, of course, as well as lay one for Dick. This is what actually happened. At 10am Dick set out for Epping. On arrival he waited in a small copse of trees until brother Harry came riding by. He stepped out and Harry, recognising him, but no doubt puzzled as to why he should appear in that place at that time, reined in. He dismounted. Presumably Dick spun some sort of tale as to why he was there and they probably talked together for a few minutes until a suitable moment when Harry turned his back and was struck down by Dick. He carried a weapon and bludgeoned his brother to death. After that he returned to London, arriving at his club about 12.30 to take his place on a committee and later to dine there, play billiards and return home at 3pm. There were no witnesses, nobody noticed him on the train in either direction. Very anonymous up to 12.30, then in the centre of a crowd of chaps thereafter. All clear so far?"

"No, Holmes. You say Harry was bludgeoned to death. How come poor Brutus the horse got blamed?" I asked.

"That's right. When our men were called in they saw the marks of horseshoes all over the body. The doctor who was called wrote it all in his statement and the coroner gave the cause of death as trampling by a horse," agreed Lestrade.

"These men were diabolically ingenious. Machiavelli himself could learn from them," said Holmes.

"Who's he, Macky Velli? That's a new one on me, where does he come in?" asked Lestrade.

"Holmes is comparing the brothers to a notorious politician in 14th century Italy," I explained.

"What you must realise is that Tom and Dick were planning this to look like an accident. The alibis that they were to create were a fall-back plan. Should the death be taken as an accident, which it was, then they were home and dry, the alibis unnecessary."

"Go on. What about the trampling of the horse?" asked Lestrade.

"I examined the horse's legs and hooves. There was no trace of blood on them. No blood anywhere. The brothers constructed some sort of club with a ball at the end. To the ball were fixed two or three horseshoes. Thus, when belaboured with this fiendish weapon, the marks of horseshoes were inflicted on the body."

"Good God, like one of those maces of old when knights in armour bashed each other about," I said. "To treat you own brother so." I was speechless.

"How do you know this, Mr Holmes? Have you found this weapon?"

"Alas no. I should imagine it was destroyed after use, or cast somewhere never to be found."

"Then how do you know it existed at all?" demanded Lestrade.

"Because the horseshoes worn by Brutus were much larger in all respects. He was a big horse. The shoe marks on Harry's body were caused by smaller shoes. I took measurements and sketches at the time.

"Perhaps he was trampled by a different horse? Dick could have come on a horse and made it trample the body after he felled Harry."

"If that is the case it was still no accident. I doubt if another horse was involved, I found no traces of a second horse, but clear evidence of two different footprints. I think my theory is correct. I agree it was well done. I myself might have been fooled if I had not had the warning from Penrose."

"Oh, him. He started all this when he came nattering to me months ago," grumbled Lestrade.

"Now that was what Dick really did. What was Tom doing during this time? First of all he set up his own alibi by behaving exactly as he always did. He went to his office at 10am, he asked not to be disturbed. He came out at 1pm and went to lunch with friends at the Savoy Hotel. His secretary in the outer office knew he was there all morning because he heard drawers slamming and the flushing of the wc. That was Tom's alibi. But what Tom actually did was far more devious. He allowed another person to enter by the window and take his place. I suspect, but cannot prove, that the other person was, in fact, Mrs Harry Harling the victim's wife. However, Tom left the office and travelled to Esher in the persona of his brother Dick. You will know Tom is clean shaven and Dick has a moustache. Tom had stuck a false moustache to his lip and wore a brand new top hat.

At Esher he dropped his topper on the rails and made a fuss. He left his card, which was, of course, one of Dick's. He took a pony trap, he visited his Aunt. This is where his careful planning had not been careful enough. When he had started visiting Aunt Phoebe several weeks before, Tom had not thought about being clean shaven. He had even given his aunt a photograph of himself clean shaven, and signed it as from Dick. I saw that photograph when we visited the cottage and I slipped into the house on the excuse of using the privy. So for his deception to work on the women in the cottage he had to remove the false moustache. This he did, and had the usual meeting with chocolates etc. They sat in the garden and he had a glass of elderberry wine and a piece of cake before leaving, when once again the moustache went back on. At the station he created another fuss about the topper. On the train he made sure the inspector knew who he was, another of Dick's cards came out. At Waterloo more fuss at the ticket office. Dick's card proffered again. After all that, Tom reverted to being Tom again, disposed of hat and moustache, climbed back into his office via the window and let his accomplice leave by the same way. Then on the stroke of 1pm he emerged. Two alibis created by one man."

"Hum," said Lestrade dubiously, "there is little actual proof in all this. I wonder if we can find the weapon. That's what we really need."

"I could not begin to suggest where you look. Is all now clear to you both?"

"Just a minute, Holmes, what about the cigarettes?" said I.

"Ah, yes, the cigarette stubs. The stubs were undoubtedly of the kind that Tom smoked, but they are not exclusive to him and may be bought at several high-class tobacconists."

"So did Dick smoke the same kind?" I asked.

"Not at all; except on this occasion when he did it for self-protection."

"Self-protection?"

"Although the two brothers were accomplices through necessity, neither trusted the other. After all they were after the big prize. Why settle for half when you can have it all?"

"A double-cross, you mean?" asked Lestrade.

"Not quite that. You must understand what type of men these were. They both had devious minds and whatever one thought, he knew the same thought would occur to his brother. I think they both suspected the other might try and pull off a double-cross. If suspicion should fall on Dick, the evidence of the cigarettes at the scene would incriminate Tom. I think Dick over-estimated the reasoning powers of the average policeman."

"Now, Mr Holmes, I can't accept that. We are upholders of the law, not university professors."

"Tom was a very astute man. He was, after all, a successful banker, but like most criminal minds he was not good at self-censoring. When he got away with his disguise he grew careless. What alerted me at first was Aunt Phoebe telling me about Dick having to buy a new ticket. In spinning his alibi Tom had sought to strengthen his story by describing an incident that was yet to happen. He had planned everything so meticulously but forgot an essential known to every actor. Though you have learned your lines you have to deliver them as though they are newly formed on the tongue. Hamlet does not know in act one that he will be dead in act five, even though the actor does."

"As you say, Holmes, positively Machiavellian. What a family!"

"And you think Harry's wife is also involved in all this?" asked Lestrade.

"Certainly they were lovers," assured Holmes. "The two brothers had planned so precisely that they never met up afterwards but, as far as possible, carried on as normal."

"What about Tom's death, then?"

"Ah, yes. That was a stroke of luck."

"Not for Tom, it wasn't," replied Lestrade.

"If it were not for Tom being poisoned by the elderberry wine, then my suspicions of the impersonation of Dick would not have been confirmed. What I did not realise, until Tom took a turn for the worse, was he had brought the rest of the bottle home at his aunt's insistence. Just when he was getting better he consumed some more and that extra dose was his death blow."

"So he poisoned himself without knowing?"

"Yes."

"But surely we can get this Aunt Phoebe for murder if she supplied it?" asked Lestrade.

"I think it was a pure accident. I suspect when she made the wine she mistook deadly nightshade for elderberries. She is very old and feeble-minded."

"So Dick had nothing to do with that at all?"

"I think not."

"I have taken your advice and my men are watching for Richard Harling's return. We'll get the truth out of him. I think it's fortunate you were in at the beginning of this stunt or those two would have got away with it. Still, there's only one to go to trial now. Imagine what some men will do for money. Slay your own brother for gold." Lestrade rose, shaking his head.

"Many men would be tempted by a quarter of a million pounds, Lestrade."

"Yes. Still, your own brother."

"Surely the lesson here is that a father should not have a favourite son, but treat them all the same. It was Mr Ferguson Harling's will that caused it all," I said.

"I wonder if the whole purpose of that bizarre will was to find out his sons' true colours?"

"Well, he won't know where he is, will he?" said Lestrade.

"No, but we do, and soon the whole world will."

The message eventually reached Richard Harling at Deauville and he returned to be arrested by Lestrade's waiting men and taken into custody. Holmes then lost interest in the case as it was always the problem and the chase that appealed to him. Although, of course, standing up for justice and the law, he was always content to let the official authorities take over, this being why Lestrade received far more praise for his acumen than he deserved, and why Sherlock Holmes himself rarely appeared in the courtrooms of the land. Once the case was solved he moved on to new things, there was always something fresh awaiting his attention, and it was about this time he was called in to investigate the strange affair of the disappearing Punch & Judy man on Ullacombe beach.

However, I was still concerned about the bottles of poisoned elderberry wine that had circulated at Esher, and why there were no reports of death or severe illness from that quarter. So I was relieved when one morning Holmes handed me a letter addressed to Dr Watson, C/o Mr Sherlock Holmes. I tore it open to read the following:

Dear Dr Watson,

Re: Distribution of Miss Harling's Elderberry Wine. Miss Marley has now returned from visiting her sister in Lancashire so I have been able to address the problem of the wine bottles I can set your mind at rest. The bottles were not given out as supposed. Miss Marley is a staunch member of the Temperance Union and has a great reluctance to disseminate alcohol. It now appears that for some years when any alcoholic bottle is given as a gift for our Deserving Poor Collections she has taken it upon herself to pour the contents away and replace the donated bottles with cordials and mineral waters purchased by herself. She continued in this practice secretly as she did not wish to cause offence to the donors, Miss Harling being the principal one to supply alcohol. It appears that prior to my becoming the incumbent here, Miss Marley made her views known and these are adhered to by all except Miss Harling, a lady well-respected in our community and now, through age, often irrational. Rather than cause further dispute over the issue Miss Marley adopted the above clandestine procedure. My own opinion is that in the circumstances it was an excusable method.

However, your concern is whether persons consumed the contaminated liquor and the answer is clearly no – it has all been poured away.

I am, sir, your obedient servant,

Giles Tooley (Rev)

I passed the letter to Holmes. "The last link finally solved. I must say Holmes I think you have outdone yourself in this affair, it must be your greatest triumph." Holmes gave that familiar airy wave of the hand one sees when he is highly praised.

We had occasional visits from Lestrade as he prepared the evidence for the public prosecutor and wished to clarify points with Holmes who found it tedious having to hark back when he had moved on to new pastures. For his part, Lestrade grumbled at the constant presence of the lawyer Penrose who was determined to keep his finger on the pulse of the affair.

When the trial took place at the Old Bailey I went, out of interest, and sat in the public gallery. Astonishingly, the case was not regarded as a triumph for Holmes, just the opposite. Holmes's name was slandered and mocked in the court, and it was my distressing experience to read newspaper headlines in the gutter press proclaiming *Sherlock Holmes Laughed Out of Court* and *Great Detective Blunders*.

Richard Harling had briefed the eminent QC Edward Carson to defend him, whilst the Crown was represented by Percival Trubshawe QC. Lestrade was the expert witness for the prosecution and I thought made an excellent job of presenting facts of the case when questioned by Trubshawe. However, when cross-examined by Carson, his natural doggedness appeared churlish, and his wits not nimble enough to see when he was being led into a corner to be trapped. Carson was one of those QCs who rely on repeating statements with heavy irony.

"You say Harry Harling was not trampled by a horse, but beaten by a club?"

"Yes, sir."

"Please tell us again about this club."

"It was studded with horseshoes," replied Lestrade.

"A club studded with horseshoes," repeated Carson "a singular weapon indeed. May we see this extraordinary implement?"

"No, sir."

"Why not, Inspector?"

"I do not have it."

"Then where is it?"

"I don't know."

"You don't know?" repeated Carson. "Have you seen this club?" Lestrade was obliged to admit that he had not. "Then how do you know it exists?"

"I was told by Mr Sherlock Holmes." The familiar name caused a murmur throughout the court.

"Mr Sherlock Holmes the well known detective whose adventures appear in a monthly magazine?"

"Yes, sir."

"He told you, or he showed you, this curious implement?"

"He told me about it."

"He told you about it," repeated Carson. "Why did he not hand it to you as a representative of the law?"

"He did not have it," replied Lestrade, uncomfortably.

"So you never saw it and Mr Holmes the great detective did not have it. Did Mr Holmes see it?"

"I think not."

"You think not. So you have belief in a club that neither you nor Mr Sherlock Holmes have seen. How do we know that this mysterious club exists at all if nobody has seen it? From whence did the idea of this imaginary club arise?"

"It was deduced by Mr Holmes."

"Deduced? May I remind the jury of the meaning of the word deduce. It means to infer from something which precedes, to draw from the general facts a particular truth. Would you agree with that definition, Inspector Lestrade?"

"If you say so."

"I do not say so, Inspector, the English Dictionary says so." This raised a laugh in the court. "In this case an unfortunate man is trampled by his own horse and covered in the marks of the horse's hooves. That is what precedes; those are the general facts. From those facts Mr Holmes infers a particular truth, and the truth he infers is that Mr Harling's own brother comes along with a gigantic club studded with horseshoes and belabours him to the ground with it. I think Mr Holmes reads too many of the fictional magazines in which his adventures appear." Another laugh in court. "Or perhaps he prefers fairy tales?" This was too much and there was much laughter and counter-consternation, with the judge banging his gavel and calling for order. I felt sick.

Lestrade tried to explain about the measurements of Brutus's hooves compared with the body marks, but nobody took him seriously and Carson demolished that theory by drawing marks on a strip of paper and stretching it around his thigh, calf and different objects. "In each case the marks would measure differently, one does not need to be a mathematician to see how curvature affects distance."

Later, when other witnesses were called to verify that they had seen Richard Harling at Esher at the time of the accident, the stationmaster, porter and pony-trap driver all swore they had seen him there, as did the ticket inspector and two men at the ticket kiosk at Waterloo. "Six men, six honest English working men who have no interest or benefit from the outcome of this case except that justice be done, have testified the man in the dock is the man they saw at Esher."

Trubshawe did his best to counter this, as one or two of the six had been less than dogmatic. "If you have the slightest doubt about the identity of the man you must not ignore those doubts. You have to be certain, positive, one hundred per cent sure. It is not enough to say 'I think so'. I remind you a man's life is at stake here. You cannot send a man to the gallows simply because you think he has a passing resemblance to a man you saw on the platform at Esher, or Waterloo. You must be certain." It was a good try, but hopeless. Even if it had succeeded, what followed destroyed all. Miss Phoebe Harling was put in the witness box and her senility caused much laughter.

"I am going to ask you some questions, Miss Harling," said Trubshawe.

"Is it an examination? I used to love exams when I was at school. I went to school, you know. That was unusual, girls didn't go to school when I was young." Trubshawe tried valiantly, but the poor lady's mind was so far shot that she had no idea what it was all about and was allowed to stand down. Carson did not even attempt to question her. However, the greatest damage was done by Lydia Bonneville.

"You are Lydia Bonneville, employed as a companion to Miss Harling?" asked Trubshawe.

"Yes."

"Do you recognise the man in the dock?"

"Yes."

"And who is he?"

"Mr Richard Harling, nephew of Miss Phoebe Harling."

"How do you know him?"

"He came to visit us every week at Miss Harling's cottage in Esher."

"Now I ask you to remember specifically Tuesday, 6th June earlier this year." Miss Bonneville remained silent. "Can you cast your mind back to that day?"

"Yes. What do you wish to know?"

"Did Richard Harling, the man you see now before you, visit the cottage on that day?"

"Yes."

"Do you recall the exact time?" asked Trubshawe.

"Not the exact time, but it was in the morning about a quarter to eleven. He always travelled on the 10.13 train which arrives at Esher at 10.35."

"That was the time he arrived?"

"Yes."

"And what time did he leave?"

"About an hour later. He usually stayed about an hour. Miss Harling gets wearied with visits that last longer than that."

"I see. So he left at about 11.35?"

"Yes, he wanted to catch the 11.45 train back to London as he had a committee meeting to attend."

"And you swear to those times?"

"The times are correct and I have already sworn on the Holy Bible."

"Thank you. No more questions, m'lud."

I could not believe my eyes and ears. Surely Lydia Bonneville could not mistake Tom for Dick? There was certainly a strong resemblance, everybody in the Harling family always acknowledged that, but even I could tell them apart and I had seen the men but rarely. I found this inexplicable.

The trial had promised to be a sensation lasting several days as Harry Harling was a popular public figure and, though his brothers less well-known, the story of the wealth in the family had become common knowledge. It was turning out completely the opposite. It was not a sensation, it was a farce and when, in the afternoon, Lestrade was called back to explain how the alibi was carried out, he got no further than explaining the part Tom had played.

"Let me get this straight, Inspector. You are trying to tell the court that the late Thomas Harling, brother of the accused, who was on the morning of 6th June in his office from 10am to 1pm, was not in fact actually in his office?" asked Edward Carson QC.

"No, sir."

"But we have just heard Mr Hopkinson, Thomas Harling's secretary, who was seated in an outer office through which Mr Harling had to pass to gain ingress and egress from his office, make a sworn statement that he was there throughout and heard the sound of his employer in his office. He mentioned the sound of opening desk drawers, the flushing of the wc and so on. Are you telling us now that Mr Hopkinson is a liar?"

"No, sir."

"Then please explain to the court and the jury exactly what you mean."

"Mr Harling was not actually in his office, though it appeared to be so."

"Indeed. That sounds very mysterious. If he were not there, how had he vanished? Was Mr Harling not actually a respectable banker, but some sort of ghost or spirit that came and went by supernatural forces?" Laughter.

"No. He climbed out of the window," said the unhappy Lestrade. More laughter.

"I see. This director of Harling & Groots Bank, a financial enterprise of much wealth and status, this director of probity and rectitude, a pillar of the community, eschewed the door to his office, but preferred to come and go by the window!" This sally brought forth howls of laughter during which Carson thundered "I suppose Mr Sherlock Holmes told you that too!"

Trubshawe quickly scribbled something on a piece of paper which was passed to the judge. The laughter in the court was still simmering when the judge banged his gavel. "I believe you wish to speak, Mr Trubshawe?"

Percival Trubshawe QC rose "Yes, m'lud. The prosecution wishes to withdraw the charges."

"I think you are wise. Very well. Case dismissed."

And that was the outcome of Holmes's masterly deduction. He was ridiculed and held up as a buffoon in the public press. I determined to speak to Lydia Bonneville and was fortunate to catch her leaving with Miss Harling.

"Miss Bonneville, may I have a word?" She turned and looked blankly at me.

"Dr Watson, or Dr Flegg rather," I explained.

"Of course, hello, Doctor. Forgive my not recognising you but I have not got my spectacles on."

"Spectacles?"

"Yes."

"I did not realise you wore spectacles," said I.

"I'm afraid so," she said with a sigh.

"But you didn't have spectacles on when I came to your house."

"No, I whip them off when visitors arrive; a lady's vanity I'm afraid."

"So there in court, you couldn't see clearly?"

"Oh, I can see well enough. I mean I recognise you now. It was just that I have only seen you once or twice and did not expect to see you here. Of course I would have recognised you had you been expected."

"I see."

"You're the doctor who came to see me at my cottage," said Miss Harling. "I do hope you will call again. We do so like visitors."

I was dumfounded and could only stutter "Yes, of course, I would be delighted."

"Good bye, Dr Flegg."

"Good bye."

I had to tell Holmes about the debacle, of course, loathe that I was to do so, but he could not avoid seeing the public prints. To my surprise he was not insulted, or even cast down.

"Cheer up, Watson, I know I am not wrong in my deductions. As you know, I do not solve all my cases by any means, it is only through your good offices that my triumphs are known at all. The newspapers will soon forget. There will be more important things to write about next week."

"I shall certainly write up this one and tell the world the truth," said I vigorously.

"Ah, Watson, what is truth? As Giambattista Vico stated, *verum ipsum factum*. I cannot be certain when I am right, I can only be sure when I am wrong."

Some weeks later I was astonished to read a paragraph in the newspaper stating Mr Richard Harling was emigrating to Canada and had left on the new White Star liner *Oceanic*, accompanied by his personal assistant Miss Lydia Bonneville. I was even more astonished when a post card arrived for Holmes bearing a picture of the *Oceanic* and franked with the words 'Posted at Sea'.

The message simply read "Spot on, Mr Holmes".

A CHRISTMAS INTERLUDE

I was tempted to call this piece *The Singular Adventure of the Adipose Advocate* but feared that would gull my readers into assuming it was another of the intriguing cases in the files of my friend Mr Sherlock Holmes. This would be deceitful as Holmes has no place at all in the following narrative. A more accurate title would be, as the essays of all our schooldays, *What I did in the Holiday*. More accurate, but far too whimsical for the unusual and tragic circumstance that faced me on a Christmas visit to Great Wishford in the county of Wiltshire. Thus I have merely called it *A Christmas Interlude*.

It was early in December when I received a letter from an old acquaintance from my university days. Charles Marlowe had been a student of law at that time, and we were both members of the same tennis club, as was a young lady by the name of Susan. Marlowe and Susan were married when he graduated and I went to their wedding. As Marlowe had still to find his place in the world, it was considered in those days extraordinarily young to marry so soon after graduation. However, he rapidly established himself as a solicitor, buying himself into a partnership in the town of Salisbury. There the couple remained, a contented pair rearing a small family, though he, lacking in further ambition, was content to minister to the modest legal requirements of the citizens of that town, seemingly suited to a harmless existence of wills, probate, deeds and conveyances. His wife was a prominent figure in local social events and charities.

I had rather lost touch with them when I joined the Indian Army and knew nothing of their lives as related in the above paragraph. But a few years ago, when I first started bringing the exploits of Sherlock Holmes before an indulgent public, Marlowe wrote to me care of my publisher enquiring if I were the same John Watson who played mixed doubles with him all those years ago. As indeed I was, we carried on a fairly regular correspondence thereafter. The intervening years were glossed and we became friends anew, although only by letter.

Thus the missive that came was in no way unusual except that it contained an invitation to spend Christmas with the couple at what they were pleased to call their country cottage. Their children, having reached adulthood, were dispersed in various manners and would not be at home. Marlowe explained it was their custom or tradition to spend

Christmas, not at their house in Salisbury city, but at a country cottage a short distance away – the former home of Susan's parents that she had inherited on their deaths. They had kept this modest dwelling as a retreat from city cares and, as their children grew, they in turn had made use of it. Reading on, it was clear there was an ulterior purpose in this invitation.

When at college, I had a great chum, a hearty fellow called Anthony Amberston always known as 'AA'. We were both regulars in the college rugby team and knocked about in the sporty drinking crowd of the college. He, too, was training to be a medic and when I joined the Indian Army he purchased a practically defunct practice at Clifton, a suburb of the mighty port of Bristol. We completely lost touch and I had had no word of him since those youthful days. Now it transpired that Marlowe, through the years, had kept up his friendship with AA and he too would be a guest. AA had married a lady of Bristol and they had produced a son who was accidentally drowned at the age of twelve. A second child was stillborn and further issue proved impossible. AA had built up his practice and was well regarded professionally, but after some years had settled for a harmless, blameless life reconciling himself to growing old with his dear wife, like Derby and Joan. Six months ago Mrs Amberston had died leaving her husband bereft in a slough of despair. As Marlowe pointed out, all three of us were of an age which was far too young for AA to become a valetudinarian. He had been trying to jockey his friend out of that gloomy frame of mind when every ache and pain presaged a mortal illness and imminent death.

Thus the invitation to me which Marlowe thought would revitalise our old friend. "*You were such pals in the old days sharing great fun. I am sure he would love to meet you again after all these years. It would help him shed some of the cares of the world that have lately beset him.*" It was a noble motive and one with which I was pleased to go along. Besides, a Christmas in the country would be a great treat, for, truth to tell, Christmas has always been a dull time for me since the death of my own dear wife.

A further exchange of letters brought me the arrangements for the party. It was only a cottage so the party would be small and informal. There would be eight of us altogether including our hosts, and there would be a housekeeper/cook and a maid-of-all-work to see to our wants. I was to arrive in time for tea on Christmas Eve. We would have dinner, then transport had been arranged to take us to the Midnight Mass at Salisbury Cathedral. This was another tradition of the Marlowes and promised to be a moving and spiritual event of some grandeur. On Christmas Day we were to rise at leisure after the late night and those who wished could attend the morning service at the local church. After lunch an expedition to Stonehenge was planned to see the astonishing ancient boulders. Should it be inclement and we were confined indoors, we would occupy ourselves pleasantly with games and festive diversions. It was intended to return from Stonehenge in time for tea. Dinner would be the grand main meal of Christmas, after which we would entertain each other and ourselves with music, songs and other amusements. I realised that this would entail my having some kind of party-piece for my contribution. Alas, I have no musical skill. At school, whilst urging the others to 'Sing-up!', the choirmaster pleaded with me to do just the opposite. In adult life I have not ventured to give voice apart from joining in chorus songs while in the audience at the music hall. I thought I might try to learn a couple of card tricks or something.

On Boxing Day after breakfast we were at liberty until 11.30, when the whole lot of us had been invited to the home of a prominent inhabitant who, though not the squire, but living in a grand house acted as though he were. As yet another tradition, this man gave a large buffet-lunch party each year to which practically the entire village was invited. This affair generally broke up about two o'clock when we would return, pack our bags and depart. The arrangements suited me admirably and I returned my acceptance eagerly.

The journey to Salisbury was uneventful, but cold, so it was with some relief and positive glee that I entered the spacious living room of the cottage to be greeted by an enormous roaring log fire in the massive ingle. I warmed my hands then, turning my back on it, warmed my nether regions. Over to one side of the room three earlier arrivals were seated in a row on the sofa, two young ladies with a man between them. The ladies were paying great attention to the man, who was speaking. He then looked up and saw me. "Rhino Watson! You haven't changed a bit. I would have recognised you anywhere!" Leaping up he came to greet me with a firm handshake, pumping my hand up and down in both of his hands.

"I have not heard that nickname for over twenty years," I said, "Not since I ceased playing rugger." I was always known by my team-mates for my strength and bulk, rather than speed and deft footwork. "How are you, AA?"

"Very well, Watson, old chap, very well. I had a rough time in the spring. I lost my wife, but time heals, you know."

I assured him I knew all about his predicament, I too suffering anguish in exactly the same way and for the same reason.

"I heard you had chosen a career in the army," said AA.

"A very brief career, brought to a sudden halt by a bullet from a

Jezail rifle," I replied. As we caught up briefly with the news of twenty years I studied my old companion, my practiced eye telling me that there was, indeed, little amiss with him. He was far slimmer than in his youth, but his frame was by no means frail, and, although his face was lined perhaps a little more than would be expected in a man of his years, the greatest sign of his troubles was that he had lost almost all of his hair which, in his youth, had been a mass of tumbling curls that for some reason used to set the girls in a whirl. Now his head was crowned with a thin layer of grey, slightly wavy hair.

"But I am being rude, Watson!" AA turned to the seated ladies. "I do apologise, but I have not seen this man for over twenty years."

"Yes, we gathered that," giggled one of them.

I was introduced to the Misses Pembury; the elder was Phoebe, whom I judged about twenty-five, with a pleasant enough sympathetic face, but no great beauty. The younger sister Rhoda was conventionally pretty, with a pert little nose.

"Why do you call Mr Amberston AA?" asked Miss Pembury.

"His initials, Anthony Amberston," I explained.

"I don't recall Sir Anthony Absolute having that nickname," said Miss Rhoda to her sister, and the two giggled.

I had no idea what she was talking about, and over the course of the visit there were many occasions when these two sisters exchanged cryptic remarks that usually led to silly tittering.

Our host Marlowe entered, apologising for his brief greeting on my arrival. "I was summoned to the kitchen to tussle with the goose. I see you have all made yourselves known to each other. Well done! We do not stand on ceremony here, you know. The drinks are all on the sideboard there and you must help yourselves and each other. Clara will be with us shortly, she is making last minute preparations to the table. We must not go into the dining room until dinner time. We will take tea in here as soon as Mr and Mrs Fuller arrive. They only live in Salisbury; typical for the nearest guests to arrive the last, eh?"

The Fullers arrived and I was astonished by the appearance of Mr Fuller. He was a small, stout man, but his girth was quite prodigious in regard to his height. When we were all introduced to each other he winked at the Pembury sisters and said: "Do you know what my clerks call me behind my back? Mr Five-by-five!" then laughed uproariously. Seeing the sisters looking baffled, he explained: "They say I am five feet tall and five feet in circumference!" and roared with laughter again, the sisters joining in with their irritating giggles.

I will not bore my readers by relating the details of this country vacation, suffice it to say that the planned itinerary was followed.

Christmas Eve dinner revealed the splendid dining room with heavily beamed ceiling and linen-fold panelling on the walls. Mrs Marlowe had followed the delightful tradition imported to this country by Prince Albert and there was a decorated fir tree, not only in the dining room, but another one in the living room. To add a festive trim to the room she had festooned it using holly, mistletoe and ivy and a twisting vine with fruit which she told me was a hopbine. The cottage may have been small but it was no hovel. Marlowe said his wife's family had improved it over the years, preferring to do that rather than move elsewhere. Gas was not available in the village, so for lighting we were dependent on oil lamps and candles but, due to generous quantities of both, the table with its silver and glassware sparkled.

The excursion to Salisbury Cathedral was something I shall remember for the rest of my life. To hear the voices of the choir soaring upwards into that mighty void was as if the angels themselves were singing. The spire, man's earthly aspiration to reach heaven, is a wonder to behold and those who only know it from the famous painting by Constable have no conception of its true majesty. Even the journey homeward was a delight, with a full moon illuminating a sparkling frost as we jogged through the countryside.

The following morning's service in the village church was totally different; modest, homely and sincere as such things are when carried out with true devotion and a lack of pomp. The trip to Stonehenge was a great success, with Fuller holding forth about Merlin, Druids and pagan rituals, much to the delight of the ladies in the party. Amberston wandered off and found himself in a bog, coming back looking rueful, with mud enveloping his boots.

At dinner on Christmas night Mrs Marlowe had provided snap-crackers which when pulled disgorged a small gift and a piece of paper with a riddle. We all had to read out our own riddle. I cannot remember the others, but mine was "Why is the sun like a coin of the realm?" Miss Rhoda suggested the answer was that they were both round and shiny, but the correct answer was "Because they are both a far-thing." After dinner, Miss Pembury played the piano and then accompanied Miss Rhoda who sang some pretty little songs. Fuller told several so-called humorous stories, but desisted when Mrs Fuller stopped him part way through one that she claimed "Was not suitable for this occasion." Amberston surprised me by playing and singing at the keyboard, as I had no idea he possessed such talents. His repertoire comprised two or three songs that appeared to be of a sentimental or mournful nature but ended with a satirical humorous twist.

As I feared, I was called upon to do something, so I produced the pack of cards I had brought with me. I had found the trick in a magazine and it involved having the pack arranged in a special order in advance. This I had prepared before leaving London, and now had in my pocket. According to the article I was to "shuffle the cards at the start using your favourite false shuffle." Well I did not know any false shuffles, much less possessing a favourite one, so I had decided to eschew that part. The idea was that some person cuts the cards, looks at the card they have cut to and replaces it in the same place. The conjuror (that was me) then picks up the pack and gives it a shuffle, using his favourite false shuffle again so the order of the pack is not disturbed. Even I could see this was essential at this stage in the trick, so I had attempted to substitute the false shuffle with a few cuts that would look as though the cards were being mixed, but retained the order. The point of the trick was the person named their card and, dealing one card for each letter, spelled out the name of the card. Having done that, the next card was turned over and that was the chosen card. Mrs Fuller was the chooser and had to spell Queen of Diamonds. Alas, when the card was turned over it was the four of spades. Clearly something had gone wrong with my cutting procedure and I had destroyed the order, as when I searched the through the pack, the Queen was in a completely different place. However, I sought to redeem myself by another card trick, or rather a puzzle where the aces, twos, threes and fours have to be arranged in four rows and four files with no same numbers or suits in any one row or file. This kept the party amused for some time as each person attempted to perform the feat singly, then combined forces. Having puzzled for some time, I was then challenged to show the solution. I had copied this on to a piece of card and intended to glance at it secretly while pretending to do it from memory. However, I could not find the card in any of my pockets and had to try and do it from recollection. I failed and was given one of those vulgar noises known as a raspberry by Fuller. The rest of the company was also displeased so I went to bed – my reputation as a conjuror thoroughly destroyed.

I have said the cottage was small. Downstairs was a large living room and a dining room of adequate size. There was a kitchen and staff room somewhere behind, but I am not clear about those. The staircase rose in a straight line and was only a yard wide. At the top was a very small landing, hardly wider than the stairs, with five matching doors, two on the left, two opposite on the right and one immediately in front. These were the bedrooms. The first one on the left was occupied by Mr & Mrs Fuller, the adjacent one by Mr & Mrs Marlowe. On the right the first one, opposite the Fullers, was taken by the two Miss Pemburys, and the remaining one had to be shared by Amberston and myself. There was one bed in there, but a truckle bed had been installed for the occasion. After some polite banter, when each urged the other to take the proper bed, we decided to toss for it. Amberston won so he had it the first night, and we agreed to swop for the second one.

The fifth door that faced the stairs opened to reveal a WC. This had been installed at some recent time utilising the end of the landing corridor. As the space was limited by the two bedroom doors adjacent, the area in the WC was very cramped and the door had been made to open outwards. Of course, this was not a true WC, but a facility for use in the night, a servant tipping water into it in the morning to flush any night soil down a pipe that ran to the outside. A modern version of the garderobe of old, and much more satisfactory than a chamber-pot in each room. All the doors upstairs were exactly alike – made of planks in the country fashion, with metal catches in place of knobs or handles.

I have dwelt at some length on the above description as the reader will find it a necessary adjunct when I relate my investigations.

Just as we were going to bed on Christmas night Amberston remembered his filthy boots and asked Marlowe about the possibility of getting them cleaned.

"Put them outside your door, old chap, and in the morning when Sally brings your hot water she'll take them away and clean them for you. You can do the same, Watson," said Marlowe. I declined as I had no wish to burden the maid who had enough to do in this old-fashioned household with lighting fires and oil lamps, carrying heated water upstairs and maintaining burning candles.

As I lay in bed that second night, Amberston taking his turn on the truckle bed, I realised that Marlowe had not been completely frank with me about the need to jolly Amberston along. He seemed to be in a remarkable good shape compared to what I had expected, and it had become clear to me that the Marlowes were trying to do a bit of match-making. The point of all this was to introduce Amberston to the Pembury sisters, and the Marlowes made this rather obvious by persistently placing him between the sisters, even when in the carriage to Stonehenge and Salisbury, as well as the seating plan of the table. As if reading my mind Amberston spoke in the darkness. "Those sisters are rather vacuous creatures, don't you think?"

"They are both very young," I replied.

"You will have gathered Marlowe is trying to palm one of them off on me."

"It has been rather obvious, old man."

"Why he thinks I would be interested in somebody young enough to be my daughter I cannot imagine."

"I think you exaggerate there, the elder must be all of twenty-five."

"Perhaps so. That is still sixteen years difference. But more than that both their characters are ones of mindless frivolity. Neither is suited to be a doctor's wife in Clifton."

"They are probably trying to enter the spirit of Christmas and jolly you along."

Amberston laughed in the darkness. "Jolly me along! Is that why you're here, too? Marlowe is a good soul and a dear friend."

"He was most concerned about you, AA. He told me you were devastated when your wife died."

"Not so. I was relieved when she died. That was when my burden was lifted. He's right that I was in despair and despondency. You see, I loved my wife dearly, but she was struck with tuberculosis and I her husband, a doctor, could do nothing to save her. She was a long time suffering, Watson. You're a doctor, you know what these pernicious wasting diseases are like. All one can do is watch and wait and try and ease the patient's suffering in some way."

"It can be seen as a blessed relief when your loved one slips away," I murmured.

"There's more to it, Watson, if I may confide in you. My receptionist is a lady of mature years, a sensible, good-looking woman and some time ago, to put it bluntly, we fell in love with each other. I, a married man with a dying wife, was in an awful position. No man of honour could contemplate betraying his dying wife so I kept my natural feelings in check. Our positions remained strictly professional, but an understanding had arisen that things would change when I was a free man. You can imagine the anguish I was in, and, yes, that was when Marlowe saw the change in me. But, eventually, my wife died and the barrier was lifted. I am still in mourning. We have agreed to wait a full year before announcing our engagement. There must be no hint of scandal, Watson. I cannot allow the thought that I should have conducted an *affaire* whilst my wife lay dying. Because I did not. So, old man, that is the position. I was in gloom and despair but now I am a happy man gradually travelling slowly uphill into the sun. I hope you understand."

"Of course. Your confidence is safe with me."

"Good night."

"Good night, AA."

As I lay there I thought of the life my friend had suffered, losing two children, one stillborn, one by drowning, losing a beloved wife, and tortured by his feelings for another woman. Then I thought of my life since we had parted at college. Joined the Indian army, shot and invalided out with a miserable pension. Struggled to build up a decent practice.

Married to the most wonderful wife a man could hope for, and then losing her. But, chiefly, to have the immense good fortune to meet Mr Sherlock Holmes and share rooms with the cleverest and wisest man I have ever known. It is a blessing that when we are young we have no idea how our lives will unfold. With these thoughts I drifted off to sleep.

I was suddenly aroused by a thumping on the door and a voice crying "Amberston! Watson! Wake up!" I lurched out of bed and, having saved space in my packing by not bringing a dressing gown, grabbed my overcoat to pull over my nightgown. I was aware of Amberston bestirring behind me. When I opened the door it was to reveal the ghastly pale face of Marlowe.

"Come quickly, something awful has happened. Fuller is dead." He gestured down the stairs.

"What is it?" demanded Amberston, appearing at my shoulder.

The three of us were now in very close proximity at the top of the stairs when the door to the Pembury sisters' room opened and Phoebe Pembury peered out. "What's the matter?" she demanded.

"Stay in your room and close the door," ordered Amberston peremptorily. The woman obeyed, instantly shooting out of sight.

"Come," said Marlowe, leading the way downstairs. At the bottom was a crumpled heap. Fuller was lying there in his night attire. Standing at a short distance were the two servants looking terrified. I knelt alongside the body to examine it.

"Not much point checking pulses and so on, Watson. The man's broken his neck," said Amberston. I stood up. It was true. Fuller's head was in a position that clearly indicated the poor fellow had broken his neck.

"He must have fallen down the stairs," said Amberston.

"Some hours ago," said I. "His body is quite cold."

"Probably arose in the night to use the urinal, lost his footing on returning to his room, and tumbled down the stairs," said Amberston.

"Good God! Would that have been sufficient to kill him?" asked Marlowe.

"The stairs are wooden, but your ground floor is comprised of flagstones. He had only to fall awkwardly in some strange position, his head hitting the ground. He was a heavy man," said Amberston. "Don't you agree, Watson?"

"Yes, yes. Surprisingly easily done."

"What should we do now?" asked Marlowe helplessly.

"Send for your local medic," replied Amberston.

"Is that necessary? With two doctors on the premises?"

"I don't carry my pad of blank death certificates around with me on social occasions, do you, Watson?" replied Amberston.

"No, no, of course not," said I. "But I think there is more to this than an accident." I had spotted some blood seeping from under the body. "Help me roll him over." We placed Fuller on his back, and there on the front of his nightgown was a patch of blood, and a rent in the centre. On lifting up his gown I discovered near his navel a bloody wound. The abdomen had been punctured.

"This man has been stabbed with a knife," I declared.

"A knife?" echoed Marlowe incredulously.

"Were all the doors locked last night?" I demanded.

"Of course they were. I suppose they still are."

I went to look. The front door was securely fastened, but the kitchen door was unlocked. The two servants had followed me into their domain.

"This door is not locked," said I.

"No, sir. It was locked as usual last night. I saw to it myself, and I opened it myself this morning not half an hour ago," said the house-keeper.

"I see."

"We were both up betimes heating the water to take up to the bedrooms. Sally was carrying the first jug when she found Mr Fuller at the foot of the stairs."

"It really frightened me, that heap of white in the gloom. I hurried back to Mrs Dean to tell her," said the maid.

"I see. Then what did you do?"

Mrs Dean continued, "I went to look and felt Mr Fuller's hand. It was icy cold and I could not detect a pulse. I thought he must be dead and said Mr Marlowe must be told. I had to step over Mr Fuller to climb the stairs. I roused Mr Marlowe and he came down and took command. I thought we were lucky to have two doctors in the house, sir."

"I'm afraid a hundred doctors would prove useless, Mrs Dean. We cannot raise the dead."

"No, sir," said she, taking up the corner of her apron and wiping a tear from her eye.

I went round checking the windows, finding them all secure. There was no likelihood of a person having entered during the night.

While I was conducting my investigations, Marlowe and Amberston were manhandling the body to lay it on the dining room table, all traces of last night's feast having been swept away by the two efficient servants when we moved into the living room to entertain ourselves. I may have proved an inept conjuror but I had assisted Sherlock Holmes long enough to have picked up a trick or two. Here was a chance to redeem myself.

The situation now was as follows – Mrs Marlowe was in the Fullers' bedroom comforting Mrs Fuller. Marlowe and Amberston were coping with the body, the maid Sally had been dispatched to summon the local doctor, Mrs Dean was in the kitchen making tea for everybody, and the Pembury sisters were still closeted in their room.

One thing was clear to me: if nobody had entered the house from outside, Fuller must have been stabbed by a person already in the house. Who would want to murder Mr Fuller? He seemed a gregarious and likable man and he was amongst friends. There was no doubt that he had met his end by falling down the stairs, but somebody had stabbed him at the top which had caused him topple. That person must have meant him to die. You do not stab a man in the stomach unless you intend him harm. I proposed to Marlowe we should all gather in the living room after getting dressed. As we returned to our rooms, Miss Pembury peeped cautiously out and asked if they could come out now.

We gathered in the living room where Mrs Dean served tea.

"This is a grave situation," I said. "A murder has been committed in this house." I was interrupted by a gasp and a cry respectively from the Misses Pembury. Of course they had no idea of what had transpired. "In the night Mr Fuller arose from his bed, possibly hearing a noise or even been deliberately lured from his bed, and whilst at the top of the stairs he was stabbed. As a result he tumbled down the stairs to the floor below where his neck was broken." Mrs Fuller let out a series of huge sobs. "I have ascertained by thorough examination that nobody could have entered via doors or windows in the night. That points to only one thing. Mr Fuller was stabbed by a person already in the house."

"Preposterous!" said Marlowe. "Who would do such a thing? We are all friends here!"

"So it would appear. But I need not remind you, I am sure, that no one expected King Duncan to be murdered by his hosts Lord and Lady Macbeth."

"Are you suggesting I am a man who would kill one of his dearest friends? Are you out of your mind, Watson?" demanded Marlowe.

"No. But you may not be aware that most murders are committed by people who are the nearest and dearest of the victim," I explained patiently.

Amberston laughed. "Well seeing how Mrs Fuller slept through the whole thing, and it was difficult to rouse her this morning to tell her the tragic news, I think you can dismiss her from your suspects, Watson."

Having myself given her a sleeping draught before going to bed, I had to admit that was unlikely. She said she had slept badly on Christmas Eve and never could sleep in a strange bed, so I had obliged her by offering the remedy. I very often carry with me a basic medical kit for emergencies.

"The man fell down the stairs in the night. A tragic accident. I really don't know why you are persisting in this amateur detective pose, Watson," said Amberston.

I have to confess this statement annoyed me, but realised that these people could not know of the many cases I have followed at the elbow of my friend Mr Sherlock Holmes. Indeed, were they likely to have even heard of that man of prodigious ability? I bit my tongue and continued, "I agree it seems improbable that a person in this room should have stabbed our friend but, when you have eliminated the impossible, whatever remains, no matter how improbable, must be the truth."

"So you claim one of us stabbed Fuller and hurled him down the stairs?" asked Amberston.

"That is the only conclusion," I asserted.

"You are one of us," said Marlowe.

"Or supposed to be," added Mrs Marlowe frostily.

Then Amberston spoke up, "Look at your list of suspects, Watson. Mrs Fuller can be eliminated – she was asleep throughout and cannot possibly have wished her husband dead." This provoked a further bout of loud wailing from Mrs Fuller. "Mr & Mrs Marlowe are the Fullers' dearest friends and are unlikely to want to kill either of them. Should they wish to do away with Mr Fuller they would hardly be likely to do so when inviting him for Christmas with other guests. Marlowe could have pushed him under a train or thrown him in the river anytime when the two of them were alone. The Misses Pembury had never met the man before and could have no possible motive for wishing him dead. No matter how tedious or offensive his jokes, they would part this afternoon and never see him again. That leaves the two servants, you and me, Watson, and I certainly did not do such a thing."

Amberston left the sentence hanging in the air and everybody looked at me in the ensuing silence. The investigation was not following the lines I had intended.

Amberston laughed again. This was, in itself, suspicious. A man had died in mysterious circumstances and he kept laughing. For a doctor it was particularly offensive.

"Come, Watson, this has gone on long enough. Follow me. You too, Marlowe."

Leaving the group of wailing women, we three men went into the dining room. The rotund body of Fuller was clearly discernible under the sheet that now covered him. Amberston raised the sheet.

"Have a closer look at the stab wound, Watson," commanded Amberston. "That man's hypodermis has layers of subcutaneous fat. One would need a long knife to even reach his vital organs."

I now saw the wound – having been swabbed by Amberston – was not very deep and, indeed, looked superficial. I was at fault for jumping to conclusions and not examining the injury more closely. I was compelled to agree that it was a trivial affair unlikely to have caused much bodily damage or even pain.

"But how and where did it arise?" said I, thoroughly baffled.

"Perhaps as he fell his gown caught on something on the stairs on the way down? A protruding nail, maybe?" suggested Marlowe.

"That is very likely!" I cried. "Let us look."

We three examined the stairs thoroughly, but there seemed to be nothing protruding that might have torn a nightgown and scratched the skin.

We found ourselves at the top of the stairs, again in close proximity because of the restricted space. Amberston spoke: "Look at the door of the urinal." He opened it. The latch on the inside of the door was, of course, protruding. It was made of flat metal and had been filed to make the edge very thin. It was obvious that had been done to make it fit the bracket on the door jamb, as there was a slight mismatch of levels. Amberston continued: "That edge is like a knife."

"My God!" said Marlowe in disbelief. "I, myself, ordered that doing because the door would not close properly. My God, I am responsible for the death of my friend! How terrible!" he moaned.

"Nonsense! It was falling down the stairs that killed him, not that scratch," snapped Amberston. "Normally it would not matter because the door opened sufficiently wide, but Fuller, being so corpulent, could not get through without brushing his belly against the sharp edge."

"I cannot agree with you there, Amberston," I said. "Look how wide the door opens. There is ample room even for a man of Fuller's girth. There would be no need for him to squeeze through."

"That's right, Watson," said Marlowe eagerly, snatching on the hope he was absolved from blame. "There is ample room for entry and exit."

"Unless something prevented the door from opening to its full width," I said.

"But there is nothing," said Amberston, swinging the door. "There is no carpet or anything to foul it."

"No, not now, but last night you placed your boots outside our door and they would have prevented the WC door from opening to its full extent," said I.

"Where are your boots, Amberston?" asked Marlowe.

"I put them back in the room when we returned to get dressed."

"Fish them out," demanded Marlowe.

The boots were placed in position. Marlowe opened the door. The boots prevented the door reaching its full extent.

"Well, I'm damned!" said Marlowe.

"An unfortunate series of coincidences, don't you agree, gentlemen?" said Amberston.

"Indeed," said I. "A catch that was dangerously sharp from work that should never have been done, boots placed in a position where they caused an accident that might have been anticipated in such cramped conditions, and an overweight man who lost his balance at the top of a flight of stairs."

"The poor chap had taken too much drink. He was clearly unsteady when climbing the stairs to bed," said Marlowe.

"It must be difficult maintaining his balance at the best of times with such excess weight," said Amberston.

"Yes, indeed," agreed Marlowe.

"Tragic," said Amberston, shaking his head, staring at the ground.

"An unfortunate accident," said Marlowe, "with no one to blame."

"When the local medic comes it will be clear that death was caused by a fall in the dark. It is not unlikely that superficial scratches may be found on the body after such a tumble," said Amberston. "As a medical man, don't you agree, Rhino, old man,?"

"Indubitably, AA," I agreed. We all shook hands and returned to the ladies.

THE THREE WISE MONKEYS

It was late afternoon and Mr Sherlock Holmes and I were toasting ourselves before a blazing fire in our rooms at 221b Baker Street. Mrs Hudson had recently delivered a plate of hot crumpets and a pot of tea to us, and we were desultorily consuming the same when she returned within minutes bearing a telegram that had just arrived.

"Ah, perhaps this will be something to stir excitement into this rather chill and gloomy afternoon," suggested Holmes, tearing open the envelope. The pause was as short as the message which he handed to me, saying: "How extraordinary!"

Very urgent come at once Diogenes Club Mycroft were the words I read. "What can it mean?" I asked.

"Let us go and find out, Watson!" replied Holmes rising. "You can be sure that if brother Mycroft states a matter is urgent then he surely means it. What time is it?"

"Just gone half-past five."

"Mycroft's habits are as fixed as the pole star. He arrives at the Diogenes club at a quarter to five and leaves at twenty minutes to eight. As it is only forty-five minutes ago we may be sure that on his arrival at the club he found something very amiss. Come, Watson!"

It was the time of day when twilight falls and the streets of London are at their busiest with home-going workers, business men and shoppers. Thus it was far quicker to walk the short distance to Pall Mall, via Bond Street, than go through the difficulty of procuring a cab, which in any case would have made very slow progress at that stage of the day. So we strode along as a matter of urgency, and gained the entrance to the club to find the door closed. A handwritten notice pinned to it bore the message: CLUB CLOSED TONIGHT, OPEN TOMORROW AS USUAL. Half a dozen men were standing aimlessly about the entrance like lost souls as Holmes and I pushed through to rap on the door. "It's closed," said the plaintive voice of one of the men. "They won't open the door," proclaimed another in hurt tones. But the door did open a chink and, on Holmes uttering our names, opened wider to allow us passage through, closing immediately behind us.

Inside, the formidable presence of the corpulent Mycroft Holmes loomed large. Although I had previously met Mycroft and, indeed, been with Holmes on the premises before, I remained in awe of my friend's elder brother. Living a circumscribed life that revolved round the three points of his Whitehall office, his rooms in Pall Mall and the Diogenes Club opposite, Mycroft was a figure of great influence in the government and had the ear of many ministers who would not make any decision without consulting Mycroft Holmes.

Two more figures also occupied space in the small entrance lobby. "Thank God, you've arrived, Sherlock," said Mycroft Holmes, "I was beginning to fear you were out of town. I really cannot delay too long before sending for the police, but I wanted you to see the scene of the crime before the official authorities became involved." He turned to the two men with him. "You two wait here, please, we will need to speak to you shortly. Good evening, Dr Watson, forgive my not greeting you before, I confess I am somewhat overwrought. Come through, both of you."

Mycroft led us forward into the luxurious club room. The Diogenes Club is unique in that it is a club comprised of anti-social men. The members are forbidden by the rules of the club from talking to fellow members, with three transgressions leading to permanent dismissal. The only sound permitted to be uttered will be an order to the waiter, and even these are rare as each chair is equipped with its note pad and pencil. Such I had learned from Holmes on a previous visit when we were confined to the Strangers' Room, the only place where visitors are allowed to tread, and talk permitted. To be allowed into the hallowed club room itself was a privilege that could only be granted through some tremendous peculiar circumstance.

Now, entering the room, I realised how extraordinary it was. It was furnished with deep pile carpets and large comfortable wing chairs, but each chair, reposing in its own niche, was arranged so that it ignored its immediate neighbours. Indeed some were placed outrageously, with the chair back towards the room so that the occupant faced the wall. Alongside each chair at elbow height was a small table with an ashtray and a notepad and pencil.

All this I took in with a sweep of the eyes, the immediate centre of focus being a huddled figure sprawled on the carpet in front of one of the chairs as though he had just toppled out of it. However, in his hand was a gun, and in his temple a bloody gaping wound. Holmes dropped to his knees and produced his lens. Mycroft stood looking down and I took the opportunity to look around. The man was clearly dead having shot himself in the head, but why he should choose to do it in that place at that time was beyond my comprehension. There was nothing I could do to either explain or assist.

Apart from ourselves and the dead man, there were three members only, seated in the room. They were widely spaced out, one with his back to the room reading a newspaper and completely oblivious to anything taking place, another gentleman eating a sandwich and drinking from a cup and taking no interest, whilst the third was waving a piece of paper excitedly and pointing in a jabbing motion at the body on the floor. As Mycroft was ignoring this man, I did not think it behove me to attend to him.

Holmes stood up. "It is not a suicide," he said.

"I know that, Sherlock," snorted Mycroft, "otherwise I would not have summoned you."

"Perhaps you could explain how it happened, Mycroft?" asked Holmes.

"Not really. I arrived at my usual time to be greeted by Billings the porter and Arthur our waiter – those are the chaps in the foyer as you came in – who told me one of the members had shot himself. I immediately came to look and found things just as you see them now."

"You mean those three men were seated as they are now?"

"Yes, I asked them not to disturb themselves until you arrived."

"I see. Though were they present when the man was shot?"

"Indeed two of them were," replied Mycroft.

"Then I do not see the difficulty."

"Then let me introduce you to each of them. Firstly, Mr Frank Dawlish, the gentleman taking a snack. Customarily he would be in the dining room, but on my insistence he has remained here, sustained by a sandwich sent in by Chef." We walked over to Dawlish who was seated near the door by which we had entered.

"Mr Dawlish, I have two men with me, may I present Mr Sherlock Holmes who is my brother and a noted detective, and his colleague Dr Watson. Gentlemen, Mr Frank Dawlish."

"Very pleased to meet you." Dawlish held out his hand which Holmes took, saying: "Sherlock Holmes at your service."

"Ah, a fine sensitive hand, long, tapering fingers. The hand of a musician, perhaps?" asked Dawlish.

"An amateur of the violin only," replied Holmes.

"John Watson, late of the Indian Army," said I, shaking hands.

"Ah, an army man."

"No longer, I'm afraid. I was wounded in Afghanistan and invalided out. I am a doctor but could not prevail against a Jezail bullet."

"War is a beastly business, but you are fit and well now?" asked Dawlish.

"Apart from the twinges when the weather is damp, I am grateful to be in perfect health."

"Would my wound had been so trivial, Doctor. You can still see the world around you which is something I have not been able to do for many years."

"You are aware of the death of one of your fellow members whose body lies on the floor only a few feet away?" asked Holmes.

"Oh, yes. I am conversant with what has happened. I was just entering the club when I stumbled and fell. Fortunately Billings was on hand and he summoned Arthur and between them they helped me up and into the club. While they were doing that I heard a loud bang. I have heard many a gun explode in my time and knew at once it was a pistol shot. When we got into the room Billings and Arthur sat me down while they found out what had happened. That's why they plonked me here in the nearest chair. Not my chair at all. Then I wanted to dine but they would not let me go to the dining room, so I've had to put up with Chef's cold beef sandwich. Not the same thing at all. But it's an emergency, so I know we will be all upset until the police have been."

"So you were not in the room when the shot was fired?" asked Holmes.

"No. As I have said, I was with Billings and Arthur in the lobby."

"Well, in that case, I thank you for your reply, but doubt if I need trouble you any more, Mr Dawlish," said Holmes.

"One wonders what led the poor chap to do himself in. Probably lost a fortune on the Exchange," surmised Dawlish.

"Thank you, Mr Dawlish. We are now leaving you to talk to another member at the other side of the room," said Mycroft. We three went over to the man reading the paper who was sitting facing the wall. Mycroft gently placed a hand on his shoulder and the man immediately turned to gaze up at him as he spoke to us. "This gentleman is Mr Repton-Davis."

"Ah, Mr Holmes, have you brought news of the police?" he said, looking from Mycroft, to Holmes and myself. Mycroft grabbed the note-pad from the table and hastily scribbled *Sherlock Holmes – Detective* and handed it to the seated man who rose as Mycroft indicated his brother. Shaking hands with Holmes, he said "An honour to meet you, sir. I am an avid follower of your work as relayed by Dr Watson, whom I presume is your friend here?" Turning to me, he shook my hand as I assented by nodding my head.

"I have the misfortune to be stone deaf so I regret I cannot hear a word you say. However, my brain and speech are in no way impaired so I can converse readily, but regrettably the conversation from the other party is constrained by having to be in written form. I am told that I should be able to lip-read but, alas, it is an art I have never mastered.

Perhaps if I had been born deaf I may have acquired the knack as a boy. I was known for my keen hearing until it was shattered by an explosion when I was serving my country. So if you have questions regarding this poor fellow's suicide, pray write them down and I will do my best to satisfy you." During this speech we had manoeuvred ourselves so that we peered down on to the dead figure.

"What is the dead man's name, Mycroft?" asked Holmes.

"Coverdale. Malcolm Coverdale."

"Do you know anything about him?"

"Not really. That is the point of the Diogenes Club. The members ignore each other. It is a club for unclubable men. As I function as secretary, treasurer and undertake the administration, I know a little about all of them, but usually nothing more than name and address. There is an application form for each member on my file, placed there when they joined. Again, we are unlike other clubs where new members are proposed and seconded by existing members. Here an individual applies himself and usually he is unknown to the existing members."

"So you are saying that no member knows another member?" asked Holmes.

"That is so whilst on club premises. Of course in the world outside they may be well acquainted, perhaps even do business together, though that is unlikely as on the whole we attract shy or misanthropic individuals."

Holmes lowered his voice. "And, it would appear, more than the average number of physically afflicted."

"True. We have the advantage of being a refuge for such men seeking the amenities of a club but who would be at a disadvantage in a more conventional one."

Holmes took up the pad, writing *Did you see Coverdale do the deed?* before handing it to Repton-Davis who had been standing patiently during the brother's conversation.

"I take it Coverdale is the dead chap's name? I knew him by sight, of course, that's the only way we know each other here. I think only Arthur and Billings know all our names. Oh, and presumably you too, Mr Holmes, since you run the place. But to answer your question Mr Sherlock Holmes: no, I came in this evening, seated myself in my usual chair, which as you will note faces away from the rest of the room. Arthur brought me a whisky and soda and the evening newspaper and I read that. Of course I can hear nothing – not even the bang of a gun – so I was not aware that a man had killed himself behind my back. The first thing I knew was when your brother came to me and, by gesture, encouraged me to rise and turn round, whereupon I saw the body on the floor exactly as you see it now."

"Thank you," said Holmes smiling and nodding. "Just one more of your eccentric members was present, Mycroft. The gentleman who has for the last ten minutes waved a piece of paper and excitedly pointed at the dead man. Shall we speak to him now?"

"Mr Edward Connor. I'm afraid that whilst you can speak to him, he is unable to speak to you. He is dumb."

"Really, Mycroft, your members are like the three wise monkeys," said Holmes with a sigh. We approached Mr Connor who held out his paper which had the words *Shot himself* scrawled upon it.

"Mr Connor, this is Sherlock Holmes the famous detective who happens to be my brother. This is Dr Watson his colleague. I have asked them to investigate this affair. They will wish to ask you some questions," explained Mycroft.

"Good evening, Mr Connor," said Holmes. "May I sit down?" Holmes perched on the foot-stool that was set before Mr Connor's chair. "I understand you are unable to speak but I will try and phrase my questions so that you may nod for 'yes' and shake for 'no'. If that does not suffice please write down anything further. We have infinite patience. Were you sitting in this chair facing the direction you are now?" Connor nodded. "Did you see Mr Coverdale clearly?" Another nod. "Did he take out the pistol secretly, in a surreptitious manner?" Connor shook his head. "He did it quite openly?" Connor nodded vehemently. "Did he put the gun to his temple?" Another nod. "Did he stand?" Connor hesitated as if he did not understand the question, then nodded. "He stood up and pulled the trigger?" Another vehement nod. "One bang and then he fell to the floor?" Another nod. "Or did he put the trigger to his head whilst seated?" Again Connor hesitated before shaking his head vigorously. "Thank you, that all seems perfectly clear, Mr Connor. I may need to speak to you again, but the three of us must now confer and arrange for the body to be taken away."

Holmes had a final look round the room, crouching from time to time as he examined the floor around the chairs, then suggested to Mycroft that we repaired to the Strangers' Room. Once there, Mycroft asked "What do you think, Sherlock?"

"Patently Mr Connor is lying. We know Coverdale did not shoot himself – "

"Just a moment, Holmes," said I. "How do you know that?"

Holmes gave a theatrical sigh and said "Will you explain, Mycroft, or shall I?"

"The dead man was left-handed," said Mycroft.

"So?" asked I, when no further explanation was offered.

"The gun was under the man's right hand. The wound was in his right temple," said Sherlock Holmes.

"He could have used his right hand even if he were left-handed. Anyway, how do you know he was left-handed?" I demanded.

"Did you not see his table was placed at the left of his chair? All the others are placed on the right. Our members arrange things to their special preferences," said Mycroft.

"If you examine Coverdale's hands you will see that the left is clearly better developed than the right, and on the inner edge of the middle finger is a callus consistent with holding a pen in that position. No doubt Coverdale did a great deal of writing through the years," said Sherlock Holmes.

"I still don't see why he could not have used his right hand even though he was normally left-handed. Perhaps his left hand was damaged in some way so that he could not use it? Perhaps that is why he committed suicide, because he was unable to write with his left hand any more," I proffered.

"Watson, you are trying to build up a theory on foundations of sand," said Holmes. "Even ignoring the possibility that he did in fact use his weaker hand – very unlikely for such a major operation as putting a gun to your head and blowing your brains out – even ignoring that, there is other evidence."

"The trajectory of the bullet shows that the barrel was pointing downwards," said Mycroft.

"Quite so. Normally when you place a pistol to your temple, on whichever side, the barrel will be pointing upwards, or at most level, because it is impossible to raise the elbow high enough and the only way would be to bend the wrist downwards, a weak position that makes it extremely awkward to pull the trigger. No, Watson, this shot was fired from a standing man alongside the sitting one."

"But Mr Connor insisted he saw Coverdale draw a pistol and shoot himself."

"The man is lying," said Holmes calmly.

"It would seem so," agreed Mycroft.

"Did you not note the hesitation with which he answered my question as to whether Coverdale was sitting or standing? If he had seen him, as he claimed, he would have answered instantly as he did my other questions. He hesitated because he did not know whether it was better to claim he shot himself while seated or standing. Of course the murderer then pushed the gun under his victim's hand to make it appear he had shot himself."

"You are both implying that Mr Connor shot Mr Coverdale," said I.

"Not necessarily, but that would seem to be the logical explanation for his obvious lie," said Holmes.

"He did seem very insistent from the start. Ever since we entered the room he was waving his paper and pointing. And, if Mr Repton-Davis had his back to it all, he wouldn't know anything different anyway," I agreed.

"How many men were in the building when the shot was fired? Two in the room with the victim, three in the lobby – Dawlish, Arthur the waiter and Billings – anyone else, Mycroft?"

"Only Chef in the kitchen," he replied.

"Ah, let us examine that worthy man now. Lead the way, Mycroft."

We made our way to the kitchen via the dining room which was arranged as bizarrely as the lounge. All the tables were small, set for one person only, and arranged so that the diner would face the wall with his back to the room. Anti-social indeed!

The Chef was a young man, I judged no more than thirty, and was not a foreigner as many London chefs are; he seemed a breezy, cheerful sort of fellow rather than the highly strung *prima donnas* one hears about at the top restaurants.

"You will be able to leave early tonight, Chef. There will be no diners," said Mycroft.

"Billings told me about poor Mr Coverdale. I realised the club would have to close," said Chef.

"Did you hear the sound of the pistol shot, Chef?" asked Holmes.

"No, sir, not a thing. I was firing up my ovens and the noise from the gas takes all my attention. When first lit, I get a lot of popping and if I don't woo it along it blows out and I have to start again."

"So when were you told of the shooting?"

"As soon as it had happened. Arthur came dashing in, said to come immediately then dashed out again. Well, normally, I do not enter the members' room, my province is kitchen and dining room, but I could tell something was seriously wrong and dropped what I was doing to chase after him. I went in and saw Mr Coverdale on the floor. Mr Connor was waving and pointing, he is dumb you know; he scribbled 'shot himself' on his notepad. Billings took charge, he said everybody must keep their places until Mr Holmes arrived and he would know what to do. We all know you arrive on the dot of a quarter to five, Mr Holmes, which was not very long to wait, so that is what we did. I came back here and waited, Arthur went and polished some glasses in his bar, and Billings went and manned the door."

"You all acted very responsibly," said Holmes. "I will speak to Billings and Arthur, then we will have done everything and the police may be called. Thank you, Chef."

The three of us returned to the Strangers' Room.

"Do you think you could look out the application forms for the four members in the room this evening, Mycroft?" asked Holmes.

"Certainly, I will get them immediately. Shall I send Billings in here for you to interview?"

"If you please, Mycroft."

Billings was an open and helpful man and answered the questions frankly and honestly. It seemed to me that, whilst the members may be misanthropic, the Diogenes Club's staff was just the opposite.

"What time did Mr Dawlish arrive at the club, do you know?"

"Yes, sir, exactly at half-past four," replied the porter.

"That is very precise, how can you be so sure?" asked Holmes.

"I could hear Big Ben striking. Arthur and I have a bit of a game about it. He says you can't hear Big Ben from here and I say you can. Well, I certainly can and listen out for it. Of course it depends on the time of day, amount of traffic and wind direction, but I can hear it without any difficulty though Arthur never seems to be able to."

"I see. So Mr Dawlish entered as the clock was chiming," affirmed Holmes.

"Yes, sir, but he stumbled on the steps. He is blind so I'm not surprised he missed his step, but that's the first time he's blundered. He said he'd fallen outside and I could see he was limping badly. I think that's why he fell again on the step. I tried to help him up and he said I'd better get Arthur to assist so I went and got him and together we hauled him up."

"When did you hear the pistol shot?"

"While we were struggling up the steps with Mr Dawlish."

"So what did you do?"

"I said to Arthur one of us better see what it was as I could tell the sound came from the Members' Room but, before we could decide who should go, Mr Dawlish lost his footing again. So we practically carried him between us to the Members' Room where we put him in the first chair we came to. Then I saw the body on the floor."

"How long do you think it was between hearing the clock chimes and seeing the body?"

Billings looked suspiciously at Holmes. "I don't rightly know. I've not thought about it. Does it matter?"

"I just wondered, had two minutes or five minutes elapsed?" asked Holmes diffidently.

"Between the two I'd say. More than two, but not as long as five. Perhaps three? I really couldn't say."

"But you looked at the time at some point because you knew it would not be long before Mr Holmes came at his regular time of a quarter to five," said Holmes.

"I don't know that I did, sir. Arthur went to get Chef and the three of us debated what to do and decided to wait for Mr Holmes because we knew he was due shortly. I suppose I knew it would not be long because of what had passed since half-past four."

"Very good, Billings, you have been most helpful," said Holmes.

"Can you ask Arthur to step in, please, then can you summon the police?" asked Mycroft, who had rejoined us during the interview, bearing membership forms.

"Yes, sir." The stout fellow knuckled his forehead and went out.

Arthur's testimony was exactly the same as Billings's except that he was not aware of the time to the same degree, but it was clear that the whole business, including the discussion between the three servants about what they should do, must have been over within ten or twelve minutes as, according to Arthur, Mycroft Holmes arrived within a very short time.

Arthur was dismissed and asked to attend to the wants of the three men patiently sitting in the Members' Room. "We must insist they stay until the police arrive, so the least we can do is see to their comfort," said Mycroft, after the man had gone. "We must try and keep this matter quiet. Even a suicide is a scandal the club cannot afford, much less a murder. What should I do, Sherlock?" asked Mycroft.

This question greatly surprised me as Mycroft Holmes was a powerful man in the government, indeed, according to my friend Holmes, the most indispensible man in the country. He had the same intellectual facilities as his brother but to a mightier degree and, whereas Sherlock used his resources to fight crime, Mycroft used his mighty brain to store and sort knowledge. Every department in the government passed their conclusions to Mycroft, and his brain accumulated, sifted and sorted these matters, compared how one thing affected another, until a logical conclusion was reached. His brain, like Sherlock's, was organised like a filing cabinet and the owner could instantly find the information required. It seems on many occasions Mycroft's decision has dictated national policy, and yet this man was asking his younger brother what he should do.

"Coverdale is dead. We can't bring him back to life. You have acted correctly in summoning the police. Tell them a member has committed suicide, let them come and see everything we have seen. There is no necessity to say that I have been here, I have touched nothing, disturbed nothing, they will be able to see everything I have seen. If they believe

Connor when he tells them he saw it all, then so be it, we know differently. If they have doubts you must not hinder them, but allow them to proceed in their own fashion," said Holmes.

"In other words act as though I believe Connor, and that we all regard it as a suicide?" confirmed Mycroft.

"Just so. I expect they will look no further than their nose end and accept the thing at face value. In the meantime I will conduct further enquiries. I am confident I can find the truth of this matter. I have already discovered two things."

"What's that, Holmes?" I asked.

"How difficult it is to phrase questions that require only a 'yes' or 'no' in reply, and how very much harder it must be to say what you mean by answering such questions."

On emerging from the club and finding that the disaffected members outside had drifted away, we walked back towards our rooms in Baker Street.

"The human body is a wonderful creation," said Holmes.

"Indeed," I agreed. "In what particular do you refer?"

"Brother Mycroft has no interests but his work. He is a human calculating machine. He sifts and sorts in his head all the reports from the various government departments, analyses them and draws conclusions that affect how the country is run. His reports dictate government policy and, no doubt, through his work he has sent many a man to his death by advising on conflicts with hostile nations. Yet a man lies dead at his feet in his club, and he asks his little brother what he should do!"

"It's not so strange, Holmes. I have seen many a dying man. I have ordered amputations that have killed rather than saved. I have seen all kinds of diseases and sufferings and not turned a hair yet, when my own brother died in wretched circumstances, do you think I was not affected just as the next man? We are all mortal, and subject to the same fears and feelings when it affects our friends and families. What we do in our professional lives is a totally different matter."

"No doubt you are right, Doctor," said Holmes, and we walked along in silence.

"Do you think the police will believe it is a suicide?" I ventured to ask.

"Who knows? I don't see why not. You did."

"At first, yes. But now you and Mycroft have explained your reasoning I see how impossible that is."

"The police, of course, will not have the benefit of Mycroft's and my conclusions."

"It is clear the poor fellow was murdered by Mr Connor."

"Is it?" asked Holmes.

"Well, surely, that is where your conclusions lead?" I protested.

"If we discount Billings, Arthur and Dawlish there are three men in the club with the opportunity. Apart from Connor there are also the Chef and Repton-Davis."

I was somewhat surprised by this statement, never having contemplated alternative possibilities. The fact that Connor, whilst insisting that Coverdale had shot himself, had been proved to be lying, surely pointed the finger of suspicion at Connor himself. Otherwise would he not have said that the Chef shot Coverdale, or Repton-Davis shot him? I puzzled with this as we walked along in silence. Of course it was possible that one of the other men could have done the deed, but why would Connor lie about it? Finally I voiced my concerns to Holmes.

"If the Chef killed Coverdale why would Connor not tell us that? Why would he lie and say Coverdale shot himself?"

"Why indeed?" We walked along in further silence then Holmes spoke again. "The Chef had a grudge against Coverdale."

"A grudge?"

"Yes. One day the Chef served some bad fish to Coverdale. It made him ill so he reported the Chef and tried to get him sacked."

"How can you know that?" I asked incredulously.

"The Chef is Mr Connor's son. So, when the Chef shot Coverdale, Connor could not turn in his own son though he saw him do it, thus pretended it was Coverdale committing suicide."

I stopped in amazement and grabbed Holmes's arm. "Are you serious? The idea is preposterous!"

"Of course it's preposterous, Watson. But you asked why Connor should lie when he knew very well who killed Coverdale, so I have just furnished you with a reason. Walk on."

"But none of that is true, you just made it up," I said hotly, as we resumed our pace.

"Of course I did, Watson. How many times have I said that to theorise without facts is pointless. I referred to the men as the Three Wise Monkeys."

"I understood the reference, Holmes. 'See no Evil, Hear no Evil, Speak no Evil'"

"That is how it is rendered in this country today, but the proverb is from ancient Japan, the original eighth century version was simply '*mizaru, kikazaru, iwazaru*' – don't see, don't hear, don't speak'. I rather think that is the true position at the Diogenes Club."

"But surely the proverb is merely an admonishment to mind your own business? The poor fellows at the club are actually unable to hear, see and speak. Each lacks one of the five senses that we all should possess."

"Of course, and so elicits our sympathy. We are grateful that we are not similarly impaired. But does that mean we, ourselves, should be metaphorically blind and deaf, and not speak out if such a man commits a crime – exactly as we would if it concerned a man with all his senses and faculties?"

"Of course we should," said I. "It makes no difference to moral scruples."

"I know you stand firm for justice and the law, Watson, and I hope I shall not have to remind you of this conversation before this case is concluded. I see Wilton's ahead, shall we call in for a few oysters?"

I saw little of Holmes during the next few days, but that was nothing unusual when he had a case in hand. I scoured the newspapers to see if anything had been reported regarding the death at the Diogenes Club, but there was nothing. It looked very much as though the police had accepted the idea of suicide and Mycroft had managed to hush things up. I was absorbed with my stamp collection when I was aware of the door opening and glanced up to see an aged clergyman making his entrance. Leaping to my feet, I was about to accost him for entering unannounced without warning, when I heard Holmes's familiar tones wishing me 'Good Evening'.

"Good Lord! You gave me a fright, Holmes. I take it you are garbed as a gentleman of the cloth for some investigative purpose?"

"Yes, Watson, I am the Reverend Augustus Dalrymple, the chaplain at the Diogenes Club."

"I was not aware the club had a chaplain."

"It didn't until three days ago when I became one. Permit me to remove my make-up and costume and I will acquaint you with my recent activities which I think will be of interest to you."

Having put my stamp collection away, I listened to Holmes with some surprise.

"You will recall Mycroft gave me the addresses of Repton-Davis, Dawlish, Connor and Coverdale. These I have visited in my clergyman's guise, making sure I called when the gentlemen were out. My ploy was to gain access to the men's wives, if they had one, or some other close relative. I said that I had been told about the distressing incident at the Diogenes Club and had come to offer any spiritual assistance to combat the dreadful shock that their husband/father/brother or whoever had suffered.

Mr Repton-Davis I found living in an affluent manner and clearly a man of private means. The butler took me to see Mrs Repton-Davis but, I regret to say, she clearly has no idea what her husband does, where he is, or very little else about him. It seemed Repton-Davis owns another house convenient to the Brighton line and, as far as she knows, spends much of his time there but, basically, they live separate lives. So that was a failure. I had a little more success with Mr Connor although his wife is dead. I saw his sister who lives with him and runs his household. Mr Connor is a business man who imports carpets, silks and artefacts from India. He has two sons out in that country, one in Delhi and one in Benares, buying at low prices. They bring crates of stuff back here which their father sells high in an emporium in New Bond Street. The sister knows nothing about the Diogenes Club, much less the suicide there, so I had to be extremely circumspect when speaking. I rather think I gave her the impression there had been an explosion caused by a gas leak."

"Smart thinking, Holmes. But I cannot see you have gained much there, or did she reveal more?"

"Yes. According to his sister, Mr Connor's love of Indian goods stems from his time in the Indian Army."

"That does not seem too significant, Holmes. I served in the Indian Army in Afghanistan and it certainly didn't give me a love of the place. But some chaps are attracted by foreign realms, and a good job too, or we would never have built an empire."

"I agree there is not much significance in the fact itself, but hear me out, old friend. My visit to Mr Dawlish was the most fruitful. He lives in a modest apartment with a very sweet wife who welcomed me in, made me a cup of tea with a buttered scone, and chatted amicably and widely. She and Mr Dawlish (Frank), had met when very young and they were always expected to marry. Then to Mrs Dawlish's distress (she was Vivien Gallagher then) Frank went to India getting a commission in the Bengal Lancers. However, they still professed their love for one another and Vivien agreed to wait until he had finished his first tour of duty and they would marry on his first leave. I believe after two years the junior officer is entitled to three months home leave, or something of the sort. However, when Frank returned, he returned as a blind man. Apparently, he had been buried in a landslide and lost his sight as a result. And, all credit to the woman, though Frank released her from her promise, she stuck by him and married as agreed. He had been honourably discharged as wounded in battle with a medal and a small pension. They reared a family of seven children, five of whom reached maturity, and Frank made his living as a piano tuner. I must say she seemed a contented lady considering that she must have anticipated a very different kind of married life. She said all her children had married well and left home and she now delighted in her grandchildren. Frank still tuned pianos but now it was not so much a necessity as obliging a few long standing customers."

"Did she say anything about the Diogenes Club?"

"Yes, although she obviously thought of it as a conventional men's club as she was pleased that Frank could mix with friends socially, on an equal footing, without his lack of vision being a handicap. I had no need to even hint at the suicide business as she seemed to think it the most natural thing in the world for a club to have a chaplain who looked after the members' spiritual welfare."

"So what deductions have you made from these visits?" I asked.

"I have not told you the most important fact I gleaned. Once a year Frank goes to a reunion with old army comrades."

"Is that important? Many men do that – school reunions, college reunions, regimental reunions."

"Yes, men who are proud of the connection, but hark! When Frank's eldest son wanted to pursue a military career, his father went insane. That was the word Vivien Dawlish used – 'insane'. He expressly forbade any of his sons to join army or navy and was so angry that father and son came to blows and didn't speak for weeks. In all the shouting, Frank, who had appeared resigned to his lot, revealed how bitter he was about being blind and blamed it all on the futility of war, saying that until the carnage ceased, men of all nations would suffer death and mutilation. Fortunately, the sons were obedient to their father and peace was restored to the household. I think the good lady was using the word insane to express the extremity of her husband's anger rather the clinical condition."

"I can readily sympathise, Holmes. A Jezail bullet put an end to my soldiering days too, remember."

"Quite. But this is the interesting thing that intrigued me. If the man was so vehemently against war and the army, why attend an annual reunion?"

"Um, does seem a bit odd."

"Ah, it turned out it was not a formal reunion at all. Frank simply got together with a couple of chums once a year quite informally – met in some restaurant, I believe."

"What about Coverdale?"

"His address was a false one. It does not exist."

"That seems strange. Are you sure?"

"Watson, of course I am sure."

"I would appreciate your conclusions from all this, Holmes."

"I asked Mycroft to get somebody in the War Office to search the army records for the names Dawlish, Repton-Davis, Connor – and Coverdale. I await his reply."

"It might be among your correspondence – there are a couple of telegrams." I nodded to the mantelpiece where they reposed. Holmes, leaping to his feet, tore open a telegram that he immediately discarded and ripped open the other one.

"Aha! I have it, Watson! Dawlish, Repton-Davis and Connor all enlisted in the Bengal Army on the same date, 22nd April 1856. All were discharged in September 1858 as unfit to serve through injuries received in the Mutiny! Coverdale, Malcolm, not known."

We met Mycroft at the Diogenes Club and found that of the three ex-soldiers only Mr Dawlish was there. Holmes asked if he could be brought to the Strangers' Room.

"Good evening, Mr Dawlish," said Holmes, shaking hands. "Do you remember me?"

"Yes, of course, the gentleman with the hands of a violinist."

"But, may I remind you, Mr Dawlish, Mr Sherlock Holmes is my brother and also a detective whom I have engaged to investigate the death of Mr Coverdale," said Mycroft. Dawlish inclined his head in response.

"I regret to inform you that I suspect that you, together with Mr Repton-Davis and Mr Connor conspired to kill Malcolm Coverdale. I further suspect that as the three of you were companions in the army in India and suffered physically in the atrocities of the Mutiny in 1857 that the murder of Mr Coverdale is connected with that event."

"Very perceptive of you, Mr Holmes. Yes, we three were all in the Bengal Army in India. We joined in 1856 as three raw subalterns and hit it off with each other straight away. We were not always broken old men, you know. The three of us were jolly daring fellows and insepar-able. They called us the three musketeers, after the fellows in the story, you know. Comrades – one for all and all for one. We were always up for some lark or madcap venture and truly we feared nothing. We were young – the oldest of us no more than twenty-two. There were few British officers in the Bengal Army at that time and we expected pretty rapid promotion. Our immediate superior was Captain Beauregard, a very popular man with the Indian rank and file. He could speak all the lingoes, he'd been born in India, I believe. We new chaps were very envious of him and tried to emulate him but I'm afraid we were too arrogant and full of our English ways from home, whereas he under-stood the sepoys and sowars like one of their own.

"Anyway, we were right there when the Mutiny broke out. It's one thing to fight an enemy, but it's a very different thing when your own men turn against you. If we'd had five thousand English soldiers we could have beaten the lot of them, but we hadn't. The first I knew about it was being woken in the night by a tremendous explosion very near at hand. The sepoys had blown up the officers' quarters. I was unscathed, but Rupert had his eardrums shattered and that bang was the last sound he ever heard. There were wooden splinters flying everywhere and Teddy Connor got one that pierced his neck. He was in a terrible mess but the only lasting damage was that he had lost his voice box. It may not sound like it to you, Mr Holmes, but we were lucky because our men didn't turn on us and hack us to death in our beds as happened at some forts. They fled to join the army of that arch-fiend Nana Sahib. We were left behind – just a handful of English officers against that devil who headed a screaming fury of 25,000 disaffected natives.

"We were defending the garrison at Panduphur. Not just soldiers were there, but European civilians too. Supplies were low, disease rife and our major at death's door. It was decided that we would leave the fort and make for Cawnpore. It seemed feasible at the time. The fact was that the military could have hot-footed to Cawnpore in no time. There was a good road, but a train of over a hundred Europeans, many of them women and children, was incredibly slow. Captain Beauregard knew the area well and said there was a way across country that was shorter than the road which had to deviate to avoid a mountain range.

"So we abandoned the fort, taking all the remaining supplies with us. Captain Beauregard volunteered to go on ahead to spy out the lie of the land. He would gallop off forward, returning a few hours later, to tell us about the conditions ahead and the way to go. So we crawled along. There was no proper road, we were cutting across country to shorten the journey but, as a result, we had to get across all sorts of wild terrain.

"The major had died and we buried him before we left. There were a couple of dozen English military and a hundred and twenty-three civilians. We had a hotch-potch of ensigns, lieutenants and a captain to control this wagon train. The captain was, of course, Beauregard, so we others deferred to him through his rank and his knowledge, but we were concerned that we seemed to be heading straight towards the mountain range ahead of us. Beauregard assured us there was a way through the range, he knew it well. Captain Beauregard had been gone some time and we were pulled in and encamped awaiting his return and guidance, for we had come to an abrupt halt, our way blocked. Suddenly a wall of wailing banshees came hurtling down upon the wagon train, the enemy was upon us. Nana Sahib was not a man to observe any rules of war or recognise non-combatants, he was the devil in disguise. It was bloody butchery, the whole lot were slaughtered, soldiers, civilians, women and children, all alike.

"So, how did we three escape? I'll tell you. By pure fluke. The three of us chums had elected to recce the lie of the land and had climbed into the mountains to try to find this promised passage through. So we were away from the camp, round the side of the immediate mountain, and totally out of sight of camp and hilltop from whence the enemy swooped on horseback. The enemy had no idea we were there, even existed. The mass of horsemen started a landslide at our side of the hill and we were engulfed in rocks, sand and God knows what else. We were entombed in all of this. I thought my last hour on earth had arrived. But it was not to be. We were all still alive and, though I couldn't see a thing, the other two said they could actually see daylight, so started crawling towards it. God knows how long it took but we got out. That was when I realised I would never see daylight again. So I never saw the results of the massacre as Rupert and Teddy did. The enemy had flown. To be brief, we made our way to Kathmandu with help from Indians friendly to the British. The trouble with India is it is not one nation. There are Brahmins, Moslems, Sikhs, Hindoos and what-have-you, tribal loyalties, a rigid caste system and most of them hate each other more than they hate the British, so we did get help in friendly territory.

We sat it out in Nepal, then heard Nana Sahib had fled there, so realising things had turned our way we made our way back to Delhi which, thanks to Campbell and Rose, was back in British hands and the Retribution had begun. When it was all over and the damage assessed we three musketeers were all honourably discharged as war wounded, with a pension, and that was that.

"And what had happened to Captain Beauregard?" asked Holmes quietly.

Dawlish gave a mirthless laugh. "What indeed? It was discovered he had joined Nana Sahib's troops, changed his name to Mangal Pande Sahib and led one of his brigades. In 1858 when the British reprisals took place he was nowhere to be found, disappeared off the face of the earth."

"But you did find him, didn't you?" said Holmes.

"Yes. Forty years later. We found him."

"He had changed his name again, now he was Malcolm Coverdale, wasn't he?"

"Correct, Mr Holmes."

"Good God!" I could not forbear exclaiming.

"Surprising, isn't it, Dr Watson? But we three had got out of it alive. We could still have been in Nepal unknown to all. Beauregard was much more wily than we simple subs. The three of us went our separate ways, living ordinary lives as well as we were able. The only time we met again was an annual lunch at Simpson's. Then Rupert joined the Diogenes Club, found it congenial and mentioned it to Teddy and me, so we joined too. As you know it's a queer club, the members not being allowed to acknowledge each other. Rupert joined about eight years ago, Teddy and I joined a couple of years later."

"Mr Connor in April 1889, you in January 1890," said Holmes.

"Was it? You know better than me. Well about three months ago Repton-Davis left a message at the club for me to meet him. He told me a new member had appeared and that he was Beauregard. Of course I could not see to check his assertion, but Connor had confirmed it."

"How could you be sure? A man changes in forty years," said I.

"He looked exactly the same only older. Repton-Davis watched him carefully and said he recognised certain of the same mannerisms as of old, but there was a more positive clue. Beauregard had a duelling scar. He was proud of it and would boast of it. He said he had been in the Crimea and had a dispute with a nobleman of the German Legion. Coverdale had an identical scar. There was no doubt."

"So the three of you plotted your revenge," said Holmes.

"Not revenge, Mr Holmes, belated justice. He was a perfidious traitor, he deliberately led us into a trap and betrayed us to the enemy. He caused the slaughter of many innocents."

"You have spoken at length, Mr Dawlish, perhaps I may finish your story for you? You timed your assault for exactly four-thirty so you, outside the club, would hear Big Ben chime. You then called for help pretending you had fallen. Billings came to assist, but you were afraid Arthur may either be in the Members' Room, or rush to it, when he heard the pistol shot, so you insisted Arthur was fetched to assist. Thus as soon as your poised fellow plotters saw Arthur go out to the vestibule they did the deed, you playing-up on the stairs to detain the servants as long as possible. By the time they got you into the room and saw for themselves the body on the floor, your chums were back in their chairs. Mr Repton-Davis, no doubt heart pounding and breathless, facing the wall pretending he had heard nothing, and Mr Connor all excited and pointing at the body."

"That's about it, Mr Holmes," affirmed Dawlish.

"But who actually pulled the trigger?" I asked.

"Mr Repton-Davis. You will have noticed the luxurious pile on the carpets downstairs. They are swept daily before the club opens for the evening. I clearly discerned that feet had passed between Mr Repton-Davis's chair and the dead man's place. Around Mr Repton-Davis's chair the pile was singularly awry and I think he positively scrambled back and hurled himself into his chair, which had slightly moved as a result. The impression of the chair legs on the carpet was quite distinctive. A mere observation at the time, it was only later the significance struck me. By the time I had deduced the three of you were in the plot, it was clear that you were not the murderer as you were not in the room, so, out of the two remaining, which one was it? Hardly likely to be the gentleman with a footstool who suffers from gout."

"Oh, yes, be in no doubt we were all involved – the three musketeers – one for all and all for one. Perhaps you can arrange for us all to hang together, Mr Holmes?" said Dawlish.

"Watson and I had a very interesting talk the other day about law and justice. Dr Watson thinks they are the same thing and all must obey the law whatever the circumstances. I disagree. Furthermore, I am of the opinion that sometimes justice can be done without recourse to the law of the land. I am very pleased to note that Mr Coverdale alias Captain Beauregard acted like an officer and a gentleman and took such an honourable way out. Come, Watson, Mrs Hudson has promised a steak and kidney pie!"

THE ANCIENT RING OF THE PROPHET

My friend Mr Sherlock Holmes is a man of enormous intellect with extraordinary deductive powers. Most of the adventures that I have laid before an indulgent public have been expressly chosen to show these particular talents of this prodigious man. However, in his career as a consulting detective there have been occasions when these powers, exceptional though they are, have not been sufficient and he has had to call on other skills in his armoury of weapons. He is a master of disguise and a consummate actor, qualities he has often utilised to the full. A rarer technique that Holmes has at his command is 'The Bluff'. This method he uses when he finds himself lacking in concrete evidence. Put simply, he conveys the impression that he knows more than he actually does and, by his assertions, convinces his listener to divulge the information he requires. The following adventure is an excellent example of this *modus operandi*.

Most people come to see Sherlock Holmes by prior appointment, so it was with some surprise that such an august personage as Lord Peverill should be announced by Mrs Hudson as begging an immediate audience with Mr Holmes. It was a Sunday and we had recently finished tea.

"Show him in, Mrs Hudson," said Holmes cheerfully, "perhaps the noble lord has something worthy of my attention." It was Holmes's constant complaint that the criminals of London were no match for his formidable intellect.

Lord Peverill was not known to me by photograph or description but, even so, I was surprised to find him a younger man than I had supposed; no older than forty years. After formal introductions the noble gentleman seated himself.

"It's very good of you to see me, Mr Holmes, and I apologise for disturbing you at Sunday tea, but I have come straight from my country home to request your urgent attention to a most mysterious affair."

"I am at your disposal for the next hour, my lord, so please acquaint me with the reason for your precipitate visit."

"This weekend I have had a few guests to stay at my home. A very few guests. It was quite informal and in no way to be construed as the usual kind of house party. My visitors came yesterday afternoon and eight of us sat at table last night. These were my wife and myself, our daughter Sophia, Captain Regulus of the Guards, Mr and Mrs Granby – he is the owner of Granby's Bank – and the remaining persons were Arthur Chudleigh the MP for Brighton, and the Ayatollah Uzma Sayyid Saduq a leading cleric from Persia."

"An eclectic mix," remarked Holmes.

"The Granbys are probably our dearest friends, we see them often. Captain Regulus is very close to an understanding with my daughter. However, the other two gentlemen were not known to me. Well, Arthur Chudleigh I know through the House, but on no more than a nodding acquaintance. The Ayatollah Uzma is on a short visit to this country. I, to be perfectly honest, had no idea he even existed until introduced to him by Chudleigh."

"But you invited this Persian to your home?"

"The circumstances were rather singular. This is how it came about. My lineage stretches back to the Norman Conquest. One Hugh de Peverill was a leading figure in the ninth crusade of 1271. When he returned from the Holy Land he brought with him a gold ring. It is a simple thing almost lacking in any decoration and cannot be of any great monetary value. However, this ring, supposed to have been the property of Mohammed the Prophet himself, was venerated in a shrine in Qaqun. To be blunt, my ancestor plundered this artefact and brought it home in triumph. As he had nothing but contempt for the heathen – as he called the Moslem peoples – he, himself, did not regard the ring as something of inestimable value. And, of course, one wonders how many of these religious relics – saints' finger bones and so on – are actually genuine. There must be enough fragments of the True Cross to build a brigantine. Hugh de Peverill had an ornate box made for the ring and, at some time in recent years, it was moved from that box to be kept in a normal jewellers' ring box. This is all background to the point, Mr Holmes. Now we come to the present. This Ayatollah Uzma Sayyid Saduq, a man whom in Persia I understand to be in a position similar to the Archbishop of Canterbury in our country, is visiting several European countries on some sort of goodwill mission.

The ruler of Persia is Naser od-Din Shah. He has offended many of the leading imams of the country by giving the sale of tobacco rights to the British. The strict Moslems regard tobacco as a sin, though it seems most of the population, women included, are puffing away. So the Shah has asked this Ayatollah Uzma fellow to tour Europe on a goodwill mission to try and build bridges. The Shah is very friendly with this country and we do a lot of trade with the Persians. As you will know, previous Shahs aligned themselves with Russia but, since the last caper when they lost half their kingdom to the Russians, they have dropped Russia and wooed us. This cleric's visit to London was engineered by Arthur Chudleigh who, it appears, has a great interest in Persian affairs, being a frequent correspondent with the royal family and high nobles of that country. Indeed he has visited the country on no fewer than four occasions.

Of course, the Moslems know all about the theft of their Prophet's ring all those centuries ago, but in the intervening years their influence has diminished as that of all the European countries has grown. They would greatly love to have the ring returned, but they realise that after six hundred years the chances are negligible. But the Ayatollah Uzma asked his friend Chudleigh if it would be possible for him to see the ring on his visit to London. Chudleigh approached me and, quite candidly, as it means as little to me as it did to my long-gone ancestor, I invited both of them for the weekend, mainly to have a look at the ring."

"An interesting story, my lord, but clearly there is more," said Holmes.

"Indeed. The ring is normally kept in a strong box at Granby's Bank, so I invited him and Barbara his wife to bring it over and then join us. Thus the eight of us assembled."

"And was the Grand Ayatollah suitably impressed by the Prophet's ring?"

"Enchanted. He kissed it and held forth in some gibberish language of his own. But he was a charming fellow and, after handling the ring, declared how honoured he was as the only living Moslem to have put the Prophet's ring on his own finger. With a sigh he returned it to the box, and that was that. The rest of yesterday evening was spent in a conventional manner. We left the table and sat round the fire chatting and finishing the opened wine. The cleric, of course, was not allowed by his religion to imbibe, but he was jolly enough on fruit cordials. As eleven struck, the ladies proposed retiring to bed, the Ayatollah Uzma also making his way upstairs. We four chaps had a another snifter before breaking up, and Regulus said we must all watch the Ayatollah Uzma and keep him away from the ring as he might be tempted to steal it. We made a vow that between us we would make sure the man was nowhere near the ring and, to be fair, he never mentioned the ring again before he left earlier this afternoon. Last night, as we were leaving the room and I called on the servant to extinguish the lights, Chudleigh said 'I say, Peverill, are you not going to put the ring somewhere safe.' It still reposed on a side table where I had put it earlier in the evening and Chudleigh handed it to me. It seemed a sensible idea so I took the box, went into the library and placed it in the top drawer of my desk, which is the only one with a lock. I locked the drawer, and in emerging from the room locked the door and pocketed the key. By then all had dispersed to their separate quarters."

"Your account is very explicit, my lord, but I am still unclear why you have called to tell me about your social affairs."

"Believe me, Mr Holmes, I tell you nothing that is not essential. All I have said is leading up to a most mysterious crime. The following morning, today, Sunday, we were all up betimes to breakfast as we had promised to take the Ayatollah Uzma fishing. The idea was to spend the morning on the river, return for a snack lunch, and the guests would then depart. So, again, we four English fellows took our foreign guest to see a spot of English fishing. He had expressed a wish to see such things. I gather his country is not very advanced mechanically and these traditional pursuits are not done as sport, as in this country, but essential for life. They suffer regular famines, I believe. It was not exactly a spectacular session, but we were really demonstrating our techniques for his interest. He seemed to enjoy himself and, as he speaks excellent English, we had a great interchange of information. To be honest we were really only pottering about for a couple of hours to fill in the time until lunch and their leaving."

"Again, my lord, we still seem no nearer the point of your visit," protested Holmes.

"You will very soon. Suffice it to say that we were all enjoying ourselves in this quiet way, we even had the unexpected treat of the sight of a heron swooping down and making off with a fish from very near where Chudleigh was casting his line. The Ayatollah Uzma said such birds in his country were called cormorants, so perhaps he was right and it was not a heron; he is surely more knowledgeable about birds than I am. The other bit of jollity was the rowing boat lurching as Granby was getting out and he ended up, not in the drink, but with wet legs up to the knees. Then it was all back for an early snack lunch and we bade farewell to our visitors. Mr & Mrs Granby hung back for half an hour or so and, as they were leaving, we both bethought ourselves of the ring in the library. I went to get it so David, that's Mr Granby, could take it away with him. I gave him the box and he idly opened it up as we said our farewells, only to gasp and show me the box was quite empty, the white padded satin interior clearly seen, but no ring nestling in there."

"Ah!" said Holmes in quiet satisfaction, rubbing his hands together between his knees like a child. "So what did you then do?"

"We were both flabbergasted, being unable to conceive how the ring, reposing behind two locks, could have been abstracted."

"Are there duplicate keys?" asked Holmes.

"No, indeed, in both cases, drawer and door, I have the only key I do not often use them. Normally these things are not locked and it was only the comments made by Capt Regulus that made me lock them last night. Also it was impossible for the Ayatollah Uzma to know where I had placed the ring, as he had retired to bed some time before."

"You suspect the Grand Ayatollah as being the thief?"

"It could be no other. The rest of the party are true born Englishmen. Besides, whilst the ring is gold, it can be worth no more than ten pounds, if that. It is only to a devout Moslem that the ring has inordinate value."

"Did you not call the police?" asked Holmes.

"That was my first instinct, but wiser heads prevailed. My sensible daughter pointed out the scandal it would cause if a foreign clergyman, a guest in our country, should be accused of theft. It would be like the Archbishop of Canterbury being accused of theft in Persia. Our government would not countenance that. It was my wife who suggested you were the man to consult, Mr Holmes. You have a reputation for discretion, as well as an incredible talent for catching rogues."

"You certainly set me a pretty problem," said Holmes, "all the suspects have dispersed and, whilst I will come to your home, I cannot imagine there is anything that will provide a clue."

"It is essential the ring is retrieved."

"Do you still have the box?"

"Yes."

Having said nothing throughout the noble lord's story, I felt compelled to say "If the ring has little value does its loss matter to you? If it is normally secreted away in a bank vault?"

"That ring has been in my family for six hundred years, that is its value to me, Doctor. But to a Moslem in Persia the value is incalculable. Chudleigh explained to me how matters stood. The Shah is not in a strong position. He is not a worldly man, having ruled for years swayed by other countries, principally Russia. Some of his clerics agree with this, but others are bitterly opposed, some decrying the moves to modernity and dealing with the infidel, while others don't think the Shah is progressive enough. Some of these latter imams are conspiring with the Shah's son – who sees the future of his country in industry and trade – to depose his father and strengthen their own religious base. There are rival clerics vying for power in the country; an ayatollah who can produce the authentic ring of their Prophet will have tens of thousands of followers flocking to him. Such a thing could destabilise the country."

"I see," I replied, somewhat chastened.

"It is late in the day, my lord," said Holmes. "I will come to your house in the morning and commence my investigations."

"I am exceedingly gratified, Mr Holmes. I feel instant relief by placing my problem in your hands."

"I can promise nothing, but I will see what I can do."

"Until tomorrow then," agreed Lord Peverill, rising to his feet.

Lord Peverill's country house was situated two or three miles inland from the coast near Jerrold's Gap, a rugged stretch of coastline in the county of Sussex. We were shown into the dining room where the company had eaten.

"This is where we were, Mr Holmes. I have set out the place cards again just as they were arranged on Saturday evening."

Holmes took in the situation at a glance. "After you had admired the ring where did you then place it?"

"Ah, the ring never came into this room. Come through." Lord Peverill led us into an adjacent room, a pleasant sitting room with an expansive view which I judged to be in the general direction of the sea, as beyond the formal garden the land fell away exposing a great expanse of sky.

"So the box with the ring was produced in here?"

"Correct. We were all in a group here and, after some general conversation, Chudleigh asked about the ring. We all knew this was the purpose of arranging the gathering so I had it ready on that small side table there." He indicated a semi-circular table pressed up again the wall alongside a finely wrought stone fireplace. "I picked it up and handed it to Chudleigh who, raising the lid admired it, and with some flowery phraseology which I don't recall precisely – but which I thought was unnecessary – handed it to the Ayatollah Uzma. This chap went into ecstasies, babbled in his own language, holding the box up to heaven and generally carrying on in an excessive manner that no Christian bishop would have done. He then asked permission to remove the ring from the box and place it on his own finger. This meant nothing to me so I said 'Go ahead'. He was transported with delight and clearly thrilled to bits with whole affair."

"It would be a most sacred relic in his religion, my lord," said I.

"Indeed. But, after all, we were merely looking at a gold ring in a jeweller's box. After a while the butler announced dinner and the ring was put back in the box – "

"One moment," interrupted Holmes. "Who actually replaced the ring?"

"I, myself," said Lord Peverill. "I put it back, closed the lid and replaced it on the table. We then all went into dinner and the matter was not referred to again."

"And after dinner, you returned to this room?" asked Holmes.

"Yes, the ladies returned first while we smoked, then we joined them in here. We chatted amicably about this and that, and then the ladies went off to bed about eleven o'clock. The Ayatollah Uzma went at the same time. We fellows sat on a little longer, half an hour at the most, before we too broke up. It was while we were going out that Chudleigh picked up the box and handed it to me, saying that I ought to place it somewhere safe."

"Were you intending to leave it there?"

"To be honest, Mr Holmes, I had forgotten about the wretched thing once I had replaced it before dinner. But, after the Ayatollah Uzma had left us, Captain Regulus had made the suggestion that the fellow might be inclined to attempt to steal it. Perhaps sneak down in the night or something. I told him it was an outrageous thing to say about my guest, an honoured clergyman of the highest rank in his own country. Alas, Captain Regulus being a young man and a soldier, his opinion of the non-English person is one of distrust, if not down-right contempt. He made some remarks about foreign religions that I had to ask him to retract. He was right to some extent, of course, but it was rather hot-headed to utter such things before Chudleigh who is a personal friend of Ayatollah Uzma Sayyid Saduq and a regular visitor and correspondent with the royal family of the Shah in Persia."

"It was then you took it to the library?"

"Yes. The others went upstairs and I went to the library."

"May we go there now?" asked Holmes.

"Certainly."

Lord Peverill took us along a short corridor that led alongside the bottom of the stairs into the library. "This is the room, and this the desk," said he. We three gathered at the desk as Lord Peverill produced a key from his pocket and unlocked the top right-hand drawer of the desk and, pulling it out, revealed the jewel box reposing inside.

"This is the box," said the noble lord, taking it up and handing to Holmes. It was a typical ring box such as all reputable jewellers provide on the sale of a ring. Even a cockney buying a ring for his donah would be given it in such a box. Holmes looked at it and replaced it on the desk.

"I cannot imagine how a thief could have entered the library when the door was locked, much less opened the drawer which was also locked," said Lord Peverill. "Not only that, but nobody other than myself knew where I had put the ring. While I was locking it away the rest had gone to bed. Even Gromby, my man extinguishing the lights in the sitting room, had departed."

"The matter seems very clear. When you picked up the box in the sitting room you did not look inside, did you?"

Lord Peverill thought a moment, but only a moment. "No. You are quite right. I did not. I brought it here and put it away."

"It is obvious that you put away an empty box."

"The ring had already been abstracted?" asked Peverill.

"Yes."

"But when?"

"The opportunities are manifold. The box reposed on the side table throughout dinner, the room was empty for some time, perhaps several hours."

"Yes, indeed. We were at dinner for some two hours."

"So who took the ring? One of your servants, perhaps?" asked Holmes.

Peverill looked shocked. "Out of the question! My staff have been with me for years and all loyal to a man and woman."

"I'm sure we would all like to think that, my lord, but as the bard said 'It is a wise father that knows his own child,' and Homer said 'It is a wise child that knows his own father.' I would suggest the relationship between a man and his servant is even more tenuous."

"Even so, Mr Holmes, I do not wish to even consider that likelihood."

"Then permit me to offer you an alternative suggestion. The three ladies in your party left the gentlemen at dinner and were in the room for half an hour. They had ample time to abstract the ring."

"Mr Holmes! That is unworthy of you! It is a direct insult to my womenfolk!"

Holmes shrugged. "You asked me to investigate the theft of the ring, I am merely pointing out the possibilities. It is clear that is the time it was taken, the opportunity was open for all. You want to know the person responsible. I am stating to you that it could have been anybody, I stress anybody, who was in this house at the time, whether servant, family or guest."

Lord Peverill looked downcast. "I suppose you are right. But many can be eliminated as being highly improbable," he said, looking up.

"Oh, yes," agreed Holmes, "many suspects are improbable but not impossible. However, when you have eliminated the impossible whatever remains, no matter how highly improbable, must be the truth."

"Then what now? We could search the servants' rooms, loath as I am to do such a thing."

"I think that would yield nothing. A ring is a tiny object, very easy to conceal. A search would have to be far more thorough than normal proceedings would allow. We return to your honoured guests, I think, to find the most likely perpetrators. The ring was not really important to anybody but the Grand Ayatollah. You have told us how he venerated the object. Religious zealots are notorious for losing their sense of proportion."

"You think he took the ring? But when did he have the opportunity?"

"That is the supreme difficulty in this case. The only man who seems to have benefitted, a man who openly showed how much he coveted the ring, is the only person who was denied the opportunity of gaining access to it. A pretty problem indeed," stated Holmes.

"Could you not interview him, Holmes? If he knew you were involved, your reputation might scare the truth out of him," I suggested.

Holmes gave a laugh. "I would be surprised if my name meant anything to a Persian clergyman, no matter how highly placed. I think you flatter yourself, Watson, if you believe your tales of a London detective have reached the souks of the mysterious east."

"An interview would be impossible in any case. The Ayatollah Uzma has left the country. He sailed this morning," said Peverill.

"Then the thief has evaded our clutches!" I wailed.

"Speaking of boats, I wonder if we can have a look at the river where your friend Mr Granby almost fell out of the rowing boat?" asked Holmes, of Lord Peverill.

That gentleman looked astonished and spluttered "Why, yes, yes, most certainly. But what has that to do with the theft?"

"Probably nothing at all," said Holmes, airily wafting his hand, "but please humour me in this. I believe in being thorough in my investigations."

The noble lord led us out into his garden and then beyond into parkland. The river that we approached was in fact the boundary of Peverill land. It seems the opposite bank was common land, or as good as so, because the local inhabitants were allowed to roam freely over there and, indeed, did their own fishing from the other bank.

"We were all grouped about here by the landing stage," explained Lord Peverill.

"What a charming scene," remarked Holmes. "And this pretty little boat was the one that almost capsized your friend?"

"Yes."

"I see the land across the river rises up to that woodland on the brow. Is that part of your property?"

"No, the river is my boundary. Beyond those trees there is a splendid view of the sea."

"Really? We are so close?"

"No, not close. We are about three miles distant as the crow flies."

"Ah, yes, as the crow flies; but the river meanders no doubt?"

"Oh yes, possibly adds as much as a mile."

"Well, that seems to be all there is to see here, my lord," said Holmes.

"Have you formed any theories, Mr Holmes?"

"Oh, no. It is always a mistake to theorise before having all the facts. You see there is a danger of seeking for facts that will fulfil one's theory, and risk overlooking matters that will point to the truth."

"Shall we then return to the house?" asked Lord Peverill.

"Actually, I noted the charming village clustered at your entrance gate. I thought we might take a look before departing."

"Departing? I expected you to be more thorough. I thought you might care to stay for lunch."

"That's very kind of you, but the truth of the matter is that the good doctor here is very partial to country ales and likes to try out the local brew whenever we have opportunity to visit the countryside. Isn't that so, Watson?"

"Why, yes, yes, indeed. A little foible of mine," I managed to splutter in response to this outrageous statement. Holmes does and says nothing idly, so I knew he had some purpose in mind, but why that purpose involved missing out on a pleasant lunch with the aristocracy in surroundings that a doctor on an army pension rarely has chance to savour, I don't know.

"If you will excuse us we will leave you here. Will you be at home for the rest of the afternoon?"

"Normally I would return to Town. I have stayed today especially for your visit."

"I see. As yet I do not know when we will leave the area. It may be that I may wish to speak with you again later today."

"In that case I will wait here."

"That's very good of you, my lord. Come, Watson. I can almost see your parched throat from here!"

With that sally we left Lord Peverill and made our way to the village. "What was all that about, Holmes? Making me out to be like some drunken yokel. Apart from causing me to miss out on lunch."

"I'm sure the village inn will supply you with some good wholesome country food, Watson."

And it was to the inn that we repaired precipitately. It was not long past noon and the inn was very quiet, with a pair of local working men, presumably taking a lunch break from their daily toil, quietly murmuring alongside the bar, and nobody else in the place.

"Two pints of your best brew, landlord," cried Holmes jovially.

"Certainly, sir, coming right up. Are you gentlemen on a visit or passing through?" The landlord was clearly a pleasant garrulous type and not one of the surly devils one often finds in a country inn, begrudging the very presence of a stranger.

"My friend here would like some food. Can you offer anything to stave his hunger?"

The landlord turned to me. "I have some rabbit pie, or ham and eggs." I elected for the rabbit pie.

"We're here for a spot of fishing," said Holmes.

"Then you want to head for the sea at Jerrold's Gap. There's fine sea fishing there."

"I have little experience of sea fishing, I prefer the quiet rivers that meander through pleasant countryside."

"So where have you been this morning?" asked the landlord, placing two pint tankards on the counter.

"Just up the road. We came to Lewes on the train, then followed the Ouse until we found a likely spot. Your health!" toasted Holmes.

"And did you have success?" asked the landlord.

"Oh, we found an ideal spot opposite a great house."

"That's Lord Peverill's place. All the land on the opposite bank is his."

"Really? Quite magnificent it looked from a distance."

"There's not usually much sport in that stretch."

"No, indeed. And what's more, one of my catch was snatched away immediately by some great seagull thing."

The landlord laughed, and the workmen looked across to see the cause of the laughter. "This gentleman says he had his fish grabbed by a seagull." This was greeted by laughter from the two men.

"I didn't find it amusing," protested Holmes in a rather pettish manner.

"Bless you, sir, you don't know why we're laughing. That bird is well known round here; it's a cormorant not a seagull."

"Well, whatever it was, it snatched my fish."

"It's a trained cormorant, sir. It belongs to Captain Jacob. He's the lighthouse keeper at Jerrold's Gap."

"A trained cormorant? Well, I'm damned! I've read about such things out in China. I didn't know we had any in this country."

"It's an old tradition, sir. In the old days they used cormorants like they used falcons. We don't have them nowadays. I think Captain Jacob brought his back from overseas."

"Well, what do you think to that, Ted?" said Holmes, addressing me. "It's wonderful what they can train animals and birds to do, isn't it? I believe they tie a thread round the bird's throat to stop it swallowing the fish, is that right?"

"That's it, sir. They can swallow the small fish but not the big ones, and they take it back to their master. A bit easier than sitting for hours with a fishing rod, eh, sir?"

While this conversation had been taking place, the landlord's wife, or perhaps it was his daughter, it was hard to say, brought me my food. The slice of pie was clearly a leftover hastily warmed up, hot on the outside and tepid within, accompanied by a heap of mashed turnips. To think I had been deprived of lunch with Lord Peverill for this. I should have known; at least the ham and eggs would have been edible.

"You say Captain Jacob is the lighthouse keeper?" asked Holmes.

"Yes, sir."

"We didn't have a lighthouse in the old days," chimed in one of the working men. "They used to go down on the cliff with lanterns. My granddaddy told me they used to put them up in the wrong places when they knew a ship was off the coast in a storm and seeking a safe harbour. They were supposed to guide them into Jerrold's Gap, but they put them so the ship was driven on to the rocks."

"How awful," said Holmes.

"Oh, yes, sir," went on the worker, "they deliberately wrecked the ship for the cargo. Wicked it were. There was a gang from a place up on the border with Kent, the Hawkhurst gang, and they would come down here and do that. They were smugglers and allsorts, those villains."

"Aye, then building the lighthouse stopped that little game," said the other worker.

"A good thing too, I should say," said Holmes. "Is Captain Jacob a local man?"

"Nobody rightly knows where he hails from. He has sailed the seven seas but he is getting on now and he got this lighthouse job. It don't pay much, but all he has to do is light the light every night and extinguish it in the morning. He gets a free house though. He lives in the light-house."

"Well, I'm glad we called in on you, landlord, I have learned things of interest I didn't know before. But we must be on our way. Is there a path up to that little copse of trees above the river where we were fishing?"

"Indeed there is, sir, a well-worn path goes up at the back of the inn here, right up to the crest and beyond. The copse is just off to the side.

Would you like some more, sir?" asked the landlord, addressing me. I declined as graciously as I could muster considering I was still gagging from the last forkful.

Outside the inn Holmes said "How was your lunch?"

"Disgusting," could be the only reply.

"The ale wasn't up to much either, was it? Let's have a look at the copse." I could not imagine why Holmes should be interested in that, but I have long given up querying and merely go along with him. Peverill was right, it was a gorgeous view from the top of the hill. One could see the land stretched out below for miles, with a distant view of the sea glinting in the sunlight. I do believe there is a theory that where we were standing was originally the coastline and centuries ago the sea receded to its present position. I was suddenly aware that I was alone, Holmes having gone off to look at the trees. I followed and found him on his knees, peering at the ground with his lens.

"There are signs that a man stood here for some time. You can see how he shifted his position, shuffling up the soil, but not moving away. There is no clear print, but I suspect from the marks I can see that the man was wearing boots without studs, and certainly not elegant shoes. I think perhaps a rubber sea boot or something of that nature. There are traces of tobacco ash and pipe dottle. I would say the tobacco is a coarse shag, not one I would care to smoke."

"What is the significance? Many a man might stand here and contemplate the views and the wonders of nature. I, myself, had to tear myself away from the vista to seek you out," said I.

"The possible significance is that from this spot there is a direct view of the landing stage where Lord Peverill's fishing party took place. But come, the game's afoot! To the lighthouse!"

We returned to Peverill Hall and sought transport. Lord Peverill offered a pony and trap with a stable lad to drive, and soon we were off to Jerrold's Gap. I think Peverill had come to the conclusion that Holmes was quite mad and had given up trying to fathom his peculiar ways. As we drove along Holmes asked me if I had any large money. I had ensured I had sufficient money for the trip so a couple of sovereigns reposed in the pocket of my jacket. I proffered those.

On gaining the lighthouse, Holmes boldly knocked. There was a long delay before the door was opened to disclose a small wizened man, obviously a seafarer in every respect down to his gumboots, an ancient pipe clamped in his mouth giving forth a most noxious smell.

"What do you want?" he almost snarled.

"Captain Jacob, we have come to see you. Our boss has sent us," said Holmes.

"Has he? And who's he when he's whitewashed?"

"We can't talk here. Let us in." Holmes, pushing the man aside, strode into the room and I, of course, followed.

"Here, who do you think you are, barging in here?" protested the captain.

"Don't get upset, old boy. The boss is very pleased with you and there may be something extra in it for you," said Holmes, holding up my coins.

"I don't know what you're talking about," said the captain, his eyes glinting as he regarded the sovereigns.

"Your clever bird brought you the ring all right, didn't he? Very smart. Have you passed it on yet, as you were told to?"

"'Course I have, what is this? I did exactly as I was told. The foreign man was on the boat waiting and I took it straight to him. Straight away. I only paused to swish it in water 'cause it had been inside the fish, that was all."

"Excellent, you have done well. You saw the boat get away?"

"Yes, I waited until it was on the horizon before I sent the telegram."

"The boss will be pleased. You have done exactly as instructed."

"Did he doubt it? He paid me before the job. I wouldn't do it otherwise, too risky."

"So you've got your money?"

"Yes. I'm not complaining. I did what I was told."

"And it all went to plan?"

"What is this? Is something wrong? It's not my fault if there is. I did my part properly."

"I said the boss is very pleased with you."

"Did he not get my telegram? I sent it just like I was told: 'mission accomplished'."

"Yes," said Holmes heartily, "he got the telegram. As I said, he's very pleased with you. So he's sent you a little bonus." Holmes indicated the coins that he had been holding aloft all the while.

"What d'ye mean?" asked Captain Jacob suspiciously.

"This is an extra bonus because you carried out the job so efficiently." He then grabbed the man by the scarf round his throat. "If you so much as blab a word about this to anybody, we'll be back. And we won't be bringing you pieces of gold. If anybody comes calling asking questions you say nothing, right? You know nothing. Ted here, he's the strong and silent type, his language is the cosh and blackjack. I learned my skills with the stiletto in Italy. We're both the tops in our field, that's why the boss employs us. So don't be a foolish man and start blabbing. People round here know all about your thieving cormorant, so just watch it, right?"

The man was thoroughly terrified by this performance of Holmes, and through chattering teeth said "I won't say a word, believe me."

"Right. Here's your bonus," said Holmes, placing my two sovereigns on the deal table. "Come on, Ted, we'd better report back to the boss."

And with that Holmes swaggered out and I followed. I could not resist turning at the door and uttering a snarl at the poor shivering seaman.

Back in the pony trap Holmes said brightly "That seemed to go well. Do you know the nearest telegraph office, young man?" He did not, but an enquiry of a local woman led us there. Once again the lad with the trap waited while we went inside.

"Good afternoon," said Holmes, "I wonder if you could help me. Captain Jacob sent me a telegram yesterday and it didn't arrive."

"Captain Jacob sent it, you say?" asked the man at the counter.

"Yes, do you know him?"

"Everybody round here knows Captain Jacob, but he's not the sort to send telegrams."

"Well he sent one to me yesterday."

"Yesterday was Sunday."

"Indeed it was," agreed Holmes.

"We are not open on a Sunday."

"Ah! Then from whence would a telegram have been sent?"

"He would have to go into Brighton and catch the office open there. But it closes at 4 o'clock on a Sunday."

"I see. Perhaps that is where the error occurred. Thank you so much for your help."

Back in the trap Holmes commanded "To Brighton, boy!"

At the telegraph office Holmes was at his most ingratiating. "I wonder if you could kindly assist me."

"I'll do my best, sir."

"A gentleman by the name of Captain Jacob sent me an urgent telegram from here yesterday afternoon. It was succinct; it merely said 'mission accomplished'. But unfortunately it was not delivered to me. I am a member of parliament and the telegram, though brief, was an important message. I waited in London to see if it arrived this morning, but as it did not I came especially to Brighton to see Captain Jacob. He swears he sent the telegram. Could you check that it was, in fact, transmitted?"

"Let's have a look. I wasn't on yesterday, it being Sunday. My day off. Here we are, it's almost the last one sent yesterday. Timed at 3.19."

"Perhaps Captain Jacob misspelled the address?"

"It's not very clear, it looks like Vincent Street?"

"May I see?" The clerk laid the pad on the desk. "Oh, I see what has happened. I am a member of parliament and the message was sent to my office rather than my home. Captain Jacob must have misunderstood. I am so sorry to have troubled you. The fault is certainly not with the telegraph office. I do apologise."

"That's quite all right, sir. It's no trouble."

"Thank you, you're very kind."

Back in the trap Holmes cried: "To the station, boy!"

It was not until we were comfortably settled on the train as it sped metropolis bound that I was able to catch my breath and accost Holmes. "I would appreciate a little forewarning if I am to be presented to the aristocracy as some kind of low-life toper, and to a perfect stranger as a silent hoodlum with a predilection for beating people to order."

Holmes laughed. "Don't be so sensitive, my friend. You have the perfect appearance that fits many types of different people. If you were dressed in military uniform you would be taken for a general, if in jodhpurs and hacking jacket, a racehorse trainer, if in clerical garb you would be undoubtedly a bishop at the very least."

"That's all very well, Holmes, but you should not spring these wild identities upon me without warning."

"I have to improvise, Watson. When clues are thin on the ground or non-existent, other ploys must come into play. You will have realised how little factual information was to be gleaned in this case. What progress that has been made has been by manipulating the slight knowledge we have gained."

"Perhaps you will kindly explain; I have become quite bewildered by all this dashing about."

"We have one last visit to make, then we can return home and enjoy Mrs Hudson's usual excellent dinner, over which I shall satisfy any outstanding queries you may have."

On gaining Town we made our way to 17 Vincent Street which proved to be a small turning in the Whitehall area dominated by government offices. It was a mansion of apartments, clearly of a superior type, with an entrance lobby guarded by a uniformed attendant.

"May I help you?" enquired the man.

"Thank you. I am Captain Jacob and I sent a telegram to Mr Chudleigh the MP yesterday afternoon, and as it was most urgent and I have had no reply I feared it might have miscarried."

"A telegram, you say? All telegrams are delivered here to me or my colleagues, and I, myself, was on duty yesterday afternoon," replied the uniformed one.

"Ah, well perhaps you recall this particular one," said Holmes, glancing round in a conspiratorial manner and lowering his voice. "It was addressed to Mr Brooke." Holmes tapped the side of his nose in a gesture copied from men generally known as 'sporting types'.

The attendant smiled. "Have no fear, sir, that telegram certainly arrived. Mr Chudleigh had prepared me to look out for it especially. I delivered it into his hands myself."

"Oh, that is a relief. Thank you. I am much obliged to you," said Holmes, and we left the building.

Two days after the events related above, Holmes informed me that he had been asked to visit Lord Peverill at his London home. "I am sure, having taken such an active part, you would like to be there when the villain is unmasked."

"I certainly would, Holmes."

Lord Peverill inhabited a very grand town house in St James's Square. We were shown into an elegant reception room where, alongside Lord Peverill, stood a small stout man of around fifty years.

"Good morning, Mr Holmes, Dr Watson. This gentleman is my parliamentary colleague Mr Arthur Chudleigh the MP for Brighton. You requested that I invited him to meet you here. Arthur, may I present Mr Sherlock Holmes the eminent detective, and his colleague Dr John Watson."

"Late of the Indian Army, I believe, Dr Watson?" said Chudleigh pleasantly as we shook hands.

"Now, sir," said Peverill to Holmes, "you requested I told Mr Chudleigh nothing about the reason for this meeting. I have obeyed your instruction, but may I say I have not been impressed by the way you have conducted your investigation. Not at all impressed. In fact, whilst your high reputation precedes you, I, myself, am profoundly disappointed."

"I regret to hear you say that, my lord," said Holmes breezily, "but I hope this little meeting will restore me into your good faith. Perhaps we may sit?" We settled ourselves around a low table, like the points of a compass. "During the recent weekend when Lord Peverill entertained guests at his country house a gold ring of considerable importance went missing."

"Mr Chudleigh knows nothing of the matter, Mr Holmes. Apart from Mr Granby and myself, I have confided in no-one except my wife and daughter; and of course yourselves."

"Then I will explain, although I think you will find Mr Chudleigh knows more about the business than any of us. But to our muttons.

After your guests had left on Sunday following lunch, you, my lord, while handing the box to your friend the banker Mr Granby, found the contents were no longer present. You were handing over an empty box. The ring had apparently been stolen, so you called on my services to investigate the theft. I attended on you during Monday and these are the results of my investigation. The ring, which had been admired during the evening on Saturday, was placed to one side in its box. It remained thus, right up to the time the party broke up to go to bed. At that point, you, Mr Chudleigh, took up the box, extracted the ring, closed the lid and handed it to Lord Peverill with the statement that he should put it somewhere safe."

"Ridiculous, I did no such thing," drawled Chudleigh.

"It was a very clever ploy, which I greatly admire, Mr Chudleigh, as it ensured that the box would be locked away, there being no likelihood that it would be produced again during the weekend. You took the risk that the lid may be opened at that point and the box seen to be empty, but you calculated that the company wending its way bedwards full of repast, good wine and pleasant company was sufficient to prevent the possibility. So Lord Peverill, by locking the box away in a very convincing manner in his library desk, assisted you in your theft."

"I hope you can prove this, Mr Holmes, otherwise it is a slander on a British member of Parliament," said Peverill.

"On Sunday morning the gentlemen of the party went fishing on the river to provide entertainment for the Grand Ayatollah Sayyid Saduq. During that time Mr Chudleigh placed the ring inside a fish –"

"Inside a fish?" exclaimed Peverill incredulously.

"The man's clearly not in his right mind, Peverill, do we have to listen to this?" said Chudleigh.

"Please hear me to the finish, then you may proceed entirely as you wish. When I have told you the entire fruits of my investigations my function is at an end and I shall leave with Dr Watson. I think you will agree that is what you have employed me to do?"

"Yes, well, I suppose it is," agreed Peverill.

"The fish containing the ring was placed deliberately accessible to allow a trained cormorant to swoop down and carry it away –"

Chudleigh laughed. "This is better than a fairy story. Do go on, Holmes, I am all agog to hear what happens next. Perhaps a witch flies in on a broomstick!"

"The cormorant belongs to one Captain Jacob, the lighthouse keeper at Jerrold's Gap. Dr Watson and I interviewed Captain Jacob and he confessed that he had been paid in advance to carry out this deed. He then passed the ring to a foreign man in a boat. This man, no doubt of

Persian nationality – but that I cannot prove – then disappeared over the horizon. Captain Jacob stood and watched until the boat was out of sight as he had been ordered to do by you, Mr Chudleigh. He then travelled to Brighton in order to send a telegram, again as you had instructed him. But, of course, you were too clever to do all this in your own name. You adopted the name Mr Brooke and the telegram was sent to a person of that name."

"Then perhaps you ought to seek this mysterious Mr Brooke instead of trying to accuse me," said Chudleigh, no longer languid but getting angrier by the minute.

"I have found Mr Brooke. It is no coincidence that Mr Brooke resides at 17 Vincent Street which is your address, because Mr Brooke is a pseudonym for yourself. The telegram which comprised the two words 'mission accomplished' was delivered to the porter at your mansions, who gave it into your hands. That, my lord, is how the theft was carried out. Mr Chudleigh is the perpetrator. What his motives were I have no idea and do not concern me."

"Is this true, Chudleigh?" demanded Peverill.

"Of course not. It's a completely fanciful tissue of lies," riposted Chudleigh angrily.

"Mr Holmes sounds very convincing," said Peverill doubtfully.

"Of course he does. He has to say something to warrant his fee. Let him prove it in a court of law."

"If proof should be needed we have the testimony of the telegraph operator, the porter at your apartment and, most importantly, Captain Jacob himself," said Holmes smoothly, rising to his feet. "I have fulfilled my obligation to you, Lord Peverill, so if you wish to notify the police I will hand my evidence to them on request. The decision is yours. I will send you my account, my lord, and consider the matter closed unless you contact me again. Perhaps, as you seem to doubt the way I proceed, I must confirm that there is total confidentiality between Dr Watson and myself and our clients. I bid you good day."

Thus we left the two politicians to ponder the situation between themselves.

The weeks passed, Holmes's account was paid promptly, but we heard no more of the affair. When I ventured to mention this, Holmes said he was not surprised as it was commonplace for politicians to close ranks to protect one another.

The adventure described above happened in the year 1895. On opening my newspaper on the 2nd May the following year, to my horror I read the following:

Assassination of the Shah of Persia
Shot with Pistol

(Reuter's Telegram) Teheran Friday 6.58pm

As the Shah was this afternoon entering the inner court of the shrine of Shah Abdul Azim, six miles south of this city, he was shot and killed. The assassin, who was arrested, is said to be a sayed from Kernan in the Southern Province. It is believed other persons were connected with the crime.

Press Association Report   Teheran Saturday

Immediately after the assassination of Nasr-ed-Din in the fiftieth year of his reign, the Shahzadehs (the Princes of the Royal blood), the chief Ulemas (high priests or doctors of divinity and law), and the various high functionaries were immediately called to the palace. The Valiahd (Heir Apparent) was proclaimed the new Shah. Named Muzaffer-ed-Din, he is the second son of the late monarch. It was announced that the important Ministerial functionary known as the Sudar Azam (or Grand Vizier) would be dispensed with henceforth.

Telegrams to date have not announced names of the new Shah's ministers, but the *urf*, or secular law of Persia, is below, far below, the *Shahr*, or religious law. Great power, therefore, resides in the person of the Ayatollah Uzma, the highest cleric in the nation. The former holder of the office, Sayyid Saduq, has been replaced by Ali Muntajabuddīn, a man who has in recent months gained an enormous following. The accession of the new ruler is unlikely to be a peaceful transition, states Mr Arthur Chudleigh the MP for Brighton, who is an intimate of Muzaffer-ed-Din Shah and a friend of the new Ayatollah Uzma, as many of the 'old guard' are resistant to change. Mr Chudleigh, already with several business interests in Persia, has recently formed Anglo-Persian Oil Prospectors Ltd with Lord Peverill as Chairman.

THE ESCAPE OF THE WOLVES

In recording the many fascinating cases of my friend Mr Sherlock Holmes I fear I have given the impression that my entire life is occupied in supporting him in his anti-criminal endeavours. It is true that I am privileged to be his confidant on many occasions, but my life has other aspects and, because these parts of my life are as mundane as the next man's, I can see no interest in them, or demand to disclose them from the followers of Mr Sherlock Holmes. However, I do not compartmentalise my life and sometimes my private life and Holmes's professional one coincide, such as the odd occasion when an old university chum appears from the void of history seeking Holmes's assistance.

Any idle curiosity on the part of my readers may be appeased, however, when I briefly write of my visit to Sanger's Amphitheatre (formerly Astley's). This place of entertainment has stood on Westminster Bridge Road, Lambeth since anybody can remember. For the last twenty years, Lord George Sanger has been the proprietor, purveying a vast quantity of shows of the circus type with acrobats, jugglers, clowns, wild animals, horses and so on. His shows often include pantomimes and melodramas with the emphasis on horsemanship. It is quite amusing how Mr Sanger became a 'Lord' for his cognomen is no more than a *nom de théâtre*. It seems that he had a legal dispute with the Yankee showman William Cody, known as Buffalo Bill, and in the court Cody, being a Justice of the Peace in Nebraska, was consistently referred to as the Honourable William Cody. This so incensed Sanger that he declared "If he's an Honourable then I'm a Lord!" He repainted his circus wagons as Lord George Sanger, and his brother John – who also owned a circus – decided he, too, would be a Lord. Other circus proprietors followed suit, with Mr Fossett becoming Sir Robert Fossett, and Mr Ross becoming Count Rosaire, and so on.

I was eager to see the current programme at Astley's as my friend Thurston, who likes a rollicking night out, had said there was one Antonio di Mezma on the bill who got people up from the audience and hypnotised them into eating onions thinking they were apples, making them dance and perform other embarrassing acts. I am very sceptical about hypnotism, not having much experience of it, and assume it is all done by suggestibility, physical manipulation, stagecraft, and trickery. Thurston claimed it was 'a good laugh'. However, when we got there we found out that di Mezma was no longer appearing, his place being taken by Professor R Dunning, the most Powerful Ventriloquist with his Merry Family. The other performers that evening were Madame Poole Garland – Soprano, The Great Alvantee – King of the Sloping Wire, Professor Devereux with his renowned troupe of Performing Dogs and Monkeys, Miss Lulu – contortionist, M Le Monte – Unique Lightning-Change Artiste, the Acrobatic Sherman Sisters, Herr Shultz – Wizard of the Indian Clubs and Captain Sydney and his Forest Bred Lions. There was also a troupe of clowns with names like Bumble, Tiny and so on. However, the star attraction was the old melodrama *Mazeppa or the Wild Horse of Tartary* from the poem by Byron; the role of the youth Mazeppa being played by that fine strapping lass Miss Maude Forrester.

I always have a good time with Thurston, he is one of the jolliest of fellows, and we really enjoyed the show, although I was surprised to see so many empty seats. One thing that turned out rather annoying was the fact that during the performance clowns wandered about the audience doing comic little stunts over and over. One particular clown kept hovering near to us and did nothing but blow a party squeaker that shot out with a feather at the end. However, the circus is a place where you can see the most stunning ladies at their best. Not only are they good lookers, they are the cleverest and most astonishing in their abilities. This clown fellow seemed to delight in blowing his stupid feather squeaker in my face just when I was particularly enjoying Miss Lulu and the Acrobatic Sherman Sisters.

Anyway, he had cleared off when the play of *Mazeppa* started. The story is not very involved; a handsome youth falls in love with the wife of a Baron who is thirty years her senior. The two lovers are caught consummating their love, the youth is hauled before the powerful Baron and his punishment decreed. He is to be tied naked on to the back of a wild horse which is painfully goaded and set loose into the wild Tartar mountains. So we had the edifying sight of Miss Forrester in flesh-coloured tights secured sprawled over the back of a horse that made its way up ramps disguised as rocks and romantic mountain passes. Of course, it all ended happily and we could emerge into the dark night having enjoyed some harmless pleasure and fooling ourselves into thinking that, because the tale was loosely based on Byron's poem, it had been a cultural experience.

Next morning, I was breakfasting whilst reading the morning newspaper and Holmes perused his voluminous correspondence; we are not very sociable at breakfast.

"Did you enjoy the circus last night, Watson?"

Jerked out of my self-imposed cocoon, I stared at Holmes. "How on earth do you know I went to Sanger's? I never told you. I didn't even know I was going myself until the last minute when Thurston suggested it."

"You know my methods, Watson," he smirked.

"Very well. Let me see. You could not have seen the programme protruding from my pocket because I didn't buy one. Thurston did and took it home with him. So it's not that. Don't tell me my coat smells of horses, lions, and orange peel?"

"My sense of smell is acute, but I have not been sniffing at your coat."

"Let's see, ah, an omnibus ticket dropped on the floor, perhaps?" I suggested, gazing around.

"I was not aware you travelled by omnibus, Watson."

"My shoes, perhaps? Some peculiarity about the ground around the end of Westminster Bridge Road that clings to my shoes?"

"Rather fanciful, don't you think?"

"Very well. I give up. I know in the olden days you would have been burned as a witch. How can you tell I was at Sanger's last night?"

Holmes, plunging his hand into his dressing gown pocket, pulled out an object and, placing it in his mouth, blew a party squeaker and the feather at the end shot out into my face. I gaped in astonishment. "Don't tell me you were that tiresome clown!"

Holmes laughed. "I'm afraid so, Watson. You must forgive me, I could not resist the opportunity of impressing you with my amazing deductive powers."

"But this is astonishing, Holmes. Surely you are not so strapped for cash you are resorting to paid employment at the circus?"

"Certainly not, Watson. But I was working. I have been engaged by Mr Sanger to investigate a series of incidents at the amphitheatre."

"You mean criminal acts?"

"No. As yet nothing criminal seems to have occurred. They are rather peculiar and may be no more than practical jokes, but they may well affect the quality of his entertainments."

"In what way?"

"Sanger was not sure when they started as some things seem so slight they are barely noticeable. For example, it seems that one night the orchestra leader's band parts were all mixed up."

"That sounds like a prank by one of the band," said I.

"Exactly, so it was not thought much of at the time. However, since then other, more serious things have come to light. When Captain Sydney came to dress for the show, his coat was missing and he was obliged to borrow one from elsewhere."

"Another prank, surely?"

"As you will know, Sydney is the lion trainer. Lions are used to doing their performance with the same person in the same way. They are unsettled by changes such as different lighting, or if the pedestals are wrongly placed. It is a moot point that Sydney, lacking his usual red coat with gold frogging, may even have been thought to be a different person by his animals. If a joke, it could have been a fatal one."

"Ah, I see what you mean."

"On another occasion the juggler found problems with his Indian clubs. After his act he discovered they had been interfered with. One had been drilled out and some lead inserted, thus disturbing the weight and balance. It is far harder to juggle with objects of different sizes and weights than identical ones. Sanger is concerned that some person is deliberately and malevolently interfering with his artistes to impair their efficiency, and thus appear sub-standard to the audience. No doubt you saw the remarkable performance of the quick-change artiste Monsieur Le Monte, and how by simply crossing behind a screen he comes out in a different character from when he went in?"

"Indeed, quite astonishing."

"At one performance his act was ruined by pins being inserted in the sleeves of some of his costumes. Because of that he was unable to emerge in a change of costume, causing the audience to laugh and jeer, with the poor fellow fleeing the stage assaulted by catcalls."

"I see why Sanger is concerned. Does he have any suspicion who this joker is?"

"He suspects it is somebody working at the behest of Buffalo Bill the American showman who is now in this country with his show 'Buffalo Bill's Wild West and Congress of Rough Riders of the World'."

"But why? Buffalo Bill's show is no longer in London. I think it's now gone to Birmingham. He is no competition."

"Sanger seems to think Cody has taken against him because of their court case."

"I see. So you are at the circus every night on watch?"

"I have been there a few nights but seen nothing suspicious."

Holmes had no sooner confided the above information to me when Mrs Hudson appeared bearing a telegram for him. "Ah, Watson, things are developing!" He passed me the telegram that briefly read *Wolves out. Come at once. Sanger.*

"Do you wish to accompany me, Watson?"

"Of course."

So once again I made the rare jaunt south of the river to Astley's where, on arrival, we found the foyer full of gentlemen from the newspapers, and several police constables. Sanger was prominently amongst them being assailed by questions on all sides. On seeing our entrance he boomed out "See, gentlemen, here is Mr Sherlock Holmes! I have called upon the services of the great detective to investigate the matter! Come, Mr Holmes, into my sanctum. Please bide, gentlemen, and shortly I will give you a statement." With that, Holmes and I were ushered into Sanger's office.

"Phew!" he said when the door was closed against the rabble.

"This is my colleague, Dr Watson. What's this about wolves, Mr Sanger?"

"I received eight untamed wolves yesterday afternoon and had them put in a cage in the stables. After last night's performance, when all but a couple of keepers, the gasman and the night watchman had left the building, a great racket was heard from the stables. The keepers immediately rushed there, finding to their horror that the wolves were loose, having attacked a horse that now lay dead and was being feasted upon by the wolves. Frank Taylor, my head man, realising that the other horses were in peril – there are sixteen more besides the slaughtered one – sent the night watchman for me and my son while he got the horses out by crawling along a beam and cutting their halters, enabling the other keepers to get them out. They then sealed up the stables with a massive wooden door, leaving the wolves at their dinner. That was the position when I got here."

"How terrible!" I cried.

"You say the wolves had only just arrived?" demanded Holmes.

"Yes, they are from Siberia and were destined for the Belgian Exhibition. For some season they were never sent and were languishing in London, so I bought them. They were brought in by a very experienced beast man called Alpine Charlie. They are not for use here. I intend to have them trained for my provincial tour."

"Perhaps you could show me the stables?" asked Holmes.

"I am afraid not, Mr Holmes. The position is still the same. I am awaiting the arrival of my full staff and a new cage. When all is in position we shall remove the temporary barrier and drive the wolves into the new cage. Not until then will the stables be open for inspection. I am sure you will appreciate the difficulty. We cannot, under any circumstances, risk ravenous wolves escaping from the building."

"Then I can do nothing at the moment. Have you no idea how the wolves got free?" asked Holmes.

"I cannot imagine. The door was secured by a large iron cross-bar that had to be lifted to enable the door to be opened. I can only hazard that the door was not securely fastened and when all was dark and quiet the wolves pressed themselves against it and, smelling horseflesh, burst through."

"Unless some disgruntled employee deliberately opened it," suggested Holmes.

"We don't have disgruntled employees, Mr Holmes. My staff has been with me a long time and we are like a family. Of course, the booked-in performers are different. As you probably know, I change my programme frequently and engage speciality performers, many of whom, coming from an agency, are unknown to me. They are not 'family'. I did have to dismiss such a man a few weeks ago, an Italian who got in a fight with our musical director."

"A fight? On what cause?" asked Holmes.

"The usual, a woman," said Sanger gloomily. "Di Mezma was enamoured of Lulu the contortionist and thought that Osbert – that's the MD – was paying her too much attention. Osbert wouldn't hurt a fly and was certainly not interested in Lulu. Not in that way. Osbert's a happily married man, but you know what these Italians are like. So he had to go."

"Could he have opened the cage, this Di Mezma?"

"No! Apart from the fact he was a timid little thing, there is no way he could have got into the theatre. All my staff, both front of house and backstage, have instructions not to admit him under any circumstances."

We were interrupted by the entrance of Mr Oliver the assistant manager. "Inspector Jackson of L Division is here, sir. He wishes to ascertain that the wolves are secure and there is no danger of them escaping into the street."

"I'll come and see him."

"Mr Humphreys says the horse that was killed is Shrewsbury."

"Oh, the poor mare. Her sacrifice saved her stable mates. It was only because the wolves were engrossed with feeding off her poor carcass that we were able to get the others out," said Sanger.

"Shrewsbury was not the horse that carries the naked Mazeppa?" I asked.

Sanger looked startled. "Oh no, that is a gelding. I never thought of that, Doctor. It would not be good if the public thought it so, that could harm business."

"You are clearly very occupied, Mr Sanger. When do you think you will be able to confine the wolves so that I can examine the stables?" asked Holmes.

"I doubt if it will be before tomorrow. Fortunately today is Sunday and we have no performance. We will be able to keep the beasts fed by throwing meat through the window, and that will make them more docile for when the new cage is ready. I suggest you come along at mid-day tomorrow when all should have been accomplished."

With that assurance we took our leave, pushing through the clamour of pressmen, ignoring their cries for news.

As suggested, we were there on Monday at noon, and all had been achieved under guidance of Mr Sanger and his head groom Frank Taylor. A new cage housed the wolves, and very disagreeable the vile beasts looked, glaring at us with their malevolent eyes.

"So where were the horses tethered, Mr Sanger?" asked Holmes.

"All along here in a double line, nose to nose. They were tethered to that beam above."

"An unusual arrangement, surely?" asked Holmes.

"We have to contrive many unusual methods in the circus, Mr Holmes. Fortunately, Frank here, was able to crawl along the beam with a knife and cut them free so the other grooms could lead them away."

Holmes turned to the head groom. "I congratulate you, Mr Taylor. A feat worthy of a skilled mountaineer. How did you get up to the beam?"

"There was a ladder, Mr Holmes," said Sanger.

Holmes looked around. "Where is the ladder now?"

"It is in use elsewhere. In the circus a ladder is indispensible and is used constantly for many different jobs."

"I see. However, I note that, should a ladder have been to hand, it would have been a simple task for a man to use it to climb on top of the cage, and from that position lift up the iron bar holding the cage door closed. The door could then have been opened, the wolves allowed to escape, and the man could easily have gained that window to provide his own exit from danger."

Sanger looked at Holmes with some astonishment. "Very true, Mr Holmes. That is most likely what happened."

"Could you bring me the ladder now?" asked Holmes, turning to Taylor.

"I'm not sure where it is," he replied hesitantly, looking at Mr Sanger.

"I'm sure it's not far away, Frank, go have a look," said Sanger. The groom hurried away and Holmes roamed about the stable.

"Where was the unfortunate mare felled?"

"Oh, just here," said Sanger, walking over and indicating a particular spot.

"Um," said Holmes, "a tragic business. One of your finest horses I believe?"

"Yes, indeed, and a valuable one."

"But not the one that stars in *Mazeppa*?" I confirmed.

"No. I have inserted an advertisement in the newspapers to assure the public that the play is unaffected by this unfortunate affair."

Sanger and I watched somewhat aimlessly as Holmes strode about peering at one thing after another, and the wolves, as if in imitation, padded round and round their cage. After some time Taylor reappeared with a ladder.

"Excellent," said Holmes. "Please prop it against the empty cage." After the man had done so, Holmes re-arranged it to his satisfaction, then mounted it to gain the top of the cage. Lying down he reached down to grasp the iron bar. "Ah, it is beyond my reach."

"The fellow could have had a walking stick," said Sanger eagerly.

"He could, but is that likely?" asked Holmes from his elevated position.

"Certainly. We use walking sticks to control the elephants. The keepers hook them over the animals' ears to guide them. The *mahouts* of India use a pole with a metal hook and spike at the end. We prefer the much gentler method of a common walking stick."

"And these walking sticks would be readily available to all?"

"Oh, yes, there are several knocking about."

Holmes took out his lens and minutely examined the window and the top of the cage before descending.

"Well, Mr Sanger, it looks as though your joker is increasing the severity of his 'jokes'. This is far in excess of the previous tricks."

"Er, yes, yes, indeed so. That is if there is a connection between them," replied Sanger.

"That must surely be the logical assumption? We must all be on our guard for further increasingly violent and dangerous incidents."

"Yes, indeed. I must warn my staff to be extra vigilant."

Before we bade our farewell to Astley's (or rather Sanger's as it is now called, but the habit of a hundred years is hard to break), Holmes, Sanger and Taylor discussed a strategy to limit the possibility of further misdemeanours arising.

The next morning we were at breakfast when I came across the following in my newspaper:

ESCAPE OF WOLVES AT SANGER'S

Eight untamed wolves arrived at Mr Sanger's theatre, Westminster-bridge-road, on Saturday afternoon, and were placed in a cage or den in one of the stables at the rear of the building, in which stable, also, 17 valuable performing horses were housed. After the evening performance the theatre was closed, the only persons left behind being a few of the attendants and keepers of the numerous animals. A few minutes after midnight the keepers on the premises were alarmed at hearing a great commotion in the stable where the wolves had been housed, and on going there, to their horror, they found that the animals had escaped from their cage by some means at present unknown, and were attacking the celebrated mare Shrewsbury in a most ferocious manner, tearing the flesh from the neck and abdomen in a very terrible fashion. One of the keepers, named Frank Taylor, perceiving the danger the remaining sixteen horses were in, with marvellous coolness and bravery entered the stable, and, notwithstanding that several wolves attacked him at intervals for his intrusion, the courageous keeper succeeded in getting the other sixteen horses out of the stable while the wolves were engaged devouring the carcass of the horse which they had killed. A large and massive iron gate was placed at the doorway of the stable in question, where the wolves were caged with the remaining portion of the horse's carcass which they continued to devour. Inspector Jackson of the L division of the police, on Sunday visited the stable and premises with a view of ascertaining whether there was any possibility of the wolves making their escape into the public street, the result of the visit being quite satisfactory to the inspector.

Mr John Dee Humphreys, better known as Captain Sydney, the well-known lion and elephant trainer, said Shrewsbury was still alive when the grooms entered the stable, with the wolves gnawing at her neck and belly, the entrails protruding and blood flowing. She died within twelve minutes. Mr Sanger, who had been sent for, deemed it prudent to allow the remains of the mare to lie where she was killed by the ravenous wolves.

Mr Sanger, the proprietor of the circus, in an interview with our reporter yesterday said: "The wolves arrived on Saturday morning, were fed, and I saw everything was right. How they got out I do not know, but it is impossible to believe they got out without assistance. This afternoon the eminent detective Mr Sherlock Holmes visited the scene and commended the skill in which Mr Taylor my head groom had made his way along a beam to cut the halters of the horses. He described the feat as 'worthy of a mountain climber'. Mr Holmes also pointed out how easy it would be for a man to stand on top of the cage, lift up the bar on the door, and then to jump out of the stable window, which is only a few feet away. Two grooms were discharged on Saturday evening for misconduct. I have had enquiries made, and I find that these two men took the Continental train from Waterloo on Sunday, and are now in Paris. The public need not have any fear, as the wolves are safe, and will be looked after very closely."

The wolves were successfully secured by Monday afternoon. A new large iron cage had been received, an interior door at one end of the stable was opened, being guarded by a party of men, armed with sticks, who drove the wolves to the opposite side till the new cage was placed in position and the door was closed. The stable, which is built in the form of a triangle, was then surrounded to prevent the escape of any of the brutes. The men then proceeded to the opposite corner, where a door was opened, and Alpine Charlie, with an assistant, entered the den. The wolves resented this intrusion, and snarled ferociously, and for some minutes it was expected that they would fly at the keepers. By the vigorous use of sticks, however, the animals were kept at a distance, while a barrier was fixed up to lead them to the cage. While this was being done one of the largest of the wolves showed fight and flew viciously at the men, but, on receiving a severe blow from the stick that the keeper carried, it retired sullenly to the darkest corner. For some time all the efforts of the attendants to make them enter the cage were futile, but eventually, after about twenty minutes' driving, the animals were all securely fastened in their new cage, the door of which was doubly locked, and the keys handed over to Mr Oliver, the assistant manager. He gave orders that no strangers were to be allowed near the stables, as it was feared that the animals might again be let loose.

The wolves will be on show at every performance this week. See advert.

"I say, Holmes, you have got your name in the newspapers. It seems

Sanger knows the men responsible for the wolves' escape."

"Indeed?" said Holmes in surprise, holding out his hand for the paper which he perused with increasing indignation. "What is the man up to? He has misrepresented all my conclusions."

"Well you showed us how it was done, Holmes."

"How it could have been done, Watson. But what is this about disgruntled employees? Sanger assured us that his employees were like a family and that he never had to dismiss them. He said he had only ever turned out one man, he being a visiting performer who had instigated a fight. Now he talks of two men dismissed on the very Saturday night in question and blames them for releasing the wolves as revenge. The man is either a fool or a double-dealer. I fear I shall have to drop this case," said Holmes, returning the paper.

"It seems odd, I agree." As Holmes seemed reluctant to discuss the matter further, I turned to the advertisements for London entertainments where I read:

Sanger's Amphitheatre (late Astley's)

Every night at 8pm.

MAZEPPA; or The Wild Horse of Tartary

Mazeppa: Miss Maude Forrester; The Wild Horse: the

original horse Pegasus; plus Capt Sydney and his Forest Bred

Lions, Miss Lulu, Professor Dunning and his Merry Family

and many other talented and clever artistes.

NB: The ravenous wolves will be displayed at every

performance.

In spite of Holmes's wrath in the morning, we both went to the amphitheatre that evening as previously arranged. I was astonished to see large queues waiting for admission to every part of the house. "Good Lord, Holmes, it wasn't like this when I came to the show last week."

"No, Watson, and there is why." Holmes indicated a large highly-coloured poster showing a pack of voracious wolves attacking a horse. The artist had allowed his imagination to run riot, setting his scene in trees, increasing the wolves to a countless number, and giving the horse the aspect of a kindly well-loved family pet.

"It looks more like Africa than Siberia," I grunted, as we forced our way through the crowds and eventually gained Sanger's office.

"Welcome, gentleman," said the beaming proprietor. "Business looks very good tonight."

"You must be highly gratified," said Holmes drily.

"Indeed, indeed. Misfortune has been turned to good account."

"You do not seem as apprehensive of further outrages as you were yesterday."

"We had a very successful show last night. A full house. Nothing untoward took place. I am hoping that our precautions will have succeeded. I trust you will be watching tonight. I am not complacent."

"According to the newspaper you have traced the miscreants to Paris, so all should be well," said Holmes sarcastically.

"Come, come, Holmes. Do not believe everything you read in the newspapers. It was necessary to show the public that the wolves had not escaped through any negligence on the part of the circus staff. Your suggestion about disgruntled staff and how the cage could have been tampered with was an excellent explanation, and one that would set the public's mind at ease. Now they are assured that the wolves are under control they are prepared to flock to see the beasts."

"You are a cynical manipulator, sir," said Holmes.

"I am a showman, Mr Holmes," smiled Sanger. "Whilst that glib explanation was made for the consumption of the public at large, you and I know that there is a saboteur who is doing his best to ruin my show and keep the public away. Cody is behind all this and when we find his man, Heaven help him!"

The show was about to start and we were taken into the auditorium. I was placed high up with the limelight man where I could look down on the greater part of the audience. Holmes was at the side of the stage where he was able to gaze upon the audience through a secret spy-hole. The show went on its merry way to an enthusiastic audience right up to the performance of the Acrobatic Sherman Sisters. These two girls carried out feats of balance on a high pedestal. Just as they were attempting a hand-to-hand balance, the pedestal lurched, pitching the girls from the top down on to the floor below. There was a mighty gasp from the audience as the poor girls remained sprawling. I heard a whistle blow and immediately into the ring tumbled the troupe of clowns, the ringmaster and attendants hastening in also, the two girls carried out, and the apparatus dragged away. The clowns indulged in a lot of noise and nonsense until the whistle blew again and Professor Devereux entered with his troupe of performing dogs and monkeys. I was astonished at the rapidity with which all these actions took place. Under the control of the red-coated ringmaster, he, by signals on his whistle, had ensured hardly any interruption to the show, and the audience was already rollicking to the hilarious antics of the dogs and monkeys.

Of course, I presumed the phantom joker had struck once more but, trapped as I was in my precarious position, I could not leave my place until the interval. As soon as possible I made my way backstage, fearful of what injuries those two charming sisters had sustained in the dreadful calamity. I was much relieved, therefore, to find Holmes, Mr Sanger, and Mr Oliver surrounding the two girls, one who seemed none the worse for her tumble, the other white-faced but voluble. On enquiry, I found that she had damaged her ankle and was in pain in that region. On examination I deduced that it was a bad sprain rather than anything broken, although, as anyone who has suffered a sprained ankle will know, the excruciating pain is as bad as a break, but, fortunately passes off relatively quickly. I tended to the wound in the time-honoured manner of a tight cold compress.

Having dealt with that, I could give my attention to the discussion of how the accident had happened. It was not, of course, an accident.

"See, Watson," said Holmes, holding up a leg from the apparatus on which the girls performed. "This leg has been sawn through, not completely of course, still sufficiently strong to support the table. When both ladies started their manoeuvres the weight and action caused the leg to collapse at the saw cut, with the result that we all witnessed."

"Diabolical," I breathed. "The intent was plainly to injure the performers."

"That would seem to be so, doctor," agreed Sanger. "This cannot go on, one thing after another. The plan is obviously intended to put me out of business." Realising that the acrobatic sisters were present and likely to gossip, he addressed them: "Well, my dears, I am pleased to see you are not too badly hurt. It could have been so much worse."

"We could have been killed!" expostulated the elder Sister Sherman.

"This is not the first of these dangerous antics, by any means," said the younger Sister Sherman. "Not only the wolves being loosed, but Captain Sydney had his coat stolen. It's still not turned up and the lions had been most unsettled until they got used to his new outfit. Then Herr Shultz had his juggling clubs tampered with. Why are the performers being attacked in this way? What are you going to do about it? You should get the police in."

"Hush! Hush! My dears," said Sanger benevolently, lowering his voice and adopting a confidential tone. "I know you artistes like to gossip to one another, but I am going to ask you to put your trust in me and say nothing to your fellow artistes. I am actively dealing with this matter, but I cannot be seen to be doing something openly because that will put the villain responsible on his guard. You see, it must be some-body working here who is responsible for initiating all these terrible accidents. There are many people employed here, as you know – artistes, grooms, beast men, stage crew, front of house staff, gas men, limelight operators – the villain could be anyone of them. I do not want you all gossiping, suspecting each other. There is only one person who is the bad man, everybody else is your trusted colleague. So please keep everything you know to yourself. If anybody asks, say it was an accident, a flaw in the pedestal leg. We cannot let this villain get the upper hand, which he will if we all start suspecting each other. My dears, have confidence in me. Have I not been good to you in the past? Have I not given you lots of work? Am I not going to take you on my next provincial tour? You know I like to use people who are loyal to me. Do not disappoint me, my dears. I have great things in mind for you. Next season here I am planning a grand spectacle in which I intend featuring the Sherman Sisters on a high podium surrounded by water fountains. Fountains that change colour throughout the act, culminating in a vision of silver and gold. You, of course, will have new glittering silver and gold costumes. With cloaks. White cloaks, trimmed with ermine. So trust me, my dears. Do not worry, I have everything under control. The villain will be found and unmasked." He patted the girls avuncularly, turned to us and said "Please come to my office, gentlemen."

As we walked along the corridor, I ventured to say to Mr Sanger how well he had set the girls' minds at rest.

"Ah, Doctor," he said, with a wink, "the shit rolls off the tongue."

Back in Sanger's office he revealed his true thoughts. "It cannot be other than Cody who is using these dastardly antics imported from the Wild West. He is trying to kill my business."

"Your business hardly seems to be suffering at the moment, Mr Sanger. A packed house and many more clamouring for entrance," said Holmes drily.

"A flash in the pan, Mr Holmes. The wolves are of hot interest at present, but the public's memory is fickle. We may get full houses for a week or two, but the novelty will wear off, believe me. I have spent a lifetime endeavouring to please the public's taste. It is a never-ending quest."

"Surely we should call in the police, sir. We cannot continue with the risk of our artistes getting maimed. Apart from anything else we will find performers reluctant to work here if they perceive actual danger," said Oliver.

"You are right, Mr Oliver. But what can the police do that we cannot do ourselves, with the guidance of Mr Holmes?"

"With all due respect to you and Mr Holmes, he has attended here on several occasions, observing throughout the show, but has prevented nothing," replied Oliver.

"I agree, Mr Oliver," said Holmes. "The tactics are not suitable. You will, no doubt, have realised that these incidents are pre-meditated. They are set-up before the performance and come to fruition during the show. What we have to do is catch the miscreant prior to the show, in the action of plotting his next attack."

"How can we do that, Mr Holmes? All the staff and company are occupied with their various preparations. I could bring in extra men for the sole purpose of watching over each individual person, but that would double the number of people backstage and front of house, and make the performance impossible to carry out."

"As well as that, Mr Sanger, all such a scheme would do is alert the villain and he would attempt nothing," replied Holmes. "I suggest Dr Watson and I adopt some disguise that would enable us to roam freely throughout the building from the time the staff arrives for the start of the performance."

"You tried dressing as a clown, Mr Holmes, that did no good," sniffed Oliver.

"There must be something that would not cause suspicion," mused Sanger. "As I told you, Mr Holmes, my people are pretty constant. We all know each other. It would be difficult to interject two strangers on a flimsy pretext. I will think of something."

The play *Mazeppa* had now started. "Do you think we should resume our positions?" I asked.

"It is not necessary, Watson. Tonight's incident has already taken place. So far, these outrages have occurred spasmodically, one per night, but to no pattern. It may be that the culprit will perpetrate two on one evening, but he has not done so far and I do not think he will. His object is to cast doubt and uncertainty – what will he do next? Will it be tonight?"

"The man must be a maniac!" I cried.

"Or being well paid by my rival," growled Sanger. "I have it! I could pretend there was something amiss with the gas and you two, disguised as gas men from the gas company, have come to investigate."

"I thought you wished to have Mr Holmes and Dr Watson here every evening, sir?" said Oliver. "It would not be necessary for gas men to come every single night looking for a fault. Mingling with beast men and artistes in the process. I do have some experience, Mr Sanger. Gas men will come during the day when the theatre is empty to trace a fault."

"Dash it! Of course you are right, Oliver. Hm. Have you any ideas?"

"Yes, I have actually, sir. It is rather bold and I do not know these gentlemen's abilities to carry it off."

"Well, speak out, man!"

"I wondered if they could perform as mesmerists."

"Mesmerists?" asked Sanger with incredulity.

"Allow me to explain. Signor di Mezma, whom you quite rightly dismissed for insubordination, presented such an act. I watched it many times. A lot of it was trickery. If these two gentlemen put their minds to it, I think we could reproduce a great part of it. It would not be as good as di Mezma, he was a seasoned professional of many years standing, but we are not interested in entertaining the public, we simply want a feasible cover for their presence. It does not have to be a lengthy affair, just sufficient to excuse their permanent presence in the theatre every night."

"You may have it, Oliver. Of course I know it was faked, he used some of my lads as stooges."

"What would we have to do?" I asked nervously.

"One of you would be the mesmerist, the other would be a plant in the audience."

"A plant?"

"That's what we call a secret confederate."

"I see."

"If you were the plant, Dr Watson, you would, in fact, be an actor playing the role of an unsuspecting member of the public."

"You're quiet, Mr Holmes. What think you to Oliver's suggestion," asked Sanger.

"I like it! I approve of it as I think it will work. But surely the mesmerist would need more than one person to work with?"

"Yes, of course," said Oliver. "What he does is get up about fifteen people, including his stooges. He then tries a simple test that they all do, and from that he can tell which are the susceptible ones and he retains those, sending the others back to their seats. So he has six or seven people, including a couple of stooges, that he actually works with. In fact, he never uses some at all. It's all a big bluff really, but the comical antics are what matter."

"Do you think you can do it, Mr Holmes."

"Certainly."

"And you, Doctor?"

"I'm willing to try," said I.

As we had been seen around the amphitheatre in our normal personas we were obliged to adopt heavy disguises to carry out the scheme. Holmes being the natural leader and I the follower, it was agreed he should be the hypnotist under the name of Professor d'Albert, and I would be his hidden plant from the audience. My name would be Ernest should it be required. Our rehearsals were necessarily intensive and at first I was totally inept, but gradually, under the expert coaching of Mr Oliver, I began to get the hang of things. Holmes, slipping into character without too much bother, proved to be superb in his role. I have always said that the stage lost a great actor when he chose to be a criminologist. As Mr Oliver described what we had to do, it became apparent that the whole thing depended on tricks and subterfuges. It seems that 10% of the population are extremely good at going into a quick hypnotic trance on the mere word of the hypnotist, so out of every fifteen or twenty called up there will be at least one good subject. When calling for volunteers you inevitably get the exhibitionists and, of course, your own confederates. So from this group the hypnotist is able to select his subjects with some success. As Mr Oliver pointed out, no hypnotist succeeds all the time, and the art of his show is to immediately switch from a failure to a guaranteed comical stunt with a stooge. "Mr d'Albert you are an entertainer, not a wonder worker," asserted Mr Oliver.

I had to eat an onion with all the relish of a juicy apple. I was astonished to find that this was not at all difficult. It is merely the thought that deters one, and whilst not tasting like an apple, it is quite easy to eat a raw onion in such a manner. Another hilarious trick is where the hypnotist tells his subjects that the audience looks funny and they are to point and laugh at them. As soon as the stooges do this the others copy them and, laughter being infectious, the audience themselves laughing, so it spreads. Another great stunt is the 'electric chair'. In this, every time a certain chair is sat upon the sitter immediately leaps up pretending he has had a shock. This is a 'running gag' as Mr Oliver called it. The stooges do it at first, but eventually all do it because the hypnotist whispers instructions to them. It is all bluff, but harmless fun. By the end of the very full day I was beginning to enjoy my training.

We had a second intensive day, at the latter end of which we were joined by Herbert, a young stage hand. He was only about eighteen but said he had been with Mr Sanger for four years, indicating, as Sanger had stated, how loyal his staff were. Herbert had acted as stooge for the previous hypnotist, or, as Mr Oliver preferred to call him, a 'mesmerist'. "It has a more theatrical ring to the word. It sounds more mysterious, don't you think?"

Fortunately, no further untoward incidents had occurred and, as we were to make our debut that evening, would be on the spot to keep a watch. I must confess in the excitement of becoming an artiste I had rather forgotten the true purpose of the exercise.

Before the audience was admitted, we were called to the stage by the ringmaster to liaise with the musical director about the music for our act. One of the stunts was that the subjects were controlled to fall asleep when a lullaby was played, then wake up when the music changed to a lively polka.

As the music played, Holmes nudged me and nodded over to the side of the stage where Herbert was going about his stagehand's duties preparing for the performance. To my surprise he stopped what he was doing, sat down on a convenient bench and closed his eyes. Then when the polka was played he opened his eyes and resumed his work. A true professional, I thought, always ready to rehearse!

I will not bore my readers with a blow-by-blow description of our performance. Suffice it to say that it passed off without too much error but, it has to be said, without a great deal of applause. I was a little disappointed but, as Holmes reminded me in our privacy, the performance is only a subterfuge to allow us to be constantly present and alert. However, nothing untoward occurred.

We repeated our little show for two more evenings, improving all the time, with the applause and laughter increasing as we became more proficient. Herbert was a great asset, but, of course he had more experience than any of us as, over his years with Mr Sanger, apart from assisting the previous mesmerist, he had undertaken all kinds of stooge work. He told me that on one occasion he even had to come out from the audience to try and ride an unrideable mule!

On the fourth night, I was beginning to think that we had seen the end of the mysterious 'joker' incidents as nothing further had occurred. To tell truth, I was beginning to tire of having to step into the ring each night and go through the same routine. It astonishes me that actors often play the same role for a hundred nights, whilst some of the circus performers have done exactly the same routine for many years! No doubt that is why they are so proficient.

It was our custom, on regaining our dressing room, to split up and keep separate watches by idly strolling around. We had, of course, to observe the rules that we must not place ourselves where we interfered with other people's work. But there is an air of controlled casualness that enables these performances to run smoothly and efficiently. Each person in the building knows what he has to do, when to do it, and can be relied upon without constant supervision. Overt management only needs to click into place when something untoward happens out of the regular proceedings.

Professor d'Albert appeared early in the programme so Holmes and I were free to do the job we were really there for – to keep a close watch backstage. Mr Oliver had been very clever in coming up with this idea for our disguise because, as well as our act, we had to stay for the finale at the end of the evening as all the performers were obliged to do. For most, this would not be a chore as they also appeared playing roles in the hippodrama *Mazeppa*, but we were not called upon to do that so our fellow performers were very sympathetic at our having to stay right to the end. "Poor you. Mr Sanger shouldn't make you stay for the finale," they said. Little did they know that was the whole purpose of our being there!

Already in those few days I could see that every evening the same things happened at the same time and place. As Mr Oliver said: "That is the art of the theatre and the circus, Ernest, ensuring that each night is an exact repetition of the one before. That is why we rehearse so meticulously." My reverie was interrupted by a shout of "Fire!" and I hastened towards the stables from whence the cry had come. I was not the first on the scene. My gaze beheld Holmes sprawled on top of a figure, some straw blazing in a corner, with several men throwing water and beating the flames. Fortunately, the fire was soon defeated. Having been discovered early, it had not had time to spread. The worst calamity that can befall a theatre, more than any other public building, is fire. Over the years many have burned down. The building we were in was, in fact, the fourth incarnation, the previous three having being destroyed by fire.

The performance was continuing undisturbed and Holmes, consulting with the ringmaster, had released the man who was frog-marched into the tiny harness room. There, Holmes and I, joined by Mr Oliver and Mr Sanger faced the miscreant who, to my astonishment, turned out to be Herbert.

"What is all this, Mr Holmes?"

"I saw Herbert deliberately put a match to the straw. I called to some grooms who instantly leapt into action to put it out while I prevented Herbert from escaping. I have to say he made no attempt to do so," replied Holmes.

"Why did you do that heinous deed, Cooper?" demanded Sanger.

The boy just stared blankly before him.

"Do you hear me, Herbert Cooper?" demanded Sanger, fiercely shaking him.

The boy coming to his senses, stared in bewilderment at us all closely closeted in the tack room.

"What's the matter?" he said. "Why am I here?"

"You have just tried to burn the whole building down, that's why! Why do you think?" shouted the livid Sanger.

"Burn the building?" replied Herbert somewhat blankly.

"You deliberately set light to a bundle of straw, Herbert," said Oliver in measured tones. "Why did you do that?"

"I didn't! I don't know anything about it!" protested the youth.

"Don't lie to me, boy!" shouted Sanger.

"You were seen, Herbert" said Oliver.

"I never did that! I wouldn't do a thing like that!" said the youth, struggling to his feet.

"Don't try to escape. I am sending for the police," said Sanger.

"Not yet, if you please, Mr Sanger," said Holmes, speaking for the first time.

"No? Why not? You caught the villain red-handed!"

"I would like to question him further. I would be obliged if you would permit me to do this privately with only Dr Watson present."

"Are you mad, Holmes? You've found our man and well done to you! Now the law can take its course!"

"Your shouting and bluster is not of assistance, Mr Sanger. You frighten the boy," said Holmes.

"I'll frighten him! The young hooligan! Trying to destroy my circus! Whose pay are you in? Did Cody put you up to this?" demanded Sanger.

"Can you see my point, Mr Oliver?" asked Holmes calmly.

"As I am an expert in theatrical matters, I acknowledge you are an expert in criminal affairs. I am content to leave the next stage to you," said Oliver.

"Are you, Oliver? Well, who is the boss here?" asked Sanger.

"You, sir, indubitably," replied Holmes, "but if you take my advice, the advice that you requested and are paying for, you will permit me to question this man in private and get to the bottom of this whole affair. As yet there is more to discover. Herbert may, as you say, be working for Cody. These things I can ascertain with more diligence and skill than you or your local policeman. Have no fear, he will not escape punishment. I suggest you speak to your staff and ensure the news of the fire does not leave the building otherwise, should it get into the newspapers, your business will be ruined, wolves or no wolves."

Sanger, seeing the sense in this statement and, eventually calming down, he and Oliver left to allow us free access to Herbert.

"Now, Herbert. Do you remember setting light to the straw?" asked Holmes kindly.

"Yes."

"You do?"

"Yes, I do now."

"Why did you do it?"

"I don't know."

"You don't know why you did it?"

"No."

"Well something must have made you do it."

"I suppose so."

"It's a very serious thing, you know. I fear you will go to prison. Have you nothing to say?"

"No."

"Did somebody tell you to do it?"

There was a long silence as Herbert clearly tried to remember why he had set light to the straw.

"I don't know. I don't know why I did it! I can't remember! I just went in the stable and saw the straw and thought I would set light to it! I don't know why!" He buried his face in his hands, clearly distressed.

"Why did you have matches in your pocket?"

Herbert stared. "Matches?"

"You must have had the matches in your pocket. Where did you get them?"

"I don't know. I can't remember."

"Did somebody give them to you?" asked Holmes.

Herbert thought. "Yes. Somebody gave them to me. A box of matches."

"Who gave the matches to you, Herbert?"

"I can't remember."

"You can, Herbert, you can remember. Who gave you the matches?"

"I don't know!"

"Where did he give you the matches?"

"Where?"

"Yes. You must have met a man who gave you the matches. Where did you meet him?"

"Meet him?"

"Yes; where did you meet the man who gave you the matches?"

"I don't know!"

"You do, Herbert, you know very well. You always meet the man, the same man. Where do you meet this man?"

"In a pub."

"A pub? Which pub?"

"The one opposite the theatre."

"You meet a man there?"

"I think so."

"Do you go in every night?"

"Yes, yes. I go in on my way to work."

"Mr Sanger does not like his staff to drink alcohol before the show. You are not supposed to go to the pub before the show, Herbert."

"I know."

"You know you shouldn't go in the pub. Why do you go in?"

"To meet a man."

"What man?"

"I can't remember."

"You must remember. Which man?"

"I don't know!"

"You do know. You have met him many times. Who is the man?"

"I can't remember. I can't remember." The boy drooped his head in despair.

"All right, Herbert. I shall ask you no more questions."

"Can I go home now?"

"No, Herbert. You cannot go home. You have done a wicked thing. You will have to go to jail."

"I don't want to go to jail!" cried the poor lad, burying his head in his hands. "It will kill my mother if I am sent to jail!" He burst into floods of tears.

"Watson, what can we do with this boy? We cannot allow him to go free. He has conducted a criminal act, but my investigations must continue. There is more in all this than meets the eye. Can we place him somewhere safe before informing the police?"

"I don't know about that, Holmes. We cannot defy the law of the land. In any case Sanger will insist on the police being called."

"True. Wait here. I'll see Oliver again."

I waited with the poor boy for Holmes's return.

"Don't weep, Herbert," I said, laying my hand on the boy's arm.

"I cannot bring shame upon my mother," he moaned.

"Mothers are usually very understanding. And forgiving," I assured him. "We all know you are not a wicked boy, though you have done a very bad thing. You have done other bad things too, haven't you? You let out the wolves."

"No! I never did that! I was never told to do that!"

"Who never told you?"

"The man, the man . . . I can't remember."

"What did the man tell you to do?"

"I can't remember. I tell you. I don't know! I can't remember."

So I got no further than Holmes, my much praised bedside manner being of no use here. Sitting there in the gloom Herbert eventually dozed off to sleep. I'm surprised I did not do so myself, as it was so warm and stuffy. I could not tell how long we had been there, but the show had finished when Herbert awoke.

"You've had a good sleep, my boy," I remarked heartily.

He stared around. "Why are we in the tack room, Ernest?"

"Oh, we have to wait here until Mr Holmes returns."

"Who's Mr Holmes?"

I had forgotten that the lad only knew us through our adopted *noms de théâtre*. "Professor d'Albert, I mean. That is only a stage name. His real name is Mr Holmes."

"He's not a real mesmerist, is he, Ernest? Not like Signor di Mezma. Signor di Mezma! That's the man who I meet in the bar."

"You see Antonio di Mezma every evening before coming into work?" I asked incredulously.

"Yes, we have a beer and a chat. I think it was rotten of Mr Sanger to throw him out. He wasn't to blame for that fight. The other man started it."

Surely this was the explanation for Herbert starting the fire? He had been hypnotised by di Mezma. Where was Holmes? What was keeping him? He should be made aware of my discovery. I was relieved when, shortly after this revelation, he reappeared.

"There you are, Holmes. I say you look dishevelled," I greeted him.

"I'm sorry for leaving you so long, Watson, but I've been involved in a bit of a rumpus since leaving you."

"I must tell you what I've discovered, Holmes. The man in the pub who Herbert meets is Antonio di Mezma."

"I know, Watson. Come with me to see Sanger in his office and I will explain all. Herbert you must go straight home now. It is very late. Your poor mother will be getting anxious. But before you go, listen to me very carefully. You must never go into that pub again. Ever. There are bad men in there who will harm you. They know you, Herbert Cooper, and want to harm you. When you come to work, you come straight here, do you understand? If you go in that pub again, Mr Sanger will dismiss you, give you the sack, throw you out unwanted. Do you understand?"

"Yes, sir."

"You would not want that, would you?"

"No sir. No. Mr Sanger has been good to me."

"Then behave yourself. And do not ever again meet the man called Antonio di Mezma. He is evil. If you ever see him, do not speak to him. Turn and run away as if your life depended on it. For, in truth, it may. You may not understand why I say this, but it is essential that you obey. These are Mr Sanger's orders. And tomorrow, when you come in to work, Mr Oliver wants to speak to you. He will explain everything. He is a good man and you must listen to what he says to you. Now off you go home."

Herbert hastened off whilst Holmes and I went through the auditorium to the foyer where Sanger's office was situated. Both Oliver and Sanger awaited us there.

"Well, Mr Holmes, it has proved an eventful evening," said Sanger.

"Indeed. As Dr Watson is still ignorant of our adventure, and you deserve a fuller explanation, may I give a resumé of the whole matter?" asked Holmes.

"I would be pleased if you would," said Sanger.

"You dismissed the performer Antonio di Mezma some weeks ago. Considering that an injustice, he brooded on his hurt. He took to loafing around the area, principally in the Cock public house opposite. He saw Herbert, the lad who had helped in his act, and befriended him by arranging to see him prior to the performance each evening. I imagine they sat and chatted and di Mezma bought him a drink or two. After establishing this pleasant routine he then began to hypnotise the lad and thereby persuaded him to carry out the subversive deeds which caused havoc to your shows. di Mezma was very clever, he did not attempt too much. He started by ordering Herbert to steal the lion trainer's coat. Then a few days later he ordered him to change the juggler's clubs. You see it is difficult to hypnotise a person to do something unwillingly. These 'jokes' did not strike the boy as being wicked or wrong, but his own mind would have rebelled if he had been told to carry out some dastardly deed that offended his moral conscience."

"But what about the wolves?" I said. "He must surely have realised that was a dangerous thing to do?"

"I will return to the wolves later, Watson, permit me to continue. By gradually increasing his demands, the boy's moral sense was not alerted. One 'joke' after another. The next thing was to saw through the leg of the acrobats' podium. You see, the clever thing about hypnosis is that you can persuade a person to do something he would not normally do, and then command him to forget about it. So Herbert did not know he had done these things. He had been ordered to forget. This is why he had such difficulty when I questioned him. He knew he had been ordered to set fire to the straw, but he could not remember who had made the order. His conscious mind was being suppressed by the command in his subconscious mind."

"This all seems very high-falutin' to me, Mr Holmes. As you now know yourself, all this mesmerism is mere stage flummery. Mr Oliver taught you how it all works," said Sanger.

"Indeed such entertainments rely on confederates, compliant exhibitionists and secret instructions. But proper hypnotism is a scientific fact. Oriental religions make use of self-hypnosis. Think of the Magi of Persia and the Yogi of India. The Hindu take sick people to sleep temples and cure them by hypnosis. I have studied the *Dabistān-i Mazāhib*. Before Anton Mesmer there were Paracelsus, Gassner and Maximilian Hell. After Mesmer, Esdaile performed operations on patients who had been hypnotised. I commend the work of James Braid to your attention, Watson. You should read his *Neurypnology*, I have it on my shelves. The Frenchmen Liébault and Bernheim have made discoveries that cannot be dismissed."

"I can see a person using power over another by hypnosis when they are present. But you are asking us to believe that they control a person at long distance," I protested.

"Baird tells us that a man was hypnotised to fall asleep when the hypnotist merely placed a finger on his forehead. Fifteen years later they met again and the hypnotist did nothing but place his finger on the man's forehead, whereupon he promptly fell asleep."

"This is all very interesting, Mr Holmes, but hardly to the point as regards our Herbert," said Oliver.

"The latest 'joke' that Herbert was asked to carry out was to give him a box of matches and instruct him to set light to straw in the stables. This was to be the final triumph; di Mezma expected the fire to catch hold, unnoticed, while the show was on, and be beyond control when it came to attention. He sat in the bar over the road nursing a beer and his grievance, waiting for the smoke and flames to issue forth. Fortunately, suspecting for some time that Herbert was involved through hypnosis, I kept a close watch. When he fell asleep as the band played a lullaby and awoke on cue when the music changed, a trick in the repertoire of di Mezma, I suspected he was still under the influence of that man. He did as he was told, setting light to the straw, but he did not know why he did it or by whom he had been told. When I questioned him I realised he was doing his best to answer, but was prevented by the instructions he had been given to forget about the deed."

"So where is di Mezma now?" I asked.

Sanger laughed. "Hightailing it out of town at a guess!"

"After leaving you with Herbert, I sought out Mr Sanger and Mr Oliver and, with a couple of stout men, we went over to the Cock Inn. As soon as di Mezma saw Mr Sanger he leapt up and tried to flee," said Holmes.

"He went to the back door, but little did he know I had my men there waiting for him," said Sanger. "I have not been the manager of the amphitheatre all these years without learning something of the neighbourhood. The back door leads to an alley. The fellow was well and truly trapped. My men in front, we three behind. I gave him a sound thrashing and I am certain we will have seen the back of him."

"But surely the police should be called?"

"With Mr Holmes's invaluable assistance, I think we have solved the case 'in house'," smirked Sanger complacently.

"But should the danger be hushed up? First the threat of loose wolves, and then a fire? The public was placed in mortal danger!" I said.

"Ah, yes, the wolves. I'm glad you reminded me, Watson. Herbert had nothing to do with the wolves, had he Mr Sanger?"

"No, no. You are quite right," he agreed.

"Would you like to explain, or shall I?" asked Holmes.

"You are very astute, sir, I should have realised I could not pull the wool over your eyes," said Sanger.

"It was obvious to me that the antics you assigned to Taylor your head groom – crawling along a beam and cutting halters and so on – were highly unlikely, seeing the man's physique. A much younger, fitter man would have had great difficulty. Indeed I would be surprised for there even to be a ladder to hand. Also the idea that the malefactor escaped via the window was impossible. That window had not been opened for many years. Then when you issued that preposterous story about chasing disgruntled employees to Paris – really, Mr Sanger!"

"You are right, Mr Holmes. The whole thing was dreamt up for publicity purposes. Our business has been faltering of late. I blame the visit of Cody, Buffalo Bill with his Wild West show. They did packing business while in Town and there's no doubt it's a cracking good show. I can't compete with sharpshooters like Annie Oakley and Frank Butler, and genuine Red Indians, much less the Cossack riders and Gauchos from South America. I suppose our shows seem a bit tame after all that. But we need to keep going. I have no difficulty with my touring show under canvas, we are still highly successful, but here I admit we struggle."

"Hence the wolves?"

"Yes. I really bought them for the tenting show but, as they were here, I wondered what I could do with them. It will take time to train them. Then I suddenly came up with the idea. If they got loose it would be quite a story. Then if I put them on show, people would flock to see them."

"A showman's stunt, eh?" said Holmes.

"I'm afraid so, Mr Holmes, but not one that you didn't see through."

"How many of you were in the plot?"

"Just Mr Oliver, Frank Taylor and myself."

"Just a minute," I cried hotly. "Are you telling me you risked all those valuable horses, even to the extent of getting one killed, just for a stunt? What about the danger involved?"

Sanger laughed. "Your concern does you credit, Doctor. But rest assured it was all carefully planned. The horses were led out of the stables in the normal manner before we opened the cage. Alas, one horse had to be left."

"You deliberately sacrificed a horse for this mad scheme? I cannot believe your heartlessness, sir!" I declared vehemently.

"The horse in question was an old horse and was very ill. She had the staggers and was in great pain and distress. We had to shoot her. It was performing this act of clemency that gave me the idea. How to get rid of the poor thing's carcass? We could not allow any contagion to spread. Hence the wolves devoured her."

Whilst to the showman this explanation may have seemed a satisfactory way of carrying on, I thought the whole scheme repulsive from beginning to end. If we cannot trust our public figures to tell the truth, the country will descend into anarchy. What would we do if the great and good of our land concealed the truth in such an underhand manner?

I ventured to express this view to Holmes when we returned home.

"Well, Watson, we must remember that Mr Sanger calls himself Lord George Sanger. He pretends he is lord, so perhaps he has gulled himself into thinking that he has the right to behave in a manner similar to genuine nobility."

"And in doing so allows a felon to go scot free!"

"The law is all very well but, in this case, poor Herbert Cooper would have had a difficult time defending his actions. Can you see any magistrate swallowing the fact he had been made to do the crimes by hypnosis? The lad is a simple fellow, he would soon be bewildered by a clever lawyer. And di Mezma would have claimed it was all nonsense and he was nothing more than a fairground charlatan. I should imagine the average judge would be more willing to believe in stage trickery than genuine hypnotism. You, yourself, a learned doctor admitted you have little knowledge of hypnotism."

"Perhaps, you are right, Holmes, but I cannot believe it is right that di Mezma should not have been arrested."

"Often closed societies have their own very effective way of dealing with matters, Watson. It's called rough justice."

There is a strange epilogue to my tale. In 1893 Lord George Sanger was obliged to close his amphitheatre on orders of the London County Council. In 1905 he finally retired to a farm at East Finchley where, on the night of 28th November 1911, George Sanger was murdered, for reasons unknown, by a blow from a hatchet by an employee, one Herbert Charles Cooper, who then committed suicide.

THE GREAT TRAIN ROBBERY

My friend Mr Sherlock Holmes does not believe in luck. We were sitting chatting desultorily after breakfast instead of stirring ourselves and getting on with the day. The rain, lashing down and beating against the window, was no incentive to bestir ourselves from the comfort of our rooms. Holmes, as so often when under-employed, was in a peevish mood. He always bemoaned that he could not hone his faculties unless he had some new case in hand. The conversation turned to some of his past triumphs and I ventured to remark that Holmes had had a bit of luck when snow had fallen during the case I have called *The Singular Adventure of the Abandoned Bicycle*.

Holmes snorted saying "It's very strange that the more perspicacious I am, the luckier I become."

I thought it wiser not to argue, but could not resist pointing out the obvious. "If I had not met Stamford in the Criterion bar when I was looking for diggings, he would not have introduced me to you and we would never have met, much less shared rooms all these years," I replied, trying to placate him.

"You are referring to mere chance."

"But I could have ended up sharing with a drunken oaf who scrounged money out of me, living in a wretched hovel with some slatternly landlady. I call it good luck that things fell out very differently."

"Equally, by chance, you could have been introduced to a well-born fellow who had a beautiful sister who fell madly in love with you, and a father of great wealth who provided his new son-in-law with a castle in the highlands and a well paid sinecure in the family firm."

"Well, should that have happened, I would call it exceedingly good luck, indeed," I replied jovially.

"I would call this conversation fatuous," said Holmes, rising. "It is time I was dressed instead of wasting time on inanities." Thus saying he went to his room, leaving me to ruminate on what difference there could be between chance and luck.

The trouble with Holmes was that everything he undertook was directed at improving himself in his position as this country's leading detective. He had little interest in activities that did not lead directly to bear upon his work. Whereas a clergyman might spend his leisure hours hunting, or on archaeological explorations, and a financier while away his leisure hours cultivating orchids or shooting grouse, Holmes incessantly turned to crime and the methods of combating it.

Thus, apart from his professional activities, he took the same interest as any man in the street in reading about the many criminal events reported in the daily newspapers that he read so assiduously. It is not too fanciful to claim that he solved more than one crime without stirring from his fireside, making his deductions from the facts printed in the daily press. He regarded such matters as an intellectual pursuit and, of course, never became involved in any way, merely making notes in his extensive files for future reference.

Therefore, there is nothing interesting in my relating such a case in a similar manner to that which many of my readers are likely to perform for themselves, especially should such a crime remain unsolved and a satisfactory dénouement unprovided. However, there was one case – at the time widely debated as it affronted the entire nation – and as there is a conclusion (provided entirely by luck, Mr Holmes), I think my readers will be satisfied. I refer to that heinous crime dubbed by the press *The Great Train Robbery*.

The year was 1889, the month was June, and Holmes was in a sour mood as he had not been consulted on any matter for several days. Thus, whilst deploring the outrageous crime, another part of me was pleased that Holmes had something to get his teeth into although, in fact, to my great surprise he was not professionally consulted.

The first anyone knew about the robbery was a brief note in the evening newspapers that said the 10.28 train to Birmingham had been halted because of an obstacle on the line. While this was being dealt with by the driver and fireman, a gang had invaded the guard's van and stolen a large amount of money.

By the following morning's newspapers, reporters had been out in force, and what had already become known as the Great Train Robbery was the main story in all the papers concerned. The train was the normal LNWR passenger train, but in the guard's van it was also carrying a consignment of newly minted gold coins worth £20,000. Some papers stated these coins had been dispatched from the Royal Mint, while others said the sender was the Bank of England. Whichever consigner it was, all agreed the value of the coins was £20,000 in sovereigns. Shortly after leaving Rugby, in open country where the train has to slow, the driver was aware that ahead, on the track itself, was some kind of obstructtion, at first merely a white blob that, as the engine neared, resolved itself into a man waving a white flag. Bringing the train to a halt, both driver and stoker jumped down and ran forward. There propped up on the track they found a board with the word HALT painted in large letters, whilst the man was waving in the air a pole with a bed sheet attached.

The man was very agitated and said further down the line a bridge had collapsed, blocking the line.

However, on going to investigate, the railwaymen found the situation not as dire as they had been informed. The parapet of the bridge had lost some of its coping stones which were, indeed, scattered on the carriageway, but the two men, aided by the good Samaritan, were able to manoeuvre them out of the way. Having succeeded in clearing the line, the men shook hands with the 'Samaritan' who immediately made off as the railwaymen returned to the train.

The journey was resumed, but at the next stop – which was Brandon – as the driver reported the incident it was found that the guard was trussed up with a gag in his mouth. Only then was it realised that a robbery had taken place. The guard said that, on the stoppage of the train, a gang of four masked men had immediately entered his van, hit him over the head and tied him up. The only thing stolen was the wooden chest containing the gold coins. Inspector Gregson of Scotland Yard was assisting the LNWR police.

"What do you make of this, Holmes?" I asked when we had perused all the newspapers.

"I have two comments, Watson. If the authorities, be it Bank of England or Royal Mint, think sending a valuable cargo by an ordinary unprotected passenger train is a sensible procedure, then they deserve all they get. Secondly, I would be interested to know if the paint on the sign be still wet, how it was supported in an upright position, and how the bed sheet was attached to the pole."

"Are those things of importance, Holmes?"

"Not now, but at the time supremely important. Should the paint on the signboard be dry and the method of supporting not some clearly *ad hoc* improvisation, then I would have been immediately suspicious, would you not, Watson?"

"Well, now you point it out, but hardly at the time, I don't think," I replied.

"Furthermore, I would be intrigued by the presence of a bed sheet in open country. From whence had it come? How was it attached to the pole? Had it been done with hammer and nails? All these things would indicate that advance preparation had been made to halt the train, rather than some 'Good Samaritan' – as the newspapers like to call this thieves' accomplice – doing his civic duty on chancing to find boulders on the line."

"I understand your deductions, Holmes, but they are unnecessary. The crime has been committed and we know the man was in league with the robbers."

"Quite so. No doubt further information will be forthcoming in due course."

"Is that all you have to say?"

"Apart from the fact that the perpetrators of this crime will, no doubt, turn out to be the Pryce gang."

"Pryce gang?"

"Mortimer Pryce is a well-respected artisan. He runs a jobbing building and decorating trade employing a team of four craftsmen. His firm is used extensively throughout the capital; I believe Mrs Hudson has used Pryce's services in the past. He lives in an Italianate villa in St John's Wood with a respectable wife who is well-liked and accepted by other women of her class. However, this man leads a double life, that's the wonder of it. Unbeknownst to all, especially his customers, Pryce and his team are also a gang of villains. Pryce organises the robberies which are carried out by his minions, the very same team that gives such satisfaction with its building and decorating craftsmanship. Pryce is a clever man, not attempting more than half-a-dozen thefts in the year, ensuring that these crimes are meticulously planned to the smallest detail. Not one of these crimes can be traced to him or any of his men."

"Good Lord, Holmes, surely something can be done?"

"Oh, the police are fully aware of Mr Mortimer Pryce, and are eagerly awaiting him to put a foot wrong. Alas, he is too clever for the average policeman. But I, too, am awaiting that wrong foot, then I'll have him, Watson. Never fear, I will get him."

The following day one of Holmes's complaints was echoed by correspondents in the newspapers. Why was such a valuable cargo transported without armed guards in an everyday regular passenger train? It appears that special trains were normally employed that, indeed, had armed guards and carried nothing else but the newly minted coins from the Royal Mint. However, lately it had been thought that such a special called undue attention, making it a more obvious target for bank robbers. An unmarked chest on an unremarkable train would be far more anonymous and safe. It seems William Lidderdale the Governor of the Bank of England, Charles Fremantle the Deputy Master of the Royal Mint and Sir Richard Moon Chairman of the LNWR had previously met to discuss the problem and, as a result, it was determined that this new method would be tried. It was never made clear who was responsible for putting the scheme into practice, and this was only the third time it had been used. Some newspapers hinted that the idea was simply to save money, special trains and armed guards being, of course, a considerable expense.

Sir Richard Moon was also quoted as saying that police investigations were proceeding satisfactorily and arrests were expected very soon.

"Clearly somebody knew about this unremarkable anonymous train, or Mortimer Pryce could not have gained knowledge of it," said Holmes.

The next couple of days brought no new information and the press, reluctant to drop the story, kept it simmering by repeating the known facts, and printing a great deal of conjecture and surmise. One journal, which I shall not insult by naming, had an article which was more like an attempt at romantic fiction as it dwelt on "the sun was high in the heavens and the passengers blithely ensconced in the carriages, gay in their 'plum and spilt milk' livery, as the train sped on to meet its doom."

Then on a particularly gloomy day as I breakfasted alone, Holmes not having yet surfaced, I was gratified to see the headlines GREAT TRAIN ROBBERS ARRESTED with the following text appended:

"We must congratulate the astute Inspector Gregson who has been indefatigable in hunting down the dastardly robbers who perpetrated the Great Train Robbery. This newspaper is gratified to be informed that the four masked men who assaulted the railway guard Mr Albert Rigby (47), leaving him tightly bound and gagged, have been arrested. It will be recalled that the train was halted by a mysterious stranger standing on the trackway. Inspector Gregson invited the engine-driver Mr Horace Cranshaw (42), and the fireman Mr Alfred Hunter (25), to visit Scotland Yard where they were shown a collection of photographs of known villains. This grisly exhibition is nicknamed 'The Rogues' Gallery'. In short order both railwaymen independently identified the man who had masqueraded as a Good Samaritan.

Inspector Gregson is now hot on the heels of Mortimer Pryce who is actually the leader of this gang. Although Pryce has never been accused of any previous crime, the police have had many suspicions that he is responsible for several robberies over a period of some years. A clever and devious crook, Pryce has eluded the police time after time but, on the present occasion there being no doubt of his involvement, he will soon be brought to book."

I must say I enjoyed my breakfast after reading that news, and couldn't wait for Holmes to join me so that I could congratulate him on the accuracy of his diagnosis. Coincidentally, outside, the day became brighter as Holmes entered to partake of breakfast.

"You were right about that aspect of the Great Train Robbery, Holmes. The police say it was the Pryce gang. Four masked men carrying out the robbery and Pryce himself stopping the train."

Holmes stared. "Pryce was the man who stopped the train?"

"So it says here," I affirmed, holding up the newspaper. Holmes rudely snatched it from my grasp and his eyes almost gobbled up the newsprint.

"This cannot be right, Watson," said Holmes, tossing the paper aside, not back to me, but aside.

"Why not, Holmes?"

"Pryce would not be likely to show his face."

"He was not going to wear a mask, was he? Even the densest railwayman would have been suspicious then!" I exclaimed facetiously.

Holmes looked stunned.

"What's the matter, Holmes?" I asked.

"This case has extraordinary aspects, Watson. It is exceedingly bizarre."

"Gregson seems to be on top of things. He's arrested Pryce's workers, if not the man himself."

After a long silence, Holmes murmured "I wonder if this is a clever ploy on Gregson's part?"

"How do you mean, Holmes?"

"Clearly Gregson's suspicions were the same as mine and he assumed the Pryce gang was responsible. He could have taken it upon himself to swoop down on them and arrest them without any definite proof."

"But the photograph?"

"There may not have been one. It could be a fabrication on Gregson's part to persuade the gang he knows more than he actually does."

"Oh, I never thought of that," I conceded. "It's a pity they have not sought to call upon your assistance."

"Gregson's a good man, he knows his job. He also knows he can come to me if he gets stuck."

The following day a full report explained Gregson's work in detail. The man dubbed the Good Samaritan had not been in any kind of disguise, but simply appearing to be a helpful citizen doing his best to assist the railwaymen. He had declined to give his name before making off. Gregson had, indeed, taken the driver and fireman to examine photographs which they had been shown independently, both instantly recognising Mortimer Pryce out of dozens shown to them. The man has a large and bulbous nose making his face the more easily recognisable. Gregson had then taken a group of constables to Pryce's house, which contained one servant only, who told the inspector that Mr & Mrs Pryce had gone on holiday. Gregson had then gone to Pryce's yard where he learned that the team of workmen were painting and decorating a house in Maida Vale.

On reaching the property, the men were found cheerfully attending to their various tasks, and protested they knew nothing of the robbery, or of Pryce's whereabouts. It seems that the procedure was for Pryce to take his men to the place of work, leave them, collecting them at the end of the day, returning them to the yard. However, Gregson arrested the men and took them into custody where they remained.

Although the men had been masked, the guard had heard their voices, and one of the men had been named as Pong. Gregson ascertained the four men's true names, but none admitted to being known as Pong. However, by some clever sleuthing in the public bars which these men frequented, he soon learned that the four men were well-known and the one called Herbert Allison was called Pong by, not only his workmates, but other customers of the bars. It seems this curious nickname had started out one day when Allison had entered a bar after spending some hours working in a sewer. The barman had dubbed him Pongy because of the noxious smell he carried with him into the bar. Taken up by the customers, and very soon shortened to Pong, this name had stuck with the unfortunate man ever since.

The four men were paraded in front of the guard, both with and without masks concealing their faces. They were also told to speak, and, whilst endeavouring to alter their voices, the guard was in no doubt these were the same men who had bound and gagged him. Gregson, by interrogating the four men separately, cleverly played them off against each other and eventually the youngest of them confessed all. He not only admitted to the Great Train Robbery, but poured out details of other robberies the gang had perpetrated. Pryce, who planned the thefts, normally took charge of the booty, mostly valuable items such as jewellery that had to be converted into cash. When that had been achieved the cash was divided fairly between the gang in six portions, each man taking one share, Pryce taking two. The men trusted Pryce implicitly, obeying him whilst carrying out robberies in exactly the same way as they did when he was giving them their daily orders for building and decorating.

However, it was certain that none of the men knew what had happened to Pryce. They were actually bereft without their leader. After previous thefts he had been there, allowing them to carry on normally as boss and workmen. Gregson was now actively looking for Mortimer Pryce. As he suspected Pryce might intend leaving the country, all the ports were being watched. Pryce's picture was printed in some of the newspapers and many people voiced their knowledge of him and his team, praising them for work done in the past, all appalled at the news he was a villain.

So the position stood when next Holmes and I discussed the matter.

"Gregson seems to have been particularly astute in dealing with this case," said I.

"Indeed, he is a smart fellow. I cannot fault him," agreed Holmes. From his tone of voice I could tell that Holmes had reservations. "Pryce is not a fool, so why did he not get somebody else to halt the train? Why, if he found it necessary to do it himself, did he not attempt some disguise?"

"To engage someone else would have meant letting another man into the gang, perhaps somebody that might not be trustworthy," I said.

"Tush! One of his men could have done the part and Pryce could have taken his place with the other three."

"But Pryce would not have known that the police had a photograph of him on their files," I pointed out.

"It won't do, Watson. Mortimer Pryce deals with the public, he moves all over London doing work for them. He may not be a public figure in the usual sense, but hundreds of honest citizens know his name and what he looks like. Even the railwaymen themselves could have known him by sight. He is wise enough to know that the police, whilst not having any proof of his nefarious activities, will be aware of them and have a file of suspicions. Why should he take those risks of recognition? Risks that could so easily have been avoided?"

All newspaper conjecture was stifled and Gregson's plans rendered redundant when an unknown assailant entered the bedroom of Mr and Mrs Pryce at the Marine Hotel Folkestone in the middle of the night, and with a hammer battered Mortimer Pryce to death.

The Marine Hotel was an over-grand nomenclature for what was nothing more than a boarding house in a back street of the port. According to the proprietor, the couple had arrived several days previously, in fact, the very day after the Great Train Robbery was perpetrated. They registered as Monsieur and Madame Duvalier, saying they had just arrived from France after a long journey from the south of the country. Their intention was to stay awhile to recover from the fatigues of their journey before travelling on to Edinburgh.

The couple had been quiet and discreet, causing no trouble at all, until the terrible events of the fateful night. The proprietor had overheard them speaking to one another in a foreign language that he assumed was French, though both spoke excellent English, albeit Mrs Duvalier with a very strong accent.

On hearing Mrs Pryce's screams, the proprietor had hurried to the room but, by the time he got there, she had fainted away. Her husband's head was beaten to a pulp by a man who must have been completely insane, such was the ferocity of the attack.

Mrs Pryce was on the floor in a dead faint, and there was no sign of an intruder. Immediately he had called the police who had swung into action without delay. They found traces of a hurried exit through the still-open window, but little else, and immediate efforts to find the murderer proved fruitless.

On subsequent questioning by the police, Mrs Duvalier confessed that they were really Mr and Mrs Pryce, whereupon the Folkestone police immediately informed Inspector Gregson that they had found the couple that he so earnestly sought. Mrs Pryce, who is French by birth, freely admitted her identity and claimed they were simply on their way to Paris for a holiday. Her husband had suggested staying in Folkestone while he booked passages on the ferry. She did not know why there was a delay, she thought perhaps that the immediate ferries were all full and her husband was having difficulty in obtaining tickets because of the influx of visitors to the Exposition Universelle. She said she had no idea of the robbery, had never even heard of it, and did not read the newspapers as, though she spoke excellent English, she could not read the language very well.

When challenged by Gregson as to why they were travelling under assumed names she wept, saying it was a romantic fancy of her husband. They were going to Paris on what Mrs Pryce termed "a second honeymoon" and, as Duvalier was her maiden name, they were pretending they were newly-weds. Clearly all this nonsense with which Pryce had stuffed his wife's vacuous brain was nothing more than an excuse to explain the delay in leaving the country, rather than the fact that Pryce was aware that all the ports were being watched.

The identity of the night-time intruder could not even be guessed at. Gregson had now to completely alter his search, the man he had hunted now being the victim. Mr and Mrs Pryce had been fast asleep when they were suddenly awoken by a noise. Stealthily creeping into the room was a man carrying a bull's eye lantern that he shone on to Pryce, dazzling him in the eyes. By this light the assailant could aim at the head of the recumbent man with a claw hammer. There was no doubt about the weapon, as it still lay on the pillow among the remains of what had been a human head. Otherwise there were no clues.

As I relayed these latest developments to Holmes, he snorted "Of course there were clues, the dolts simply did not know how to recognise them."

"Perhaps you should volunteer your services, Holmes?" I suggested.

"If Gregson needs me, he'll send a message."

But Holmes was not called for, and a few days later, on the last day of June, the funeral of Mr Mortimer Pryce took place at St John's Wood. By all accounts it was a strange affair as, until the robbery, Pryce had been a well-respected figure in the community and would normally have had a large congregation for his funeral rites. However, the knowledge, now common, that he was the leader of the gang of train robbers alienated the many friends and neighbours who might have been expected to be present. The Pryces had no children, but the greater family rallied round in spite of the disgrace the departed had brought upon his kin. I understand that relatives of Mrs Pryce even came over from France to support the grieving widow.

Again Holmes was cynical, saying: "Grieving widow! How do they know it was not she who battered her husband's head in?" As I have said many times, Holmes was not an admirer of women and distrusted the whole sex. I have always suspected that he must have had some profound emotional cause for this, emanating from his youth.

Strangely, the funeral seemed to be the end of the affair. Gregson had found Pryce, but he was dead. The four accomplices were tried and jailed, the youngest receiving a lesser sentence for turning Queen's Evidence. It was true that a murderer was still at large, but even Gregson was at a loss how to proceed with further enquiries. It seems the police attitude was that the murder was perpetrated by a rival villain, perhaps a disaffected former gang member, and eventually such a person may be apprehended for some other crime. The stolen money that the imprisoned men had handed over to their boss remained missing. Mrs Pryce, not being able to stand the ignominy, sold up the house in St John's Wood and was thought to have returned to France.

Holmes, who had been making notes of the case based purely on the information he read in the newspapers, filed them away, and the world rolled on.

It was a harsh winter that saw the end of 1889 and the start of 1890. London was inundated with frequent sulphurous fogs that each lasted several days. I had much bronchial trouble throughout the winter months that I did not really shake off until well into May. Holmes had many cases with which to occupy himself, but I have to confess my interest in them was somewhat subdued. A permanent state of lassitude seemed to have covered me, and a feeling of lethargy was difficult to throw off. Toward the end of summer, which had not been particularly pleasant, I noticed an advertisement for Cook's Tours. There was nothing unusual in this as most newspapers carried such things almost daily. However, instead of promoting one of the trips to Egypt that were currently so popular, this particular advertisement was offering excursions to Paris. Many of these had taken place the previous summer for the Exposition Universelle, the World's Fair that commemorated a hundred years since the French Revolution. Though the Fair had ended at the end of last October, Cook's were still running similar excursions during the current year. My heart lifted at the idea and, considering this just the sort of tonic I needed, forthwith took myself to Thomas Cook's office in Piccadilly.

All the clerks seemed to be occupied with dealing with customers so, while I waited, I glanced at maps and brochures and admired the large and magnificent photographs adorning the wall. There was a particularly fine one of the Pyramids and another excellent one of the inspiring iron lattice tower that had been erected in Paris for the World's Fair. I thought how much I would like to ascend that tower and view Paris all around from a great height. I knew it remained there and was not due to be dismantled until 1909. Another picture of Paris showed a typical street scene with Parisians sitting outside one of the cafés that are so much a feature of life in the city. I imagined myself sitting there sipping coffee or wine, smiling at the charming mam'selles and tipping my hat to them.

Then to my amazement I recognised a man in the picture! I had not seen the man before, but I had seen his photograph many times, not much more than a year ago. The large bulbous nose was quite distinct; the man was indubitably Mortimer Pryce. My ennui disappeared in an instant and I excitedly returned to Baker Street to tell Holmes.

"Holmes! Guess whose photograph I have just seen at Cook's Tours?"

"I have no idea, Watson. Do you expect me to deduce, or simply guess?"

"Mortimer Pryce."

"Indeed?"

"You remember Mortimer Pryce of the Great Train Robbery?"

"Of course."

"Well it is clearly the man himself in the picture. He is sitting at a table outside a cafe in Paris."

"That is not so surprising. We were told that his wife was a French lady."

"Oh, yes, yes, of course." I had forgotten that fact and was instantly deflated. It was not unlikely they would often be in France, visiting relatives perhaps; or Pryce may even have had business interests there. Just because Mrs Pryce lived in England it did not preclude her from going to her home country.

"I doubt if it tells us anything we do not know, Watson. There is nothing to stop a robber imbibing at a bar, any more than an honest man."

"No, of course not. You are quite right Holmes. The photograph could have been taken at any time. It is pure chance that they are included in the picture."

"You say 'they', Watson?"

"Well, yes. I cannot remember who else was at his table, but no doubt his French wife was with him. I would not know. I do not know what she looks like."

"Are you thinking of taking a holiday, Watson?"

"What? Oh, yes. I thought I might try an excursion to Paris. That's why I was in the Cook's Tours office."

"I understand spring is the time to visit Paris, Watson," said Holmes, puffing at his pipe. "We are now in September."

"That's true, Holmes. It doesn't have to be Paris. I might try Italy."

The day after the incident related above, I returned to our rooms after a most invigorating walk in Regent's Park – my late ennui totally forgotten – to find the dinner table set for three. "Are we expecting a guest, Holmes?" I enquired.

"I have asked Inspector Gregson to call; he claimed dinner was his most convenient time."

"Indeed? May I enquire the purpose? Has he consulted you on a case?"

"No. I'm sure you will forgive me, Watson, if I delay my tale until his arrival. It would be tedious for me to relate it twice and, I am sure, even more so for you to hear it repeated."

With that, as usual, I had to be content. Holmes can be insufferably secretive at times.

We had a pleasant meal, with all of us doing more than justice to Mrs Hudson's pickled herrings, rabbit pie and baked apple pudding, before Holmes announced "I have kept you in suspense long enough, gentlemen. Watson, be so good as to charge our brandy glasses and I will tell you of the purpose of our gathering. You will both, of course, recall the audacious theft commonly referred to as the Great Train Robbery. You must know, Gregson, that Watson and I followed the case closely via the public prints."

"Yes, the affair was well thrashed out by know-all reporters telling me what I should be doing to apprehend the criminals."

"I made a few notes at the time which I have in this file. No doubt you, too, from the start had the idea the robbery was carried out by the Pryce gang, Inspector?"

"Indeed, yes. It had all the hallmarks of that devious gentleman Mortimer Pryce. I was determined to nail him this time round," replied Gregson grimly.

"Did you not find it inexplicable that Pryce himself should have stopped the train without making any attempt to conceal his face?"

"How do you mean?" asked Gregson.

"Surely the fact that you had a photograph of the man in your files, by which the railwaymen were able to confirm the identification of the man, was taking a risk of such foolishness that even the most inept criminal would not have blundered in that way."

"Pryce was not to know we had him on file. Even the cleverest villain slips up, Mr Holmes. Surely you, of all people, know that."

"Of course it was not a slip-up, as you call it. Pryce deliberately ensured he was recognised. The wonder is that he did not give his name as well!"

"But why should he wish to be identified, Holmes? Surely he would do all he could to deflect suspicion from himself, not deliberately court it?" I asked.

"The deviousness of this man knows no bounds, Watson. This was merely the first step in a very cunning plot. It ensured friend Gregson was able to arrest his men."

"That I did, and they are all in jail as a result," said Gregson smugly.

"Note that Pryce had already taken all the loot and disappeared. His men knew not where he had gone, and neither did the police."

"He couldn't get far, Mr Holmes, all the ports were guarded. Don't forget we had a good photograph of him. That was issued to all the ports. That great bulbous conk of his was very prominent."

"Indeed, the gentleman's nose was distinctive. That fact took on a great importance in what subsequently happened."

"You talk in riddles, sir," said the Inspector, becoming annoyed.

"The riddle will become all too clear. We now know that Mr & Mrs Pryce hid in a Folkestone boarding house. Pryce knew it was foolish to attempt to leave the country with all forces being alert. He also knew that as soon as he was dead, the search would be called off and he would be safe. Thus he arranged his own death."

"I am beginning to see your reasoning, Holmes," said I excitedly.

"I'm damned if I am," grumbled Gregson.

"To be brief, then. He found a person sufficiently like himself in build and took him to the hotel in secret. Not difficult, I should imagine, as the place was described as nothing much more than a boarding house."

"No, it was more like a common lodging house," agreed Gregson.

"But who was this other man?" I asked.

"Who knows?" shrugged Holmes. "The back streets of a port are full of derelicts. Pryce probably plied some poor tramp with drink, or rendered him insensible otherwise. Once in the privacy of his bedroom Pryce battered the man to death with a claw hammer, smashing his face to a pulp so that recognition was impossible."

"Just a minute, Holmes, that means Mrs Pryce was an accessory to all this," said I.

"Of course, Watson. At first I suspected her of doing the deed on her husband for some private purpose. But it seemed unlikely that, whilst she might wish him dead, she would have gone on to pulverise his head after killing him. She had no cause to obliterate his features, including the prominent nose. She also seems to have been strangely quiet after the police came. Perhaps you can confirm this, Gregson. Did she keep hounding the police to find her husband's murderer?"

"No, now you mention it, she didn't. She actually said to me at one point 'I am sure you are doing all you can.' She is a French lady, Mr Holmes, I don't know how good is her command of English."

"I would think quite excellent. The deed being done, the pair waited until the early hours of the morning. Pryce hopped over the window sill and fled. I do not know where he went, but I doubt it was very long before he made his way to France. If I had been called in I should have found several clues. The amount of blood and the dryness of it on the bed sheets will surely have given an indication that the deed had been perpetrated not at the time presumed, but much earlier in the evening."

"So you are saying that Pryce, after killing this poor derelict, then casually made off via the window, leaving his wife alone with the body for several hours before she started screaming and fainting away?" I asked.

"That is so. Pryce could, of course, have easily gone out through the hotel door, but to live up to the story of the intruder he had to leave evidence of a man making his exit via the window. No doubt you found traces, Gregson?"

"I did. There were blood splashes on the pavement outside, and the villain had dropped the lantern in his flight."

Holmes laughed and clapped his hands. "Excellent! One has to admire Pryce for his thoroughness. The lantern is an excellent touch. He had, as we know, also left the hammer on the pillow."

"This is all surmise, Mr Holmes. The police surgeon examined the body before releasing it for burial, you know."

"I'm sure he did. But no doubt about the cause of death, I think? Having one's head pulverised to mash is fairly conclusive without searching much further. With Mrs Pryce in her night attire, screaming, fainting and jabbering about a fleeing villain in the night, and sobbing over her unfortunate dead husband, a coroner is not likely to suspect she was doing all that over a corpse she knew full well was not the person it purported to be."

"You are telling me you deduced all this from the newspaper reports?" asked Gregson incredulously.

"No, though I think if I had been on the spot I may have done so. The circumstances were bizarre throughout. From the beginning I knew there must be some reason why Pryce wanted to be known as the mastermind of the Great Train Robbery. I confess it baffled me. Then later, when I read of the body with the head so heavily beaten as to be unrecognisable, things started to fall into place."

"I don't see the point of it, Mr Holmes. Even if you're right – and I don't for a minute agree that you are – but allowing that, what was the point of this elaborate charade?" asked the Inspector.

"That is surely obvious. If the Great Train robber is dead and buried, the police will cease to look for him. If, thereafter, he keeps low and commits no more robberies, lives a modest unremarkable life, does not attract attention, he will be safe. The man has £20,000 in ready money, without counting any proceeds from earlier thefts, plus the money from the sale of his house and business which I believe Mrs Pryce undertook almost immediately. Such a sum will be ample to fund the rest of their lives. Who will seek them out in a foreign country that probably has never even heard of the English train robbers."

"So I was right! Pryce is alive and well and living in Paris!" I cried.

"What do mean, Doctor?" asked Gregson.

Holmes reached out and produced a large flat object wrapped in brown paper. When unwrapped I saw it was the very same photograph I had seen the previous day in Cook's Tours offices.

"Dr Watson saw this picture yesterday and called my attention to it. This morning I went to see it for myself. I agree the man here is indubitably Mr Mortimer Pryce. Please look." Holmes, holding out the picture to Gregson, pointed to the figure in question.

"You may be right, it does look like him. But I can positively state the lady next to him is Mrs Pryce."

"Aha!" cried Holmes. "As neither Watson nor myself have ever seen the lady or her picture we could not make any such assumption. Your confirmation makes my thesis even more plausible."

Inspector Gregson studied the whole picture for a long time before speaking. "Alas, Mr Holmes, it sounds convincing the way you tell it, though I cannot see my superiors swallowing it. Permit me to say it sounds rather fanciful. And you must surely be aware this photograph is no proof at all. It could have been taken years ago, even before Pryce did any robberies at all."

"I agree that is the difficulty. We need to prove that this photograph was taken some time after 30th June 1889. That was when Pryce was buried at St John's Wood."

"Correct, Mr Holmes."

"Of course I realised the difficulty as soon as I saw the picture. I also saw an opportunity to furnish such proof. Hence I persuaded the manager to take down the picture and lend it to me for further examination. You will note here at the left side of the picture is a newspaper seller. At his feet is a board which, as in our country, advertises the day's leading news item. If that can be identified and the date traced we can find the very day when this picture was taken."

"Ridiculous!" snorted Gregson. "The thing is illegible. It's small and blurred. Hopeless!"

"Not quite," said Holmes smoothly. "Borrow my lens, you may be able to make out some of the words."

Gregson, moving nearer the gas bracket, peered at the notice. "I can make out four words. Two long words and two short. I think the short words are 'DO' and 'VERY' in capital letters. The other two are just a jumble. Has Dr Watson had a go?"

"No, I welcome the opportunity," said I, taking the picture and lens. I could see the words that Gregson had seen but, like him, I could make nothing of the longer ones, though I thought I discerned what could be two 'O's in the top word.

"Splendid. You concur with me. The first word at the top is a long word that I, too, thought contained two round letters – possibly O, or perhaps C, G, or Q. I also think the third letter is an X.

Leaving that, the second word is in less doubt, it is DU. The third word presents a great difficulty, the only letter I can make out may be a U. See it makes a kind of break halfway through the word. I think it may be a U as it seems to follow the clearer U printed above it. However, our conjectures are saved by the last word which you both think is the word VERY."

"I can't see much sense in very as a last word, Holmes, even on a terse newsboard. It might say 'minister very ill' or something, but it would not say 'minister ill very'," I said.

"That is true, Watson, but we are not looking at English words, but words in the French language."

"Of course!" I exclaimed, but immediately had doubts again. "Very in French is 'très' if I recall my schoolboy French correctly."

"You are correct, Watson. That is not relevant. Very in this instance is the French word."

"So what does that word mean in English?"

"There is no equivalent. Very is a French name. There is an accent over the E."

"This is all very well, Mr Holmes, but it doesn't get us anywhere," said the Inspector.

"On the contrary, now I can tell you exactly what the board says," replied Holmes.

"Then tell us, for God's sake, if it's so important!" cried Gregson.

"Humour me a minute more as I tell you how I deciphered it. All I could be certain of was the word DU which is 'of' in French. So I thought I would take it to a French speaker. Where is the most convenient place to find a French speaker in London? A French restaurant. The two that came to mind were the Café Royal and Verrey's."

"Verrey's Restaurant, Holmes! The newsboard says 'very', the long word could be 'restaurant'!"

"Exactly so. The idea of going to seek a translation itself revealed that probability. However, Verrey is not spelled the same. So I kept to my plan and visited the manager at Verrey's in Regent Street. Instantly he told me that Restaurant Véry near the Gare du Nord in Paris had been bombed by anarchists earlier this year. The French anarchist Ravachol had been arrested by the police some time before. They found him dining at the Restaurant Véry, having been tipped off by the owner Monsieur Véry. The evening before Ravachol was due in court, as a reprisal, fellow anarchists threw a dynamite bomb into the restaurant causing an explosion when many were injured and the owner killed.

The notice actually reads

L'EXPLOSION
DU
RESTAURANT
VÉRY

Being a Parisian and a restaurateur himself, the poor fellow remembered it very well, though he could not state the precise date, but it was definitely in April of this year. So I then sent a telegram to Monsieur Le Villard, a fellow detective in Paris, asking for the date of the atrocity. His answer was 25th April 1890. Thus the newspapers had the information the following day. We can be certain this photograph was taken on 26th April this year, almost ten months after Pryce's presumed death."

"Amazing, Holmes!" said I in wonderment.

"You will find the event was extensively covered in our own newspapers also on 26th April, the information conveyed by Reuter's Telegram."

"Mr Holmes, I do not know what to say. If it is as you assert then we must contact the French police to see if they can locate the Pryces in Paris. Not an easy task."

"I agree. But it might be useful to try the name Duvalier as a start."

"But I still do not see why Pryce resorted to this extraordinary plan," said the Inspector.

"It is bizarre. I think, perhaps Pryce, suspecting his luck would not hold out much longer, wanted to cease his criminal activities before he was caught. The Great Train Robbery was probably intended to provide for his needs for the rest of his life. Having successfully gained that enormous amount, I think he probably wished to live a life of peace and quietude with his wife in Paris."

"Well, with any luck we may put a stop to that little scheme," said Gregson. "Indeed it was a lucky day when Dr Watson walked into Cook's Tours, otherwise we would have known nothing of this."

"Mr Sherlock Holmes does not believe in luck," said I.

"A last brandy before you go, Inspector?" asked Holmes, turning away to reach for the decanter.

NOTES

THE CASE OF THE CRYPTIC CAPITALS
The Louisiana State Lottery Company, a private corporation formed in the mid-19th century, had a reputation for swindling and corruption. Most of the tickets were sent to agents throughout America and abroad who would sell them in their respective areas. In 1890, the United States Congress banned the interstate transportation of lottery tickets and lottery advertisements, thus depriving the company of 90% of its revenue.

Death by stabbing with an icicle has been mooted many times in detective fiction. My claim to originality with the idea is having it fired from a crossbow, probably as unlikely a method as all its predecessors.

THE ORDEAL OF OSCAR WILDE
The story has no basis in fact other than Oscar Wilde was pestered by low-life blackmailers. It is entirely fictional, though Oscar Wilde and Robert Ross were, of course, real historical persons. Ross was born in Tours, France, attending King's College, Cambridge in 1888. He is thought to have been Oscar Wilde's first male lover. Following Wilde's disgrace and imprisonment in 1895, Ross went abroad for safety's sake, but he returned to offer both financial and emotional support to Wilde during his last years. Ross remained loyal to Wilde and was with him when he died on 30th November 1900.

Ross became Wilde's literary executor, tracking down and purchasing the rights to all of Wilde's works, which had been sold off when the playwright was declared bankrupt. Ross gave Wilde's sons the rights to their father's entire works, along with the monies earned whilst he controlled them.

THE SURREY MAN-MONKEY
1) George Augustus Conquest (1837 – 1902), a playwright, acrobat, pantomimist and manager hailed from a famous theatrical dynasty. He managed the Surrey Theatre from 1881 to his death in 1902. I have depicted him in a totally fictitious manner.

2) The man-monkey character appeared in straight plays as well as pantomimes. *Perouse; or the Desolate Island* a play by John Fawcett, based on a former one by Kotzebue, first appeared in London in 1801. The play was a fictional concept of what might have happened to the

inhabitants of a real-life French shipwreck in 1785. La Pérouse, his wife, and their son are all about to be killed, but are saved through the intervention of a loyal and intelligent chimpanzee. E J Parsloe first played the role as a boy at Covent Garden in 1816. Parsloe was also a noted clown in pantomime, and in 1831 took a pantomime company to the Bowery Theatre in New York. This was an ill-starred venture as Parsloe seriously injured himself falling on board ship. On the fourth night of the pantomime he broke down mid-show, overwhelmed by his mental anxieties, his injuries and the poor reception of his company, dying the following day. However, this recognised biography is contradicted by a letter dated 23rd January 1832 from RS to the *Tatler* which corrects the facts, saying Parsloe had not died, but withdrawn from the pantomime *Mother Goose* for several days on the advice of two doctors.

Perouse; or the Desolate Island with its monkey role was a great favourite for many years, the man-monkey character becoming almost a sub-genre of melodrama adopted by subsequent performers, the most notable being Monsieur Gouffé who had a very long career at the Surrey Theatre by actually being two different men – John Hornshaw in the 1820s and Sam Todd in the late 1830s. In *Annals of the New York Stage 1835/36* it states that "Jacko the Brazilian ape was performed by Monsieur and Madame Gouffé, Parslow now resigning monkey business to his superior" and taking a lesser role.

I have been cavalier with dates and facts and used the name Parsloe simply in tribute to these sterling acrobats.

3) Transportation to the British colonies in North America was a common punishment handed out for both major and petty crimes in the seventeenth and eighteenth centuries. After the American War of Independence and the discovery of Australia, transportation was transferred to the new country. The practice had mainly ceased by the 1850s as, because of the gold rush and farming opportunities, people were settling voluntarily. Between 1803 and 1853 around 75,000 convicts were transported to Tasmania. Transportation finally ceased in 1868, but the lower orders had long memories, still living in fear long after the practice had ceased.

THE BLACK PEARL OF RAJASTHAN
Robert Arthur Talbot Gascoyne-Cecil, 3rd Marquess of Salisbury, KG, GCVO, PC, (1830 –1903) was Prime Minister 1886–1892 and 1895–1902. A very capable politician and far more intelligent than he may appear from my fictional version of the man.

THE DEMISE OF THE FAVOURITE SON

The case of the Punch & Judy man at Ullacombe beach is related as *The Singular Adventure of the Disappearing Bubbles*, one of the seventeen stories in *The Singular Adventures of Mr Sherlock Holmes*.

Edward Carson was an eminent QC of the day, his name becoming known to the man in the street as the prosecutor of Oscar Wilde.

THE THREE WISE MONKEYS

The Indian Mutiny is well documented. I have taken events, names and other elements of that history and, regardless of accuracy, mingled them fictionally with my own original fabrication.

THE ANCIENT RING OF THE PROPHET

Aficionados will recognise this story attempts to explain the background to Watson's remark prior to *The Adventure of the Veiled Lodger* that "the whole story concerning the politician, the lighthouse, and the trained cormorant will be given to the public."

Apart from the names of Persian royalty in the authentic news bulletins of the Shah's assassination, on which my report is based, the names of my fictional characters from that land are taken from a mixture of previous ayatollahs throughout history.

THE ESCAPE OF THE WOLVES

Astley's was a well-known London landmark from 1773 until closure in 1893. Starting as an outdoor school of trick-riding, it developed in successive phases until it was an amphitheatre, with circus ring and theatre stage. Pantomimes, melodramas and even Shakespeare were presented as equine entertainments. The Greek word Hippodrome – which originally meant a horse-racing stadium – was adopted by theatres that presented these hippodramas. The present theatres bearing the title Hippodrome such as at Birmingham and Bristol are, of course, conventional theatres. Interestingly, at Great Yarmouth in Norfolk, England there is still a functioning building rather tautologically known as the Hippodrome Circus which stages non-animal circus shows.

The basis for this tale is the real-life event of the escape of wolves from Astley's which took place exactly as described. The press report is elaborated from an authentic and genuine specimen. The characters Lord George Sanger, his groom Frank Taylor (known as Alpine Charlie) and Inspector Jackson were real historical persons, here used fictionally. All the others – staff, employees and artistes are fictional, although some of the artistes' names are taken from old playbills.

I have taken the name Herbert Charles Cooper from the genuine employee who killed Sanger, using it for the deluded hypnotised youth.

THE GREAT TRAIN ROBBERY
The story where the snow was a fortunate factor is *The Singular Adventure of the Abandoned Bicycle* which can be found in *The Singular Adventures of Mr Sherlock Holmes*. (3rd Revised Edition - Vesper Hawk 2010)

The French anarchists' atrocities actually took place two years later than I have placed them, the bomb explosion at the Restaurant Véry taking place on 25th April 1892 and reported extensively the next day. The Great Train Robbery is entirely fictitious.

PRAISE FOR PREVIOUS SHERLOCK HOLMES BOOKS
by
ALAN STOCKWELL

The Singular Adventures of Mr Sherlock Holmes
ISBN 978-0-9565013-0-1

"One of the best collections of Holmes pastiches for some time. Recommended." *Sherlock Magazine*

"These tales are different from the usual run of pastiches . . a fascinating read." *The Torr*

"A superbly crafted and grippingly entertaining collection of stories. . . enthusiastically recommended." *Midwest Book Review.*

"A sparking collection well worthy to be considered in the lineage of tales penned by Dr Watson. . . 'Let me recommend this book . . . remarkable'" *Auberon Redfearn, Sherlock Holmes Society of London*

Sherlock Holmes and the Singular Adventure of the Gloved Pianist
ISBN 978-0-9565013-1-8

"As in his previous volumes, Alan Stockwell gets close to the authentic Watsonian narrative style, and the reader is transported convincingly back into the ambience of the (here) Edwardian era. The story introduces a very ingenious basic idea, whereby the latest technology of the age conspires to produce a crime unique in the annals of malefaction. The tale is strongly plotted, and all the loose ends of the suitably tangled skein are neatly teased out and tied together at the end, with a satisfying profusion of false trails along the way. . . . To paraphrase a closing remark by Holmes, the demonstration of method in the one case, and the murder in the other, were both effected by means which 'would have been impossible just a few years ago'. If this intriguing fact does not make you yearn to read the book, then it jolly well should!"
The Sherlock Holmes Society of London Journal

www.ingramcontent.com/pod-product-compliance
Lightning Source LLC
Chambersburg PA
CBHW020743250626

47155CB00003B/901